# The Riddle of the Sands

DOVER · THRIFT · EDITIONS

# The Riddle of the Sands

## ERSKINE CHILDERS

DOVER PUBLICATIONS, INC.
Mineola, New York

# DOVER THRIFT EDITIONS

GENERAL EDITOR: PAUL NEGRI
EDITOR OF THIS VOLUME: KATHY CASEY

## Bibliographical Note

This Dover edition, first published in 1999, is an unabridged republication of the work originally published in 1903 by Smith, Elder & Co., London. It includes an Introduction written by Norman Donaldson for the 1976 Dover edition.

## Library of Congress Cataloging-in-Publication Data

Childers, Erskine, 1870–1922.
    The riddle of the sands / Erskine Childers.
        p.   cm. — (Dover thrift editions)
    "Includes an introduction written by Norman Donaldson for the 1976 Dover edition"—T.p. verso.
    ISBN 0-486-40879-5
    1. Great  Britain—History—Invasions—Fiction.  2. Secret  service—Great
Britain—Fiction.  I. Title.  II. Series.
PR6005.H52R52     1999
823'.912—dc21
                                                                    99-29902
                                                                    CIP

Manufactured in the United States of America
Dover Publications, Inc., 31 East 2nd Street, Mineola, N.Y. 11501

# Contents

# Maps and Charts

# Introduction to the Dover Edition

EVEN IF its author had died peacefully in bed instead of before a firing squad in a dingy barracks, *The Riddle of the Sands* would have been a noteworthy book, possessing as it does a threefold attraction. To Christopher Morley it was the classic Secret Service novel; to successive generations of amateur yachtsmen it has been the preeminent yarn about inshore sailing in fair weather and foul; while to its author and original readers it was above all a cautionary tale, admonishing the British Government and people to look to their North Sea defenses while there was yet time. Patriotism—though he seldom employed the word—was the key to the author's life. Loyalty to his native England was the mainspring of this, his only work of fiction; devotion to his mother's land led to his death.

Robert Erskine Childers was born in London on June 25, 1870, to Robert Caesar Childers, a scholar of Oriental languages, and his wife, Anna. After the early deaths of both parents, he was brought up in easy circumstances by his mother's people, the Bartons, at Glendalough House in the Wicklow hills south of Dublin. At Trinity College, Cambridge, where he went after Haileybury, his exceptional debating powers were widely remarked on; but away from the rostrum he was a quiet, often preoccupied young man. During the vacations he learned the art of sailing over sandy bottoms in and around Wicklow harbor. His first yacht was the *Vixen*, a shallow-draft, gaff-rigged, 30-foot sloop—heavy and uncomfortable, but solidly built with double-diagonal teak planking and a large centerboard. When this was raised, the craft drew almost no water, and running aground was scarcely a hazard in fair weather. The *Vixen* was to become the model for the fictional *Dulcibella*.

In 1895, Erskine Childers (the name rhymes with *furskin builders*) became a committee clerk at the House of Commons, where the lengthy vacations gave him plenty of leisure for extended yachting trips of just the kind his novel portrays, exploration—alone or with one or two friends—of the shoals off the German, Danish and Baltic coasts.

When the Boer War began he volunteered for service in the City Imperial Volunteers (part of the Honourable Artillery Company) and endured (even enjoyed) looking after the horses of his troop en route for South Africa. His eight months of war experience provided him with material for several books, and for that part of The [London] Times History of the War in South Africa dealing with guerrilla warfare. Moreover, his earlier conservative colonialist views gave way to a new sympathy for those who, like the Boers, were fighting for their independence.

It was after a season of sailing in his new and bigger yacht, the Sunbeam, that he wrote The Riddle of the Sands. His devotion to England then was absolute, uncomplicated by his later anguish over the Irish question.

During a visit to the United States in 1903, the year his novel was published in London, he met petite, auburn-haired Mollie Osgood, daughter of a Boston physician, and the pair were married four months later. Though disabled by a spinal injury at an early age—for much of her life she needed the support of two canes—Mrs. Childers was an accomplished helmsman and a source of strength to her husband in all his tribulations. The Osgoods had a 50-foot gaff ketch, the Asgard, built for the newlyweds in Norway, and, together with one or two friends or a hired crew, the Childerses sailed regularly out of Southampton to the usual North Sea and Baltic haunts.

During a tour of Ireland's southwest counties in 1908 Childers so far revised his Unionist position as to espouse Home Rule in the orthodox sense, thereby going far beyond what most Englishmen were then willing to accept. Characteristically, he gave himself wholeheartedly to his new cause, resigning his House of Commons post to write The Framework of Home Rule (1911), a closely reasoned case for giving Ireland dominion status like Canada—that is, independence in internal affairs under the British flag.

In 1914 a Home Rule Bill which had been passed by the Asquith administration evoked violent opposition among the Protestant majority in Ireland's northern counties and its terms were suspended. The Ulster Volunteers armed themselves, and the Volunteers in the South were put at a disadvantage. Childers's Asgard and Conor O'Brien's Kelpie kept a rendezvous with a German tug off the Belgian coast one night in July, 1914, and by dawn 1500 Mauser rifles and 45,000 rounds of ammunition were stowed aboard the two yachts, every cubic inch of space being pressed into service. Childers, his wife and a small crew brought the Asgard, in a hazardous, uncomfortable journey of thirteen days, into Howth harbor just north of Dublin, where they were met according to plan by the eager Volunteers. During the trip they had un-expectedly sailed through the British fleet, which was being inspected by George V off Spithead, and survived a gale in the Irish Sea. The double cargo—*Kelpie* arrived a week later—was credited with arming the Irish republicans for the Easter uprising of 1916 and subsequent military campaigns.

Childers volunteered for British service again when the First World War began a few days after the gunrunning episode. His knowledge of the German coast proved invaluable for seaplane reconnaissance. He took part in the Cuxhaven raid of November, 1914, and was later active in naval intelligence. On one occasion he is reported to have crashed into a coastal mine field and sailed home by rigging up a makeshift boat from pieces of wing fabric. Leaving the service in March, 1919, as a major with the Distinguished Service Cross, he again became preoccupied by Irish affairs and moved his family to Dublin. By this time, he felt, something more than the still uncon-summated Home Rule was necessary, and he devoted his energies to securing full independence.

In 1920 the British government divided the rebellious island into two parts, giving Northern Ireland (six of the nine Ulster Counties) and the remaining twenty-six counties separate but limited powers. In the general election of that year nearly all southern constituencies returned nationalist candidates, who refused to assemble as Dáil Éireann until after a truce was signed in July, 1921, when the members took an oath of allegiance, not to the Crown but to the Irish republic. Delegates dis-patched to London by the Irish republican leader, de Valera, ham-mered out a treaty with the Lloyd George government. Childers played a much more important role than his position as secretary might indi-cate. Recently elected as member for Wicklow, he looked by this pe-riod a physical wreck: white-haired, pale and thin, with a constant cough, he scribbled into the night at his memoranda for use at the next day's discussions. His analysis of the Canadian analogy was considered especially brilliant. Others distrusted his hardening fanaticism; the del-egation's leader, Arthur Griffith, even suspecting him of being an English spy. Lloyd George, by threats of "war—and war within three days," forced the exhausted plenipotentiaries to sign an agreement on December 16, 1921, that gave the Irish only limited autonomy. The na-tion would remain divided and an oath of allegiance to the Crown was still required. A provisional Free State government was to be set up for the South to which some powers would be handed over; within a year, if the treaty were ratified, the Irish Free State would achieve permanent status.

Bitter impassioned debates took place in the Dáil early in 1922.

Childers argued that, as a practical matter, the state had come out of the talks with even less than Canada had; cession of her ports alone meant abdication of the right of self-defense. The treaty's supporters claimed that it offered all that could be obtained short of a war that Ireland could not win. When the vote went narrowly in favor of the treaty, de Valera resigned the presidency and was succeeded by Childers's enemy, Griffith. The May, 1922, election showed a strong feeling in favor of the treaty. When Childers (who lost his Wicklow seat) elected to join Liam Lynch's republican forces around Cork as a staff-captain he must have been well aware that he was acting against the wishes of the majority of his fellow-countrymen. But he wrote to a friend, "No one dies for Home Rule in any country. . . . The thing [they] die for—freedom—is not a thing that can be whittled away by limitations."

We are fortunate to be able to see him in his last unhappy months through the eyes of a youth who was later to adopt his mother's surname and become the noted writer "Frank O'Connor." Michael O'Donovan, still in his teens, drifted into the republican forces for no better reason than that a friend and mentor favored that side of the conflict. A poor Cork boy, so ashamed of his attraction to the literature of the English overlords that he escaped when he could into the Gaelic and even into German, O'Donovan never forgot his first sight of Childers, limping and frowning as he came down the stairs of a Cork hotel. He recalled him forty years later in *An Only Child* as

> a small, slight, grey-haired man in tweeds with a tweed cap pulled over his eyes, wearing a light mackintosh stuffed with papers and carrying another coat over his arm. Apart from his accent, which would have identified him anywhere, there was something peculiarly English about him; something that nowadays reminds me of some old parson or public-school teacher I have known, conscientious to a fault and overburdened with minor cares. His thin, grey face, shrunk almost to its mould of bone, had a coldness as though life had contracted behind it to its narrowest span; the brows were puckered in a triangle of obsessive thought like pain, and the eyes were clear, pale and tragic.

A day or two later, O'Donovan and a companion observed him "drifting aimlessly down King Street. . . . He had a sort of doddering drooping absent-mindedness that at times resembled that of a parson in a comedy." Noticing that he was being ineptly shadowed by a shabbily dressed man, they drew him into an entry and suggested he give up his gun.

> He was very alarmed at our manner, but with old-fashioned politeness he turned aside, unbuttoned one mackintosh, then another, then a jacket, and finally a vest. Just over his heart and fixed to his braces by a safety-pin was a delicately made gun such as a middle-aged lady of timid disposition might carry in her handbag.

This tiny weapon, not recorded as being fired while Childers possessed it, was to spell his doom.

Though the provisional government viewed him as de Valera's evil genius and the most dangerous man in the country, he seems to have been alternately distrusted and ignored by his companions. A Protestant Englishman whose every word and gesture recalled their ancient enemy, he was an unhappy misfit. At a country house commandeered as headquarters, it was country youths, O'Donovan saw, who occupied the upholstered furniture.

> There being no chair for Childers, nor anyone who valued his advice on military matters, he sat on a petrol can by the open door, his cap over his eyes and his mackintosh trailing on the floor, and went on scribbling his endless memoranda, articles and letters, like some old book-keeper who fears the new directors may think him superfluous.

In the retreat from Cork, O'Donovan spied Childers racing by, perched on the running board of a car. "Naturally, nobody had thought of offering the 'damned Englishman' his seat." Later, in Macroom, Childers gave up his bed in the middle of the night to newly arrived soldiers, and tramped the town till dawn. By this time the rebel army was melting away, and Childers was repeatedly warned that his life was in danger. "Oh, why does everyone tell me that?" he answered wearily on one occasion. An entire edition of the republican newssheet he managed to publish regularly was ditched when it became too dangerous to distribute, and his portable press was lost in a bog. Thereafter he was reduced to addressing envelopes for the cause. When local officers quashed a scheme to have Childers spirited away to France his fate was sealed.

Recalled to Dublin by de Valera, he set off with a cousin, David Robinson, in a hectic flight across the southern counties, mainly by dark, and reached his boyhood home on November 10. There, among the old well-loved scenes, he relaxed his guard. During the night Free State soldiers surrounded and entered the house. Though Childers seems to have pulled out his tiny Colt automatic, a servant thrust herself in the way, and he and Robinson were taken without a shot being fired.

In prison the two men used a tiny hole in the wall between their cells to play chess, with a board marked on the floor and pieces cut from newsprint. While Childers awaited trial, Winston Churchill denounced him in a speech as being actuated by hatred of his native land. Rumors were spread in high places about his outstanding wickedness, but at his secret court-martial on November 17 the only charge presented was unauthorized possession of an automatic pistol. He was speedily found guilty and sentenced to death. Although he refused to recognize the court's jurisdiction, a motion of *habeas corpus* was made on his behalf to the civil court. This delayed his execution from day to day. His elder son, Erskine Hamilton Childers, a future president of Ireland, was asked by his father during their final meeting at Beggar's Bush Barracks, Dublin, to seek out and shake the hands of all those who had signed the death warrant and to allow no bitterness to linger. To his wife, who was to outlive him by more than forty years, he wrote:

> I am fully prepared. . . . Serenity? Serenity, yes: I have that at last if never before. I die full of intense love for Ireland. . . . I felt what Churchill said about hatred against England. How well we know it is not true. I die loving England and passionately praying that she may change completely and finally towards Ireland.
>
> It is now 6 A.M. You will be pleased to know how imperturbably normal and tranquil I have been this night and am. It all seems perfectly simple and inevitable, like lying down after a long day's work. I shall have on my rosary, crucifix and our locket.

He spent his last hour with an old friend, the Protestant dean of Kildare, and ate his breakfast calmly. Telling the dean he was at peace with the world and bore no grudges, he was taken out by a party of Free State soldiers through the archway into an inner courtyard. At the time finally set for the execution, 7 A.M. on November 24, 1922, it had been dark; now, nearly an hour later, the light was still poor. He asked that he not be blindfolded. Walking across to the nervous young members of the firing squad, he calmly shook their hands, bidding them be of good cheer and do their duty as soldiers. While his grieving pastor watched from a distant window, he resumed his position against the wall and uttered his last words: "Come closer lads; it will be easier for you." As the rifles were raised, he looked proudly and steadfastly over them. . . .

Although other executions took place before "the troubles" came to an end, many of them without trial, the dispatching of Childers sent a chill through friends and foes alike, and his execution while the appeal from the *habeas corpus* decision was pending outraged the legal community. Still, there was little argument over the merits of the case. The

*Nation* in New York asked in a headline whether the Free State had gone mad, but it did not condone Childers's actions, merely feared that new passions would be aroused. Much of the London press was openly gleeful that an England-hater had received his deserts, but the *Times* at least shook its head over the spectacle. Should Childers's eminence have saved his life? The newspaper thought not.

> We hold that the only means for the Free State to establish its authority is to make that authority real, cost what it may. . . . In renouncing his country he took his life in his hands, and, with a personal courage beyond cavil, faced the consequences of his action. He challenged the only constituted authority in his adopted country and he has met his doom.

It is to his personal friends that we must look for an ultimate verdict on his actions. Two of them, one English and one Irish, are on record in the case. Alfred Ollivant, soldier turned novelist, who had been Childers's sailing companion, wrote:

> I loved Childers; but had I been President of the Irish Free State I should have signed his death warrant as surely if not as gladly as I should have signed away those greater rebels and lesser men who preceded him down the path of disruption and anarchy.

Desmond MacCarthy, who had "played with [Childers's] children and talked round his fire," declared, "I could not sign the petition for his pardon," and abhorred his friend's role as a leader of "martyrs and blackguards" in his last months. Yet he disagreed with those who believed his friend to have been actuated by hatred of England. "Indeed, his nature was singularly gentle and magnanimous." His error was in believing that "an Independent Republic could alone satisfy the national aspirations of Irishmen, and he died for that mistaken idea."

*The Riddle of the Sands* concerns the holiday adventures off Germany's Frisian and Baltic shores of two young men one summer in the late 1890s. A jaded young civil servant, Carruthers, is summoned to the Baltic by his friend, Arthur Davies, who is an accomplished yachtsman. After an awkward few days, during which the snobbish Carruthers fails to "hit it off" on the shabby old *Dulcibella* with his gauche, hesitant host, confidence is gradually established. Bit by bit, Davies discloses his suspicions of what the Germans are up to in the shallow waters behind the North Frisian Islands, and together the friends set about foiling these Prussian designs.

One may speculate on just how many real espionage missions, professional and amateur, were engendered by the fictional one. We know that two officers, Capt. B. F. Trench and Lt. V. R. Brandon, were caught in August, 1910, on the island of Borkum, inspecting German gun emplacements and newly installed searchlights. These tight-lipped men were surely professionals, but Bertrand Stewart, a young London attorney who was arrested in Bremen a year later, was more nearly an amateur spy of the Davies–Carruthers school. The Leipzig trials and the imprisonment of these men not only heightened anti-German feeling in Britain but increased the demand for *The Riddle of the Sands*, which was published in the United States for the first time in 1915.

Surprisingly, it is not Carruthers, the narrator, but Davies, exhibited in a cool, even unsympathetic light, who represents the author. Childers, in fact, permits us to see him as others only gradually learned to know him—awkward and gentle, but single-minded and implacable. This rare ability to view himself objectively was in itself an interesting facet of his character. Carruthers depicts Davies as "resourceful, skilful, and alert, but liable to lapse into a certain amateurish vagueness, half irritating and half amusing." This is paralleled by O'Donovan's description of Childers's "doddering drooping absent-mindedness" when wandering in Cork and even when inspecting the front line under the very barrels of the enemy guns.

Davies talks in the public-schoolboy manner that never fully deserted Childers after he left Haileybury, the "damned English" tone which was later to affront so grievously his Irish comrades-in-arms, but which in both men—the real and the created—served to disguise their sterner natures and passionate purposes. When Childers wrote of Davies's sense of mission he penned his own epitaph:

> Not that Davies ever doubted. Once set on the road he gripped his purpose with childlike faith and tenacity. It was his "chance."

War-scare fiction in Britain between about 1870 and the outbreak of World War I is a sub-genre that deserves a historian of its own. When it finally receives one he must surely take note of *The Battle of Dorking* (1871) at one extreme and P. G. Wodehouse's *The Swoop* (1909) at the other. Wodehouse's little-known novel tells the story of how England, invaded by Germans, was saved by a Boy Scout, Clarence MacAndrew Chugwater. *The Battle of Dorking*, which first appeared anonymously in *Blackwood's Magazine*, is a much more earnest work by Sir George Chesney. It is significant in drawing attention away from Britain's traditional enemy, France, to focus on a new threat. Chesney, alarmed by France's recent defeat by Germany, told the story of the British Army's defeat at Dorking after a German invasion at Worthing. The account engendered great interest for a while, but the old enmity with France gradually reasserted itself.

In 1900, under Germany's new Chancellor, von Bülow, a Navy law was promoted that had the aim of gradually giving the nation a great fleet in keeping with world-power status. Most Britons took little heed of these plans until the German navy became an obvious threat around 1908, but Childers, taking to heart the writings on sea-power by the American strategist Alfred T. Mahan, was early in the field with his fictional warning.

More significantly for the modern reader, *The Riddle of the Sands* is the first important British spy novel. Eric Ambler, himself a leading writer in the genre, has indeed described Childers's book as the earliest of all spy novels, recognizing the prior claim of James Fenimore Cooper's *The Spy* (1821) only to dismiss the book, which treats of the American War of Independence, as unreadable. Rudyard Kipling's *Kim*, which appeared the year before Childers's romance, clearly falls outside the canon; the eponymous hero's apprenticeship in the Secret Service is not central to the book's theme, serving merely to educate him in the shady walks of Anglo-Indian life.

Childers was followed by Joseph Conrad with his masterpiece, *The Secret Agent* (1907), and by the innumerable novels of E. Phillips Oppenheim and, on a lower level, William Le Queux. John Buchan's *The Thirty-Nine Steps* (1915) was the first of several adventures of Richard Hannay. W. Somerset Maugham's highly realistic *Ashenden* was published in 1928 and Compton Mackenzie's lighthearted but important *The Three Couriers* a year later. Several of Graham Greene's novels, including *The Confidential Agent* (1939), qualify on anyone's list of the best spy novels. More recently the fantasy of Ian Fleming's James Bond novels has been balanced by the shabby realism of John Le Carré's *The Spy Who Came In from the Cold* (1963).

Although *The Riddle of the Sands* was the earliest of this long line of British spy novels, it is in many ways quite unlike most of its successors. First, the spies are amateurs, self-appointed to their task; and second, the richness of technical detail, especially in the yachting sequences, would have made it an outstanding and unforgettable volume of adventure even if the intelligence-gathering episodes had been replaced by, say, a treasure hunt or a search for the great auk.

NORMAN DONALDSON

*Columbus, Ohio*
*October 1975*

# Preface to the Original Edition

A WORD about the origin and authorship of this book.

In October last (1902), my friend "Carruthers" visited me in my chambers, and, under a provisional pledge of secrecy, told me frankly the whole of the adventure described in these pages. Till then I had only known as much as the rest of his friends, namely, that he had recently undergone experiences during a yachting cruise with a certain Mr. "Davies" which had left a deep mark on his character and habits.

At the end of his narrative—which, from its bearing on studies and speculations of my own, as well as from its intrinsic interest and racy delivery, made a very deep impression on me—he added that the important facts discovered in the course of the cruise had, without a moment's delay, been communicated to the proper authorities, who, after some dignified incredulity, due in part, perhaps, to the pitiful inadequacy of their own secret service, had, he believed, made use of them, to avert a great national danger. I say "he believed," for though it was beyond question that the danger was averted for the time, it was doubtful whether they had stirred a foot to combat it, the secret discovered being of such a nature that mere suspicion of it on this side was likely to destroy its efficacy.

There, however that may be, the matter rested for a while, as, for personal reasons which will be manifest to the reader, he and Mr. "Davies" expressly wished it to rest.

But events were driving them to reconsider their decision. These seemed to show that the information wrung with such peril and labour from the German Government, and transmitted so promptly to our own, had had none but the most transitory influence on our policy. Forced to the conclusion that the national security was really being neglected, the two friends now had a mind to make their story public; and it was about this that "Carruthers" wished for my advice. The great drawback was that an Englishman, bearing an honoured name, was disgracefully implicated, and that unless infinite delicacy were used, innocent persons, and, especially, a young lady, would suffer pain and indignity, if his identity were known. Indeed, troublesome rumours, containing a grain of truth and a mass of falsehood, were already afloat.

After weighing both sides of the question, I gave my vote emphatically for publication. The personal drawbacks could, I thought, with tact be neutralized; while, from the public point of view, nothing but good could come from submitting the case to the common sense of the country at large. Publication, therefore, was agreed upon, and the next point was the form it should take. "Carruthers," with the concurrence of Mr. "Davies," was for a bald exposition of the essential facts, stripped of their warm human envelope. I was strongly against this course, first, because it would aggravate instead of allaying the rumours that were current; secondly, because in such a form the narrative would not carry conviction, and would thus defeat its own end. The persons and the events were indissolubly connected; to evade, abridge, suppress, would be to convey to the reader the idea of a concocted hoax. Indeed, I took bolder ground still, urging that the story should be made as explicit and circumstantial as possible, frankly and honestly for the purpose of entertaining and so of attracting a wide circle of readers. Even anonymity was undesirable. Nevertheless, certain precautions were imperatively needed.

To cut the matter short, they asked for my assistance and received it at once. It was arranged that I should edit the book; that "Carruthers" should give me his diary and recount to me in fuller detail and from his own point of view all the phases of the "quest," as they used to call it; that Mr. "Davies" should meet me with his charts and maps and do the same; and that the whole story should be written, as from the mouth of the former, with its humours and errors, its light and its dark side, just as it happened; with the following few limitations. The year it belongs to is disguised; the names of persons are throughout fictitious; and, at my instance, certain slight liberties have been taken to conceal the identity of the English characters.

Remember, also that these persons are living now in the midst of us, and if you find one topic touched on with a light and hesitating pen, do not blame the Editor, who, whether they are known or not, would rather say too little than say a word that might savour of impertinence.

E. C.

*March 1903*

NOTE

The maps and charts following p. xv and facing pp. 46, 97, and 150 are based on British and German Admiralty charts, with irrelevant details omitted.

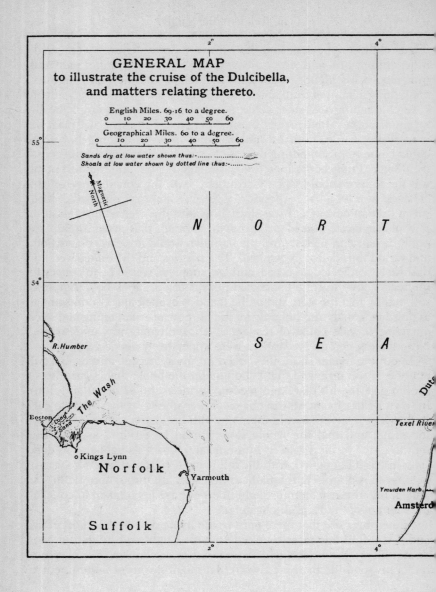

GENERAL MAP
to illustrate the cruise of the Dulcibella,
and matters relating thereto.

English Miles. 69·16 to a degree.
0   10   20   30   40   50   60

Geographical Miles. 60 to a degree.
0   10   20   30   40   50   60

Sands dry at low water shown thus:-
Shoals at low water shown by dotted line thus:-

Magnetic North

N   O   R   T

S   E   A

R. Humber

The Wash

Boston   Long Sand

o Kings Lynn

N o r f o l k   Yarmouth

S u f f o l k

Dut

Texel River

Ymuiden Harb.

Amsterd

MAP A.

Walker & Cockerell sc

# I

## The Letter

I HAVE read of men who, when forced by their calling to live for long periods in utter solitude—save for a few black faces—have made it a rule to dress regularly for dinner in order to maintain their self-respect and prevent a relapse into barbarism. It was in some such spirit, with an added touch of self-consciousness, that, at seven o'clock in the evening of 23rd September in a recent year, I was making my evening toilet in my chambers in Pall Mall. I thought the date and the place justified the parallel; to my advantage even; for the obscure Burmese administrator might well be a man of blunted sensibilities and coarse fibre, and at least he is alone with nature, while I—well, a young man of condition and fashion, who knows the right people, belongs to the right clubs, has a safe, possibly a brilliant, future in the Foreign Office—may be excused for a sense of complacent martyrdom, when, with his keen appreciation of the social calendar, he is doomed to the outer solitude of London in September. I say "martyrdom," but in fact the case was infinitely worse. For to feel oneself a martyr, as everybody knows, is a pleasurable thing, and the true tragedy of my position was that I had passed that stage. I had enjoyed what sweets it had to offer in ever dwindling degree since the middle of August, when ties were still fresh and sympathy abundant. I had been conscious that I was missed at Morven Lodge party. Lady Ashleigh herself had said so in the kindest possible manner, when she wrote to acknowledge the letter in which I explained, with an effectively austere reserve of language, that circumstances compelled me to remain at my office. "We know how busy you must be just now," she wrote, "and I do hope you won't overwork; we shall *all* miss you very much." Friend after friend "got away" to sport and fresh air, with promises to write and chaffing condolences, and as each deserted the sinking ship, I took a grim delight in my misery, positively almost enjoying the first week or two after my world had been finally dissipated to the four bracing winds of heaven. I began to take a spurious

1

interest in the remaining five millions, and wrote several clever letters in a vein of cheap satire, indirectly suggesting the pathos of my position, but indicating that I was broad-minded enough to find intellectual entertainment in the scenes, persons, and habits of London in the dead season. I even did rational things at the instigation of others. For, though I should have liked total isolation best, I, of course, found that there was a sediment of unfortunates like myself, who, unlike me, viewed the situation in a most prosaic light. There were river excursions, and so on, after office-hours; but I dislike the river at any time for its noisy vulgarity, and most of all at this season. So I dropped out of the fresh air brigade and declined H——'s offer to share a riverside cottage and run up to town in the mornings. I did spend one or two week-ends with the Catesbys in Kent; but I was not inconsolable when they let their house and went abroad, for I found that such partial compensations did not suit me. Neither did the taste for satirical observation last. A passing thirst, which I dare say many have shared, for adventures of the fascinating kind described in the *New Arabian Nights* led me on a few evenings into some shady haunts in Soho and farther eastward; but was finally quenched one sultry Saturday night after an hour's immersion in the reeking atmosphere of a low music-hall in Ratcliffe Highway, where I sat next a portly female who suffered from the heat, and at frequent intervals refreshed herself and an infant from a bottle of tepid stout.

By the first week in September I had abandoned all palliatives, and had settled into the dismal but dignified routine of office, club, and chambers. And now came the most cruel trial, for the hideous truth dawned on me that the world I found so indispensable could after all dispense with me. It was all very well for Lady Ashleigh to assure me that I was deeply missed; but a letter from F——, who was one of the party, written "in haste, just starting to shoot," and coming as a tardy reply to one of my cleverest, made me aware that the house party had suffered little from my absence, and that few sighs were wasted on me, even in the quarter which I had assumed to have been discreetly alluded to by the underlined *all* in Lady Ashleigh's "we shall *all* miss you." A thrust which smarted more, if it bit less deeply, came from my cousin Nesta, who wrote: "It's horrid for you to have to be baking in London now; but, after all, it must be a great pleasure to you" (malicious little wretch!) "to have such interesting and important work to do." Here was a nemesis for an innocent illusion I had been accustomed to foster in the minds of my relations and acquaintances, especially in the breasts of the trustful and admiring maidens whom I had taken down to dinner in the last two seasons; a fiction which I had almost reached the point of believing in myself. For the plain truth was that my work was neither interesting nor important, and consisted chiefly at present in smoking cigarettes, in saying that Mr. So-and-So was away and would be back about 1st October, in being absent for lunch from twelve till two, and in my spare moments making *précis* of—let us say—the less confidential consular reports, and squeezing the results into cast-iron schedules. The reason of my detention was not a cloud on the international horizon—though I may say in passing that there was such a cloud—but a caprice on the part of a remote and mighty personage, the effect of which, ramifying downwards, had dislocated the carefully-laid holiday plans of the humble juniors, and in my own small case had upset the arrangement between myself and K——, who positively liked the dog-days in Whitehall.

Only one thing was needed to fill my cup of bitterness, and this it was that specially occupied me as I dressed for dinner this evening. Two days more in this dead and fermenting city and my slavery would be at an end. Yes, but—irony of ironies!—I had nowhere to go to! The Morven Lodge party was breaking up. A dreadful rumour as to an engagement which had been one of its accursed fruits tormented me with the fresh certainty that I had not been missed, and bred in me that most desolating brand of cynicism which is produced by defeat through insignificance. Invitations for a later date, which I had declined in July with a gratifying sense of being much in request, now rose up spectrally to taunt me. There was at least one which I could easily have revived, but neither in this case nor in any other had there been any renewal of pressure, and there are moments when the difference between proposing oneself and surrendering as a prize to one of several eagerly competing hostesses seems too crushing to be contemplated. My own people were at Aix for my father's gout; to join them was a *pis aller* whose banality was repellent. Besides, they would be leaving soon for our home in Yorkshire, and I was not a prophet in my own country. In short, I was at the extremity of depression.

The usual preliminary scuffle on the staircase prepared me for the knock and entry of Withers. (One of the things which had for some time ceased to amuse me was the laxity of manners, proper to the season, among the servants of the big block of chambers where I lived.) Withers demurely handed me a letter bearing a German post-mark and marked "Urgent." I had just finished dressing, and was collecting my money and gloves. A momentary thrill of curiosity broke in upon my depression as I sat down to open it. A corner on the reverse of the envelope bore the blotted legend: "Very sorry, but there's one other thing—a pair of rigging screws from Carey and Neilson's, size 1⅜, *galvanized.*" Here it is:

*Yacht "Dulcibella,"*
*Flensburg, Schleswig-Holstein, 21st Sept.*

DEAR CARRUTHERS,—I daresay you'll be surprised at hearing from me, as it's ages since we met. It is more than likely, too, that what I'm going to suggest won't suit you, for I know nothing of your plans, and if you're in town at all you're probably just getting into harness again and can't get away. So I merely write on the offchance to ask if you would care to come out here and join me in a little yachting, and, I hope, duck shooting. I know you're keen on shooting, and I sort of remember that you have done some yachting too, though I rather forget about that. This part of the Baltic—the Schleswig fiords—is a splendid cruising-ground—A1 scenery—and there ought to be plenty of duck about soon, if it gets cold enough. I came out here *via* Holland and the Frisian Islands, starting early in August. My pals have had to leave me, and I'm badly in want of another, as I don't want to lay up yet for a bit. I needn't say how glad I should be if you could come. If you can, send me a wire to the P.O. here. Flushing and on by Hamburg will be your best route, I think. I'm having a few repairs done here, and will have them ready sharp by the time your train arrives. Bring your gun and a good lot of No. 4's; and would you mind calling at Lancaster's and asking for mine, and bringing it too? Bring some oilskins. Better get the eleven-shilling sort, jacket and trousers—not the "yachting" brand; and if you paint bring your gear. I know you speak German like a native, and that will be a great help. Forgive this hail of directions, but I've a sort of feeling that I'm in luck and that you'll come. Anyway, I hope you and the F.O. both flourish. Good-bye.

Yours ever,     ARTHUR H. DAVIES.

Would you mind bringing me out a *prismatic compass*, and a pound of Raven Mixture.

This letter marked an epoch for me; but I little suspected the fact as I crumpled it into my pocket and started languidly on the *voie douloureuse* which I nightly followed to the club. In Pall Mall there were no dignified greetings to be exchanged now with well-groomed acquaintances. The only people to be seen were some late stragglers from the park, with a perambulator and some hot and dusty children lagging fretfully behind; some rustic sightseers draining the last dregs of the daylight in an effort to make out from their guide-books which of these reverend piles was which; a policeman and a builder's cart. Of course the club was a strange one, both of my own being closed for cleaning, a coincidence expressly planned by Providence for my inconvenience. The club which you are "permitted to make use of" on these occasions always irritates with its strangeness and discomfort. The few occupants seem odd and oddly dressed, and you wonder how they got there. The particular weekly that you want is not taken in; the dinner is execrable, and the ventilation a farce. All these evils oppressed me to-night. And yet I was puzzled to find that somewhere within me there was a faint lightening of the spirits; causeless, as far as I could discover. It could not be Davies's letter. Yachting in the Baltic at the end of September! The very idea made one shudder. Cowes, with a pleasant party and hotels handy, was all very well. An August cruise on a steam yacht in French waters or the Highlands was all very well; but what kind of a yacht was this? It must be of a certain size to have got so far, but I thought I remembered enough of Davies's means to know that he had no money to waste on luxuries. That brought me to the man himself. I had known him at Oxford—not as one of my immediate set; but we were a sociable college, and I had seen a good deal of him, liking him for his physical energy combined with a certain simplicity and modesty, though, indeed, he had nothing to be conceited about; liked him, in fact, in the way that at that receptive period one likes many men whom one never keeps up with later. We had both gone down in the same year—three years ago now. I had gone to France and Germany for two years to learn the languages; he had failed for the Indian Civil, and then had gone into a solicitor's office. I had only seen him since at rare intervals, though I admitted to myself that for his part he had clung loyally to what ties of friendship there were between us. But the truth was that we had drifted apart from the nature of things. I had passed brilliantly into my profession, and on the few occasions I had met him since I made my triumphant *début* in society I had found nothing left in common between us. He seemed to know none of my friends, he dressed indifferently, and I thought him dull. I had always connected him with boats and the sea, but never with yachting, in the sense that I understood it. In college days he had nearly persuaded me into sharing a squalid week in some open boat he had picked up, and was going to sail among some dreary mud-flats somewhere on the east coast. There was nothing else, and the funereal function of dinner drifted on. But I found myself remembering at the *entrée* that I had recently heard, at second or third hand, of something else about him— exactly what I could not recall. When I reached the savoury, I had concluded, so far as I had centred my mind on it at all, that the whole thing was a culminating irony, as, indeed, was the savoury in its way. After the wreck of my pleasant plans and the fiasco of my martyrdom, to be asked as consolation to spend October freezing in the Baltic with an eccentric nonentity who bored me! Yet, as I smoked my cigar in the ghastly splendour of the empty smoking-room, the subject came up again. Was there anything in it? There were certainly no alternatives at hand. And to bury myself in the Baltic at this unearthly time of year had at least a smack of tragic thoroughness about it.

I pulled out the letter again, and ran down its impulsive staccato sentences, affecting to ignore what a gust of fresh air, high spirits, and good fellowship this flimsy bit of paper wafted into the jaded club-room. On reperusal, it was full of evil presage—"A1 scenery"—but what of equinoctial storms and October fogs? Every sane yachtsman was paying off his crew now. "There ought to be duck"—vague, very vague. "If it gets cold enough" . . . cold and yachting seemed to be a gratuitously monstrous union. His pals had left him; why? "Not the 'yachting' brand"; and why not? As to the size, comfort, and crew of the yacht—all cheerfully ignored; so many maddening blanks. And, by the way, why in Heaven's name "a prismatic compass"? I fingered a few magazines, played a game of fifty with a friendly old fogey, too importunate to be worth the labour of resisting, and went back to my chambers to bed, ignorant that a friendly Providence had come to my rescue; and, indeed, rather resenting any clumsy attempt at such friendliness.

## 2

### The *Dulcibella*

THAT two days later I should be found pacing the deck of the Flushing steamer with a ticket for Hamburg in my pocket may seem a strange result, yet not so strange if you have divined my state of mind. You will guess, at any rate, that I was armed with the conviction that I was doing an act of obscure penance, rumours of which might call attention to my lot and perhaps awaken remorse in the right quarter, while it left me free to enjoy myself unobtrusively in the remote event of enjoyment being possible.

The fact was that, at breakfast on the morning after the arrival of the letter, I had still found that inexplicable lightening which I mentioned before, and strong enough to warrant a revival of the pros and cons. An important pro which I had not thought of before was that after all it was a good-natured piece of unselfishness to join Davies; for he had spoken of the want of a pal, and seemed honestly to be in need of me. I almost clutched at this consideration. It was an admirable excuse, when I reached my office that day, for a resigned study of the Continental Bradshaw, and an order to Carter to unroll a great creaking wall-map of Germany and find me Flensburg. The latter labour I might have saved him, but it was good for Carter to have something to do; and his patient ignorance was amusing. With most of the map and what it suggested I was tolerably familiar, for I had not wasted my year in Germany, whatever I had done or not done since. Its people, history, progress, and future had interested me intensely, and I had still friends in Dresden and Berlin. Flensburg recalled the Danish war of '64, and by the time Carter's researches had ended in success I had forgotten the task set him, and was wondering whether the prospect of seeing something of that lovely region of Schleswig-Holstein,* as I knew from hearsay that it was, was at all to be set against such an uncomfortable way of seeing it, with the season so late, the company so unattractive, and all the other drawbacks which I counted and treasured as proofs of my desperate condition, if I *were* to go. It needed little to decide me, and I think K——'s arrival from Switzerland, offensively sunburnt, was the finishing touch. His greeting was "Hullo, Carruthers, you here? Thought you had got away long ago. Lucky devil, though, to be going now, just in time for the best driving and the early pheasants. The heat's been shocking out there. Carter, bring me a Bradshaw"—(an extraordinary book, Bradshaw, turned to from habit, even when least wanted, as men fondle guns and rods in the close season).

By lunch-time the weight of indecision had been removed, and I found myself entrusting Carter with a telegram to Davies, P.O., Flensburg. "Thanks; expect me 9.34 p.m. 26th"; which produced, three hours later, a reply: "Delighted; please bring a No. 3 Rippingille stove"—a perplexing and ominous direction, which somehow chilled me in spite of its subject matter.

Indeed, my resolution was continually faltering. It faltered when I turned out my gun in the evening and thought of the grouse it ought to have accounted for. It faltered again when I contemplated the miscellaneous list of commissions, sown broadcast through Davies's letter, to fulfil which seemed to make me a willing tool where my chosen *rôle* was that of an embittered exile, or at least a condescending ally. However, I faced the commissions manfully, after leaving the office.

At Lancaster's I inquired for his gun, was received coolly, and had to pay a heavy bill, which it seemed to have incurred, before it was handed over. Having ordered the gun and No. 4's to be sent to my chambers, I bought the Raven mixture with that peculiar sense of injury which the prospect of smuggling in another's behalf always entails; and wondered where in the world Carey and Neilson's was, a firm which Davies spoke of as though it were as well known as the Bank of England or the Stores, instead of specializing in "rigging-screws," whatever they might be. They sounded important, though, and it would be only polite to unearth them. I connected them with the "few repairs" and awoke new misgivings. At the Stores I asked for a No. 3 Rippingille stove, and was confronted with a formidable and hideous piece of

*See Map A.

ironmongery, which burned petroleum in two capacious tanks, horribly prophetic of a smell of warm oil. I paid for this miserably, convinced of its grim efficiency, but speculating as to the domestic conditions which caused it to be sent for as an afterthought by telegram. I also asked about rigging-screws in the yachting department, but learnt that they were not kept in stock; that Carey and Neilson's would certainly have them, and that their shop was in the Minories, in the far east, meaning a journey nearly as long as to Flensburg, and twice as tiresome. They would be shut by the time I got there, so after this exhausting round of duty I went home in a cab, omitted dressing for dinner (an epoch in itself), ordered a chop up from the basement kitchen, and spent the rest of the evening packing and writing, with the methodical gloom of a man setting his affairs in order for the last time.

The last of those airless nights passed. The astonished Withers saw me breakfasting at eight, and at 9.30 I was vacantly examining rigging-screws with what wits were left me after a sulphurous ride in the Underground to Aldgate. I laid great stress on the ⅜'s, and the galvanism, and took them on trust, ignorant as to their functions. For the eleven-shilling oilskins I was referred to a villainous den in a back street, which the shopman said they always recommended, and where a dirty and bejewelled Hebrew chaffered with me (beginning at 18s.) over two reeking orange slabs distantly resembling moieties of the human figure. Their odour made me close prematurely for 14s., and I hurried back (for I was due there at eleven) to my office with my two disreputable brown-paper parcels, one of which made itself so noticeable in the close official air that Carter attentively asked if I would like to have it sent to my chambers, and K—— was inquisitive to bluntness about it and my movements. But I did not care to enlighten K——, whose comments I knew would be provokingly envious or wounding to my pride in some way.

I remembered, later on, the prismatic compass, and wired to the Minories to have one sent at once, feeling rather relieved that I was not present there to be cross-examined as to size and make. The reply was, "Not stocked; try surveying-instrument maker"—a reply both puzzling and reassuring, for Davies's request for a compass had given me more uneasiness than anything, while, to find that what he wanted turned out to be a surveying-instrument, was a no less perplexing discovery. That day I made my last *précis* and handed over my schedules— Procrustean beds, where unwilling facts were stretched and tortured— and said good-bye to my temporary chief, genial and lenient M——, who wished me a jolly holiday with all sincerity.

At seven I was watching a cab packed with my personal luggage and the collection of unwieldy and incongruous packages that my shopping had drawn down on me. Two deviations after that wretched prismatic compass—which I obtained in the end second-hand, *faute de mieux*, near Victoria, at one of those showy shops which look like jewellers' and are really pawnbrokers'—nearly caused me to miss my train. But at 8.30 I had shaken off the dust of London from my feet, and at 10.30 I was, as I have announced, pacing the deck of a Flushing steamer, adrift on this fatuous holiday in the far Baltic.

An air from the west, cooled by a midday thunderstorm, followed the steamer as she slid through the calm channels of the Thames estuary, passed the cordon of scintillating lightships that watch over the sea-roads to the imperial city like pickets round a sleeping army, and slipped out into the dark spaces of the North Sea. Stars were bright, summer scents from the Kent cliffs mingled coyly with vulgar steamer-smells; the summer weather held immutably. Nature, for her part, seemed resolved to be no party to my penance, but to be imperturbably bent on shedding mild ridicule over my wrongs. An irresistible sense of peace and detachment, combined with that delicious physical awakening that pulses through the nerve-sick townsman when city airs and bald routine are left behind him, combined to provide me, however thankless a subject, with a solid background of resignation. Stowing this safely away, I could calculate my intentions with cold egotism. If the weather held I might pass a not intolerable fortnight with Davies. When it broke up, as it was sure to, I could easily excuse myself from the pursuit of the problematical ducks; the wintry logic of facts would, in any case, decide him to lay up his yacht, for he could scarcely think of sailing home at such a season. I could then take a chance lying ready of spending a few weeks in Dresden or elsewhere. I settled this programme comfortably and then turned in.

From Flushing eastward to Hamburg, then northward to Flensburg, I cut short the next day's sultry story. Past dyke and windmill and still canals, on to blazing stubbles and roaring towns; at the last, after dusk, through a quiet level region where the train pottered from one lazy little station to another, and at ten o'clock I found myself, stiff and stuffy, on the platform at Flensburg, exchanging greetings with Davies.

"It's awfully good of you to come."

"Not at all; it's very good of you to ask me."

We were both of us ill at ease. Even in the dim gaslight he clashed on my notions of a yachtsman—no cool white ducks or neat blue serge; and where was the snowy crowned yachting cap, that precious charm that so easily converts a landsman into a dashing mariner? Conscious that this impressive uniform, in high perfection, was lying ready in my portmanteau, I felt oddly guilty. He wore an old Norfolk jacket, muddy brown shoes, grey flannel trousers (or had they been white?), and an

ordinary tweed cap. The hand he gave me was horny, and appeared to
be stained with paint; the other one, which carried a parcel, had a bandage on it which would have borne renewal. There was an instant of
mutual inspection. I thought he gave me a shy, hurried scrutiny as
though to test past conjectures, with something of anxiety in it, and perhaps (save the mark!) a tinge of admiration. The face was familiar, and
yet not familiar; the pleasant blue eyes, open, clean-cut features, unin-
tellectual forehead were the same; so were the brisk and impulsive
movements; there was some change; but the moment of awkward hesitation was over and the light was bad; and, while strolling down the
platform for my luggage, we chatted with constraint about trivial
things.

"By the way," he suddenly said, laughing, "I'm afraid I'm not fit to be
seen; but it's so late it doesn't matter. I've been painting hard all day,
and just got it finished. I only hope we shall have some wind to-morrow—it's been hopelessly calm lately. I say, you've brought a good deal
of stuff," he concluded, as my belongings began to collect.

Here was a reward for my submissive exertions in the far east!

"You gave me a good many commissions!"

"Oh, I didn't mean those things," he said, absently. "Thanks for
bringing them, by the way. That's the stove, I suppose; cartridges, this
one, by the weight. You got the rigging-screws all right, I hope? They're
not really necessary, of course" (I nodded vacantly, and felt a little
hurt); "but they're simpler than lanyards, and you can't get them here.
It's that portmanteau," he said, slowly, measuring it with a doubtful eye.
"Never mind! we'll try. You couldn't do with the Gladstone only, I suppose? You see, the dinghy—h'm, and there's the hatchway, too"—he
was lost in thought. "Anyhow, we'll try. I'm afraid there are no cabs; but
it's quite near, and the porter'll help."

Sickening forebodings crept over me, while Davies shouldered my
Gladstone and clutched at the parcels.

"Aren't your men here?" I asked, faintly.

"Men?" He looked confused. "Oh, perhaps I ought to have told you,
I never have any paid hands; it's quite a small boat, you know—I hope
you didn't expect luxury. I've managed her single-handed for some
time. A man would be no use, and a horrible nuisance." He revealed
these appalling truths with a cheerful assurance, which did nothing to
hide a naïve apprehension of their effect on me. There was a check in
our mobilization.

"It's rather late to go on board, isn't it?" I said, in a wooden voice.
Someone was turning out the gaslights, and the porter yawned ostenta-
tiously. "I think I'd rather sleep at an hotel to-night." A strained pause.

"Oh, of course you can do that, if you like," said Davies, in transparent distress of mind. "But it seems hardly worth while to cart this stuff all the way to an hotel (I believe they're all on the other side of the harbour), and back again to the boat to-morrow. She's quite comfortable, and you're sure to sleep well, as you're tired."

"We can leave the things here," I argued feebly, "and walk over with my bag."

"Oh, I shall have to go aboard anyhow," he rejoined; "I *never* sleep on shore."

He seemed to be clinging timidly, but desperately, to some diplomatic end. A stony despair was invading me and paralysing resistance. Better face the worst and be done with it.

"Come on," I said, grimly.

Heavily loaded, we stumbled over railway lines and rubble heaps, and came on the harbour. Davies led the way to a stairway, whose weedy steps disappeared below in gloom.

"If you'll get into the dinghy," he said, all briskness now, "I'll pass the things down."

I descended gingerly, holding as a guide a sodden painter which ended in a small boat, and conscious that I was collecting slime on cuffs and trousers.

"Hold up!" shouted Davies, cheerfully, as I sat down suddenly near the bottom, with one foot in the water.

I climbed wretchedly into the dinghy and awaited events.

"Now float her up close under the quay wall, and make fast to the ring down there," came down from above, followed by the slack of the sodden painter, which knocked my cap off as it fell. "All fast? Any knot'll do," I heard, as I grappled with this loathsome task, and then a big, dark object loomed overhead and was lowered into the dinghy. It was my portmanteau, and, placed athwart, exactly filled all the space amidships. "Does it fit?" was the anxious inquiry from aloft.

"Beautifully."

"Capital!"

Scratching at the greasy wall to keep the dinghy close to it, I received in succession our stores, and stowed the cargo as best I could, while the dinghy sank lower and lower in the water, and its precarious superstructure grew higher.

"Catch!" was the final direction from above, and a damp soft parcel hit me in the chest. "Be careful of that, it's meat. Now back to the stairs!"

I painfully acquiesced, and Davies appeared.

"It's a bit of a load, and she's rather deep; but I *think* we shall manage," he reflected. "You sit right aft, and I'll row."

I was too far gone for curiosity as to how this monstrous pyramid was to be rowed, or even for surmises as to its foundering by the way. I crawled to my appointed seat, and Davies extricated the buried sculls by a series of tugs, which shook the whole structure, and made us roll alarmingly. How he stowed himself into rowing posture I have not the least idea, but eventually we were moving sluggishly out into the open water, his head just visible in the bows. We had started from what appeared to be the head of a narrow loch, and were leaving behind us the lights of a big town. A long frontage of lamp-lit quays was on our left, with here and there the vague hull of a steamer alongside. We passed the last of the lights and came out into a broader stretch of water, when a light breeze was blowing and dark hills could be seen on either shore.

"I'm lying a little way down the fiord, you see," said Davies. "I hate to be too near a town, and I found a carpenter handy here—There she is! I wonder how you'll like her!"

I roused myself. We were entering a little cove encircled by trees, and approaching a light which flickered in the rigging of a small vessel, whose outline gradually defined itself.

"Keep her off," said Davies, as we drew alongside.

In a moment he had jumped on deck, tied the painter, and was round at my end.

"You hand them up," he ordered, "and I'll take them."

It was a laborious task, with the one relief that it was not far to hand them—a doubtful compensation, for other reasons distantly shaping themselves. When the stack was transferred to the deck I followed it, tripping over the flabby meat parcel, which was already showing ghastly signs of disintegration under the dew. Hazily there floated through my mind my last embarkation on a yacht; my faultless attire, the trim gig and obsequious sailors, the accommodation ladder flashing with varnish and brass in the August sun; the orderly, snowy decks and basket chairs under the awning aft. What a contrast with this sordid midnight scramble, over damp meat and littered packing-cases! The bitterest touch of all was a growing sense of inferiority and ignorance which I had never before been allowed to feel in my experience of yachts.

Davies awoke from another reverie over my portmanteau to say, cheerily: "I'll just show you round down below first, and then we'll stow things away and get to bed."

He dived down a companion ladder, and I followed cautiously. A complex odour of paraffin, past cookery, tobacco, and tar saluted my nostrils.

"Mind your head," said Davies, striking a match and lighting a candle, while I groped into the cabin. "You'd better sit down; it's easier to look round."

There might well have been sarcasm in this piece of advice, for I must have cut a ridiculous figure, peering awkwardly and suspiciously round, with shoulders and head bent to avoid the ceiling, which seemed in the half-light to be even nearer the floor than it was.

"You see," were Davies's reassuring words, "there's plenty of room to *sit* upright" (which was strictly true; but I am not very tall, and he is short). "Some people make a point of head-room, but I never mind much about it. That's the centre-board case," he explained, as, in stretching my legs out, my knee came into contact with a sharp edge.

I had not seen this devilish obstruction, as it was hidden beneath the table, which indeed rested on it at one end. It appeared to be a long, low triangle, running lengthways with the boat and dividing the naturally limited space into two.

"You see, she's a flat-bottomed boat, drawing very little water without the plate; that's why there's so little head-room. For deep water you lower the plate; so, in one way or another, you can go practically anywhere."

I was not nautical enough to draw any very definite conclusions from this, but what I did draw were not promising. The latter sentences were spoken from the forecastle, whither Davies had crept through a low sliding door, like that of a rabbit-hutch, and was already busy with a kettle over a stove which I made out to be a battered and disreputable twin brother of the No. 3 Rippingille.

"It'll be boiling soon," he remarked, "and we'll have some grog."

My eyes were used to the light now, and I took in the rest of my surroundings, which may be very simply described. Two long cushion-covered seats flanked the cabin, bounded at the after end by cupboards, one of which was cut low to form a sort of miniature sideboard, with glasses hung in a rack above it. The deck overhead was very low at each side but rose shoulder high for a space in the middle, where a "coach-house roof" with a skylight gave additional cabin space. Just outside the door was a fold-up washing-stand. On either wall were long net-racks holding a medley of flags, charts, caps, cigar-boxes, hanks of yarn, and such like. Across the forward bulkhead was a bookshelf crammed to overflowing with volumes of all sizes, many upside down and some coverless. Below this were a pipe-rack, an aneroid, and a clock with a hearty tick. All the woodwork was painted white, and to a less jaundiced eye than mine the interior might have had an enticing look of snugness. Some Kodak prints were nailed roughly on the after bulkhead, and just over the doorway was the photograph of a young girl.

"That's my sister," said Davies, who had emerged and saw me looking at it. "Now, let's get the stuff down." He ran up the ladder, and soon my portmanteau blackened the hatchway, and a great straining and squeezing began. "I was afraid it was too big," came down; "I'm sorry, but you'll have to unpack on deck—we may be able to squash it down when it's empty."

Then the wearisome tail of packages began to form a fresh stack in the cramped space at my feet, and my back ached with stooping and moiling in unfamiliar places. Davies came down, and with unconcealed pride introduced me to the sleeping cabin (he called the other one "the saloon"). Another candle was lit and showed two short and narrow berths with blankets, but no sign of sheets; beneath these were drawers, one set of which Davies made me master of, evidently thinking them a princely allowance of space for my wardrobe.

"You can chuck your things down the skylight on to your berth as you unpack them," he remarked. "By the way, I doubt if there's room for all you've got. I suppose you couldn't manage—"

"No, I couldn't," I said shortly.

The absurdity of argument struck me; two men, doubled up like monkeys, cannot argue.

"If you'll go out I shall be able to get out too," I added. He seemed miserable at this ghost of an altercation, and I pushed past, mounted the ladder, and in the expiring moonlight unstrapped that accursed portmanteau and, brimming over with irritation, groped among its contents, sorting some into the skylight with the same feeling that nothing mattered much now, and it was best to be done with it; repacking the rest with guilty stealth ere Davies should discover their character, and strapping up the whole again. Then I sat down upon my white elephant and shivered, for the chill of autumn was in the air. It suddenly struck me that if it had been raining things might have been worse still. The notion made me look round. The little cove was still as glass; stars above and stars below; a few white cottages glimmering at one point on the shore; in the west the lights of Flensburg; to the east the fiord broadening into unknown gloom. From Davies toiling below there were muffled sounds of wrenching, pushing, and hammering, punctuated occasionally by a heavy splash as something shot up from the hatchway and fell into the water.

How it came about I do not know. Whether it was something pathetic in the look I had last seen on his face—a look which I associated for no reason whatever with his bandaged hand; whether it was one of those instants of clear vision in which our separate selves are seen divided, the baser from the better, and I saw my silly egotism in contrast with a simple generous nature; whether it was an impalpable air of mystery which pervaded the whole enterprise and refused to be dissipated by its most mortifying and vulgarizing incidents—a mystery dimly connected with my companion's obvious consciousness of having misled me into joining him; whether it was only the stars and the cool air rousing atrophied instincts of youth and spirits; probably, indeed, it was all these influences, cemented into strength by a ruthless sense of humour which whispered that I was in danger of making a mere commonplace fool of myself in spite of all my laboured calculations; but whatever it was, in a flash my mood changed. The crown of martyrdom disappeared, the wounded vanity healed; that precious fund of fictitious resignation drained away, but left no void. There was left a fashionable and dishevelled young man sitting in the dew and in the dark on a ridiculous portmanteau which dwarfed the yacht that was to carry it; a youth acutely sensible of ignorance in a strange and strenuous atmosphere; still feeling sore and victimized; but withal sanely ashamed and sanely resolved to enjoy himself. I anticipate; for though the change was radical its full growth was slow. But in any case it was here and now that it took its birth.

"Grog's ready!" came from below. Bunching myself for the descent I found to my astonishment that all trace of litter had miraculously vanished, and a cosy neatness reigned. Glasses and lemons were on the table, and a fragrant smell of punch had deadened previous odours. I showed little emotion at these amenities, but enough to give intense relief to Davies, who delightedly showed me his devices for storage, praising the "roominess" of his floating den. "There's your stove, you see," he ended; "I've chucked the old one overboard." It was a weakness of his, I should say here, to rejoice in throwing things overboard on the flimsiest pretexts. I afterwards suspected that the new stove had not been "really necessary" any more than the rigging-screws, but was an excuse for gratifying this curious taste.

We smoked and chatted for a little, and then came the problem of going to bed. After much bumping of knuckles and head, and many giddy writhings, I mastered it, and lay between the rough blankets. Davies, moving swiftly and deftly, was soon in his.

"It's quite comfortable, isn't it?" he said, as he blew out the light from where he lay, with an accuracy which must have been the fruit of long practice.

I felt prickly all over, and there was a damp patch on the pillow, which was soon explained by a heavy drop of moisture falling on my forehead.

"I suppose the deck's not leaking?" I said, as mildly as I could.

"I'm awfully sorry," said Davies, earnestly, tumbling out of his bunk. "It must be the heavy dew. I did a lot of caulking yesterday, but I suppose I missed that place. I'll run up and square it with an oilskin."

"What's wrong with your hand?" I asked, sleepily, on his return, for gratitude reminded me of that bandage.

"Nothing much; I strained it the other day," was the reply; and then the seemingly inconsequent remark: "I'm glad you brought that prismatic compass. It's not really necessary, of course; but" (muffled by blankets) "it may come in useful."

## 3

### Davies

I DOZED but fitfully, with a fretful sense of sore elbows and neck and many a draughty hiatus among the blankets. It was broad daylight before I had reached the stage of torpor in which such slumber merges. That was finally broken by the descent through the skylight of a torrent of water. I started up, bumped my head hard against the decks, and blinked leaden-eyed upwards.

"Sorry! I'm scrubbing decks. Come up and bathe. Slept well?" I heard a voice saying from aloft.

"Fairly well," I growled, stepping out into a pool of water on the oilcloth. Thence I stumbled up the ladder, dived overboard, and buried bad dreams, stiffness, frowsiness, and tormented nerves in the loveliest fiord of the lovely Baltic. A short and furious swim and I was back again, searching for a means of ascent up the smooth black side, which, low as it was, was slippery and unsympathetic. Davies, in a loose canvas shirt, with the sleeves tucked up, and flannels rolled up to the knee, hung over me with a rope's end, and chatted unconcernedly about the easiness of the job when you know how, adjuring me to mind the paint, and talking about an accommodation ladder he had once had, but had thrown overboard because it was so horribly in the way. When I arrived, my knees and elbows were picked out in black paint, to his consternation. Nevertheless, as I plied the towel, I knew that I had left in those limpid depths yet another crust of discontent and self-conceit.

As I dressed into flannels and blazer, I looked round the deck, and with an unskilled and doubtful eye took in all that the darkness had hitherto hidden. She seemed very small (in point of fact she was seven tons), something over thirty feet in length and nine in beam, a size very suitable to week-ends in the Solent, for such as liked that sort of thing; but that she should have come from Dover to the Baltic suggested a world of physical endeavour of which I had never dreamed. I passed to the aesthetic side. Smartness and beauty were essential to yachts, in my mind, but with the best resolves to be pleased I found little encouragement here. The hull seemed too low, and the mainmast too high; the cabin roof looked clumsy, and the skylights saddened the eye with dull iron and plebeian graining. What brass there was, on the tiller-head and elsewhere, was tarnished with sickly green. The decks had none of that creamy purity which Cowes expects, but were rough and grey, and showed tarry exhalations round the seams and rusty stains near the bows. The ropes and rigging were in mourning when contrasted with the delicate buff manilla so satisfying to the artistic eye as seen against the blue of a June sky at Southsea. Nor was the whole effect bettered by many signs of recent refitting. An impression of paint, varnish, and carpentry was in the air; a gaudy new burgee fluttered aloft; there seemed to be a new rope or two, especially round the diminutive mizzenmast, which itself looked altogether new. But all this only emphasized the general plainness, reminding one of a respectable woman of the working-classes trying to dress above her station, and soon likely to give it up.

That the *ensemble* was businesslike and solid even my untrained eye could see. Many of the deck fittings seemed disproportionately substantial. The anchor-chain looked contemptuous of its charge; the binnacle with its compass was of a size and prominence almost comically impressive, and was, moreover, the only piece of brass which was burnished and showed traces of reverent care. Two huge coils of stout and dingy warp lay just abaft the mainmast, and summed up the weather-beaten aspect of the little ship. I should add here that in the distant past she had been a lifeboat, and had been clumsily converted into a yacht by the addition of a counter, deck, and the necessary spars. She was built, as all lifeboats are, diagonally, of two skins of teak, and thus had immense strength, though, in the matter of looks, all a hybrid's failings.

Hunger and "Tea's made!" from below brought me down to the cabin, where I found breakfast laid out on the table over the centreboard case, with Davies earnestly presiding, rather flushed as to the face, and sooty as to the fingers. There was a slight shortage of plate and crockery, but I praised the bacon and could do so truthfully, for its crisp and steaming shavings would have put to shame the efforts of my London cook. Indeed, I should have enjoyed the meal heartily were it not for the lowness of the sofa and table, causing a curvature of the body which made swallowing a more lengthy process than usual, and induced a periodical yearning to get up and stretch—a relief which spelt disaster to the skull. I noticed, too, that Davies spoke with a zest, sinister to me, of the delights of white bread and fresh milk, which he seemed to consider unusual luxuries, though suitable to an inaugural banquet in honour of a fastidious stranger. "One can't be always going on shore," he said, when I showed a discreet interest in these things. "I lived for ten days on a big rye loaf over in the Frisian Islands."

"And it died hard, I suppose?"

"Very hard, but" (gravely) "quite good. After that I taught myself to make rolls; had no baking powder at first, so used Eno's fruit salt, but they wouldn't rise much with that. As for milk, condensed is—I hope you don't mind it?"

I changed the subject, and asked about his plans.

"Let's get under way at once," he said, "and sail down the fiord." I tried for something more specific, but he was gone, and his voice drowned in the fo'c'sle by the clatter and swish of washing up. Thenceforward events moved with bewildering rapidity. Humbly desirous of being useful I joined him on deck, only to find that he scarcely noticed me, save as a new and unexpected obstacle in his round of activity. He was everywhere at once—heaving in chain, hooking on halyards, hauling ropes; while my part became that of the clown who does things after they are already done, for my knowledge of a yacht was of that floating and inaccurate kind which is useless in practice. Soon the anchor was up (a great rusty monster it was!), the sails set, and Davies was darting swiftly to and fro between the tiller and jib-sheets, while the *Dulcibella* bowed a lingering farewell to the shore and headed for the open fiord. Erratic puffs from the high land behind made her progress timorous at first, but soon the fairway was reached and a true breeze from Flensburg and the west took her in its friendly grip. Steadily she rustled down the calm blue highway whose soft beauty was the introduction to a passage in my life, short, but pregnant with moulding force, through stress and strain, for me and others.

Davies was gradually resuming his natural self, with abstracted intervals, in which he lashed the helm to a finger a distant rope, with such speed that the movements seemed simultaneous. Once he vanished, only to reappear in an instant with a chart, which he studied, while steering, with a success that its reluctant folds seemed to render impossible. Waiting respectfully for his revival I had full time to look about. The fiord here was about a mile broad. From the shore we had left the hills rose steeply, but with no rugged grandeur; the outlines were soft; there were green spaces and rich woods on the lower slopes; a little white town was opening up in one place, and scattered farms dotted the prospect. The other shore, which I could just see, framed between the gunwale and the mainsail, as I sat leaning against the hatchway, and sadly missing a deck-chair, was lower and lonelier, though prosperous and pleasing to the eye. Spacious pastures led up by slow degrees to ordered clusters of wood, which hinted at the presence of some great manor house. Behind us, Flensburg was settling into haze. Ahead, the scene was shut in by the contours of hills, some clear, some dreamy and distant. Lastly, a single glimpse of water shining between the folds of hill far away hinted at spaces of distant sea of which this was but a secluded inlet. Everywhere was that peculiar charm engendered by the association of quiet pastoral country and a homely human atmosphere with a branch of the great ocean that bathes all the shores of our globe.

There was another charm in the scene, due to the way in which I was viewing it—not as a pampered passenger on a "fine steam yacht," or even on "a powerful modern schooner," as the yacht agents advertise, but from the deck of a scrubby little craft of doubtful build and distressing plainness, which yet had smelt her persistent way to this distant fiord through I knew not what of difficulty and danger, with no apparent motive in her single occupant, who talked as vaguely and unconcernedly about his adventurous cruise as though it were all a protracted afternoon on Southampton Water.

I glanced round at Davies. He had dropped the chart and was sitting, or rather half lying, on the deck with one bronzed arm over the tiller, gazing fixedly ahead, with jsut an occasional glance around and aloft. He still seemed absorbed in himself, and for a moment or two I studied his face with an attention I had never, since I had known him, given it. I had always thought it commonplace, as I had thought him commonplace, so far as I had thought at all about either. It had always rather irritated me by an excess of candour and boyishness. These qualities it had kept, but the scales were falling from my eyes, and I saw others. I saw strength to obstinacy and courage to recklessness, in the firm lines of the chin; an older and deeper look in the eyes. Those odd transitions from bright mobility to detached earnestness, which had partly amused and chiefly annoyed me hitherto, seemed now to be lost in a sensitive reserve, not cold or egotistic, but strangely winning from its paradoxical frankness. Sincerily was stamped on every lineament. A deep misgiving stirred me that, clever as I thought myself, nicely perceptive of the right and congenial men to know, I had made some big mistakes—how many, I wondered? A relief, scarcely less deep because it was unconfessed, stole in on me with the suspicion that, little as I deserved it, the patient fates were offering me a golden chance of repairing at least one. And yet, I mused, the patient fates have crooked methods, besides a certain mischievous humour, for it was Davies who had asked me out—though now he scarcely seemed to need me—almost tricked me into coming out, for he might have known I was not suited to such a life; yet trickery and Davies sounded an odd conjuncture.

Probably it was the growing discomfort of my attitude which

produced this backsliding. My night's rest and the "ascent from the bath" had, in fact, done little to prepare me for contact with sharp edges and hard surfaces. But Davies had suddenly come to himself, and with an "I say, are you comfortable? Have something to sit on?" jerked the helm a little to windward, felt it like a pulse for a moment, with a rapid look to windward, and dived below, whence he returned with a couple of cushions, which he threw to me. I felt perversely resentful of these luxuries, and asked:

"Can't I be of any use?"

"Oh, don't you bother," he answered. "I expect you're tired. Aren't we having a splendid sail? That must be Ekken on the port bow," peering under the sail, "where the trees run in. I say, do you mind looking at the chart?" He tossed it over to me. I spread it out painfully, for it curled up like a watch-spring at the least slackening of pressure. I was not familiar with charts, and this sudden trust reposed in me, after a good deal of neglect, made me nervous.

"You see Flensburg, don't you?" he said. "That's where we are," dabbing with a long reach at an indefinite space on the crowded sheet. "Now which side of that buoy off the point do we pass?"

I had scarcely taken in which was land and which was water, much less the significance of the buoy, when he resumed:

"Never mind; I'm pretty sure it's all deep water about here. I expect that marks the fair-way for steamers."

In a minute or two we were passing the buoy in question, on the wrong side I am pretty certain, for weeds and sand came suddenly into view below us with uncomfortable distinctness. But all Davies said was:

"There's never any sea here, and the plate's not down," a dark utterance which I pondered doubtfully. "The best of these Schleswig waters," he went on, "is that a boat of this size can go almost anywhere. There's no navigation required. Why—" At this moment a faint scraping was felt, rather than heard, beneath us.

"Aren't we aground?" I asked, with great calmness.

"Oh, she'll blow over," he replied, wincing a little.

She "blew over," but the episode caused a little naïve vexation in Davies. I relate it as a good instance of one of his minor peculiarities. He was utterly without that didactic pedantry which yachting has a fatal tendency to engender in men who profess it. He had tossed me the chart without a thought that I was an ignoramus, to whom it would be Greek, and who would provide him with an admirable subject to drill and lecture, just as his neglect of me throughout the morning had been merely habitual and unconscious independence. In the second place, master of his *métier*, as I knew him afterwards to be, resourceful, skilful, and alert, he was liable to lapse into a certain amateurish vagueness, half irritating and half amusing. I think truly that both these peculiarities came from the same source, a hatred of any sort of affectation. To the same source I traced the fact that he and his yacht observed none of the superficial etiquette of yachts and yachtsmen, that she never, for instance, flew a national ensign, and he never wore a "yachting suit."

We rounded a low green point which I had scarcely noticed before.

"We must jibe," said Davies; "just take the helm, will you?" and, without waiting for my co-operation, he began hauling in the mainsheet with great vigour. I had rude notions of steering, but jibing is a delicate operation. No yachtsman will be surprised to hear that the boom saw its opportunity and swung over with a mighty crash, with the mainsheet entangled round me and the tiller.

"Jibed all standing," was his sorrowful comment. "You're not used to her yet. She's very quick on the helm."

"Where am I to steer for?" I asked, wildly.

"Oh, don't trouble, I'll take her now," he replied.

I felt it was time to make my position clear. "I'm an utter duffer at sailing," I began. "You'll have a lot to teach me, or one of these days I shall be wrecking you. You see, there's always been a crew—"

"Crew!"—with sovereign contempt—"why, the whole fun of the thing is to do everything oneself."

"Well, I've felt in the way the whole morning."

"I'm awfully sorry!" His dismay and repentance were comical. "Why, it's just the other way; you may be all the use in the world." He became absent.

We were following the inward trend of a small bay towards a cleft in the low shore.

"That's Ekken Sound," said Davies; "let's look into it," and a minute or two later we were drifting through a dainty little strait, with a peep of open water at the end of it. Cottages bordered either side, some overhanging the very water, some connecting with it by a rickety wooden staircase or a miniature landing-stage. Creepers and roses rioted over the walls and tiny porches. For a space on one side, a rude quay, with small smacks floating off it, spoke of some minute commercial interests; a very small tea-garden, with neglected-looking bowers and leaf-strewn tables, hinted at some equally minute tripping interest. A pervading hue of mingled bronze and rose came partly from the weather-mellowed woodwork of the cottages and stages, and partly from the creepers and the trees behind, where autumn's subtle fingers were already at work. Down this exquisite sea-lane we glided till it ended in a broad mere, where our sails, which had been shivering and complaining, filled into contented silence.

"Ready about!" said Davies, callously. "We must get out of this again." And round we swung.

"Why not anchor and stop here?" I protested; for a view of tantalizing loveliness was unfolding itself.

"Oh, we've seen all there is to be seen, and we must take this breeze while we've got it." It was always torture to Davies to feel a good breeze running to waste while he was inactive at anchor or on shore. The "shore" to him was an inferior element, merely serving as a useful annexe to the water—a source of necessary supplies.

"Let's have lunch," he pursued, as we resumed our way down the fiord. A vision of iced drinks, tempting salads, white napery, and an attentive steward mocked me with past recollections.

"You'll find a tongue," said the voice of doom, "in the starboard sofalocker; beer under the floor in the bilge. I'll see her round that buoy, if you wouldn't mind beginning." I obeyed with a bad grace, but the close air and cramped posture must have benumbed my faculties, for I opened the port-side locker, reached down, and grasped a sticky body, which turned out to be a pot of varnish. Recoiling wretchedly, I tried the opposite one, combating the embarrassing heel of the boat and the obstructive edges of the centre-board case. A medley of damp tins of varied sizes showed in the gloom, exuding a mouldy odour. Faded legends on dissolving paper, like the remnants of old posters on a disused hoarding, spoke of soups, curries, beefs, potted meats, and other hidden delicacies. I picked out a tongue, re-imprisoned the odour, and explored for beer. It was true, I supposed, that bilge didn't hurt it, as I tugged at the plank on my hands and knees, but I should have myself preferred a more accessible and less humid wine-cellar than the cavities among slimy ballast from which I dug the bottles. I regarded my hard-won and ill-favoured pledges of a meal with giddiness and discouragement.

"How are you getting on?" shouted Davies; "the tin-opener's hanging up on the bulkhead; the plates and knives are in the cupboard."

I doggedly pursued my functions. The plates and knives met me half-way, for, being on the weather side, and thus having a downward slant, its contents, when I slipped the latch, slid affectionately into my bosom, and overflowed with a clatter and jingle on to the floor.

"That often happens," I heard from above. "Never mind! There are no breakables. I'm coming down to help." And down he came, leaving the *Dulcibella* to her own devices.

"I think I'll go on deck," I said. "Why in the world couldn't you lunch comfortably at Ekken and save this infernal pandemonium of a picnic? Where's the yacht going to meanwhile? And how are we to lunch on that slanting table? I'm covered with varnish and mud, and ankle-deep in crockery. There goes the beer!"

"You shouldn't have stood it on the table with this list on," said Davies, with intense composure, "but it won't do any harm; it'll drain into the bilge" (ashes to ashes, dust to dust, I thought). "You go on deck now, and I'll finish getting ready." I regretted my explosion, though wrung from me under great provocation.

"Keep her straight on as she's going," said Davies, as I clambered up out of the chaos, brushing the dust off my trousers and varnishing the ladder with my hands. I unlashed the helm and kept her as she was going.

We had rounded a sharp bend in the fiord, and were sailing up a broad and straight reach which every moment disclosed new beauties, sights fair enough to be balm to the angriest spirit. A red-roofed hamlet was on our left, on the right an ivied ruin, close to the water, where some contemplative cattle stood knee-deep. The view ahead was a white strand which fringed both shores, and to it fell wooded slopes, interrupted here and there by low sandstone cliffs of warm red colouring, and now and again by a dingle with cracks of greensward.

I forgot petty squalors and enjoyed things—the coy tremble of the tiller and the backwash of air from the dingy mainsail, and, with a somewhat chastened rapture, the lunch which Davies brought up to me and solicitously watched me eat.

Later, as the wind sank to lazy airs, he became busy with a larger topsail and jib; but I was content to doze away the afternoon, drenching brain and body in the sweet and novel foreign atmosphere, and dreamily watching the fringe of glen cliff and cool white sand as they passed ever more slowly by.

## 4

### Retrospect

"Wake up!" I rubbed my eyes and wondered where I was; stretched myself painfully, too, for even the cushions had not given me a true bed of roses. It was dusk, and the yacht was stationary in glassy water, coloured by the last after-glow. A roofing of thin upper-cloud had spread over most of the sky, and a subtle smell of rain was in the air. We seemed to be in the middle of the fiord, whose shores looked distant and steep in the gathering darkness. Close ahead they faded away suddenly, and the sight lost itself in a grey void. The stillness was absolute.

"We can't get to Sonderburg to-night," said Davies.

"What's to be done then?" I asked, collecting my senses.

"Oh! we'll anchor anywhere here, we're just at the mouth of the fiord; I'll tow her inshore if you'll steer in that direction." He pointed vaguely at a blur of trees and cliff. Then he jumped into the dinghy, cast off the painter, and, after snatching at the slack of a rope, began towing the reluctant yacht by short jerks of the sculls. The menacing aspect of that grey void, combined with a natural preference for getting to some definite place at night, combined to depress my spirits afresh. In my sleep I had dreamt of Morven Lodge, of heather tea-parties after glorious slaughters of grouse, of salmon leaping in amber pools—and now—

"Just take a cast of the lead, will you?" came Davies's voice above the splash of the sculls.

"Where is it?" I shouted back.

"Never mind—we're close enough now; let—Can you manage to let go the anchor?"

I hurried forward and picked impotently at the bonds of the sleeping monster. But Davies was aboard again, and stirred him with a deft touch or two, till he crashed into the water with a grinding of chain.

"We shall do well here," said he.

"Isn't this rather an open anchorage?" I suggested.

"It's only open from that quarter," he replied. "If it comes on to blow from there we shall have to clear out; but I think it's only rain. Let's stow the sails."

Another whirlwind of activity, in which I joined as effectively as I could, oppressed by the prospect of having to "clear out"—who knows whither?—at midnight. But Davies's *sang froid* was infectious, I suppose, and the little den below, bright-lit and soon fragrant with cookery, pleaded insistently for affection. Yachting in this singular style was hungry work, I found. Steak tastes none the worse for having been wrapped in newspaper, and the slight traces of the day's news disappear with frying in onions and potato-chips. Davies was indeed on his mettle for this, his first dinner to his guest; for he produced with stealthy pride, not from the dishonoured grave of the beer, but from some more hallowed recess, a bottle of German champagne, from which we drank success to the *Dulcibella*.

"I wish you would tell me all about your cruise from England," I asked. "You must have had some exciting adventures. Here are the charts; let's go over them."

"We must wash up first," he replied, and I was tactfully introduced to one of his very few "standing orders," that tobacco should not burn, nor post-prandial chat begin, until that distasteful process had ended. "It would never get done otherwise," he sagely opined. But when we were finally settled with cigars, a variety of which, culled from many ports—German, Dutch, and Belgian—Davies kept in a battered old box in the net-rack, the promised talk hung fire.

"I'm no good at description," he complained; "and there's really very little to tell. We left Dover—Morrison and I—on 6th August; made a good passage to Ostend."

"You had some fun there, I suppose?" I put in, thinking of—well, of Ostend in August.

"Fun! A filthy hole I call it; we had to stop a couple of days, as we fouled a buoy coming in and carried away the bobstay; we lay in a dirty little tidal dock, and there was nothing to do on shore."

"Well, what next?"

"We had a splendid sail to the East Scheldt, but then, like fools, decided to go through Holland by canal and river. It was good fun enough navigating the estuary—the tides and banks there are appalling—but farther inland it was a wretched business, nothing but paying lock-dues, bumping against schuyts, and towing down stinking canals. Never a peaceful night like this—always moored by some quay or tow-path, with people passing and boys. Heavens! shall I ever forget those boys! A perfect murrain of them infests Holland; they seem to have nothing in the world to do but throw stones and mud at foreign yachts."

"They want a Herod, with some statesmanlike views on infanticide."

"By Jove! yes; but the fact is that you want a crew for that pottering inland work; they can smack the boys and keep an eye on the sculls. A boat like this should stick to the sea, or out-of-the-way places on the coast. Well, after Amsterdam."

"You've skipped a good deal, haven't you?" I interrupted.

"Oh! have I? Well, let me see, we went by Dordrecht to Rotterdam; nothing to see there, and swarms of tugs buzzing about and shaving one's bows every second. On by the Vecht river to Amsterdam, and thence—Lord, what a relief it was!—out into the North Sea again. The weather had been still and steamy; but it broke up finely now, and we had a rattling three-reef sail to the Zuyder Zee."

He reached up to the bookshelf for what looked like an ancient ledger, and turned over the leaves.

"Is that your log?" I asked. "I should like to have a look at it."

"Oh! you'd find it dull reading—if you could read it at all; it's just short notes about winds and bearings, and so on." He was turning some leaves over rapidly. "Now, why don't *you* keep a log of what we do? I can't describe things, and you can."

"I've half a mind to try," I said.

"We want another chart now," and he pulled down a second yet more stained and frayed than the first. "We had a splendid time then exploring the Zuyder Zee, its northern part at least, and round those islands which bound it on the north. Those are the Frisian Islands, and they stretch for 120 miles or so eastward. You see, the first two of them, Texel and Vlieland, shut in the Zuyder Zee, and the rest border the Dutch and German coasts."*

"What's all this?" I said, running my finger over some dotted patches which covered much of the chart. The latter was becoming unintelligible; clean-cut coasts and neat regiments of little figures had given place to a confusion of winding and intersecting lines and bald spaces.

"All *sand*," said Davies, enthusiastically. "You can't think what a splendid sailing-ground it is. You can explore for days without seeing a soul. These are the channels, you see; they're very badly charted. This chart was almost useless, but it made it all the more fun. No towns or harbours, just a village or two on the islands, if you wanted stores."

"They look rather desolate," I said.

"Desolate's no word for it; they're really only gigantic sandbanks themselves."

"Wasn't all this rather dangerous?" I asked.

"Not a bit; you see, that's where our shallow draught and flat bottom came in—we could go anywhere, and it didn't matter running aground—she's perfect for that sort of work; and she doesn't really *look* bad either, does she?" he asked, rather wistfully. I suppose I hesitated, for he said, abruptly:

"Anyway, I don't go in for looks."

He had leaned back, and I detected traces of incipient absent-mindedness. His cigar, which he had lately been lighting and relighting feverishly—a habit of his when excited—seemed now to have expired for good.

"About running aground," I persisted; "surely that's apt to be dangerous?"

He sat up and felt round for a match.

"Not the least, if you know where you can run risks and where you can't; anyway, you can't possibly help it. That chart may look simple to you"—("simple!" I thought)—"but at half flood all those banks are covered; the islands and coasts are scarcely visible, they are so low, and everything looks the same." This graphic description of a "splendid cruising-ground" took away my breath. "Of course there *is* risk sometimes—choosing an anchorage requires care. You can generally get a nice berth under the lee of a bank, but the tides run strong in the channels, and if there's a gale blowing—"

"Didn't you ever take a pilot?" I interrupted.

*See Map A.

"Pilot? Why, the whole point of the thing"—he stopped short—"I did take one once, later on," he resumed, with an odd smile, which faded at once.

"Well?" I urged, for I saw a reverie was coming.

"Oh! he ran me ashore, of course. Served me right. I wonder what the weather's doing"; he rose, glanced at the aneroid, the clock, and the half-closed skylight with a curious circular movement, and went a step or two up the companion-ladder, where he remained for several minutes with head and shoulders in the open air.

There was no sound of wind outside, but the *Dulcibella* had begun to move in her sleep, as it were, rolling drowsily to some faint send of the sea, with an occasional short jump, like the start of an uneasy dreamer.

"What does it look like?" I called from my sofa. I had to repeat the question.

"Rain coming," said Davies, returning, "and possibly wind; but we're safe enough here. It's coming from the sou'-west; shall we turn in?"

"We haven't finished your cruise yet," I said. "Light a pipe and tell me the rest."

"All right," he agreed, with more readiness than I expected.

"After Terschelling*—here it is, the third island from the west—I pottered along eastward."

"I?"

"Oh! I forgot. Morrison had to leave me there. I missed him badly, but I hoped at that time to get —— to join me. I could manage all right single-handed, but for that sort of work two are much better than one. The plate's beastly heavy; in fact, I had to give up using it for fear of a smash."

"After Terschelling?" I jogged his memory.

"Well, I followed the Dutch islands, Ameland, Schiermonnikoog, Rottum (outlandish names, aren't they?), sometimes outside them, sometimes inside. It was a bit lonely, but grand sport and very interesting. The charts were shocking, but I worried out most of the channels."

"I suppose those waters are only used by small local craft?" I put in; "that would account for inaccuracies." Did Davies think that Admiralties had time to waste on smoothing the road for such quixotic little craft as his, in all its inquisitive ramblings? But he fired up.

"That's all very well," he said, "but think what folly it is. However, that's a long story, and will bore you. To cut matters short, for we ought to be turning in, I got to Borkum—that's the first of the *German* islands." He pointed at a round bare lozenge lying in the midst of a

---

*See Map A.

welter of sandbanks. "Rottum—this queer little one—it has only one house on it—is the most easterly Dutch island, and the mainland of Holland ends *here*, opposite it, at the Ems River"—indicating a dismal cavity in the coast, sown with names suggestive of mud, and wrecks, and dreariness.

"What date was this?" I asked.

"About the ninth of this month."

"Why, that's only a fortnight before you wired to me! You were pretty quick getting to Flensburg. Wait a bit, we want another chart. Is this the next?"

"Yes; but we scarcely need it. I only went a little way farther on—to Norderney, in fact, the third German island—then I decided to go straight for the Baltic. I had always had an idea of getting there, as Knight did in the *Falcon*. So I made a passage of it to the Eider River, *there* on the West Schleswig coast, took the river and canal through to Kiel on the Baltic, and from there made another passage up north to Flensburg. I was a week there, and then you came, and here we are. And now let's turn in. We'll have a fine sail to-morrow!" He ended with rather forced vivacity, and briskly rolled up the chart. The reluctance he had shown from the first to talk about his cruise had been for a brief space forgotten in his enthusiasm about a portion of it, but had returned markedly in this bald conclusion. I felt sure that there was more in it than mere disinclination to spin nautical yarns in the "hardy Corinthian" style, which can be so offensive in amateur yachtsmen; and I thought I guessed the explanation. His voyage single-handed to the Baltic from the Frisian Islands had been a foolhardy enterprise, with perilous incidents, which, rather than make light of, he would not refer to at all. Probably he was ashamed of his recklessness and wished to ignore it with me, an inexperienced acquaintance not yet enamoured of the *Dulcibella*'s way of life, whom both courtesy and interest demanded that he should inspire with confidence. I liked him all the better as I came to this conclusion, but I was tempted to persist a little.

"I slept the whole afternoon," I said; "and, to tell the truth, I rather dread the idea of going to bed, it's so tiring. Look here, you've rushed over that last part like an express train. That passage to the Schleswig coast—the Eider River, did you say?—was a longish one, wasn't it?"

"Well, you see what it was; about seventy miles, I suppose, direct." He spoke low, bending down to sweep up some cigar ashes on the floor.

"Direct?" I insinuated. "Then you put in somewhere?"

"I stopped once, anchored for the night; oh, that's nothing of a sail with a fair wind. By Jove! I've forgotten to caulk that seam over your bunk, and it's going to rain. I must do it now. You turn in."

He disappeared. My curiosity, never very consuming, was banished by concern as to the open seam; for the prospect of a big drop, re-morseless and regular as Fate, falling on my forehead throughout the night, as in the torture-chamber of the Inquisition, was alarming enough to recall me wholly to the immediate future. So I went to bed, finding on the whole that I had made progress in the exercise, though still far from being the trained contortionist that the occasion called for. Hammering ceased, and Davies reappeared just as I was stretched on the rack—tucked up in my bunk, I mean.

"I say," he said, when he was settled in his, and darkness reigned, "do you think you'll like this sort of thing?"

"If there are many places about here as beautiful as this," I replied, "I think I shall. But I should like to land now and then and have a walk. Of course, a great deal depends on the weather, doesn't it? I hope this rain" (drops had begun to patter overhead) "doesn't mean that the summer's over for good."

"Oh, you can sail just the same," said Davies, "unless it's very bad. There's plenty of sheltered water. There's bound to be a change soon. But then there are the ducks. The colder and stormier it is, the better for them."

I had forgotten the ducks and the cold, and, suddenly presented as a shooting-box in inclement weather, the *Dulcibella* lost ground in my estimation, which she had latterly gained.

"I'm fond of shooting," I said, "but I'm afraid I'm only a fair-weather yachtsman, and I should much prefer sun and scenery."

"Scenery," he repeated, reflectively. "I say, you must have thought it a queer taste of mine to cruise about on that outlandish Frisian coast. How would you like that sort of thing?"

"I should loathe it," I answered, promptly, with a clear conscience. "Weren't you delighted yourself to get to the Baltic? It must be a wonderful contrast to what you described. Did you ever see another yacht there?"

"Only one," he answered. "Good night!"

"Good night!"

## 5

### Wanted, a North Wind

NOTHING disturbed my rest that night, so adaptable is youth and so masterful is nature. At times I was remotely aware of a threshing of rain and a humming of wind, with a nervous kicking of the little hull, and at one moment I dreamt I saw an apparition by candle-light of Davies, clad in pyjamas and huge top-boots, grasping a misty lantern of gigantic proportions. But the apparition mounted the ladder and disappeared, and I passed to other dreams.

A blast in my ear, like the voice of fifty trombones, galvanized me into full consciousness. The musician, smiling and tousled, was at my bedside, raising a foghorn to his lips with deadly intention. "It's a way we have in the _Dulcibella_," he said, as I started up on one elbow. "I didn't startle you much, did I?" he added.

"Well, I like the _mattinata_ better than the cold douche," I answered, thinking of yesterday.

"Fine day and magnificent breeze!" he answered. My sensations this morning were vastly livelier than those of yesterday at the same hour. My limbs were supple again and my head clear. Not even the searching wind could mar the ecstasy of that plunge down to smooth, seductive sand, where I buried greedy fingers and looked through a medium blue, with that translucent blue, fairy-faint and angel-pure, that you see in perfection only in the heart of ice. Up again to sun, wind, and the forest whispers from the shore; down just once more to see the uncouth anchor stabbing the sand's soft bosom with one rusty fang, deaf and inert to the _Dulcibella_'s puny efforts to drag him from his prey. Back, holding by the cable as a rusty clue from heaven to earth, up to that _bourgeois_ little maiden's bows; back to breakfast, with an appetite not to be blunted by condensed milk and somewhat _passé_ bread. An hour later we had dressed the _Dulcibella_ for the road, and were foaming into the grey void of yesterday, now a noble expanse of wind-whipped blue, half surrounded by distant hills, their every outline vivid in the rain-washed air.

I cannot pretend that I really enjoyed this first sail into the open, though I was keenly anxious to do so. I felt the thrill of those forward leaps, heard that persuasive song the foam sings under the lee-bow, saw the flashing harmonies of sea and sky; but sensuous perception was deadened by nervousness. The yacht looked smaller than ever outside the quiet fiord. The song of the foam seemed very near, the wave crests aft very high. The novice in sailing clings desperately to the thoughts of sailors—effective, prudent persons, with a typical jargon and a typical dress, versed in local currents and winds. I could not help missing this professional element. Davies, as he sat grasping his beloved tiller, looked strikingly efficient in his way, and supremely at home in his surroundings; but he looked the amateur through and through, as with one hand, and (it seemed) one eye, he wrestled with a spray-splashed chart half unrolled on the deck beside him. All his casual ways returned to me—his casual talk and that last adventurous voyage to the Baltic, and the suspicions his reticence had aroused.

"Do you see a monument anywhere?" he said, all at once; and, before I could answer: "We must take another reef." He let go of the tiller and relit his pipe, while the yacht rounded sharply to, and in a twinkling was tossing head to sea with loud claps of her canvas and passionate jerks of her boom, as the wind leapt on its quarry, now turning to bay, with redoubled force. The sting of spray in my eyes and the Babel of noise dazed me; but Davies, with a pull on the fore-sheet, soothed the tormented little ship, and left her coolly sparring with the waves while he shortened sail and puffed his pipe. An hour later the narrow vista of Als Sound was visible, with quiet old Sonderburg sunning itself on the island shore, and the Dybbol heights towering above—the Dybbol of bloody memory; scene of the last desperate stand of the Danes in '64, ere the Prussians wrested the two fair provinces from them.

"It's early to anchor, and I hate towns," said Davies, as one section of a lumbering pontoon bridge opened to give us passage. But I was firm on the need for a walk, and got my way on condition that I bought stores as well, and returned in time to admit of further advance to a "quiet anchorage." Never did I step on the solid earth with stranger feelings, partly due to relief from confinement, partly to that sense of independence in travelling, which, for those who go down to the sea in small ships, can make the foulest coal-port in Northumbria seem attractive. And here I had fascinating Sonderburg, with its broad-eaved houses of carved woodwork, each fresh with cleansing, yet reverend with age; its fair-haired Viking-like men, and rosy, plain-faced women, with their bullet foreheads and large mouths; Sonderburg still Danish to the core under its Teuton veneer. Crossing the bridge I climbed the Dybbol—dotted with memorials of that heroic defence—and thence could see the wee form and gossamer rigging of the *Dulcibella* on the silver ribbon of the Sound, and was reminded by the sight that there were stores to be bought. So I hurried down again to the old quarter and bargained over eggs and bread with a dear old lady, pink as a *débutante*, who made a patriotic pretence of not understanding German, and called in her strapping son, whose few words of English, being chiefly nautical slang picked up on a British trawler, were peculiarly useless for the purpose. Davies had tea ready when I came aboard again, and, drinking it on deck, we proceeded up the sheltered Sound, which, in spite of its imposing name, was no bigger than an inland river, only the hosts of rainbow jelly-fish reminding us that we were threading a highway of ocean. There is no rise and fall of tide in these regions to disfigure the shore with mud. Here was a shelving gravel bank; there a bed of whispering rushes; there again young birch trees growing to the very brink, each wearing a stocking of bright moss and setting its foot firmly in among golden leaves and scarlet fungus.

Davies was preoccupied, but he lighted up when I talked of the Danish war. "Germany's a thundering great nation," he said; "I wonder if we shall ever fight her." A little incident that happened after we anchored deepened the impression left by this conversation. We crept at dusk into a shaded back-water, where our keel almost touched the gravel bed. Opposite us on the Alsen shore there showed, clean-cut against the sky, the spire of a little monument rising from a leafy hollow.

"I wonder what that is," I said. It was scarcely a minute's row in the dinghy, and when the anchor was down we sculled over to it. A bank of loam led to gorse and bramble. Pushing aside some branches we came to a slender Gothic memorial in grey stone, inscribed with bas-reliefs of battle scenes, showing Prussians forcing a landing in boats and Danes resisting with savage tenacity. In the failing light we spelt out an inscription: "Den bei dem Meeres-Uebergange und der Eroberung von Alsen am 29. Juni 1864 heldenmüthig gefallenen zum ehrenden Gedächtniss." "To the honoured memory of those who died heroically at the invasion and storming of Alsen." I knew the German passion for commemoration; I had seen similar memorials on Alsatian battlefields, and several on the Dybbol only that afternoon; but there was something in the scene, the hour, and the circumstances, which made this one seem singularly touching. As for Davies, I scarcely recognized him; his eyes flashed and filled with tears as he glanced from the inscription to the path we had followed and the water beyond. "It was a landing in boats, I suppose," he said, half to himself. "I wonder they managed it. What does *heldenmüthig* mean?"—"Heroically."—"Heldenmüthig gefallenen," he repeated, under his breath, lingering on each syllable. He was like a schoolboy reading of Waterloo.

Our conversation at dinner turned naturally on war, and in naval warfare I found I had come upon Davies's literary hobby. I had not hitherto paid attention to the medley on our bookshelf, but I now saw that, besides a Nautical Almanack and some dilapidated *Sailing Directions*, there were several books on the cruises of small yachts, and also some big volumes crushed in anyhow or lying on the top. Squinting painfully at them I saw Mahan's *Life of Nelson*, Brassey's *Naval Annual*, and others.

"It's a tremendously interesting subject," said Davies, pulling down (in two pieces) a volume of Mahan's *Influence of Sea Power*.

Dinner flagged (and froze) while he illustrated a point by reference to the much-thumbed pages. He was very keen, and not very articulate.

I knew just enough to be an intelligent listener, and, though hungry, was delighted to hear him talk.

"I'm not boring you, am I?" he said, suddenly.

"I should think not," I protested. "But you might just have a look at the chops."

They had indeed been crying aloud for notice for some minutes, and drew candid attention to their neglect when they appeared. The diversion they caused put Davies out of vein. I tried to revive the subject, but he was reserved and diffident.

The untidy bookshelf reminded me of the logbook, and when Davies had retired with the crockery to the forecastle, I pulled the ledger down and turned over the leaves. It was a mass of short entries, with cryptic abbreviations, winds, tides, weather, and courses appearing to predominate. The voyage from Dover to Ostend was dismissed in two lines: "Under way 7 p.m., wind W.S.W. moderate; West Hinder 5 a.m., outside all banks; Ostend 11 a.m." The Scheldt had a couple of pages very technical and *staccato* in style. Inland Holland was given a contemptuous summary, with some half-hearted allusions to windmills, and so on, and a caustic word or two about boys, paint, and canal smells.

At Amsterdam technicalities began again, and a brisker tone pervaded the entries, which became progressively fuller as the writer cruised on the Frisian coast. He was clearly in better spirits, for here and there were quaint and laboured efforts to describe nature out of material which, as far as I could judge, was repellent enough to discourage the most brilliant and observant of writers; with an occasional note of a visit on shore, generally reached by a walk of half a mile over sand, and of talks with shop people and fishermen. But such lighter relief was rare. The bulk dealt with channels and shoals with weird and depressing names, with the centre-plate, the sails, and the wind, buoys and "booms," tides and "berths" for the night. "Kedging off" appeared to be a frequent diversion; "running aground" was of almost daily occurrence.

It was not easy reading, and I turned the leaves rapidly. I was curious, too, to see the latter part. I came to a point where the rain of little sentences, pattering out like small shot, ceased abruptly. It was at the end of 9th September. That day, with its "kedging" and "boom-dodging," was filled in with the usual detail. The log then leapt over three days, and went on: "13th. Sept.—Wind W.N.W. fresh. Decided to go to Baltic. Sailed 4 a.m. Quick passage E. ½ S. to mouth of Weser. Anchored for night under Hohenhörn Sand. 14th Sept.—Nil. 15th Sept.—Under way at 4 a.m. Wind East moderate. Course W. by S.; four miles; N.E. by N. fifteen miles Norderpiep 9.30. Eider River

11.30." This recital of naked facts was quite characteristic when "passages" were concerned, and any curiosity I had felt about his reticence on the previous night would have been rather allayed than stimulated had I not noticed that a page had been torn out of the book just at this point. The frayed edge left had been pruned and picked into very small limits; but dissimulation was not Davies's strong point, and a child could have seen that a leaf was missing, and that the entries, starting from the evening of 9th September (where a page ended), had been written together at one sitting. I was on the point of calling to Davies, and chaffing him with having committed a grave offence against maritime law in having "cooked" his log; but I checked myself, I scarcely know why, probably because I guessed the joke would touch a sensitive place and fail. Delicacy shrank from seeing him compelled either to amplify a deception or blunder out a confession—he was too easy a prey; and, after all, the matter was of small moment. I returned the book to the shelf, the only definite result of its perusal being to recall my promise to keep a diary myself, and I then and there dedicated a notebook to the purpose.

We were just lighting our cigars when we heard voices and the splash of oars, followed by a bump again the hull which made Davies wince, as violations of his paint always did. "Guten Abend; wo fahren Sie hin?" greeted us as we climbed on deck. It turned out to be some jovial fishermen returning to their smack from a visit to Sonderburg. A short dialogue proved to them that we were mad Englishmen in bitter need of charity.

"Come to Satrup," they said; "all the smacks are there, round the point. There is good punch in the inn."

Nothing loth, we followed in the dinghy, skirted a bend of the Sound, the opened up the lights of a village, with some smacks at anchor in front of it. We were escorted to the inn, and introduced to a formidable beverage, called coffee-punch, and a smoke-wreathed circle of smacksmen, who talked German out of courtesy, but were Danish in all else. Davies was at once at home with them, to a degree, indeed, that I envied. His German was of the crudest kind, *bizarre* in vocabulary and comical in accent; but the freemasonry of the sea, or some charm of his own, gave intuition to both him and his hearers. I cut a poor figure in this nautical gathering, though Davies, who persistently referred to me as "meiner Freund," tried hard to represent me as a kindred spirit and to include me in the general talk. I was detected at once as an uninteresting hybrid. Davies, who sometimes appealed to me for a word, was deep in talk over anchorages and ducks, especially, as I well remember now, about the chance of sport in a certain *Schlei Fiord*. I fell into utter neglect, till rescued by a taciturn person in spectacles and a very high cap, who appeared to be the only landsman present. After silently puffing smoke in my direction for some time, he asked me if I was married, and if not, when I proposed to be. After this inquisition he abandoned me.

It was eleven before we left this hospitable inn, escorted by the whole party to the dinghy. Our friends of the smack insisted on our sharing their boat out of pure good-fellowship—for there was not nearly room for us—and would not let us go till a bucket of fresh-caught fish had been emptied into her bottom. After much shaking of scaly hands, we sculled back to the *Dulcibella*, where she slept in a bed of tremulous stars.

Davies sniffed the wind and scanned the tree-tops, where light gusts were toying with the leaves.

"Sou'-west still," he said, "and more rain coming. But it's bound to shift into the north."

"Will that be a good wind for us?"

"It depends where we go," he said, slowly. "I was asking those fellows about duck-shooting. They seemed to think the best place would be Schlei Fiord. That's about fifteen miles south of Sonderburg, on the way to Kiel. They said there was a pilot chap living at the mouth who would tell us all about it. They weren't very encouraging though. We should want a north wind for that."

"I don't care where we go," I said, to my own surprise.

"Don't you really?" he rejoined, with sudden warmth. Then, with a slight change of voice. "You mean it's all very jolly about here?"

Of course I meant that. Before we went below we both looked for a moment at the little grey memorial; its slender fretted arch outlined in tender lights and darks above the hollow on the Alsen shore. The night was that of 27th September, the third I had spent on the *Dulcibella*.


6


### Schlei Fiord

I MAKE no apology for having described these early days in some detail. It is no wonder that their trivialities are as vividly before me as the colours of earth and sea in this enchanting corner of the world. For every trifle, sordid or picturesque, was relevant; every scrap of talk a link; every passing mood critical for good or ill. So slight indeed were

the determining causes that changed my autumn holiday into an undertaking the most momentous I have ever approached.

Two days more preceded the change. On the first, the southwesterly
wind still holding, we sallied forth into Augustenburg Fiord, "to prac-
tise smartness in a heavy thresh," as Davies put it. It was the day of ded-
ication for those disgusting oilskins, immured in whose stiff and
odorous angles, I felt distressfully cumbersome; a day of proof indeed
for me, for heavy squalls swept incessantly over the loch, and Davies, at
my own request, gave me no rest. Backwards and forwards we tacked,
blustering into coves and out again, reefing and unreefing, now stung
with rain, now warmed with sun, but never with time to breathe or
think.

I wrestled with intractable ropes, slaves if they could be subdued,
tyrants if they got the upper hand; creeping, craning, straining, I made
the painful round of the deck, while Davies, hatless and tranquil, directed my blundering movements.

"Now take the helm and try steering in a hard breeze to windward.
It's the finest sport on earth."

So I grappled with the niceties of that delicate craft; smarting eyes,
chafed hands, and dazed brain all pressed into the service, whilst
Davies, taming the ropes the while, shouted into my ear the subtle
mysteries of the art; that fidgeting ripple in the luff of the mainsail,
and the distant rattle from the hungry jib—signs that they are starved
of wind and must be given more; the heavy list and wallow of the hull,
the feel of the wind on your cheek instead of your nose, the broader
angle of the burgee at the masthead—signs that they have too much,
and that she is sagging recreantly to leeward instead of fighting to
windward. He taught me the tactics for meeting squalls, and the way
to press your advantage when they are defeated—the iron hand in the
velvet glove that the wilful tiller needs if you are to gain your ends with
it; the exact set of the sheets necessary to get the easiest and swiftest
play of the hull—all these things and many more I struggled to ap-
prehend, careless for the moment as to whether they were worth
knowing, but doggedly set on knowing them. Needless to say, I had no
eyes for beauty. The wooded inlets we dived into gave a brief respite
from wind and spindrift, but called into use the lead and the centre-
board tackle—two new and cumbrous complexities. Davies's passion
for intricate navigation had to be sated even in these secure and tideless waters.

"Let's get in as near as we can—you stand by the lead," was his formula; so I made false casts, tripped up in the slack, sent rivers of water
up my sleeves, and committed all the other *gaucheries* that beginners
in the art commit, while the sand showed whiter beneath the keel, till

Davies regretfully drew off and shouted: "Ready about, centre-plate down," and I dashed down to the trappings of that diabolical contrivance, the only part of the *Dulcibella's* equipment that I hated fiercely to the last. It had an odious habit when lowered of spouting jets of water through its chain-lead on to the cabin floor. One of my duties was to gag it with cotton-waste, but even then its choking gurgle was a most uncomfortable sound in your dining-room. In a minute the creek would be behind us and we would be thumping our stem into the short hollow waves of the fiord, and lurching through spray and rain for some point on the opposite shore. Of our destination and objects, if we had any, I knew nothing. At the northern end of the fiord, just before we turned, Davies had turned dreamy in the most exasperating way, for I was steering at the time and in mortal need of sympathetic guidance, if I was to avoid a sudden jibe. As though continuing aloud some internal debate, he held a one-sided argument to the effect that it was no use going farther north. Ducks, weather, and charts figured in it, but I did not follow the pros and cons. I only know that we suddenly turned and began to "battle" south again. At sunset we were back once more in the same quiet pool among the trees and fields of Als Sound, a wondrous peace succeeding the turmoil. Bruised and sodden, I was extricating myself from my oily prison, and later was tasting (though not nearly yet in its perfection) the unique exultation that follows such a day, when, glowing all over, deliciously tired and pleasantly sore, you eat what seems ambrosia, be it only tinned beef; and drink nectar, be it only distilled from terrestrial hops or coffee berries, and inhale as culminating luxury balmy fumes which even the happy Homeric gods knew naught of.

On the following morning, the 30th, a joyous shout of "Nor'west wind" sent me shivering on deck, in the small hours, to handle rain-stiff canvas and cutting chain. It was a cloudy, unsettled day, but still enough after yesterday's boisterous ordeal. We retraced our way past Sonderburg, and thence sailed for a faint line of pale green on the far south-western horizon. It was during this passage that an incident occurred, which, slight as it was, opened my eyes to much.

A flight of wild duck crossed our bows at some little distance, a wedge-shaped phalanx of craning necks and flapping wings. I happened to be steering while Davies verified our course below; but I called him up at once, and a discussion began about our chances of sport. Davies was gloomy over them.

"Those fellows at Satrup were rather doubtful," he said. "There are plenty of ducks, but I made out that it's not easy for strangers to get shooting. The whole country's so very civilized; it's not *wild* enough, is it?"

He looked at me. I had no very clear opinion. It was anything but wild in one sense, but there seemed to be wild enough spots for ducks. The shore we were passing appeared to be bordered by lonely marshes, though a spacious champaign showed behind. If it were not for the beautiful places we had seen, and my growing taste for our way of seeing them, his disappointing vagueness would have nettled me more than it did. For, after all, he had brought me out loaded with sporting equipment under a promise of shooting.

"Bad weather is what we want for ducks," he said; "but I'm afraid we're in the wrong place for them. Now, if it was the North Sea, among those Frisian Islands—" His tone was timid and interrogative, and I felt at once that he was sounding me as to some unpalatable plan whose nature began to dawn on me.

He stammered on through a sentence or two about "wildness" and "nobody to interfere with you," and then I broke in: "You surely don't want to leave the Baltic?"

"Why not?" said he, staring into the compass.

"Hang it, man!" I returned, tartly, "here we are in October, the summer over, and the weather gone to pieces. We're alone in a cockle-shell boat, at a time when every other yacht of our size is laying up for the winter. Luckily, we seem to have struck an ideal cruising-ground, with a wide choice of safe fiords and a good prospect of ducks, if we choose to take a little trouble about them. You can't mean to waste time and run risks" (I thought of the torn leaf in the log-book) "in a long voyage to those forbidding haunts of yours in the North Sea."

"It's not very long," said Davies, doggedly. "Part of it's canal, and the rest is quite safe if you're careful. There's plenty of sheltered water, and it's not really necessary—"

"What's it all *for*?" I interrupted, impatiently. "We haven't *tried* for shooting here yet. You've no notion, have you, of getting the boat back to England this autumn?"

"England?" he muttered. "Oh, I don't much care." Again his vagueness jarred on me; there seemed to be some bar between us, invisible and insurmountable. And, after all, what was I doing here? Roughing it in a shabby little yacht, utterly out of my element, with a man who, a week ago, was nothing to me, and who now was a tiresome enigma. Like swift poison the old morbid mood in which I left London spread through me. All I had learnt and seen slipped away; what I had suffered remained. I was on the point of saying something which might have put a precipitate end to our cruise, but he anticipated me.

"I'm awfully sorry," he broke out, "for being such a selfish brute. I don't know what I was thinking about. You're a brick to join me in this sort of life, and I'm afraid I'm an infernally bad host. Of course this is just the place to cruise. I forgot about the scenery, and all that. Let's ask about the ducks here. As you say, we're sure to get sport if we worry and push a bit. We must be nearly there now—yes, there's the entrance. Take the helm, will you?"

He sprang up the mast like a monkey, and gazed over the land from the cross-trees. I looked up at my enigma and thanked Providence I had not spoken; for no one could have resisted his frank outburst of good nature. Yet it occurred to me that, considering the conditions of our life, our intimacy was strangely slow in growth. I had no clue yet as to where his idiosyncrasies began and his self ended, and he, I surmised, was in the same stage towards me. Otherwise I should have pressed him further now, for I felt convinced that there was some mystery in his behaviour which I had not yet accounted for. However, light was soon to break.

I could see no sign of the entrance he had spoken of, and no wonder, for it is only eighty yards wide, though it leads to a fiord thirty miles long. All at once we were jolting in a tumble of sea, and the channel grudgingly disclosed itself, stealing between marshes and meadows and then broadening to a mere, as at Ekken. We anchored close to the mouth, and not far from a group of vessels of a type that afterwards grew very familiar to me. They were sailing-barges, something like those that ply in the Thames, bluff-bowed, high-sterned craft of about fifty tons, ketch-rigged, and fitted with lee-boards, very light spars, and a long tip-tilted bowsprit. (For the future I shall call them "galliots.") Otherwise the only sign of life was a solitary white house—the pilot's house, the chart told us—close to the northern point of entrance. After tea we called on the pilot. Patriarchally installed before a roaring stove, in the company of a buxom bustling daughter-in-law and some rosy grand-children, we found a rotund and rubicund person, who greeted us with a hoarse roar of welcome in German, which instantly changed, when he saw us, to the funniest broken English, spoken with intense relish and pride. We explained ourselves and our mission as well as we could through the hospitable interruptions caused by beer and the strains of a huge musical box, which had been set going in honour of our arrival. Needless to say, I was read like a book at once, and fell into the part of listener.

"Yes, yes," he said, "all right. There is plenty ducks, but first we will drink a glass beer; then we will shift your ship, captain—she lies not good there." (Davies started up in a panic, but was waved back to his beer.) "Then we will drink together another glass beer; then we will talk of ducks—no, then we will kill ducks—that is better. Then we will have plenty glasses beer."

This was an unexpected climax, and promised well for our prospects.

And the programme was fully carried out. After the beer our host was packed briskly by his daughter into an armour of woollen gaiters, coats, and mufflers, topped with a worsted helmet, which left nothing of his face visible but a pair of twinkling eyes. Thus equipped, he led the way out of doors, and roared for Hans and his gun, till a great gawky youth, with high cheek-bones and a downy beard, came out from the yard and sheepishly shook our hands.

Together we repaired to the quay, where the pilot stood, looking like a genial ball of worsted, and bawled hoarse directions while we shifted the *Dulcibella* to a berth on the farther shore close to the other vessels. We returned with our guns, and the interval for refreshments followed. It was just dusk when we sallied out again, crossed a stretch of bog-land, and took up strategic posts round a stagnant pond. Hans had been sent to drive, and the result was a fine mallard and three ducks. It was true that all fell to the pilot's gun, perhaps owing to Hans' filial instinct and his parent's canny egotism in choosing his own lair, or perhaps it was chance; but the shooting-party was none the less a triumphal success. It was celebrated with beer and music as before, while the pilot, an infant on each podgy knee, discoursed exuberantly on the glories of his country and the Elysian content of his life. "There is plenty beer, plenty meat, plenty money, plenty ducks," summed up his survey.

It may have been fancy, but Davies, though he had fits and starts of vivacity, seemed very inattentive, considering that we were sitting at the feet of so expansive an oracle. It was I who elicited most of the practical information—details of time, weather, and likely places for shooting, with some shrewd hints as to the kind of people to conciliate. Whatever he thought of me, I warmed with sympathy towards the pilot, for he assumed that we had done with cruising for the year, and thought us mad enough as it was to have been afloat so long, as madder still to intend living on "so little a ship" when we could live on land with beer and music handy. I was tempted to raise the North Sea question, just to watch Davies under the thunder of rebukes which would follow. But I refrained from a wish to be tender with him, now that all was going so well. The Frisian Islands were an extravagant absurdity now. I did not even refer to them as we pulled back to the *Dulcibella*, after swearing eternal friendship with the good pilot and his family.

Davies and I turned in good friends that night—or rather I should say that I turned in, for I left him sucking an empty pipe and aimlessly fingering a volume of Mahan; and once when I woke in the night I felt somehow that his bunk was empty and that he was there in the dark cabin, dreaming.

# 7

## The Missing Page

I WOKE (on 1st October) with that dispiriting sensation that a hitch has occurred in a settled plan. It was explained when I went on deck, and I found the *Dulcibella* wrapped in a fog, silent, clammy, nothing visible from her decks but the ghostly hull of a galliot at anchor near us. She must have brought up there in the night, for there had been nothing so close the evening before; and I remembered that my sleep had been broken once by sounds of rumbling chain and gruff voices.

"This looks pretty hopeless for to-day," I said, with a shiver, to Davies, who was laying the breakfast.

"Well, we can't do anything till this fog lifts," he answered, with a good deal of resignation. Breakfast was a cheerless meal. The damp penetrated to the very cabin, whose roof and walls wept a fine dew. I had dreaded a bathe, and yet missed it, and the ghastly light made the tablecloth look dirtier than it naturally was, and all the accessories more sordid. Something had gone wrong with the bacon, and the lack of egg-cups was not in the least humorous.

Davies was just beginning, in his summary way, to tumble the things together for washing up, when there was a sound of a step on deck, two sea-boots appeared on the ladder, and, before we could wonder who the visitor was, a little man in oilskins and a sou'-wester was stooping towards us in the cabin door, smiling affectionately at Davies out of a round grizzled beard.

"Well met, captain," he said, quietly, in German. "Where are you bound to this time?"

"Bartels!" exclaimed Davies, jumping up. The two stooping figures, young and old, beamed at one another like father and son.

"Where have you come from? Have some coffee. How's the *Johannes*? Was that you that came in last night? I'm delighted to see you!" (I spare the reader his uncouth lingo.) The little man was dragged in and seated on the opposite sofa to me.

"I took my apples to Kappeln," he said, sedately, "and now I sail to Kiel, and so to Hamburg, where my wife and children are. It is my last voyage of the year. You are no longer alone, captain, I see." He had taken off his dripping sou'wester and was bowing ceremoniously towards me.

"Oh, I quite forgot!" said Davies, who had been kneeling on one knee in the low doorway, absorbed in his visitor. "This is '*meiner Freund*,' Herr Carruthers. Carruthers, this is my friend, Schiffer Bartels, of the galliot *Johannes*."

Was I never to be at an end of the puzzles which Davies presented to me? All the impulsive heartiness died out of his voice and manner as he uttered the last few words, and there he was, nervously glancing from the visitor to me, like one who, against his will or from tactlessness, has introduced two persons who he knows will disagree.

There was a pause while he fumbled with the cups, poured some cold coffee out and pondered over it as though it were a chemical experiment. Then he muttered something about boiling some more water, and took refuge in the forecastle. I was ill at ease at this period with seafaring men, but this mild little person was easy ground for a beginner. Besides, when he took off his oilskin coat he reminded me less of a sailor than of a homely draper of some country town, with his clean turned-down collar and neatly fitting frieze jacket. We exchanged some polite platitudes about the fog and his voyage last night from Kappeln, which appeared to be a town some fifteen miles up the fiord.

Davies joined in from the forecastle with an excess of warmth which almost took the words out of my mouth. We exhausted the subject very soon, and then my *vis-à-vis* smiled paternally at me, as he had done at Davies, and said, confidentially:

"It is good that the captain is no more alone. He is a fine young man—Heaven, what a fine young man! I love him as my son—but he is too brave, too reckless. It is good for him to have a friend."

I nodded and laughed, though in reality I was very far from being amused.

"Where was it you met?" I asked.

"In an ugly place, and in ugly weather," he answered, gravely, but with a twinkle of fun in his eye. "But has he not told you?" he added, with ponderous slyness. "I came just in time. No! what am I saying? He is brave as a lion and quick as a cat. I think he cannot drown; but still it was an ugly place and ugly—"

"What are you talking about, Bartels?" interrupted Davies, emerging noisily with a boiling kettle.

I answered the question. "I was just asking your friend how it was you made his acquaintance."

"Oh, he helped me out of a bit of a mess in the North Sea, didn't you, Bartels?" he said.

"It was nothing," said Bartels. "But the North Sea is no place for your little boat, captain. So I have told you many times. How did you like Flensburg? A fine town, is it not? Did you find Herr Krank, the carpenter? I see you have placed a little mizzen-mast. The rudder was nothing much, but it was well that it held to the Eider. But she is strong and good, your little ship, and—Heaven!—she had need be so." He chuckled, and shook his head at Davies as at a wayward child.

This is all the conversation that I need record. For my part I merely waited for its end, determined on my course, which was to know the truth once and for all, and make an end of these distracting mystifications. Davies plied his friend with coffee, and kept up the talk gallantly; but affectionate as he was, his manner plainly showed that he wanted to be alone with me.

The gist of the little skipper's talk was a parental warning that, though we were well enough here in the "Ost-See," it was time for little boats to be looking for winter quarters. That he himself was going by the Kiel Canal to Hamburg to spend a cosy winter as a decent citizen at his warm fireside, and that we should follow his example. He ended with an invitation to us to visit him on the *Johannes*, and with suave farewells disappeared into the fog. Davies saw him into his boat, returned without wasting a moment, and sat down on the sofa opposite me.

"What did he mean?" I asked.

"I'll tell you," said Davies. "I'll tell you the whole thing. As far as you're concerned it's partly a confession. Last night I had made up my mind to say nothing, but when Bartels turned up I knew it must all come out. It's been fearfully on my mind, and perhaps you'll be able to help me. But it's for you to decide."

"Fire away!" I said.

"You know what I was saying about the Frisian Islands the other day? A thing happened there which I never told you, when you were asking about my cruise."

"It began near Norderney," I put in.

"How did you guess that?" he asked.

"You're a bad hand at duplicity," I replied. "Go on."

"Well, you're quite right, it was there, on 9th September. I told you the sort of thing I was doing at that time, but I don't think I said that I made inquiries from one or two people about duck-shooting, and had been told by some fishermen at Borkum that there was a big sailing-yacht in those waters, whose owner, a German of the name of Dollmann, shot a good deal, and might give me some tips. Well, I found this yacht one evening, knowing it must be her from the description I had. She was what is called a "barge-yacht," of fifty or sixty tons, built for shallow water on the lines of a Dutch galliot, with leeboards and those queer round bows and square stern. She's something like those galliots anchored near us now. You sometimes see the same sort of yacht in English waters, only there they copy the Thames barges. She looked a clipper of her sort, and very smart; varnished all over and shining like gold. I came on her about sunset, after a long day of exploring round the Ems estuary. She was lying in—"

"Wait a bit, let's have the chart," I interrupted.

Davies found it and spread it on the table between us, first pushing back the cloth and the breakfast things to one end, where they lay in a slovenly litter. This was one of the only two occasions on which I ever saw him postpone the rite of washing up, and it spoke volumes for the urgency of the matter in hand.

"Here it is," said Davies (see Map A), and I looked with a new and strange interest at the long string of slender islands, the parallel line of coast, and the confusion of shoals, banks, and channels which lay between. "Here's Norderney, you see. By the way, there's a harbour there at the west end of the island, the only real harbour on the whole line of islands, Dutch or German, except at Terschelling. There's quite a big town there, too, a watering place, where Germans go for sea-bathing in the summer. Well, the *Medusa*, that was her name, was lying in the Riff Gat roadstead, flying the German ensign, and I anchored for the night pretty near her. I meant to visit her owner later on, but I very nearly changed my mind, as I always feel rather a fool on smart yachts, and my German isn't very good. However, I thought I might as well; so, after dinner, when it was dark, I sculled over in the dinghy, hailed a sailor on deck, said who I was, and asked if I could see the owner. The sailor was a surly sort of chap, and there was a good long delay while I waited on deck, feeling more and more uncomfortable. Presently a steward came up and showed me down the companion and into the saloon, which, after *this*, looked—well, horribly gorgeous—you know what I mean, plush lounges, silk cushions, and that sort of thing. Dinner seemed to be just over, and wine and fruit were on the table. Herr Dollmann was there at his coffee. I introduced myself somehow—"

"Stop a moment," I said; "what was he like?"

"Oh, a tall, thin chap, in evening dress; about fifty I suppose, with greyish hair and a short beard. I'm not good at describing people. He had a high, bulging forehead, and there was something about him—but I think I'd better tell you the bare facts first. I can't say he seemed pleased to see me, and he couldn't speak English, and, in fact, I felt infernally awkward. Still, I had an object in coming, and as I was there I thought I might as well gain it."

The notion of Davies in his Norfolk jacket and rusty flannels haranguing a frigid German in evening dress in a "gorgeous" saloon tickled my fancy greatly.

"He seemed very much astonished to see me; had evidently seen the *Dulcibella* arrive, and had wondered what she was. I began as soon as I could about the ducks, but he shut me up at once, said I could do nothing hereabouts. I put it down to sportsman's jealousy—you know what that is. But I saw I had come to the wrong shop, and was just going to back out and end this unpleasant interview, when he thawed a bit, offered me some wine, and began talking in quite a friendly way, taking a great interest in my cruise and my plans for the future. In the end we sat up quite late, though I never felt really at my ease. He seemed to be taking stock of me all the time, as though I were some new animal." (How I sympathized with that German!) "We parted civilly enough, and I rowed back and turned in, meaning to potter on eastwards early next day.

"But I was knocked up at dawn by a sailor with a message from Dollmann asking if he could come to breakfast with me. I was rather flabbergasted, but didn't like to be rude, so I said, 'Yes.' Well, he came, and I returned the call—and—well, the end of it was that I stayed at anchor there for three days." This was rather abrupt.

"How did you spend the time?" I asked. Stopping three days anywhere was an unusual event for him, as I knew from his log.

"Oh, I lunched or dined with him once or twice—with *them*, I ought to say," he added, hurriedly. "His daughter was with him. She didn't appear the evening I first called."

"And what was she like?" I asked, promptly, before he could hurry on.

"Oh, she seemed a very nice girl," was the guarded reply, delivered with particular unconcern, "and—the end of it was that I and the *Medusa* sailed away in company. I must tell you how it came about, just in a few words for the present.

"It was his suggestion. He said he had to sail to Hamburg, and proposed that I should go with him in the *Dulcibella* as far as the Elbe, and then, if I liked, I could take the ship canal at Brunsbüttel through to Kiel and the Baltic. I had no very fixed plans of my own, though I had meant to go on exploring eastwards between the islands and the coast, and so reach the Elbe in a much slower way. He dissuaded me from this, sticking to it that I should have no chance of ducks, and urging other reasons. Anyway, we settled to sail in company direct to Cuxhaven, in the Elbe. With a fair wind and an early start it should be only one day's sail of about sixty miles.

"The plan only came to a head on the evening of the third day, 12th September."

"I told you, I think, that the weather had broken after a long spell of heat. That very day it had been blowing pretty hard from the west, and the glass was falling still. I said, of course, that I couldn't go with him if the weather was too bad, but he prophesied a good day, said it was an easy sail, and altogether put me on my mettle. You can guess how it was. Perhaps I had talked about single-handed cruising as though it were easier than it was, though I never meant it in a boasting way, for I hate that sort of thing, and besides there *is* no danger if you're careful—"

"Oh, go on," I said.

"Anyway, we went next morning at six. It was a dirty-looking day, wind W.N.W., but his sails were going up and mine followed. I took two reefs in, and we sailed out into the open and steered E.N.E. along the coast for the Outer Elbe Lightship about fifty knots off. Here it all is, you see." (He showed me the course on the chart.) "The trip was nothing for his boat, of course, a safe, powerful old tub, forging through the sea as steady as a house. I kept up with her easily at first. My hands were pretty full, for there was a hard wind on my quarter and a troublesome sea; but as long as nothing worse came I knew I should be all right, though I also knew that I was a fool to have come.

"All went well till we were off Wangeroog, the last of the islands— *here*—and then it began to blow really hard. I had half a mind to chuck it and cut into the Jade River, *down there*; but I hadn't the face to, so I hove to and took in my last reef." (Simple words, simply uttered; but I had seen the operation in calm water and shuddered at the present picture.) "We had been about level till then, but with my shortened canvas I fell behind. Not that that mattered in the least. I knew my course, had read up my tides, and, thick as the weather was, I had no doubt of being able to pick up the lightship. No change of plan was possible now. The Weser estuary was on my starboard hand, but the whole place was a lee-shore and a mass of unknown banks—just look at them. I ran on, the *Dulcibella* doing her level best, but we had some narrow shaves of being pooped. I was about *here*, say six miles southwest of the lightship,\* when I suddenly saw that the *Medusa* had hove to right ahead, as though waiting till I came up. She wore round again on the course as I drew level, and we were alongside for a bit. Dollmann lashed the wheel, leaned over her quarter, and shouted, very slowly and distinctly so that I could understand: "Follow me—sea too bad for you outside— short cut through sands—save six miles."

"It was taking me all my time to manage the tiller, but I knew what he meant at once, for I had been over the chart carefully the night before.† You see, the whole bay between Wangeroog and the Elbe is encumbered with sand. A great jagged chunk of it runs out from Cuxhaven in a north-westerly direction for fifteen miles or so, ending in a pointed spit, called the *Scharhorn*. To reach the Elbe from the west you have to go right outside this, round the lightship, which is off the Scharhorn, and double back. Of course, that's what all big vessels do.

---

\*See Chart A.    †See Map A.

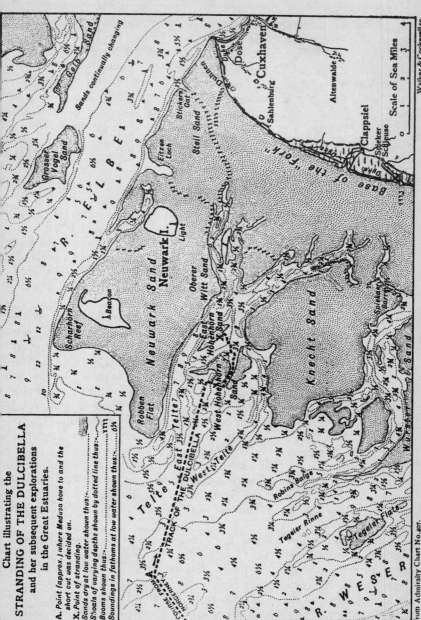

Chart illustrating the
STRANDING OF THE DULCIBELLA
and her subsequent explorations
in the Great Estuaries.

A. Point (approx.) where Medusa hove to and the
   short cut was decided on.
X. Point of stranding.
Sands dry at low water shown thus:—
Shoals of varying depths shown by dotted line thus:—
Booms shown thus:—
Soundings in fathoms at low water shown thus:—6½

CHART A.

from Admiralty Chart No.407.

Walker & Cockerell sc.

Scale of Sea Miles

But, as you see, these sands are intersected here and there by channels, very shallow and winding, exactly like those behind the Frisian Islands. Now look at this one, which cuts right through the big chunk of sand and comes out near Cuxhaven. The *Telte** it's called. It's miles wide, you see, at the entrance, but later on it is split into two by the Hohen-hörn bank; then it gets shallow and very complicated, and ends in a mere tidal driblet with another name. It's just the sort of channel I should like to worry into on a fine day or with an off-shore wind. Alone, in thick weather and a heavy sea, it would have been folly to attempt it, except as a desperate resource. But, as I said I knew at once that Dollmann was proposing to run for it and guide me in.

"I didn't like the idea, because I like doing things for myself, and, silly as it sounds, I believe I resented being told the sea was too bad for me, which it certainly was. Yet the short cut did save several miles and a devil of a tumble off the Scharhorn, where two tides meet. I had complete faith in Dollmann, and I suppose I decided that I should be a fool not to take a good chance. I hesitated, I know; but in the end I nodded, and held up my arm as she forged ahead again. Soon after, she shifted her course and I followed. You asked me once if I ever took a pilot. That was the only time."

He spoke with bitter gravity, flung himself back, and felt his pocket for his pipe. It was not meant for a dramatic pause, but it certainly was one. I had just a glimpse of still another Davies—a Davies five years older throbbing with deep emotions, scorn, passion, and stubborn purpose; a being above my plane, of sterner stuff, wider scope. Intense as my interest had become, I waited almost timidly while he mechanically rammed tobacco into his pipe and struck ineffectual matches. I felt that whatever the riddle to be solved, it was no mean one. He repressed himself with an effort, half rose, and made his circular glance at the clock, barometer, and skylight, and then resumed.

"We soon came to what I knew must be the beginning of the Telte channel. All round you could hear the breakers on the sands, though it was too thick to see them yet. As the water shoaled, the sea, of course, got shorter and steeper. There was more wind—a whole gale I should say.

"I kept dead in the wake of the *Medusa*, but to my disgust I found she was gaining on me very fast. Of course I had taken for granted, when he said he would lead me in, that he would slow down and keep close to me. He could easily have done so by getting his men up to check his sheets or drop his peak. Instead of that he was busting on for all he was worth. Once, in a rain-squall, I lost sight of him altogether;

*See Chart A.

got him faintly again, but had enough to do with my own tiller not to want to be peering through the scud after a runaway pilot. I was all right so far, but we were fast approaching the worst part of the whole passage, where the Hohenhörn bank blocks the road, and the channel divides. I don't know what it looks like to you on the chart—perhaps fairly simple, because you can follow the twists of the channels, as on a ground-plan; but a stranger coming to a place like that (where there are no buoys, mind you) can tell nothing certain by the eye—unless perhaps at dead low water, when the banks are high and dry, and in very clear weather—he must trust to the lead and the compass, and feel his way step by step. I knew perfectly well that what I should soon see would be a wall of surf stretching right across and on both sides. To *feel* one's way in that sort of weather is impossible. You must *know* your way, or else have a pilot. I had one, but he was playing his own game.

"With a second hand on board to steer while I conned I should have felt less of an ass. As it was, I knew I ought to be facing the music in the offing, and cursed myself for having broken my rule and gone blundering into this confounded short cut. It was giving myself away, doing just the very thing that you can't do in single-handed sailing.

"By the time I realized the danger it was far too late to turn and hammer out to the open. I was deep in the bottle-neck bight of the sands, jammed on a lee shore, and a strong flood tide sweeping me on. That tide, by the way, gave just the ghost of a chance. I had the hours in my head, and knew it was about two-thirds flood, with two hours more of rising water. That meant the banks would be all covering when I reached them, and harder than ever to locate; but it also meant that I *might* float right over the worst of them if I hit off a lucky place." Davies thumped the table in disgust. "Pah! It makes me sick to think of having to trust to an accident like that, like a lubberly cockney out for a boozy Bank Holiday sail. Well, just as I foresaw, the wall of surf appeared clean across the horizon, and curling back to shut me in, booming like thunder. When I last saw the *Medusa* she seemed to be charging it like a horse at a fence, and I took a rough bearing of her position by a hurried glance at the compass. At that very moment I *thought* she seemed to luff and show some of her broadside; but a squall blotted her out and gave me hell with the tiller. After that she was lost in the white mist that hung over the line of breakers. I kept on my bearing as well as I could, but I was already out of the channel. I knew that by the look of the water, and as we neared the bank I saw it was all awash and without the vestige of an opening. I wasn't going to chuck her on to it without an effort; so, more by instinct than with any particular hope, I put the helm down, meaning to work her along the edge on the chance of spotting a way over. She was buried at once by the beam sea, and the jib flew to blazes; but the reefed stays'l stood, she recovered gamely, and I held on, though I knew it could only be for a few minutes, as the centre-plate was up, and she made frightful leeway towards the bank.

"I was half-blinded by scud, but suddenly I noticed what looked like a gap, behind a spit which curled out right ahead. I luffed still more to clear this spit, but she couldn't weather it. Before you could say knife she was driving across it, bumped heavily, bucked forward again, bumped again, and—ripped on in deeper water! I can't describe the next few minutes. I was in some sort of channel, but a very narrow one, and the sea broke everywhere. I hadn't proper command either; for the rudder had crocked up somehow at the last bump. I was like a drunken man running for his life down a dark alley, barking himself at every corner. It couldn't last long, and finally we went crash on to something and stopped there, grinding and banging. So ended that little trip under a pilot.

"Well, it was like this—there was really no danger"—I opened my eyes at the characteristic phrase. "I mean, that lucky stumble into a channel was my salvation. Since then I had struggled through a mile of sands, all of which lay behind me like a breakwater against the gale. They were covered, of course, and seething like soapsuds; but the force of the sea was deadened. The *Dulce* was bumping, but not too heavily. It was nearing high tide, and at half ebb she would be high and dry.

"In the ordinary way I should have run out a kedge with the dinghy, and at the next high water sailed farther in and anchored where I could lie afloat. The trouble was now that my hand was hurt and my dinghy stove in, not to mention the rudder business. It was the first bump on the outer edge that did the damage. There was a heavy swell there, and when we struck, the dinghy, which was towing astern, came home on her painter and down with a crash on the yacht's weather quarter. I stuck out one hand to ward it off and got it nipped on the gunwale. She was badly stove in and useless, so I couldn't run out the kedge"—this was Greek to me, but I let him go on—"and for the present my hand was too painful even to stow the boom and sails, which were whipping and racketing about anyhow. There was the rudder, too, to be mended; and we were several miles from the nearest land. Of course, if the wind fell, it was all easy enough; but if it held or increased it was a poor lookout. There's a limit to strain of that sort—and other things might have happened.

"In fact, it was precious lucky that Bartels turned up. His galliot was at anchor a mile away, up a branch of the channel. In a clear between squalls he saw us, and, like a brick, rowed his boat out—he and his boy, and a devil of a pull they must have had. I was glad enough to see them—no, that's not true; I was in such a fury of disgust and shame that

I believe I should have been idiot enough to say I didn't want help, if he hadn't just nipped on board and started work. He's a terror to work, that little mouse of a chap. In half an hour he had stowed the sails, unshackled the big anchor, run out fifty fathoms of warp, and hauled her off there and then into deep water. Then they towed her up the channel—it was dead to leeward and an easy job—and berthed her near their own vessel. It was dark by that time, so I gave them a drink, and said good-night. It blew a howling gale that night, but the place was safe enough, with good ground-tackle.

"The whole affair was over; and after supper I thought hard about it all."

8

**The Theory**

DAVIES leaned back and gave a deep sigh, as though he still felt the relief from some tension. I did the same, and felt the same relief. The chart, freed from the pressure of our fingers, rolled up with a flip, as though to say, "What do you think of that?" I have straightened out his sentences a little, for in the excitement of his story they had grown more and more jerky and elliptical.

"What about Dollmann?" I asked.

"Of course," said Davies, "what about him? I didn't get at much that night. It was all so sudden. The only thing I could have sworn to from the first was that he had purposely left me in the lurch that day. I pieced out the rest in the next few days, which I'll just finish with as shortly as I can. Bartels came aboard next morning, and though it was blowing hard still we managed to shift the *Dulcibella* to a place where she dried safely at the mid-day low water, and we could get at her rudder. The lower screw-plate on the stern post had wrenched out, and we botched it up roughly as a make-shift. There were other little breakages, but nothing to matter, and the loss of the jib was nothing, as I had two spare ones. The dinghy was past repair just then, and I lashed it on deck.

"It turned out that Bartels was carrying apples from Bremen to Kappeln (in this fiord), and had run into that channel in the sands for shelter from the weather. To-day he was bound for the Eider River, whence, as I told you, you can get through (by river and canal) into the Baltic. Of course the Elbe route, by the new Kaiser Wilhelm Ship Canal, is the shortest. The Eider route is the old one, but he hoped to get rid of some of his apples at Tönning, the town at its mouth. Both routes touch the Baltic at Kiel. As you know, I had been running for the Elbe, but yesterday's muck-up put me off, and I changed my mind— I'll tell you why presently—and decided to sail to the Eider along with the *Johannes* and get through that way. It cleared from the east next day, and I raced him there, winning hands down, left him at Tönning, and in three days was in the Baltic. It was just a week after I ran ashore that I wired to you. You see, I had come to the conclusion that *that chap was a spy.*"

In the end it came out quite quietly and suddenly, and left me in profound amazement. "I wired to you—that chap was a spy." It was the close association of these two ideas that hit me hardest at the moment. For a second I was back in the dreary splendour of the London clubroom, spelling out that crabbed scrawl from Davies, and fastidiously criticizing its proposal in the light of a holiday. Holiday! What was to be its issue? Chilling and opaque as the fog that filtered through the skylight there flooded my imagination a mist of doubt and fear.

"A spy!" I repeated blankly. "What do you mean? Why did you wire to me? A spy of what—of whom?"

"I'll tell you how I worked it out," said Davies. "I don't think 'spy' is the right word; but I mean something pretty bad.

"He purposely put me ashore. I don't think I'm suspicious by nature, but I know something about boats and the sea. I know he could have kept close to me if he had chosen, and I saw the whole place at low water when we left those sands on the second day. Look at the chart again. Here's the Hohenhörn bank that I showed you as blocking the road.* It's in two pieces—first the west and then the east. You see the Telte channel dividing into two branches and curving round it. Both branches are broad and deep, as channels go in those waters. Now, in sailing in I was nowhere near either of them. When I last saw Dollmann he must have been steering straight for the bank itself, at a point somewhere *here*, quite a mile from the northern arm of the channel, and two from the southern. I followed by compass, as you know, and found nothing but breakers ahead. How did I get through? That's where the luck came in. I spoke of only two channels, that is, *round* the bank—one to the north, the other to the south. But look closely and you'll see that right through the centre of the West Hohenhörn runs another, a very narrow and winding one, so small that I hadn't even noticed it the night before, when I was going over the chart. That was the one I stumbled into in that tailor's fashion, as I was groping along the edge of the surf in a desperate effort to gain time. I bolted down it

*See Chart A.

blindly, came out into this strip of open water, crossed that aimlessly, and brought up on the edge of the *East* Hohenhörn, *here*. It was more than I deserved. I can see now that it was a hundred to one in favour of my striking on a bad place outside, where I should have gone to pieces in three minutes."

"And how did Dollmann go?" I asked.

"It's as clear as possible," Davies answered. "He doubled back into the northern channel when he had misled me enough. Do you remember my saying that when I last saw him I *thought* he had luffed and showed his broadside? I had another bit of luck in that. He was luffing towards the north—so it struck me through the blur—and when I in my turn came up to the bank, and had to turn one way or the other to avoid it, I think I should naturally have turned north too, as he had done. In that case I should have been done for, for I should have had a mile of the bank to skirt before reaching the north channel, and should have driven ashore long before I got there. But as a matter of fact I turned south."

"Why?"

"Couldn't help it. I was running on the starboard tack—boom over to port; to turn north would have meant a jibe, and as things were I couldn't risk one. It was blowing like fits; if anything had carried away I should have been on shore in a jiffy. I scarcely thought about it at all, but put the helm down and turned her south. Though I knew nothing about it, that little central channel was now on my port hand, distant about two cables. The whole thing was luck from beginning to end."

Helped by pluck, I thought to myself, as I tried with my landsman's fancy to conjure up that perilous scene. As to the truth of the affair, the chart and Davies's version were easy enough to follow, but I felt only half convinced. The "spy," as Davies strangely called his pilot, might have honestly mistaken the course himself, outstripped his convoy inadvertently, and escaped disaster as narrowly as she did. I suggested this on the spur of the moment, but Davies was impatient.

"Wait till you hear the whole thing," he said. "I must go back to when I first met him. I told you that on that first evening he began by being as rude as a bear and as cold as stone, and then became suddenly friendly. I can see now that in the talk that followed he was pumping me hard. It was an easy game to play, for I hadn't seen a gentleman since Morrison left me, I was tremendously keen about my voyage, and I thought the chap was a good sportsman, even if he was a bit dark about the ducks. I talked quite freely—at least, as freely as I could with my bad German—about my last fortnight's sailing; how I had been smelling out all the channels in and out of the islands, how interested I had been in the whole business, puzzling out the effect of the winds

on the tides, the set of the currents, and so on. I talked about my difficulties, too; the changes in the buoys, the prehistoric rottenness of the
English charts. He drew me out as much as he could, and in the light
of what followed I can see the point of scores of his questions.

"The next day and the next I saw a good deal of him, and the same
thing went on. And then there were my plans for the future. My idea
was, as I told you, to go on exploring the German coast just as I had the
Dutch. His idea—Heavens, how plainly I see it now!—was to choke
me off, get me to clear out altogether from that part of the coast. That
was why he said there were no ducks. That was why he cracked up the
Baltic as a cruising-ground and shooting-ground. And that was why he
broached and stuck to that plan of sailing in company direct to the
Elbe. It was to *see* me clear."

"He improved on that."

"Yes, but after that, it's guess-work. I mean that I can't tell when he
first decided to go one better and drown me. He couldn't count for certain on bad weather, though he held my nose to it when it came. But,
granted that he wanted to get rid of me altogether, he got a magnificent
chance on that trip to the Elbe lightship. I expect it struck him suddenly, and he acted on the impulse. Left to myself I was all right; but
the short cut was a grand idea of his. Everything was in its favour—
wind, sea, sand, tide. He thinks I'm dead."

"But the crew?" I said; "what about the crew?"

"That's another thing. When he first hove to, waiting for me, of
course they were on deck (two of them, I think) hauling at sheets. But
by the time I had drawn up level the *Medusa* had worn round again on
her course, and no one was on deck but Dollmann at the wheel. No
one overheard what he said."

"Wouldn't they have *seen* you again?"

"Very likely not; the weather was very thick, and the *Dulce* is very
small."

The incongruity of the whole business was striking me. Why should
anyone want to kill Davies, and why should Davies, the soul of modesty and simplicity, imagine that anyone wanted to kill him? He must
have cogent reasons, for he was the last man to give way to a morbid
fancy.

"Go on," I said. "What was his motive? A German finds an
Englishman exploring a bit of German coast, determines to stop him,
and even to get rid of him. It looks so far as if *you* were thought to be
the spy."

Davies winced. "*But he's not a German,*" he said, hotly. "He's an
Englishman."

"An Englishman?"

"Yes, I'm sure of it. Not that I've much to go on. He professed to know very little English, and never spoke it, except a word or two now and then to help me out of a sentence; and as to his German, he seemed to me to speak it like a native; but, of course, I'm no judge." Davies sighed. "That's where I wanted someone like you. You would have spotted him at once, if he wasn't German. I go more by a—what do you call it?—a—"

"General impression," I suggested.

"Yes, that's what I mean. It was something in his looks and manner; you know how different we are from foreigners. And it wasn't only himself, it was the way he talked—I mean about cruising and the sea, especially. It's true he let me do most of the talking; but, all the same—how can I explain it? I felt we understood one another, in a way that two foreigners wouldn't. He pretended to think me a bit crazy for coming so far in a small boat, but I could swear he knew as much about the game as I did; for lots of little questions he asked had the right ring in them. Mind you, all this is an afterthought. I should never have bothered about it—I'm not cut out for a Sherlock Holmes—if it hadn't been for what followed.

"It's rather vague," I said. "Have you no more definite reason for thinking him English?"

"There were one or two things rather more definite," said Davies, slowly. "You know when he hove to and hailed me, proposing the short cut, I told you roughly what he said. I forget the exact words, but 'abschneiden' came in—'durch Watten' and 'abschneiden' (they call the banks 'watts,' you know); they were simple words, and he shouted them loud, so as to carry through the wind. I understood what he meant, but, as I told you, I hesitated before consenting. I suppose he thought I didn't understand, for just as he was drawing ahead again he pointed to the south'ard, and then shouted through his hands as a trumpet 'Verstehen Sie? short-cut through sands; follow me!' the last two sentences in downright English. I can hear those words now, and I'll swear they were in his native tongue. Of course I thought nothing of it at the time. I was quite aware that he knew a few English words, though he had always mispronounced them; an easy trick when your hearer suspects nothing. But I needn't say that just then I was observant of trifles. I don't pretend to be able to unravel a plot and steer a small boat before a heavy sea at the same moment."

"And if he was piloting you into the next world he could afford to commit himself before you parted! Was there anything else? By the way, how did the daughter strike you? Did she look English too?"

Two men cannot discuss a woman freely without a deep foundation of intimacy, and, until this day, the subject had never arisen between us in any form. It was the last that was likely to, for I could have divined that Davies would have met it with an armour of reserve. He was busy putting on this armour now; yet I could not help feeling a little brutal as I saw how badly he jointed his clumsy suit of mail. Our ages were the same, but I laugh now to think how old and *blasé* I felt as the flush warmed his brown skin, and he slowly propounded the verdict, "Yes, I think she did."

"She *talked* nothing but German, I suppose?"

"Oh, of course."

"Did you see much of her?"

"A good deal."

"Was she—" (how frame it?) "Did she want you to sail to the Elbe with them?"

"She seemed to," admitted Davies, reluctantly, clutching at his ally, the match-box. "But, hang it, don't dream that she knew what was coming," he added, with sudden fire.

I pondered and wondered, shrinking from further inquisition, easy as it would have been with so truthful a victim, and banishing all thought of ill-timed chaff. There was a cross-current in this strange affair, whose depth and strength I was beginning to gauge with increasing seriousness. I did not know my man yet, and I did not know myself. A conviction that events in the near future would force us into complete mutual confidence withheld me from pressing him too far. I returned to the main question: who was Dollmann, and what was his motive? Davies struggled out of his armour.

"I'm convinced," he said, "that he's an Englishman in German service. He must be in German service, for he had evidently been in those waters a long time, and knew every inch of them; of course, it's a very lonely part of the world, but he has a house on Norderney Island; and he, and all about him, must be well known to a certain number of people. One of his friends I happened to meet; what do you think he was? A naval officer. It was on the afternoon of the third day, and we were having coffee on the deck of the *Medusa*, and talking about next day's trip, when a little launch came buzzing up from seaward, drew alongside, and this chap I'm speaking of came on board, shook hands with Dollmann, and stared hard at me. Dollmann introduced us, calling him Commander von Brüning, in command of the torpedo gunboat *Blitz*. He pointed towards Norderney, and I saw her—a low, grey rat of a vessel—anchored in the Roads about two miles away. It turned out that she was doing the work of fishery guardship on that part of the coast.

"I must say I took to him at once. He looked a real good sort, and a splendid officer, too—just the sort of chap I should have liked to be.

You know I always wanted—but that's an old story, and can wait. I had some talk with him, and we got on capitally as far as we went, but that wasn't far, for I left pretty soon, guessing that they wanted to be alone."

"*Were* they alone then?" I asked, innocently.

"Oh, Fräulein Dollmann was there, of course," explained Davies, feeling for his armour again.

"Did he seem to know them well?" I pursued, inconsequently.

"Oh, yes, very well."

Scenting a faint clue, I felt the need of feminine weapons for my sensitive antagonist. But the opportunity passed.

"That was the last I saw of him," he said. "We sailed, as I told you, at daybreak next morning. Now, have you got any idea what I'm driving at?"

"A rough idea," I answered. "Go ahead."

Davies sat up to the table, unrolled the chart with a vigorous sweep of his two hands, and took up his parable with new zest.

"I start with two certainties," he said. "One is that I was 'moved on' from that coast, because I was too inquisitive. The other is that Dollmann is at some devil's work there which is worth finding out. Now"—he paused in a gasping effort to be logical and articulate. "Now—well, look at the chart. No, better still, look first at this map of Germany. It's on a small scale, and you can see the whole thing." He snatched down a pocket-map from the shelf and unfolded it.* "Here's this huge empire, stretching half over central Europe—an empire growing like wildfire, I believe, in people, and wealth, and everything. They've licked the French, and the Austrians, and are the greatest military power in Europe. I wish I knew more about all that, but what I'm concerned with is their sea-power. It's a new thing with them, but it's going strong, and that Emperor of theirs is running it for all it's worth. He's a splendid chap, and anyone can see he's right. They've got no colonies to speak of, and *must* have them, like us. They can't get them and keep them, and they can't protect their huge commerce without naval strength. The command of the sea is *the* thing nowadays, isn't it? I say, don't think these are my ideas," he added, naïvely. "It's all out of Mahan and those fellows. Well, the Germans have got a small fleet at present, but it's a thundering good one, and they're building hard. There's the —— and the —— ." He broke off into a digression on armaments and speeds in which I could not follow him. He seemed to know every ship by heart. I had to recall him to the point. "Well, think of Germany as a new sea-power," he resumed. "The next thing is, what is her coast-line? It's a very queer one, as you know, split clean in two

*See Map A.

by Denmark, most of it lying east of that and looking on the Baltic, which is practically an inland sea, with its entrance blocked by Danish islands. It was to evade that block that William built the ship canal from Kiel to the Elbe, but that could be easily smashed in war-time. Far the most important bit of coast-line is that which lies *west* of Denmark and looks on the North Sea. It's there that Germany gets her head out into the open, so to speak. It's there that she fronts us and France, the two great sea-powers of Western Europe, and it's there that her greatest ports are and her richest commerce.

"Now it must strike you at once that it's ridiculously short compared with the huge country behind it. From Borkum to the Elbe, as the crow flies, is only seventy miles. Add to that the west coast of Schleswig, say 120 miles. Total, say, two hundred. Compare that with the seaboard of France and England. Doesn't it stand to reason that every inch of it is important? Now what *sort* of coast is it? Even on this small map you can see at once, by all those wavy lines, shoals and sand everywhere, blocking nine-tenths of the land altogether, and doing their best to block the other tenth where the great rivers run in. Now let's take it bit by bit. You see it divides itself into three. Beginning from the west the *first piece* is from Borkum to Wangeroog—fifty odd miles. What's that like? A string of sandy islands backed by sand; the Ems river at the western end, on the Dutch border, leading to Emden—not much of a place. Otherwise, no coast towns at all. *Second piece:* a deep sort of bay consisting of the three great estuaries—the Jade, the Weser, and the Elbe—leading to Wilhelmshaven (their North Sea naval base), Bremen, and Hamburg. Total breadth of bay twenty odd miles only; sandbanks littered about all through it. *Third piece:* the Schleswig coast, hopelessly fenced in behind a six to eight mile fringe of sand. No big towns; one moderate river, the Eider. Let's leave that third piece aside. I may be wrong, but, in thinking this business out, I've pegged away chiefly at the other two, the seventy-mile stretch from Borkum to the Elbe—half of it estuaries, and half islands. It was there that I found the *Medusa*, and it's that stretch that, thanks to him, I missed exploring."

I made an obvious conjecture. "I suppose there are forts and coast defences? Perhaps he thought you would see too much. By the way, he saw your naval books, of course?"

"Exactly. Of course that was my first idea; but it can't be that. It doesn't explain things in the least. To begin with, there *are* no forts and can be none in that first division, where the islands are. There might be something on Borkum to defend the Ems; but it's very unlikely, and, anyway, I had passed Borkum and was at Norderney. There's nothing else to defend. Of course it's different in the second division, where the big rivers are. There are probably hosts of forts and mines round

Wilhelmshaven and Bremerhaven, and at Cuxhaven just at the mouth of the Elbe. Not that I should ever dream of bothering about them; every steamer that goes in would see as much as me. Personally, I much prefer to stay on board, and don't often go on shore. And, good Heavens!" (Davies leant back and laughed joyously) "do I *look* like that kind of spy?"

I figured to myself one of those romantic gentlemen that one reads of in sixpenny magazines, with a Kodak in his tie-pin, a sketch-book in the lining of his coat, and a selection of disguises in his hand luggage. Little disposed for merriment as I was, I could not help smiling, too.

"About this coast," resumed Davies. "In the event of war it seems to me that every inch of it would be important, *sand and all*. Take the big estuaries first, which, of course, might be attacked or blockaded by an enemy. At first sight you would say that their main channels were the only things that mattered. Now, in time of peace there's no secrecy about the navigation of these. They're buoyed and lighted like streets, open to the whole world, and taking an immense traffic; well charted, too, as millions of pounds in commerce depend on them. But now look at the sands they run through, intersected, as I showed you, by threads of channels, tidal for the most part, and probably only known to smacks and shallow coasters, like that galliot of Bartels.

"It strikes me that in a war a lot might depend on these, both in defence and attack, for there's plenty of water in them at the right tide for patrol-boats and small torpedo craft, though I can see they take a lot of knowing. Now, say *we* were at war with Germany—both sides could use them as lines between the three estuaries; and to take our own case, a small torpedo-boat (not a destroyer, mind you) could on a dark night cut clean through from the Jade to the Elbe and play the deuce with the shipping there. But the trouble is that I doubt if there's a soul in our fleet who knows those channels. We haven't coasters there; and, as to yachts, it's a most unlikely game for an English yacht to play at; but it does so happen that I have a fancy for that sort of thing and would have explored those channels in the ordinary course." I began to see his drift.

"Now for the islands. I was rather stumped there at first, I grant, because, though there are lashings of sand behind them, and the same sort of intersecting channels, yet there seems nothing important to guard or attack.

"Why shouldn't a stranger ramble as he pleases through them? Still Dollmann had his headquarters there, and I was sure that had some meaning. Then it struck me that the same point held good, for that strip of Frisian coast adjoins the estuaries, and would also form a splendid base for raiding midgets, which could travel unseen right through from the Ems to the Jade, and so to the Elbe, as by a covered way between a line of forts.

"Now here again it's an unknown land to us. Plenty of local galliots travel it, but strangers never, I should say. Perhaps at the most an occasional foreign yacht gropes in at one of the gaps between the islands for shelter from bad weather, and is precious lucky to get in safe. Once again, it was my fad to like such places, and Dollmann cleared me out. He's not a German, but he's in with Germans, and naval Germans too. He's established on that coast, and knows it by heart. And he tried to drown me. Now what do you think?" He gazed at me long and anxiously.

# 9

## I Sign Articles

IT WAS not an easy question to answer, for the affair was utterly outside all my experience; its background the sea, and its actual scene a region of the sea of which I was blankly ignorant. There were other difficulties that I could see perhaps better than Davies, an enthusiast with hobbies, who had been brooding in solitude over his dangerous adventure. Yet both narrative and theory (which have lost, I fear, in interpretation to the reader) had strongly affected me; his forcible roughnesses, tricks of manner, sudden bursts of ardour, sudden retreats into shyness, making up a charm I cannot render. I found myself continually trying to see the man through the boy, to distinguish sober judgement from the hot-headed vagaries of youth. Not that I dreamed for a moment of dismissing the story of his wreck as an hallucination. His clear blue eyes and sane simplicity threw ridicule on such treatment.

Evidently, too, he wanted my help, a matter that might well have influenced my opinion on the facts, had he been other than he was. But it would have taken a "finished and finite clod" to resist the attraction of the man and the enterprise; and I take no credit whatever for deciding to follow him, right or wrong. So, when I stated my difficulties, I knew very well that we should go.

"There are two main points that I don't understand," I said. "First, you've never explained why an *Englishman* should be watching those waters and ejecting intruders; secondly, your theory doesn't supply sufficient motive. There may be much in what you say about the navigation of those channels, but it's not enough. You say he wanted to drown you—a big charge, requiring a big motive to support it. But I don't deny that you've got a strong case." Davies lighted up. "I'm willing to take a good deal for granted—until we find out more."

He jumped up, and did a thing I never saw him do before or since—bumped his head against the cabin roof.

"You mean that you'll come?" he exclaimed. "Why, I hadn't even asked you! Yes, I want to go back and clear up the whole thing. I know now that I want to; telling it all to you has been such an immense relief. And a lot depended on you, too, and that's why I've been feeling such an absolute hypocrite. I say, how can I apologize?"

"Don't worry about me; I've had a splendid time. And I'll come right enough; but I should like to know exactly what you—"

"No; but wait till I just make a clean breast of it—about you, I mean. You see, I came to the conclusion that I could do nothing alone; not that two are really necessary for managing the boat in the ordinary way, but for this sort of job you *do* want two; besides, I can't speak German properly, and I'm a dull chap all round. If my theory, as you call it, is right, it's a case for sharp wits, if ever there was one; so I thought of you. You're clever, and I knew you had lived in Germany and knew German, and I knew," he added, with a little awkwardness, "that you had done a good deal of yachting; but of course I ought to have told you what you were in for—roughing it in a small boat with no crew. I felt ashamed of myself when you wired back so promptly, and when you came—er—" Davies stammered and hesitated in the humane resolve not to wound my feelings. "Of course I couldn't help noticing that it wasn't what you expected," was the delicate summary he arrived at. "But you took it splendidly," he hastened to add. "Only, somehow, I couldn't bring myself to talk about the plan. It was good enough of you to come out at all, without bothering you with hare-brained schemes. Beside, I wasn't even sure of myself. It's a tangled business. There were reasons, there are reasons still"—he looked nervously at me—"which—well, which make it a tangled business." I had thought a confidence was coming, and was disappointed. "I was in an idiotic state of uncertainty," he hurried on; "but the plan grew on me more and more, when I saw how you were taking to the life and beginning to enjoy yourself. All that about the ducks on the Frisian coast was humbug; part of a stupid idea of decoying you there and gaining time. However, you quite naturally objected, and last night I meant to chuck the whole thing up and give you the best time here I could. Then Bartels turned up—"

"Stop," I put in. "Did you know he might turn up when you sailed here?"

"Yes," said Davies, guiltily. "I knew he might; and now it's all come out, and you'll come! What a fool I've been!"

Long before he had finished I had grasped the whole meaning of the last few days, and had read their meaning into scores of little incidents which had puzzled me.

"For goodness' sake, don't apologize," I protested. "I could make confessions, too, if I liked. And I doubt if you've been such a fool as you think. I'm a patient that wants careful nursing, and it has been the merest chance all through that I haven't rebelled and bolted. We've got a good deal to thank the weather for, and other little stimulants. And you don't know yet my reasons for deciding to try your cure at all."

"My cure?" said Davies; "what in the world do you mean? It was jolly decent of you to—"

"Never mind! There's another view of it, but it doesn't matter now. Let's return to the point. What's your plan of action?"

"It's this," was the prompt reply: "to get back to the North Sea, *via* Kiel and the ship canal. Then there will be two objects: one, to work back to Norderney, where I left off before, exploring all those channels through the estuaries and islands; the other, to find Dollmann, discover what he's up to, and settle with him. The two things may overlap, we can't tell yet. I don't even know where he and his yacht are; but I'll be bound they're somewhere in those same waters, and probably back at Norderney."

"It's a delicate matter," I mused, dubiously, "if your theory's correct. Spying on a spy—"

"It's not like that," said Davies, indignantly. "Anyone who likes can sail about there and explore those waters. I say, you don't really think it's like that, do you?"

"I don't think you're likely to do anything dishonourable," I hastened to explain. "I grant you the sea's public property in your sense. I only mean that developments are possible, which you don't reckon on. There *must* be more to find out than the mere navigation of those channels, and if that's so, mightn't we come to be genuine spies ourselves?"

"And, after all, hang it!" exclaimed Davies, "if it comes to that, why shouldn't we? I look at it like this. The man's an Englishman, and if he's in with Germany he's a traitor to us, and we as Englishmen have a right to expose him. If we can't do it without spying we've a right to spy, at our own risk—"

"There's a stronger argument than that. He tried to take your life."

"I don't care a rap about that. I'm not such an ass as to thirst for revenge and all that, like some chap in a shilling shocker. But it makes me wild to think of that fellow masquerading as a German, and up to who knows what mischief—mischief enough to make him want to get rid of *any* one. I'm keen about the sea, and I think they're apt to be a bit slack at home," he continued inconsequently. "Those Admiralty chaps want waking up. Anyway, as far as I'm concerned, it's quite natural that I should look him up again."

"Quite," I agreed; "you parted friends, and they may be delighted to see you. You'll have plenty to talk about."

"H'm," said Davies, withered into silence by the "they." "Hullo! I say, do you know it's three o'clock? How the time has gone! And, by Jove! I believe the fog's lifting."

I returned, with a shock, to the present, to the weeping walls, the discoloured deal table, the ghastly breakfast litter—all the visible symbols of the life I had pledged myself to. Disillusionment was making rapid headway when Davies returned, and said, with energy:

"What do you say to starting for Kiel at once? The fog's going, and there's a breeze from the sou'-west."

"Now?" I protested. "Why, it'll mean sailing all night, won't it?"

"Oh, no," said Davies. "Not with luck."

"Why, it's dark at seven!"

"Yes, but it's only twenty-five miles. I know it's not exactly a fair wind, but we shall lie closehauled most of the way. The glass is falling, and we ought to take this chance."

To argue about winds with Davies was hopeless, and the upshot was that we started lunchless. A pale sun was flickering out of masses of racing vapour, and through delicate vistas between them the fair land of Schleswig now revealed and now withdrew her pretty face, as though smiling *adieu* to her faithless courtiers.

The clank of our chain brought up Bartels to the deck of the *Johannes*, rubbing his eyes and pulling round his throat a grey shawl, which gave him a comical likeness to a lodging-house landlady receiving the milk in morning *déshabillé*.

"We're off, Bartels," said Davies, without looking up from his work. "See you at Kiel, I hope."

"You are always in a hurry, captain," bleated the old man, shaking his head. "You should wait till to-morrow. The sky is not good, and it will be dark before you are off Eckenförde."

Davies laughed, and very soon his mentor's sad little figure was lost in haze.

That was a curious evening. Dusk soon fell, and the devil made a determined effort to unman me; first, with the scrambled tea which was the tardy substitute for an orderly lunch, then with the new and nauseous duty of filling the side-lights, which meant squatting in the fo'c'sle to inhale paraffin and dabble in lampblack; lastly, with an all-round attack on my nerves as the night fell on our frail little vessel, pitching on her precarious way through driving mist. In a sense I think I went through the same sort of mental crisis as when I sat upon my portmanteau at Flensburg. The main issue was not seriously in question, for I had signed on in the *Dulcibella* for good or ill; but in doing so I had outrun myself, and still wanted an outlook, a mood suited to the enterprise, proof against petty discouragements. Not for the first time a sense of the ludicrous came to my assistance, as I saw myself fretting in London under my burden of self-imposed woes, nicely weighing that insidious invitation, and stepping finally into the snare with the dignity due to my importance; kidnapped as neatly as ever a peaceful clerk was kidnapped by a lawless press-gang, and, in the end, finding as the arch-conspirator a guileless and warm-hearted friend, who called me clever, lodged me in a cell, and blandly invited me to talk German to the purpose, as he was aiming at a little secret service on the high seas. Close in the train of Humour came Romance, veiling her face, but I knew it was the rustle of her robes that I heard in the foam beneath me; I knew that it was she who handed me the cup of sparkling wine and bade me drink and be merry. Strange to me though it was, I knew the taste when it touched my lips. It was not that bastard concoction I had tasted in the pseudo-Bohemias of Soho; it was not the showy but insipid beverage I should have drunk my fill of at Morven Lodge; it was the purest of her pure vintages, instilling the ancient inspiration which, under many guises, quickens thousands of better brains than mine, but whose essence is always the same; the gay pursuit of a perilous quest. Then and there I tried to clinch the matter and keep that mood. In the main I think I succeeded, though I had many lapses.

For the present my veins tingled with the draught. The wind humming into the mainsail, the ghostly wave-crests riding up out of the void, whispered a low thrilling chorus in praise of adventure. Potent indeed must the spell have been, for, in reality, that first night sail teemed with terrors for me. It is true that it began well, for the haze dispersed, as Davies had prophesied, and Bulk Point Lighthouse guided us safely to the mouth of Kiel Fiord. It was during this stage that, crouching together aft, our pipe-bowls glowing sympathetically, we returned to the problem before us; for we had shot out on our quest with volcanic precipitation, leaving much to be discussed. I gleaned a few more facts, though I dispelled no doubts. Davies had only seen the Dollmanns on their yacht, where father and daughter were living for the time. Their villa at Norderney, and their home life there, were unknown to him, though he had landed once at the harbour himself. Further, he had heard vaguely of a stepmother, absent at Hamburg. They were to have joined her on their arrival at that city, which, be it noted, stands a long way up the Elbe, forty miles and more above Cuxhaven, the town at the mouth.

The exact arrangement made on the day before the fatal voyage was that the two yachts should meet in the evening at Cuxhaven and proceed up the river together. Then, in the ordinary course, Davies would have parted company at Brunsbüttel (fifteen miles up), which is the western terminus of the ship canal to the Baltic. Such at least had been his original intention; but, putting two and two together, I gathered that latterly, and perhaps unconfessed to himself, his resolve had weakened, and that he would have followed the *Medusa* to Hamburg, or indeed the end of the world, impelled by the same motive that, contrary to all his tastes and principles, had induced him to abandon his life in the islands and undertake the voyage at all. But on that point he was immovably reticent, and all I could conclude was that the strange cross-current connected with Dollmann's daughter had given him cruel pain and had clouded his judgement to distraction, but that he now was prepared to forget or ignore it, and steer a settled course.

The facts I elicited raised several important questions. Was it not known by this time that he and his yacht had survived? Davies was convinced that it was not. "He may have waited at Cuxhaven, or inquired at the lock at Brunsbüttel," he said. "But there was no need, for I tell you the thing was a certainty. If I had struck and *stuck* on that outer bank, as it was a hundred to one I should do, the yacht would have broken up in three minutes. Bartels would never have seen me, and couldn't have got to me if he had. No one would have seen me. And nothing whatever has happened since to show that they know I'm alive."

"They," I suggested. "Who are 'they'? Who are our adversaries?" If Dollmann were an accredited agent of the German Admiralty—But, no, it was incredible that the murder of a young Englishman should be connived at in modern days by a friendly and civilized government! Yet, if he were not such an agent, the whole theory fell to the ground.

"I believe," said Davies, "that Dollmann did it off his own bat, and beyond that I can't see. And I don't know that it matters at present. Alive or dead we're doing nothing wrong, and have nothing to be ashamed of."

"I think it matters a good deal," I objected. "Who will be interested in our resurrection, and how are we to go to work, openly or secretly? I suppose we shall keep out of the way as much as we can?"

"As for keeping out of the way," said Davies, jerkily, as he peered to windward under the foresail, "we *must* pass the ship canal; that's a public highway, where anyone can see you. After that there won't be much difficulty. Wait till you see the place!" He gave a low, contented laugh, which would have frozen my marrow yesterday. "By the way, that reminds me," he added; "we must stop at Kiel for the inside of a day and lay in a lot of stores. We want to be independent of the shore." I said nothing. Independence of the shore in a seven-tonner in October! What an end to aim at!

About nine o'clock we weathered the point, entered Kiel Fiord, and began a dead beat to windward of seven miles to the head of it where Kiel lies. Hitherto, save for the latent qualms concerning my total helplessness if anything happened to Davies, interest and excitement had upheld me well. My alarms only began when I thought them nearly over. Davies had frequently urged me to turn in and sleep, and I went so far as to go below and coil myself up on the lee sofa with my pencil and diary. Suddenly there was a flapping and rattling on deck, and I began to slide on to the floor. "What's happening?" I cried, in a panic, for there was Davies stooping in at the cabin door.

"Nothing," he said, chafing his hands for warmth; "I'm only going about. Hand me the glasses, will you? There's a steamer ahead. I say, if you really don't want to turn in, you might make some soup. Just let's look at the chart." He studied it with maddening deliberation, while I wondered how near the steamer was, and what the yacht was doing meanwhile.

"I suppose it's not really necessary for anyone to be at the helm?" I remarked.

"Oh, she's all right for a minute," he said, without looking up. "Two—one and a half—one—lights in line sou'-west by west—got a match?" He expended two, and tumbled upstairs again.

"You don't want me, do you?" I shouted after him.

"No, but come up when you've put the kettle on. It's a pretty beat up the fiord. Lovely breeze."

His legs disappeared. A sort of buoyant fatalism possessed me as I finished my notes and pored over the stove. It upheld me, too, when I went on deck and watched the "pretty beat," whose prettiness was mainly due to the crowd of fog-bound shipping—steamers, smacks, and sailing-vessels—now once more on the move in the confined fairway of the fiord, their baleful eyes of red, green, or yellow, opening and shutting, brightening and fading; while shore-lights and anchor-lights added to my bewilderment, and a throbbing of screws filled the air like the distant roar of London streets. In fact, every time we spun round for our dart across the fiord I felt like a rustic matron gathering her skirts for the transit of the Strand on a busy night. Davies, however, was the street arab who zigzags under the horses' feet unscathed; and all the time he discoursed placidly on the simplicity and safety of night-sailing if only you are careful, obeying rules, and burnt good lights. As we were nearing the hot glow in the sky that denoted Kiel we passed a huge scintillating bulk moored in mid-stream. "Warships," he murmured, ecstatically.

At one o'clock we anchored off the town.

# 10

### His Chance

"I SAY, Davies," I said, "how long do you think this trip will last? I've only got a month's leave."

We were standing at slanting desks in the Kiel post-office, Davies scratching diligently at his letter-card, and I staring feebly at mine.

"By Jove!" said Davies, with a start of dismay; "that's only three weeks more; I never thought of that. You couldn't manage to get an extension, could you?"

"I can write to the chief," I admitted; "but where's the answer to come to? We're better without an address, I suppose."

"There's Cuxhaven," reflected Davies; "but that's too near, and there's—but we don't want to be tied down to landing anywhere. I tell you what: say "Post Office, Norderney," just your name, not the yacht's. We *may* get there and be able to call for letters." The casual character of our adventure never struck me more strongly than then.

"Is that what *you're* doing?" I asked.

"Oh, I shan't be having important letters like you."

"But what are you saying?"

"Oh, just that we're having a splendid cruise, and are on our way home."

The notion tickled me, and I said the same in my home letter, adding that we were looking for a friend of Davies's who would be able to show us some sport. I wrote a line, too, to my chief (unaware of the gravity of the step I was taking) saying it was possible that I might have to apply for longer leave, as I had important business to transact in Germany, and asking him kindly to write to the same address. Then we shouldered our parcels and resumed our business.

Two full dinghy-loads of stores we ferried to the *Dulcibella*, chief among which were two immense cans of petroleum, constituting our reserves of heat and light, and a sack of flour. There were spare ropes and blocks, too; German charts of excellent quality; cigars and many weird brands of sausage and tinned meats, besides a miscellany of odd-ments, some of which only served in the end to slake my companion's craving for jettison. Clothes were my own chief care, for, freely as I had purged it at Flensburg, my wardrobe was still very unsuitable, and I had already irretrievably damaged two faultless pairs of white flannels. ("We shall be able to throw them overboard," said Davies, hopefully.) So I bought a great pair of seaboots of the country, felt-lined and wooden-soled, and both of us got a number of rough woollen garments (as worn by the local fishermen), breeches, jerseys, helmets, gloves; all of a colour chosen to harmonize with paraffin stains and anchor mud.

The same evening we were taking our last look at the Baltic, sailing past warships and groups of idle yachts battened down for their winter's sleep; while the noble shores of the fiord, with its villas embowered in copper foliage, grew dark and dim above us.

We rounded the last headland, steered for a galaxy of coloured lights, tumbled down our sails, and came to under the colossal gates of the Holtenau lock. That these would open to such an infinitesimal suppli-ant seemed inconceivable. But open they did, with ponderous majesty, and our tiny hull was lost in the womb of a lock designed to float the largest battleships. I thought of Boulter's on a hot August Sunday, and wondered if I really was the same peevish dandy who had jostled and sweltered there with the noisy cockney throng a month ago. There was a blaze of electricity overhead, but utter silence till a solitary cloaked figure hailed us and called for the captain. Davies ran up a ladder, dis-appeared with the cloaked figure, and returned crumpling a paper into his pocket. It lies before me now, and sets forth, under the stamp of the Königliches Zollamt, that, in consideration of the sum of ten marks for dues and four for tonnage, an imperial tug would tow the vessel *Dulcibella* (master A. H. Davies) through the Kaiser Wilhelm Canal from Holtenau to Brunsbüttel. Magnificent condescension! I blush when I look at this yellow document and remember the stately cour-tesy of the great lock gates; for the sleepy officials of the Königliches Zollamt little knew what an insidious little viper they were admitting into the imperial bosom at the light toll of fourteen shillings.

"Seems cheap," said Davies, joining me, "doesn't it? They've a regu-lar tariff on tonnage, same for yachts as for liners. We start at four to-morrow with a lot of other boats. I wonder if Bartels is here."

The same silence reigned, but invisible forces were at work. The inner gates opened and we prised ourselves through into a capacious basin, where lay moored side by side a flotilla of sailing vessels of vari-ous sizes. Having made fast alongside a vacant space of quay, we had our dinner, and then strolled out with cigars to look for the *Johannes*. We found her wedged among a stack of galliots, and her skipper sitting primly below before a blazing stove, reading his Bible through spectacles. He produced a bottle of schnapps and some very small and hard pears, while Davies twitted him mercilessly about his false predictions.

"The sky was not good," was all he said, beaming indulgently at his incorrigible young friend.

Before parting for the night it was arranged that next morning we should lash alongside the *Johannes* when the flotilla was marshalled for the tow through the canal.

"Karl shall steer for us both," he said, "and we will stay warm in the cabin."

The scheme was carried out, not without much confusion and loss of paint, in the small hours of a dark and drizzling morning. Boisterous little tugs sorted us into parties, and half lost under the massive bulwarks of the *Johannes* we were carried off into a black inane. If any doubt remained as to the significance of our change of cruising-grounds, dawn dispelled it. View there was none from the deck of the *Dulcibella*; it was only by standing on the mainboom that you could see over the embankments to the vast plain of Holstein, grey and monotonous under a pall of mist. The soft scenery of the Schleswig coast was a baseless dream of the past, and a cold penetrating rain added the last touch of dramatic completeness to the staging of the new act.

For two days we travelled slowly up the mighty waterway that is the strategic link between the two seas of Germany. Broad and straight, massively embanked, lit by electricity at night till it is lighter than many a great London street; traversed by great war vessels, rich merchantmen, and humble coasters alike, it is a symbol of the new and mighty force which, controlled by the genius of statesmen and engineers, is thrusting the empire irresistibly forward to the goal of maritime greatness.

"Isn't it splendid?" said Davies. "He's a fine fellow, that emperor."

Karl was the shock-headed, stout-limbed boy of about sixteen, who constituted the whole crew of the *Johannes*, and was as dirty as his master was clean. I felt a certain envious reverence for this unprepossessing youth, seeing in him a much more efficient counterpart of myself; but how he and his little master ever managed to work their ungainly vessel was a miracle I never understood. Phlegmatically impervious to rain and cold, he steered the *Johannes* down the long grey reaches in the wake of the tug, while we and Bartels held snug gatherings down below, sometimes in his cabin, sometimes in ours. The heating arrangements of the latter began to be a subject of serious concern. We finally did the only logical thing, and brought the kitchen-range into the parlour, fixing the Rippingille stove on the forward end of the cabin table, where it could warm as well as cook for us. As an ornament it was monstrous, and the taint of oil which it introduced was a disgusting drawback; but, after all, the great thing—as Davies said—is to be comfortable, and after that to be clean.

Davies held long consultations with Bartels, who was thoroughly at home in the navigation of the sands we were bound for, his own boat being a type of the very craft which ply in them. I shall not forget the moment when it first dawned on him that his young friend's curiosity was practical; for he had thought that our goal was his own beloved Hamburg, queen of cities, a place to see and die.

"It is too late," he wailed. "You do not know the Nord See as I do."

"Oh, nonsense, Bartels, it's quite safe."

"Safe! And have I not found you fast on Hohenhörn, in a storm, with your rudder broken? God was good to you then, my son."

"Yes, but it wasn't my f—" Davies checked himself. "We're going home. There's nothing in that." Bartels became sadly resigned.

"It is good that you have a friend," was his last word on the subject; but all the same he always glanced at me with a rather doubtful eye. As to Davies and myself, our friendship developed quickly on certain limited lines, the chief obstacle, as I well know now, being his reluctance to talk about the personal side of our quest.

On the other hand, I spoke about my own life and interests, with an unsparing discernment, of which I should have been incapable a month ago, and in return I gained the key to his own character. It was devotion to the sea, wedded to a fire of pent-up patriotism struggling incessantly for an outlet in strenuous physical expression; a humanity, born of acute sensitiveness to his own limitations, only adding fuel to the flame. I learnt for the first time now that in early youth he had failed for the navy, the first of several failures in his career. "And I can't settle down to anything else," he said. "I read no end about it, and yet I am a useless outsider. All I've been able to do is to potter about in small boats; but it's all been *wasted* till this chance came. I'm afraid you'll not understand how I feel about it; but at last, for once in a way, I see a chance of being useful."

"There ought to be chances for chaps like you," I said, "without the accident of a job such as this."

"Oh, as long as I get it, what matter? But I know what you mean. There must be hundreds of chaps like me—I know a good many myself—who know our coasts like a book—shoals, creeks, tides, rocks; there's nothing in it, it's only practice. They ought to make some use of us as a naval reserve. They tried to once, but it fizzled out, and nobody really cares. And what's the result? Using every man of what reserves we've got, there's about enough to man the fleet on a war footing, and no more. They've tinkered with fishermen, and merchant sailors, and yachting hands, but every one of them ought to be got hold of; and the colonies, too. Is there the ghost of a doubt that if war broke out there'd be wild appeals for volunteers, aimless cadging, hurry, confusion, waste? My own idea is that we ought to go much further, and train every able-bodied man for a couple of years as a sailor. Army? Oh, I suppose you'd have to give them the choice. Not that I know or care much about the Army, though to listen to people talk you'd think it really mattered as the Navy matters. We're a maritime nation—we've grown by the sea and live by it; if we lose command of it we starve. We're unique in that way, just as our huge empire, only linked by the sea, is unique. And yet, read Brassey, Dilke, and those 'Naval Annuals,' and see what mountains of apathy and conceit have had to be tackled. It's not the people's fault. We've been safe so long, and grown so rich, that we've forgotten what we owe it to. But there's no excuse for those blockheads of statesmen, as they call themselves, who are paid to see things as they are. They have to go to an American to learn their A B C, and it's only when kicked and punched by civilian agitators, a mere handful of men who get sneered at for their pains, that they wake up, do some work, point proudly to it, and go to sleep again, till they get another kick. By Jove! we want a man like this Kaiser, who doesn't wait to be kicked, but works like a nigger for his country, and sees ahead."

"We're improving, aren't we?"

"Oh, of course, we are! But it's a constant uphill fight; and we aren't ready. They talk of a two-power standard—" He plunged away into regions where space forbids me to follow him. This is only a sample of many similar conversations that we afterwards held, always culminating in the burning question of Germany. Far from including me and the Foreign Office among his targets for vague invective, he had a profound respect for my sagacity and experience as a member of that institution; a respect which embarrassed me not a little when I thought of my *précis* writing and cigarette-smoking, my dancing, and my dining. But I did know something of Germany, and could satisfy his tireless questioning with a certain authority. He used to listen rapt while I described her marvellous awakening in the last generation, under the strength and wisdom of her rulers; her intense patriotic ardour; her seething industrial activity, and, most potent of all, the forces that are moulding modern Europe, her dream of a colonial empire, entailing her transformation from a land-power to a sea-power. Impregnably based on vast territorial resources which we cannot molest, the dim instincts of her people, not merely directed but anticipated by the genius of her ruling house, our great trade rivals of the present, our great naval rival of the future, she grows, and strengthens, and waits, an ever more formidable factor in the future of our delicate network of empire, sensitive as gossamer to external shocks, and radiating from an island whose commerce is its life, and which depends even for its daily ration of bread on the free passage of the seas.

"And we aren't ready for her," Davies would say; "we don't look her way. We have no naval base in the North Sea, and no North Sea Fleet. Our best battleships are too deep in draught for North Sea work. And, to crown all, we were asses enough to give her Heligoland, which commands her North Sea coast. And supposing she collars Holland; isn't there some talk of that?"

That would lead me to describe the swollen ambitions of the Pan-Germanic party, and its ceaseless intrigues to promote the absorption of Austria, Switzerland, and—a direct and flagrant menace to ourselves—of Holland.

"I don't blame them," said Davies, who, for all his patriotism, had not a particle of racial spleen in his composition. "I don't blame them; their Rhine ceases to be German just when it begins to be most valuable. The mouth is Dutch, and would give them magnificent ports just opposite British shores. We can't talk about conquest and grabbing. We've collared a fine share of the world, and they've every right to be jealous. Let them hate us, and say so; it'll teach us to buck up; and that's what really matters."

In these talks there occurred a singular contact of minds. It was very well for me to spin sonorous generalities, but I had never till now dreamed of being so vulgar as to translate them into practice. I had always detested the meddlesome alarmist, who veils ignorance under noisiness, and for ever wails his chant of lugubrious pessimism. To be thrown with Davies was to receive a shock of enlightenment; for here, at least, was a specimen of the breed who exacted respect. It is true he made use of the usual jargon, interlarding his stammering sentences (sometimes, when he was excited, with the oddest effect) with the conventional catchwords of the journalist and platform speaker. But these were but accidents; for he seemed to have caught his innermost conviction from the very soul of the sea itself. An armchair critic is one thing, but a sunburnt, brine-burnt zealot smarting under a personal discontent, athirst for a means, however tortuous, of contributing his effort to the great cause, the maritime supremacy of Britain, that was quite another thing. He drew inspiration from the very wind and spray. He communed with his tiller, I believe, and marshalled his figures with its help. To hear him talk was to feel a current of clarifying air blustering into a close club-room, where men bandy ineffectual platitudes, and mumble old shibboleths, and go away and do nothing.

In our talk about policy and strategy we were Bismarcks and Rodneys, wielding nations and navies; and, indeed, I have no doubt that our fancy took extravagant flights sometimes. In plain fact we were merely two young gentlemen in a seven-ton pleasure boat, with a taste for amateur hydrography and police duty combined. Not that Davies ever doubted. Once set on the road he gripped his purpose with childlike faith and tenacity. It was his "chance."

# 11

### The Pathfinders

IN THE late afternoon of the second day our flotilla reached the Elbe at Brunsbüttel and ranged up in the inner basin, while a big liner, whimpering like a fretful baby, was tenderly nursed into the lock. During the delay Davies left me in charge, and bolted off with an oil-can and a milk-jug. An official in uniform was passing along the quay from vessel to vessel counter-signing papers. I went up to meet him with our receipt for dues, which he signed carelessly. Then he paused and muttered "Dooltzhibella," scratching his head, "that was the name. English?" he asked.

"Yes."

"Little *lust-cutter*, that is so; there was an inquiry for you."

"Whom from?"

"A friend of yours from a big barge-yacht."

"Oh, I know; she went on to Hamburg, I suppose?"

"No such luck, captain; she was outward bound."

What did the man mean? He seemed to be vastly amused by something.

"When was this—about three weeks ago?" I asked, indifferently.

"Three weeks? It was the day before yesterday. What a pity to miss him by so little!" He chuckled and winked.

"Did he leave any message?" I asked.

"It was a lady who inquired," whispered the fellow, sniggering.

"Oh, really," I said, beginning to feel highly absurd, but keenly curious. "And she inquired about the *Dulcibella*?"

"Herrgott! she was difficult to satisfy! Stood over me while I searched the books. 'A very little one,' she kept saying, and 'Are you sure all the names are here?' I saw her into her kleine Boot, and she rowed away in the rain. No, she left no message. It was dirty weather for a young fräulein to be out alone in. Ach! she was safe enough, though. To see her crossing the ebb in a chop of tide was a treat."

"And the yacht went on down the river? Where was she bound to?"

"How do I know? Bremen, Wilhelmshaven, Emden—somewhere in the North Sea; too far for you."

"I don't know about that," said I, bravely.

"Ach! you will not follow in *that*? Are not you bound to Hamburg?"

"We can change our plans. It seems a pity to have missed them."

"Think twice, captain, there are plenty of pretty girls in Hamburg. But you English will do anything. Well, viel Glück!"

He moved on, chuckling, to the next boat. Davies soon returned with his cans and an armful of dark, rye loaves, just in time, for, the liner being through, the flotilla was already beginning to jostle into the lock and Bartels was growing impatient.

"They'll last ten days," he said, as we followed the throng, still clinging like a barnacle to the side of the *Johannes*. We spent the few minutes while the lock was emptied in a farewell talk to Bartels. Karl had hitched their main halyards on to the windlass and was grinding at it in an *acharnement* of industry, his shock head jerking and his grubby face perspiring. Then the lock gates opened; and so, in a Babel of shouting, whining of blocks, and creaking of spars, our whole company was split out into the dingy bosom of the Elbe. The *Johannes* gathered way under wind and tide and headed for midstream. A last shake of the hand, and Bartels reluctantly slipped the head-rope and we drifted apart. "Gute Reise! Gute Reise!" It was no time for regretful gazing, for the flood-tide was sweeping us up and out, and it was not until we had set the foresail, edged into a shallow bight, and let go our anchor, that we had leisure to think of him again; but by that time his and the other craft were shades in the murky east.

We swung close to a *glacis* of smooth blue mud which sloped up to a weed-grown dyke; behind lay the same flat country, colourless, humid; and opposite us, two miles away, scarcely visible in the deepening twilight, ran the outline of a similar shore. Between rolled the turgid Elbe. "The Styx flowing through Tartarus," I thought to myself, recalling some of our Baltic anchorages.

I told my news to Davies as soon as the anchor was down, instinctively leaving the sex of the inquirer to the last, as my informant had done.

"The *Medusa* called yesterday?" he interrupted. "And outward bound? That's a rum thing. Why didn't he inquire when he was going *up*?"

"It was a lady," and I drily retailed the official's story, very busy with a deck-broom the while. "We're all square now, aren't we?" I ended. "I'll go below and light the stove."

Davies had been engaged in fixing up the riding-light. When I last saw him he was still so engaged, but motionless, the lantern under his left arm, and his right hand grasping the forestay and the half-knotted lanyard; his eyes staring fixedly down the river, a strange look in his face, half exultant, half perplexed. When he joined me and spoke he seemed to be concluding a difficult argument.

"Anyway, it proves," he said, "that the Medusa has gone back to Norderney. That's the main thing."

"Probably," I agreed, "but let's sum up all we know. First, it's certain that nobody we've met as yet has any suspicion of us—"

"I told you he did it off his own bat," threw in Davies.

"Or, secondly, of him. If he's what you think it's not known here."

"I can't help that."

"Thirdly, he inquires for you on his way back from Hamburg, three weeks after the event. It doesn't look as if he thought he had disposed of you—it doesn't look as if he had meant to dispose of you. He sends his daughter, too—a curious proceeding under the circumstances. Perhaps it's all a mistake."

"It's not a mistake," said Davies, half to himself. "But did he send her? He'd have sent one of his men. He can't be on board at all."

This was a new light.

"What do you mean?" I asked.

"He must have left the yacht when he got to Hamburg; some other devil's work, I suppose. She's being sailed back now, and passing here—"

"Oh, I see! It's a private supplementary inquiry."

"That's a long name to call it."

"Would the girl sail back alone with the crew?"

"She's used to the sea—and perhaps she isn't alone. There was that stepmother—But it doesn't make a ha'porth of difference to our plans; we'll start on the ebb to-morrow morning."

We were busier than usual that night, reckoning stores, tidying lockers, and securing movables. "We must economize," said Davies, for all the world as though we were castaways on a raft. "It's a wretched thing to have to land somewhere to buy oil," was a favourite observation of his.

Before getting to sleep I was made to recognize a new factor in the conditions of navigation, now that the tideless Baltic was left behind us. A strong current was sluicing past our sides, and at the eleventh hour I was turned out, clad in pyjamas and oilskins (a horrible combination), to assist in running out a kedge or spare anchor.

"What's kedging-off?" I asked, when we were tucked up again.

"Oh, it's when you run aground; you have to—but you'll soon learn all about it." I steeled my heart for the morrow.

So behold us, then, at eight o'clock on 5th October, standing down the river towards the field of our first labours. It is fifteen miles to the mouth; drab, dreary miles like the dullest reaches of the lower Thames; but scenery was of no concern to us, and a south-westerly breeze blowing out of a grey sky kept us constantly on the verge of reefing. The tide as it gathered strength swept us down with a force attested by the speed with which buoys came in sight, nodded above us and passed, each boiling in its eddy of dirty foam. I scarcely noticed at first—so calm was the water, and so regular were the buoys, like milestones along a road—that the northern line of coast was rapidly receding and that the "river" was coming to be but a belt of deep water skirting a vast estuary, three—seven—ten miles broad, till it merged in open sea.

"Why, we're at sea!" I suddenly exclaimed, "after an hour's sailing!"

"Just discovered that?" said Davies, laughing.

"You said it was fifteen miles," I complained.

"So it is, till we reach this coast at Cuxhaven; but I suppose you may say we're at sea; of course that's all sand over there to starboard. Look! some of it's showing already."

He pointed into the north. Looking more attentively I noticed that outside the line of buoys patches of the surface heaved and worked; in one or two places streaks and circles of white were forming; in the midst of one such circle a sleek mauve hump had risen, like the back of a sleeping whale. I saw that an old spell was enthralling Davies as his eye travelled away to the blank horizon. He scanned it all with a critical eagerness, too, as one who looks for a new meaning in an old friend's face. Something of his zest was communicated to me, and stilled the shuddering thrill that had seized me. The protecting land was still a comforting neighbour; but our severance with it came quickly. The tide whirled us down, and our straining canvas aiding it, we were soon off Cuxhaven, which crouched so low behind its mighty dyke, that of some of its houses only the chimneys were visible. Then, a mile or so on, the shore sharpened to a point like a claw, where the innocent dyke became a long, low fort, with some great guns peeping over; then of a sudden it ceased, retreating into the far south in a dim perspective of groins and dunes.

We spun out into the open and leant heavily over to the now unobstructed wind. The yacht rose and sank to a little swell, but my first impression was one of wonder at the calmness of the sea, for the wind blew fresh and free from horizon to horizon.

"Why, it's all sand *there* now, and we're under the lee of it," said Davies, with an enthusiastic sweep of his hand over the sea on our left, or port, hand. "That's our hunting ground."

"What are we going to do?" I inquired.

"Pick up Sticker's Gat," was the reply. "It ought to be near Buoy K."

A red buoy with a huge K on it soon came into view. Davies peered over to port.

"Just pull up the centre-board, will you?" he remarked abstractedly, adding, "and hand me up the glasses as you're down there."

"Never mind the glasses. I've got it now; come to the mainsheet," was the next remark.

He put down the helm and headed the yacht straight for the troubled and discoloured expanse which covered the submerged sands. A "sleeping whale," with a light surf splashing on it, was right in our path.

"Stand by the lead, will you?" said Davies, politely. "I'll manage the sheets, it's a dead beat in. Ready about!"

The wind was in our teeth now, and for a crowded half-hour we wormed ourselves forward by ever-shortening tacks into the sinuous recesses of a channel which threaded the shallows westward. I knelt in a tangle of line, and, under the hazy impression that something very critical was going on, plied the lead furiously, bumping and splashing myself, and shouting out the depths, which lessened steadily, with a great sense of the importance of my function. Davies never seemed to listen, but tacked on imperturbably, juggling with the tiller, the sheets, and the chart, in a way that made one giddy to look at. For all our zeal we seemed to be making very slow progress.

"It's no use, tide's too strong; we must chance it," he said at last.

"Chance what?" I wondered to myself. Our tacks suddenly began to grow longer, and the depths, which I registered, shallower. All went well for some time though, and we made better progress. Then came a longer reach than usual.

"Two and a half—two—one and a half—one—only five feet," I gasped, reproachfully. The water was growing thick and frothy.

"It doesn't matter if we do," said Davies, thinking aloud. "There's an eddy here, and it's a pity to waste it—ready about! Back the jib!"

But it was too late. The yacht answered but faintly to the helm, stopped, and heeled heavily over, wallowing and grinding. Davies had the mainsail down in a twinkling; it half smothered me as I crouched on the lee-side among my tangled skeins of line, scared and helpless. I crawled out from the folds, and saw him standing by the mast in a reverie.

"It's not much use," he said, "on a falling tide, but we'll try kedging-off. Pay that warp out while I run out the kedge."

Like lightning he had cast off the dinghy's painter, tumbled the kedge-anchor and himself into the dinghy, pulled out fifty yards into the deeper water, and heaved out the anchor.

"Now haul," he shouted.

I hauled, beginning to see what kedging-off meant.

"Steady on! Don't sweat yourself," said Davies, jumping aboard again.

"It's coming," I spluttered, triumphantly.

"The warp is, the yacht isn't; you're dragging the anchor home. Never mind, she'll lie well here. Let's have lunch."

The yacht was motionless, and the water round her visibly lower. Petulant waves slapped against her sides, but, scattered as my senses were, I realized that there was no vestige of danger. Round us the whole face of the waters was changing from moment to moment, whitening in some places, yellowing in others, where breadths of sand began to be exposed. Close on our right the channel we had left began to look like a turbid little river; and I understood why our progress had been so slow when I saw its current racing back to meet the Elbe. Davies was already below, laying out a more than usually elaborate lunch, in high content of mind.

"Lies quiet, doesn't she?" he remarked. "If you *do* want a sit-down lunch, there's nothing like running aground for it. And, anyhow, we're as handy for work here as anywhere else. You'll see."

Like most landsmen I had a wholesome prejudice against "running aground," so that my mentor's turn for breezy paradox was at first rather exasperating. After lunch the large-scale chart of the estuaries was brought down, and we pored over it together, mapping out work for the next few days. There is no need to tire the general reader with its intricacies, nor is there space to reproduce it for the benefit of the instructed reader. For both classes the general map should be sufficient, taken with the large-scale fragment (Chart A), which gives a fair example of the region in detail. It will be seen that the three broad fairways of the Jade, Weser, and Elbe split up the sands into two main groups. The westernmost of these is symmetrical in outline, an acute-angled triangle, very like a sharp steel-shod pike, if you imagine the peninsula from which it springs to be the wooden haft. The other is a huge congeries of banks, its base resting on the Hanover coast, two of its sides tolerably clean and even, and the third, that facing the northwest, ribboned and lacerated by the fury of the sea, which has eaten out deep cavities and struck hungry tentacles far into the interior. The whole resembles an inverted E, or, better still, a rude fork, on whose three deadly prongs, the Scharhorn Reef, the Knecht Sand, and the Tegeler Flat, as on the no less deadly point of the pike, many a good ship splinters herself in northerly gales. Following this simile, the Hohenhörn bank, where Davies was wrecked, is one of those that lie between the upper and middle prongs.

Our business was to explore the Pike and the Fork and the channels which ramify through them. I use the general word "channel," but in fact they differ widely in character, and are called in German by various names: Balje, Gat, Loch, Diep, Rinne. For my purpose I need only divide them into two sorts—those which have water in them at all states of the tide, and those which have not, which dry off, that is, either wholly or partly at low-tide.

Davies explained that the latter would take most learning, and were to be our chief concern, because they were the "through-routes"—the connecting links between the estuaries. You can always detect them on the chart by rows of little Y-shaped strokes denoting "booms," that is to say, poles or saplings fixed in the sand to mark the passage. The strokes, of course, are only conventional signs, and do not correspond in the least to individual "booms," which are far too numerous and complex to be indicated accurately on a chart, even of the largest scale. The same applies to the course of the channels themselves, whose minor meanderings cannot be reproduced.

It was on the edge of one of these tidal swatchways that the yacht was now lying. It is called Sticker's Gat, and you cannot miss it (Chart A) if you carry your eye westward along our course from Cuxhaven. It was, so Davies told me, the last and most intricate stage of the "short cut" which the *Medusa* had taken on that memorable day—a stage he himself had never reached. Discussion ended, we went on deck, Davies arming himself with a notebook, binoculars, and the prismatic compass, whose use—to map the angles of the channels—was at last apparent. This is what I saw when we emerged.

# 12

### My Initiation

THE yacht lay with a very slight heel (thanks to a pair of small bilge-keels on her bottom) in a sort of trough she had dug for herself, so that she was still ringed with a few inches of water, as it were with a moat.

For miles in every direction lay a desert of sand. To the north it touched the horizon, and was only broken by the blue dot of Neuerk Island and its lighthouse. To the east it seemed also to stretch to infinity, but the smoke of a steamer showed where it was pierced by the stream of the Elbe. To the south it ran up to the pencil-line of the Hanover shore. Only to the west was its outline broken by any vestiges of the sea it had risen from. There it was astir with crawling white filaments, knotted confusedly at one spot in the northwest, whence came a sibilant murmur like the hissing of many snakes. Desert as I call it, it was not entirely featureless. Its colour varied from light fawn, where the highest levels had dried in the wind, to brown or deep violet, where it was still wet, and slate-grey where patches of mud soiled its clean bosom. Here and there were pools of water, smitten into ripples by the impotent wind; here and there it was speckled by shells and seaweed. And close to us, beginning to bend away towards that hissing knot in the northwest, wound our poor little channel, mercilessly exposed as a stagnant, muddy ditch with scarcely a foot of water, not deep enough to hide our small kedge-anchor, which perked up one fluke in impudent mockery. The dull, hard sky, the wind moaning in the rigging as though crying in despair for a prey that had escaped it, made the scene inexpressibly forlorn.

Davies scanned it with gusto for a moment, climbed to a point of vantage on the boom, and swept his glasses to and fro along the course of the channel.

"Fairly well boomed," he said, meditatively, "but one or two are very much out. By Jove! that's a tricky bend there." He took a bearing with the compass, made a note or two, and sprang with a vigorous leap down on to the sand.

This, I may say, was the only way of "going ashore" that he really liked. We raced off as fast as our clumsy sea-boots would let us, and followed up the course of our channel to the west, reconnoitring the road we should have to follow when the tide rose.

"The only way to learn a place like this," he shouted, "is to see it at low water. The banks are dry then, and the channels are plain. Look at that boom"—he stopped and pointed contemptuously—"it's all out of place. I suppose the channel's shifted there. It's just at an important bend too. If you took it as a guide when the water was up you'd run aground."

"Which would be very useful," I observed.

"Oh, hang it!" he laughed, "we're exploring. I want to be able to run through this channel without a mistake. We will, next time." He stopped, and plied compass and notebook. Then we raced on till the next halt was called.

"Look," he said, "the channel's getting deeper, it was nearly dry a moment ago; see the current in it now? That's the flood tide coming up—from the *west*, mind you; that is, from the Weser side. That shows we're past the watershed."

"Watershed?" I repeated, blankly.

"Yes, that's what I call it. You see, a big sand such as this is like a range of hills dividing two plains, it's never dead flat though it looks it;

there's always one point, one ridge, rather, where it's highest. Now a channel cutting right through the sand is, of course, always at its shallowest when it's crossing this ridge; at low water it's generally dry there, and it gradually deepens as it gets nearer to the sea on either side. Now at high tide, when the whole sand is covered, the water can travel where it likes; but directly the ebb sets in the water falls away on either side the ridge and the channel becomes two rivers flowing in opposite directions *from* the centre, or watershed, as I call it. So, also, when the ebb has run out and the flood begins, the channel is fed by two currents flowing *to* the centre and meeting in the middle. Here the Elbe and the Weser are our two feeders. Now this current here is going eastwards; we know by the time of day that the tide's rising, *therefore* the watershed is between us and the yacht."

"Why is it so important to know that?"

"Because these currents are strong, and you want to know when you'll lose a fair one and strike a foul one. Besides, the ridge is the critical point when you're crossing on a falling tide, and you want to know when you're past it."

We pushed on till our path was barred by a big lagoon. It looked far more imposing than the channel; but Davies, after a rapid scrutiny, treated it to a grunt of contempt.

"It's a *cul de sac*," he said. "See that hump of sand it's making for, beyond?"

"It's boomed," I remonstrated, pointing to a decrepit stem drooping over the bank, and shaking a palsied finger at the imposture.

"Yes, that's just where one goes wrong, it's an old cut that's silted up. That boom's a fraud; there's no time to go farther, the flood's making fast. I'll just take bearings of what we can see."

The false lagoon was the first of several that began to be visible in the west, swelling and joining hands over the ribs of sand that divided them. All the time the distant hissing grew nearer and louder, and a deep, thunderous note began to sound beneath it. We turned our backs to the wind and hastened back towards the *Dulcibella*, the stream in our channel hurrying and rising alongside of us.

"There's just time to do the other side," said Davies, when we reached her, and I was congratulating myself on having regained our base without finding our communications cut. And away we scurried in the direction we had come that morning, splashing through pools and jumping the infant runnels that were stealing out through rifts from the mother-channel as the tide rose. Our observations completed, back we travelled, making a wide circuit over higher ground to avoid the encroaching flood, and wading shin-deep in the final approach to the yacht.

As I scrambled thankfully aboard, I seemed to hear a far-off voice saying, in languid depreciation of yachting, that it did not give one enough exercise. It was mine, centuries ago, in another life. From east and west two sheets of water had overspread the desert, each pushing out tongues of surf that met and fused.

I waited on deck and watched the death-throes of the suffocating sands under the relentless onset of the sea. The last strong-holds were battered, stormed, and overwhelmed; the tumult of sounds sank and steadied, and the sea swept victoriously over the whole expanse. The *Dulcibella*, hitherto contemptuously inert, began to wake and tremble under the buffetings she received. Then, with an effort, she jerked herself on to an even keel and bumped and strained fretfully, impatient to vanquish this insolent invader and make him a slave for her own ends. Soon her warp tightened and her nose swung slowly round; only her stern bumped now, and that with decreasing force. Suddenly she was free and drifting broadside to the wind till the anchor checked her and she brought up to leeward of it, rocking easily and triumphantly. Good-humoured little person! At heart she was friends alike with sand and sea. It was only when the old love and the new love were in mortal combat for her favours, and she was mauled in the *fracas*, that her temper rose in revolt.

We swallowed a hasty cup of tea, ran up the sails, and started off west again. Once across the "watershed" we met a strong current, but the trend of the passage was now more to the north-west, so that we could hold our course without tacking, and consequently could stem the tide. "Give her just a foot of the centre-plate," said Davies. "We know the way here, and she'll make less leeway; but we shall generally have to do without it—always on a falling tide. If you run aground with the plate down you deserve to be drowned." I now saw how valuable our walk had been. The booms were on our right; but they were broken reeds, giving no hint as to the breadth of the channel. A few had lost their tops, and were being engulfed altogether by the rising water. When we came to the point where they ceased, and the false lagoon had lain, I should have felt utterly lost. We had crossed the high and relatively level sands which form the base of the Fork, and were entering the labyrinth of detached banks which obstruct the funnel-shaped cavity between the upper and middle prongs. This I knew from the chart. My unaided eye saw nothing but the open sea, growing dark green as the depths increased; a dour, threatening sea, showing its white fangs. The waves grew longer and steeper, for the channels, though still tortuous, now begin to be broad and deep.

Davies had his bearings, and struck on his course confidently. "Now for the lead," he said; "the compass'll be little use soon. We must feel the edge of the sands till we pick up more booms."

"Where are we going to anchor for the night?" I asked.

"Under the Hohenhörn," said Davies, "for auld lang syne!"

Partly by sight and mostly by touch we crept round the outermost alley of the hidden maze till a new clump of booms appeared, meaningless to me, but analysed by him into two groups. One we followed for some distance, and then struck finally away and began another beat to windward.

Dusk was falling. The Hanover coast-line, never very distinct, had utterly vanished; an ominous heave of swell was under-running the short sea. I ceased to attend to Davies imparting instruction on his beloved hobby, and sought to stifle in hard manual labour the dread that had been latent in me all day at the prospect of our first anchorage at sea.

"Sound, like blazes now!" he said at last. I came to a fathom and a half. "That's the bank," he said; "we'll give it a bit of a berth and then let go."

"Let go now!" was the order after a minute, and the chain ran out with a long-drawn moan. The *Dulcibella* snubbed up to it and jauntily faced the North Sea and the growing night.

"There we are!" said Davies, as we finished stowing the mainsail, "safe and snug in four fathoms in a magnificent sand-harbour, with no one to bother us and the whole of it to ourselves. No dues, no stinks, no traffic, no worries of any sort. It's better than a Baltic cove even, less beastly civilization about. We're seven miles from the nearest coast, and five even from Neuerk—look, they're lighting up." There was a tiny spark in the east.

"I suppose it's all right," I said, "but I'd rather see a solid breakwater somewhere; it's a dirty-looking night, and I don't like this swell."

"The swell's nothing," said Davies; "it's only a stray drain from outside. As for breakwaters, you've got them all round you, only they're hidden. Ahead and to starboard is the West Hohenhörn, curling round to the sou'west for all the world like a stone pier. You can hear the surf battering on its outside over to the north. That's where I was nearly wrecked that day, and the little channel I stumbled into must be quite near us somewhere. Half a mile away—to port there—is the East Hohenhörn, where I brought up, after dashing across this lake we're in. Another mile astern is the main body of the sands, the top prong of your fork. So you see we're shut in—practically. Surely you remember the chart? Why, it's—"

"Oh, confound the chart!" I broke out, finding this flow of plausible comfort too dismally suggestive for my nerves. "*Look* at it, man! Supposing anything happens—supposing it blows a gale! But it's no good shivering here and staring at the view. I'm going below."

There was a *mauvais quart d'heure* below, during which, I am ashamed to say, I forgot the quest.

"Which soup do you feel inclined for?" said Davies, timidly, after a black silence of some minutes.

That simple remark, more eloquent of security than a thousand technical arguments, saved the situation.

"I say, Davies," I said, "I'm a white-livered cur at the best, and you mustn't spare me. But you're not like any yachtsman I ever met before, or any sailor of any sort. You're so casual and quiet in the extraordinary things you do. I believe I should like you better if you let fly a volley of deep-sea oaths sometimes, or threatened to put me in irons."

Davies opened wide eyes, and said it was all his fault for forgetting that I was not as used to such anchorages as he was. "And, by the way," he added, "as to its blowing a gale, I shouldn't wonder if it did; the glass is falling hard; but it can't hurt us. You see, even at high water the drift of the sea—"

"Oh, for Heaven's sake, don't begin again. You'll prove soon that we're safer here than in an hotel. Let's have dinner, and a thundering good one!"

Dinner ran a smooth course, but just as coffee was being brewed the hull, from pitching regularly, began to roll.

"I knew she would," said Davies. "I was going to warn you, only—the ebb has set in *against* the wind. It's quite safe—"

"I thought you said it would get calmer when the tide fell?"

"So it will, but it may *seem* rougher. Tides are queer things," he added, as though in defence of some not very respectable acquaintances.

He busied himself with his logbook, swaying easily to the motion of the boat; and I for my part tried to write up my diary, but I could not fix my attention. Every loose article in the boat became audibly restless. Cans clinked, cupboards rattled, lockers uttered hollow groans. Small things sidled out of dark hiding-places, and danced grotesque drunken figures on the floor, like goblins in a haunted glade. The mast whined dolorously at every heel, and the centre-board hiccoughed and choked. Overhead another horde of demons seemed to have been let loose. The deck and mast were conductors which magnified every sound and made the tap-tap of every rope's end resemble the blows of a hammer, and the slapping of the halyards against the mast the rattle of a Maxim gun. The whole tumult beat time to a rhythmical chorus which became maddening.

"We might turn in now," said Davies; "it's half-past ten."

"What, sleep through this?" I exclaimed. "I can't stand this, I must *do* something. Can't we go for another walk?"

I spoke in bitter, half-delirious jest.

"Of course we can," said Davies, "if you don't mind a bit of a tumble in the dinghy."

I reconsidered my rash suggestion, but it was too late now to turn back, and some desperate expedient was necessary. I found myself on deck, gripping a backstay and looking giddily down and then up at the dinghy, as it bobbed like a cork in the trough of the sea alongside, while Davies settled the sculls and rowlocks.

"Jump!" he shouted, and before I could gather my wits and clutch the sides we were adrift in the night, reeling from hollow to hollow of the steep curling waves. Davies nursed our walnut-shell tenderly over their crests, edging her slantwise across their course. He used very little exertion, relying on the tide to carry us to our goal. Suddenly the motion ceased. A dark slope loomed up out of the night, and the dinghy rested softly in a shallow eddy.

"The West Hohenhörn," said Davies. We jumped out and sank into soft mud, hauled up the dinghy a foot or two, then mounted the bank and were on hard, wet sand. The wind leapt on us, and choked our voices.

"Let's find my channel," bawled Davies. "This way. Keep Neuerk light right astern of you."

We set off with a long, stooping stride in the teeth of the wind, and straight towards the roar of the breakers on the farther side of the sand. A line of Matthew Arnold's, "The naked shingles of the world," was running in my head. "Seven miles from land," I thought, "scuttling like sea-birds on a transient islet of sand, encircled by rushing tides and hammered by ocean, at midnight in a rising gale—cut off even from our one dubious refuge." It was the time, if ever, to conquer weakness. A mad gaiety surged through me as I drank the wind and pressed forward. It seemed but a minute or two and Davies clutched me.

"Look out!" he shouted. "It's my channel."

The ground sloped down, and a rushing river glimmered before us. We struck off at a tangent and followed its course to the north, stumbling in muddy rifts, slipping on seaweed, beginning to be blinded by a fine salt spray, and deafened by the thunder of the ocean surf. The river broadened, whitened, roughened, gathered itself for the shock, was shattered, and dissolved in milky gloom. We wheeled away to the right, and splashed into yeasty froth. I turned my back to the wind, scooped the brine out of my eyes, faced back and saw that our path was barred by a welter of surf. Davies's voice was in my ear and his arm was pointing seaward.

"This—is—about where—I—bumped first—worse then—nor'-west wind—this—is—nothing. Let's—go—right—round."

We galloped away with the wind behind us, skirting the line of surf. I lost all account of time and direction. Another sea barred our road, became another river as we slanted along its shore. Again we were in the teeth of that intoxicating wind. Then a point of light was swaying and flickering away to the left, and now we were checking and circling. I stumbled against something sharp—the dinghy's gunwale. So we had completed the circuit of our fugitive domain, that dream-island—nightmare island as I always remember it.

"You must scull, too," said Davies. "It's blowing hard now. Keep her nose *up* a little—all you know!"

We lurched along, my scull sometimes buried to the thwart, sometimes striking at the bubbles of a wave top. Davies, in the bows, said "Pull!" or "Steady!" at intervals. I heard the scud smacking against his oilskin back. Then a wan, yellow light glanced over the waves. "Easy! Let her come!" and the bowsprit of the *Dulcibella*, swollen to spectral proportions, was stabbing the darkness above me. "Back a bit! Two good strokes. Ship your scull! Now jump!" I clawed at the tossing hull and landed in a heap. Davies followed with the painter, and the dinghy swept astern.

"She's riding beautifully now," said he, when he had secured the painter. "There'll be no rolling on the flood, and it's nearly low water."

I don't think I should have cared, however much she had rolled. I was finally cured of funk.

It was well that I was, for to be pitched out of your bunk on to wet oilcloth is a disheartening beginning to a day. This happened about eight o'clock. The yacht was pitching violently, and I crawled on all fours into the cabin, where Davies was setting out breakfast on the floor.

"I let you sleep on," he said; "we can't do anything till the water falls. We should never get the anchor up in this sea. Come and have a look round. It's clearing now," he went on, when we were crouching low on deck, gripping cleats for safety. "Wind's veered to nor'-west. It's been blowing a full gale, and the sea is at its worst now—near high water. You'll never see worse than this."

I was prepared for what I saw—the stormy sea for leagues around, and a chaos of breakers where our dream-island had stood—and took it quietly, even with a sort of elation. The *Dulcibella* faced the storm as doggedly as ever, plunging her bowsprit into the sea and flinging green water over her bows. A wave of confidence and affection for her welled through me. I had been used to resent the weight and bulk of her unwieldy anchor and cable, but I saw their use now; varnish, paint, spotless decks, and snowy sails were foppish absurdities of a hateful past.

"What can we do to-day?" I asked.

"We must keep well inside the banks and be precious careful wherever there's a swell. It's rampant in here, you see, in spite of the barrier of sand. But there's plenty we can do farther back."

We breakfasted in horrible discomfort; then smoked and talked till the roar of the breakers dwindled. At the first sign of bare sand we got under way, under mizzen and head-sails only, and I learned how to sail a reluctant anchor out of the ground. Pivoting round, we scudded east before the wind, over the ground we had traversed the evening before, while an archipelago of new banks slowly shouldered up above the fast weakening waves. We trod delicately among and around them, sounding and observing; heaving to where space permitted, and sometimes using the dinghy. I began to see where the risks lay in this sort of navigation. Wherever the ocean swell penetrated, or the wind blew straight down a long deep channel, we had to be very cautious and leave good margins. "That's the sort of place you mustn't ground on," Davies used to say.

In the end we traversed the Steil Sand again, but by a different swatchway, and anchored, after an arduous day, in a notch on its eastern limit, just clear of the swell that rolled in from the turbulent estuary of the Elbe. The night was fair, and when the tide receded we lay perfectly still, the fresh wind only sending a lip-lip of ripples against our sides.

## 13

### The Meaning of Our Work

NOTHING happened during the next ten days to disturb us at our work. During every hour of daylight and many of darkness, sailing or anchored, aground or afloat, in rain and shine, wind and calm, we studied the bed of the estuaries, and practised ourselves in threading the network of channels; holding no communication with the land and rarely approaching it. It was a life of toil, exposure, and peril; a struggle against odds, too; for wild autumnal weather was the rule, with the wind backing and veering between the south-west and north-west, and only for two placid days blowing gently from the east, the safe quarter for this region. Its force and direction determined each fresh choice of ground. If it was high and northerly we explored the inner fastnesses; in moderate intervals the exterior fringe, darting when surprised into whatever lair was most convenient.

Sometimes we were tramping vast solitudes of sand, sometimes scudding across ephemeral tracts of shallow sea. Again, we were creeping gingerly round the deeper arteries that surround the Great Knecht, examining their convolutions as it were the veins of a living tissue, and the circulation of the tide throbbing through them like blood. Again, we would be staggering through the tide-rips and overfalls that infest the open fairway of the Weser on our passage between the Fork and the Pike. On one of our fine days I saw the scene of Davies's original adventure by daylight with the banks dry and the channels manifest. The reader has seen it on the chart, and can, up to a point, form his opinion; I can only add that I realized by ocular proof that no more fatal trap could have been devised for an innocent stranger; for approaching it from the north-west under the easiest conditions it was hard enough to verify our true course. In a period so full of new excitements it is not easy for me to say when we were hardest put to it, especially as it was a rule with Davies never to admit that we were in any danger at all. But I think that our ugliest experience was on the 10th, when, owing to some minute miscalculation, we stranded in a dangerous spot. Mere stranding, of course, was all in the day's work; the constantly recurring question being when and where to court or risk it. This time we were so situated that when the rising tide came again we were on a lee shore, broadside on to a gale of wind which was sending a nasty sea—with a three-mile drift to give it force—down Robin's Balje, which is one of the deeper arteries I spoke of above, and now lay dead to windward of us. The climax came about ten o'clock at night. "We can do nothing till she floats," said Davies; and I can see him now quietly smoking and splicing a chafed warp while he explained that her double skin of teak fitted her to stand anything in reason. She certainly had a terrific test that night, for the bottom was hard, unyielding sand, on which she rose and fell with convulsive vehemence. The last half-hour was for me one of almost intolerable tension. I spent it on deck unable to bear the suspense below. Sheets of driven sea flew bodily over the hull, and a score of times I thought she must succumb as she shivered to the blows of her keel on the sand. But those stout skins knit by honest labour stood the trial. One final thud and she wrenched herself bodily free, found her anchor, and rode clear.

On the whole I think we made few mistakes. Davies had a supreme aptitude for the work. Every hour, sometimes every minute, brought its problem, and his resource never failed. The stiffer it was the cooler he became. He had, too, that intuition which is independent of acquired skill, and is at the root of all genius; which, to take cases analogous to his own, is the last quality of the perfect guide or scout. I believe he could *smell* sand where he could not see or touch it.

As for me, the sea has never been my element, and never will be; nevertheless, I hardened to the life, grew salt, tough, and tolerably alert. As a soldier learns more in a week of war than in years of parades and pipeclay, so, cut off from all distractions, moving from bivouac to precarious bivouac, and depending, to some extent, for my life on my muscles and wits, I rapidly learnt my work and gained a certain dexterity. I knew my ropes in the dark, could beat economically to windward through squalls, take bearings, and estimate the interaction of wind and tide.

We were generally in solitude, but occasionally we met galliots like the *Johannes* tacking through the sands, and once or twice we found a fleet of such boats anchored in a gut, waiting for water. Their draught, loaded, was from six to seven feet, our own only four, without our centre-plate, but we took their mean draught as the standard of all our observations. That is, we set ourselves to ascertain when and how a vessel drawing six and a half feet could navigate the sands.

A word more as to our motive. It was Davies's conviction, as I have said, that the whole region would in war be an ideal hunting-ground for small free-lance marauders, and I began to know he was right; for look at the three sea-roads through the sands of Hamburg, Bremen, Wilhelmshaven, and the heart of commercial Germany. They are like highways piercing a mountainous district by defiles, where a handful of desperate men can arrest an army.

Follow the parallel of a war on land. People your mountains with a daring and resourceful race, who possess an intimate knowledge of every track and bridle-path, who operate in small bands, travel light, and move rapidly. See what an immense advantage such guerillas possess over an enemy which clings to beaten tracks, moves in large bodies, slowly, and does not "know the country." See how they can not only inflict disasters on a foe who vastly overmatches them in strength, but can prolong a semi-passive resistance long after all decisive battles have been fought. See, too, how the strong invader can only conquer his elusive antagonists by learning their methods, studying the country, and matching them in mobility and cunning. The parallel must not be pressed too far; but that this sort of warfare will have its counterpart on the sea is a truth which cannot be questioned.

Davies in his enthusiasm set no limits to its importance. The small boat in shallow waters played a mighty *rôle* in his vision of a naval war, a part that would grow in importance as the war developed and reach its height in the final stages.

"The heavy battle fleets are all very well," he used to say, "but if the sides are well matched there might be nothing left of them after a few months of war. They might destroy one another mutually, leaving as nominal conqueror an admiral with scarcely a battleship to bless himself with. It's then that the true struggle will set in; and it's then that anything that will float will be pressed into the service, and anybody who can steer a boat, knows his waters, and doesn't care the toss of a coin for his life, will have magnificent opportunities. It cuts both ways. What small boats can do in these waters is plain enough; but take our own case. Say we're beaten on the high seas by a coalition. There's then a risk of starvation or invasion. It's all rot what they talk about instant surrender. We can live on half rations, recuperate, and build; but we must have time. Meanwhile our coast and ports are in danger, for the millions we sink in forts and mines won't carry us far. They're fixed—pure passive defence. What you want is *boats*—mosquitoes with stings—swarms of them—patrol-boats, scout-boats, torpedo-boats; intelligent irregulars manned by local men, with a pretty free hand to play their own game. And what a splendid game to play! There are places very like this over there—nothing half so good, but similar—the Mersey estuary, the Dee, the Severn, the Wash, and, best of all, the Thames, with all the Kent, Essex, and Suffolk banks round it. But as for defending our coasts in the way I mean—we've nothing ready—nothing whatsoever! We don't even build or use small torpedo-boats. These fast "destroyers" are no good for *this* work—too long and unmanageable, and most of them too deep. What you want is something strong and simple, of light draught, and with only a spar-torpedo, if it came to that. Tugs, launches, small yachts—anything would do at a pinch, for success would depend on intelligence, not on brute force or complicated mechanism. They'd get wiped out often, but what matter? There'd be no lack of the right sort of men for them if the thing was *organized*. But where are the men?

"Or, suppose we have the best of it on the high seas, and have to attack or blockade a coast like this, which is sand from end to end. You can't improvise people who are at home in such waters. The navy chaps don't learn it, though, by Jove! they're the most magnificent service in the world—in pluck, and nerve, and everything else. They'll *try* anything, and often do the impossible. But their boats are deep, and they get little practice in this sort of thing."

Davies never pushed home his argument here; but I know that it was the passionate wish of his heart, somehow and somewhere, to get a chance of turning his knowledge of this coast to practical account in the war that he felt was bound to come, to play that "splendid game" in this, the most fascinating field for it.

I can do no more than sketch his views. Hearing them as I did, with the very splash of the surf and the bubble of the tides in my ears, they made a profound impression on me, and gave me the very zeal for our work he, by temperament, possessed.

But as the days passed and nothing occurred to disturb us, I felt more and more strongly that, as regards our quest, we were on the wrong tack. We found nothing suspicious, nothing that suggested a really adequate motive for Dollmann's treachery. I became impatient, and was for pushing on more quickly westward. Davies still clung to his theory, but the same feeling influenced him.

"It's something to do with these channels in the sand," he persisted, "but I'm afraid, as you say, we haven't got at the heart of the mystery. Nobody seems to care a rap what we do. We haven't done the estuaries as well as I should like, but we'd better push on to the islands. It's exactly the same sort of work, and just as important, I believe. We're bound to get a clue soon."

There was also the question of time, for me at least. I was due to be back in London, unless I obtained an extension, on the 28th, and our present rate of progress was slow. But I cannot conscientiously say that I made a serious point of this. If there was any value in our enterprise at all, official duty pales beside it. The machinery of State would not suffer from my absence; excuses would have to be made, and the results braved.

All the time our sturdy little craft grew shabbier and more weather-worn, the varnish thinner, the decks greyer, the sails dingier, and the cabin roof more murky where stove-fumes stained it. But the only beauty she ever possessed, that of perfect fitness for her functions, remained. With nothing to compare her to she became a home to me. My joints adapted themselves to her crabbed limits, my tastes and habits to her plain domestic economy.

But oil and water were running low, and the time had come for us to be forced to land and renew our stock.

# 14

### The First Night in the Islands

A LOW line of sandhills, pink and fawn in the setting sun, at one end of them a little white village huddled round the base of a massive four-square lighthouse—such was Wangeroog, the easternmost of the Frisian Islands, as I saw it on the evening of 15th October. We had decided to make it our first landing-place; and since it possesses no harbour, and is hedged by a mile of sand at low water, we had run in on the rising tide till the yacht grounded, in order to save ourselves as much labour as possible in the carriage to and fro of the heavy water-breakers and oil-cans which we had to replenish. In faint outline three miles to the south of us was the flat plain of Friesland, broken only by some trees, a windmill or two, and a church spire. Between, the shallow expanse of sea was already beginning to shrink away into lagoons, chief among which was the narrow passage by which we had approached from the east. This continued its course west, directly parallel to the island, and in it, at a distance of half a mile from us, three galliots lay at anchor.

Before supper was over the yacht was high and dry, and when we had eaten, Davies loaded himself with cans and breakers. I was for taking my share, but he induced me to stay aboard; for I was dead tired after an unusually long and trying day, which had begun at 2 a.m., when, using a precious instalment of east wind, we had started on a complete passage of the sands from the Elbe to the Jade. It was a barely possible feat for a boat of our low speed to perform in only two tides; and though we just succeeded, it was only by dint of tireless vigilance and severe physical strain.

"Lay out the anchor when you've had a smoke," said Davies, "and keep an eye on the riding-light; it's my only guide back."

He lowered himself, and I heard the scrunch of his sea-boots as he disappeared in the darkness. It was a fine starry night, with a touch of frost in the air. I lit a cigar, and stretched myself on a sofa close to the glow of the stove. The cigar soon languished and dropped, and I dozed uneasily, for the riding-light was on my mind. I got up once and squinted at it through the half-raised skylight, saw it burning steadily, and lay down again. The cabin lamp wanted oil and was dying down to a red-hot wick, but I was too drowsy to attend to it, and it went out. I lit my cigar stump again, and tried to keep awake by thinking. It was the first time I and Davies had been separated for so long; yet so used had we grown to freedom from interference that this would not have disturbed me in the least were it not for a sudden presentiment that on this first night of the second stage of our labours something would happen. All at once I heard a sound outside, a splashing footstep as of a man stepping in a puddle. I was wide awake in an instant, but never thought of shouting "Is that you, Davies?" for I knew in a flash that it was not he. It was the slip of a stealthy man. Presently I heard another footstep—the pad of a boot on the sand—this time close to my ear, just outside the hull; then some more, fainter and farther aft. I gently rose and peered aft through the skylight. A glimmer of light, reflected from below, was wavering over the mizzen-mast and bumpkin; it had nothing to do with the riding-light, which hung on the forestay. My prowler, I understood, had struck a match and was reading the name on the stern. How much farther would his curiosity carry him? The match went out, and footsteps were audible again. Then a strong, guttural voice called in German, "Yacht ahoy!" I kept silence. "Yacht ahoy!" a little louder this time. A pause, and then a vibration of the hull as boots scraped on it and hands grasped the gunwale. My visitor was on deck. I bobbed down, sat on the sofa, and I heard him moving along the deck, quickly and confidently, first forward to the bows, where he stopped, then back to the companion amidships. Inside the cabin it was pitch dark, but I heard his boots on the ladder, feeling for the steps. In another moment he would be in the doorway lighting his second match. Surely it was darker than before? There had been a little glow from the riding-lamp reflected on to the skylight, but it had disappeared. I looked up, realized, and made a fool of myself. In a few seconds more I should have seen my visitor face to face, perhaps had an interview: but I was new to this sort of work and lost my head. All I thought of was Davies's last words, and saw him astray on the sands, with no light to guide him back, the tide rising, and a heavy load. I started up involuntarily, bumped against the table, and set the stove jingling. A long step and a grab at the ladder, but just too late! I grasped something damp and greasy, there was tugging and hard breathing, and I was left clasping a big sea-boot, whose owner I heard jump on to the sand and run. I scrambled out, vaulted overboard, and followed blindly by the sound. He had doubled round the bows of the yacht, and I did the same, ducked under the bowsprit, forgetting the bobstay, and fell violently on my head, with all the wind knocked out of me by a wire rope and block whose strength and bulk was one of the glories of the *Dulcibella*. I struggled on as soon as I got some breath, but my invisible quarry was far ahead. I pulled off my heavy boots, carried them, and ran in my stockings, promptly cutting my foot on some cockle-shells. Pursuit was hopeless, and a final stumble over a bit of driftwood sent me sprawling with agony in my toes.

Limping back, I decided that I had made a very poor beginning as an active adventurer. I had gained nothing, and lost a great deal of breath and skin, and did not even know for certain where I was. The yacht's light was extinguished, and, even with Wangeroog Lighthouse to guide me, I found it no easy matter to find her. She had no anchor out, if the tide rose. And how was Davies to find her? After much feeble circling I took to lying flat at intervals in the hopes of seeing her silhouetted against the starry sky. This plan succeeded at last, and with relief and humility I boarded her, relit the riding-light, and carried out the kedge anchor. The strange boot lay at the foot of the ladder, but it told no tales when I examined it. It was eleven o'clock, past low water. Davies was cutting it fine if he was to get aboard without the dinghy's help. But eventually he reappeared in the most prosaic way, exhausted with his heavy load, but full of talk about his visit ashore. He began while we were still on deck.

"Look here, we ought to have settled more about what we're to say when we're asked questions. I chose a quiet-looking shop, but it turned out to be a sort of inn, where they were drinking pink gin—all very friendly, as usual, and I found myself under a fire of questions. I said we were on our way back to England. There was the usual rot about the smallness of the boat, etc. It struck me that we should want some other pretence for going so slow and stopping to explore, so I had to bring in the ducks, though goodness knows we don't want to waste time over *them*. The subject wasn't quite a success. They said it was too early— jealous, I suppose; but then two fellows spoke up, and asked to be taken on to help. Said they would bring their punt; without local help we should do no good. All true enough, no doubt, but what a nuisance they'd be. I got out of it—"

"It's just as well you did," I interposed. "We shall never be able to leave the boat by herself. I believe we're watched," and I related my experience.

"H'm! It's a pity you didn't see who it was. Confound that bobstay!" (his tactful way of reflecting on my clumsiness); "which way did he run?" I pointed vaguely into the west. "Not towards the island? I wonder if it's someone off one of those galliots. There are three anchored in the chan- nel over there; you can see their lights. You didn't hear a boat pulling off?"

I explained that I had been a miserable failure as a detective.

"You've done jolly well, I think," said Davies. "If you had shouted when you first heard him we should know less still. And we've got a boot, which may come in useful. Anchor out all right? Let's get below."

We smoked and talked till the new flood, lapping softly round the *Dulcibella*, raised her without a jar.

Of course, I argued, there might be nothing in it. The visitor might have been a commonplace thief; an apparently deserted yacht was a tempting bait. Davies scouted this possibility from the first.

"They're not like that in Germany," he said. "In Holland, if you like, they'll do anything. And I don't like that turning out of the lantern to gain time, if we *were* away."

Nor did I. In spite of my blundering in details, I welcomed the inci- dent as the first concrete proof that the object of our quest was no mare's nest. The next point was what was the visitor's object? If to search, what would he have found?

"The charts, of course, with all our corrections and notes, and the log. They'd give us away," was Davies's instant conclusion. Not having his faith in the channel theory, I was lukewarm about his precious charts.

"After all, we're doing nothing wrong, as you've often said yourself," I said.

Still, as a true index to our mode of life they were the only things on board that could possibly compromise us or suggest that we were any- thing more than eccentric young Englishmen cruising for sport (witness the duck guns) and pleasure. We had two sets of charts, German and English. The former we decided to use in practice, and to hide, together with the log, if occasion demanded. My diary, I resolved, should never leave my person. Then there were the naval books. Davies scanned them with a look I knew well.

"There are too many of them," he said, in the tone of a cook fixing the fate of superfluous kittens. "Let's throw them overboard. They're very old anyhow, and I know them by heart."

"Well, not here!" I protested, for he was laying greedy hands on the shelf; "they'll be found at low water. In fact, I should leave them as they are. You had them when you were here before, and Dollmann knows you had them. If you return without them, it will look queer." They were spared.

The English charts, being relatively useless, thought more suitable to our *rôle* as English yachtsmen, were to be left in evidence, as shining proofs of our innocence. It was all delightfully casual, I could not help thinking. A seven-ton yacht does not abound in (dry) hiding-places, and we were helpless against a drastic search. If there *were* secrets on this coast to guard, and we were suspected as spies, there was nothing to prevent an official visit and warning. There need be no prowlers scuttling off when alarmed, unless indeed it was thought wisest to let well alone, if we *were* harmless, and not to arouse suspicions where there were none. Here we lost ourselves in conjecture. Whose agent was the prowler? If Dollmann's, did Dollmann know now that the *Dulcibella* was safe, and back in the region he had expelled her from? If so, was he likely to return to the policy of violence? We found ourselves both glancing at the duck guns strung up under the racks, and then we both laughed and looked foolish. "A war of wits, and not of duck guns," I opined. "Let's look at the chart."

The reader is already familiar with the general aspect of this singular region, and I need only remind him that the mainland is that district of Prussia which is known as East Friesland.* It is a short, flat-topped peninsula, bounded on the west by the Ems estuary and beyond that by Holland, and on the east by the Jade estuary; a low-lying country, containing great tracts of marsh and heath, and few towns of any size; on the north side none. Seven islands lie off the coast. All, except Borkum, which is round, are attenuated strips, slightly crescent-shaped, rarely more than a mile broad, and tapering at the ends; in length averaging about six miles, from Norderney and Juist, which are seven and nine respectively, to little Baltrum, which is only two and a half.

Of the shoal spaces which lie between them and the mainland,

*See Map B.

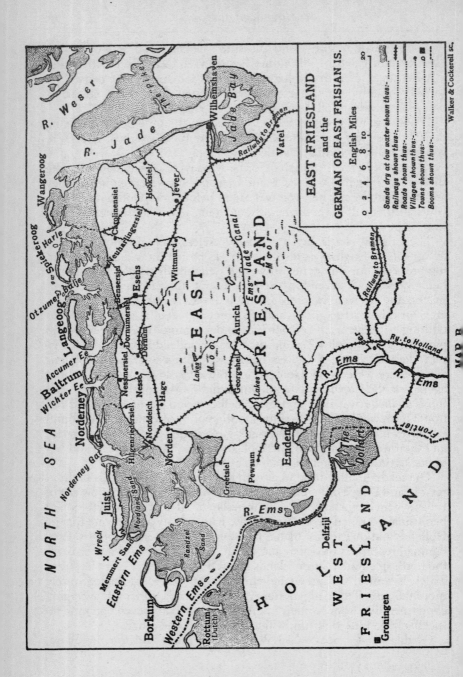

EAST FRIESLAND
and the
GERMAN OR EAST FRISIAN IS.

English Miles

0  2  4  6  8  10        20

Sands dry at low water shown thus:⋯
Railways shown thus:⋯
Roads shown thus:⋯
Villages shown thus:⋯
Towns shown thus:⋯
Booms shown thus:⋯

Walker & Cockerell sc.

MAP B

NORTH SEA

R. Weser

R. Jade

The Pike

Jade Bay

Wangeroog

Otzumer or Spiekeroog Balje

Harle

Langeoog

Accumer Ee

Baltrum

Wichter Ee

Norderney

Norderney Gat

Juist

Wreck

Memmert Sand

Nordland Sand

Eastern Ems

Borkum

Western Ems

Rottum
(Dutch)

Ramzel Sand

Hilgenriedersiel

Nessmersiel

Nessi

Norddeich

Norden

Greetsiel

Pewsum

R. Ems

Delfzijl

HOLLAND

WEST FRIESLAND

Groningen

Emden

The Dollart

R. Ems

R. Ems

Frontier

Ry. to Holland

Railway to Bremen

Ls.

Georgsheil

Lakes

Aurich

EAST FRIESLAND

Moor

Lakes

Moor

Ems Jade Canal

Moor

Hage

Dornum

Dornumersiel

Bensersiel

Esens

Neuharlingersiel

Wittmund

Carolinensiel

Hooksiel

Jever

Varel

Willemshaven

Railway to Bremen

two-thirds dry at low-water, and the remaining third becomes a system of lagoons whose distribution is controlled by the natural drift of the North Sea as it forces its way through the intervals between the islands. Each of these intervals resembles the bar of a river, and is obstructed by dangerous banks, over which the sea pours at every tide scooping out a deep pool. This fans out and ramifies to east and west as the pent-up current frees itself, encircles the islands, and spreads over the intervening flats. But the farther it penetrates the less coursing force it has, and as a result no island is girt completely by a low-water channel. About midway at the back of each of them is a "watershed," only covered for five or six hours out of the twelve. A boat, even of the lightest draught, navigating behind the islands must choose its moment for passing these. As to navigability, the *North Sea Pilot* sums up the matter in these dry terms: "The channels dividing these islands from each other and the shore afford to the small craft of the country the means of communication between the Ems and the Jade, to which description of vessels only they are available." The islands are dismissed with a brief note or two about beacons and lights.

The more I looked at the chart the more puzzled I became. The islands were evidently mere sandbanks, with a cluster of houses and a church on each, the only hint of animation in their desolate *ensemble* being the occasional word "Bade-strand," suggesting that they were visited in the summer months by a handful of townsfolk for the sea-bathing. Norderney, of course, was conspicuous in this respect; but even its town, which I know by repute as a gay and fashionable watering-place, would be dead and empty for some months in the year, and could have no commercial importance. No man could do anything on the mainland coast—a monotonous line of dyke punctuated at intervals by an infinitesimal village. Glancing idly at the names of these villages, I noticed that they most of them ended in siel—a repulsive termination, that seemed appropriate to the whole region. There were Carolinensiel, Bensersiel, etc. Siel means either a sewer or a sluice, the latter probably in this case, for I noticed that each village stood at the outlet of a little stream which evidently carried off the drainage of the lowlands behind. A sluice, or lock, would be necessary at the mouth, for at high tide the land is below the level of the sea. Looking next at the sands outside, I noticed that across them and towards each outlet a line of booms was marked, showing that there was some sort of tidal approach to the village, evidently formed by the scour of the little stream.

"Are we going to explore those?" I asked Davies.

"I don't see the use," he answered; "they only lead to those potty little places. I suppose local galliots use them."

"How about your torpedo-boats and patrol-boats?"

"They *might*, at certain tides. But I can't see what value they'd be, unless as a refuge for a German boat in the last resort. They lead to no harbours. Wait! There's a little notch in the dyke at Neuharlingersiel and Dornumersiel, which may mean some sort of a quay arrangement, but what's the use of that?"

"We may as well visit one or two, I suppose?"

"I suppose so; but we don't want to be playing round villages. There's heaps of really important work to do, farther out."

"Well, what *do* you make of this coast?"

Davies had nothing but the same old theory, but he urged it with a force and keenness that impressed me more deeply than ever.

"Look at those islands!" he said. "They're clearly the old line of coast, hammered into breaches by the sea. The space behind them is like an immense tidal harbour, thirty miles by five, and they screen it impenetrably. It's absolutely *made* for shallow war-boats under skilled pilotage. They can nip in and out of the gaps, and dodge about from end to end. On one side is the Ems, on the other the big estuaries. It's a perfect base for torpedo-craft."

I agreed (and agree still), but still I shrugged my shoulders.

"We go on exploring, then, in the same way?"

"Yes; keeping a sharp look-out, though. Remember, we shall always be in sight of land now."

"What's the glass doing?"

"Higher than for a long time. I hope it won't bring fog. I know this district is famous for fogs, and fine weather at this time of the year is bad for them anywhere. I would rather it blew, if it wasn't for exploring those gaps, where an on-shore wind would be nasty. Six-thirty tomorrow; not later. I think I'll sleep in the saloon for the future, after what happened to-night."

## 15

### Bensersiel*

THE decisive incidents of our cruise were now fast approaching. Looking back on the steps that led to them, and anxious that the reader should be wholly with us in our point of view, I think I cannot do better than give extracts from my diary of the next three days:

---

*For this chapter see Map B.

"*16th Oct.* (up at 6.30, yacht high and dry). Of the three galliots out at anchor in the channel yesterday, only one is left . . . I took my turn with the breakers this morning and walked to Wangeroog, whose village I found half lost in sand drifts, which are planted with tufts of marram-grass in mathematical rows, to give stability and prevent a catastrophe like that at Pompeii. A friendly grocer told me all there is to know, which is little. The islands are what we thought them—barren for the most part, with a small fishing population, and a scanty accession of summer visitors for bathing. The season is over now, and business slack for him. There is still, however, a little trade with the mainland in galliots and lighters, a few of which come from the "siels" on the mainland. "Had these harbours?" I asked. "Mud-holes!" he replied, with a contemptuous laugh. (He is a settler in these wilds, not a native.) Said he had heard of schemes for improving them, so as to develop the islands as health-resorts, but thought it was only a wild speculation.

"A heavy tramp back to the yacht, nearly crushed by impedimenta. While Davies made yet another trip, I stalked some birds with a gun, and obtained what resembled a specimen of the smallest variety of jack-snipe, and small at that; but I made a great noise, which I hope persuaded somebody of the purity of our motives.

"We weighed anchor at one o'clock, and in passing the anchored galliot took a good look at her. *Kormoran* was on her stern; otherwise she was just like a hundred others. Nobody was on deck.

"We spent the whole afternoon till dark exploring the Harle, or gap between Wangeroog and Spiekeroog; the sea breaking heavily on the banks outside . . . Fine as the day was, the scene from the offing was desolate to the last degree. The naked spots of the two islands are hideous in their sterility: melancholy bits of wreck-wood their only relief, save for one or two grotesque beacons, and, most *bizarre* of all, a great church-tower, standing actually *in* the water, on the north side of Wangeroog, a striking witness to the encroachment of the sea. On the mainland, which was barely visible, there was one very prominent landmark, a spire, which from the chart we took to be that of Esens, a town four miles inland.

"The days are growing short. Sunset is soon after five, and an hour later it is too dark to see booms and buoys distinctly. The tides also are awkward just now.* High-water at morning and evening is between five and six—just at twilight. For the night, we groped with the lead into the Muschel Balge, the tributary channel which laps round the inside of

---

*I exclude all the technicalities that I can, but the reader should take note that the tide-table is very important henceforward.

Spiekeroog, and lay in two fathoms, clear of the outer swell, but rolling a little when the ebb set in strong against the wind.

"A galliot passed us, going west, just as we were stowing sails; too dark to see her name. Later, we saw her anchor-light higher up our channel.

"The great event of the day has been the sighting of a small German gunboat, steaming slowly west along the coast. That was about half-past four, when we were sounding along the Harle.

"Davies identified her at once as the *Blitz*, Commander von Brüning's gunboat. We wondered if he recognized the *Dulcibella*, but, anyway, she seemed to take no notice of us and steamed slowly on. We quite expected to fall in with her when we came to the islands, but the actual sight of her has excited us a good deal. She is an ugly, cranky little vessel, painted grey, with one funnel. Davis is contemptuous about her low freeboard forward; says he would rather go to sea in the *Dulce*. He has her dimensions and armament (learnt from Brassey) at his fingers' ends: one hundred and forty feet by twenty-five, one 4.9 gun, one 3.4, and four Maxims—an old type. Just going to bed; a bitterly cold night.

"*17th Oct.*—Glass falling heavily this morning, to our great disgust. Wind back in the SW and much warmer. Starting at 5.30 we tacked on the tide over the "watershed" behind Spiekeroog. So did the galliot we had seen last night, but we again missed identifying her, as she weighed anchor before we came up to her berth. Davies, however, swore she was the *Kormoran*. We lost sight of her altogether for the greater part of the day, which we spent in exploring the Otzumer Ee (the gap between Langeoog and Spiekeroog), now and then firing some perfunctory shots at seals and sea-birds . . . (nautical details omitted) . . . In the evening we were hurrying back to an inside anchorage, when we made a bad mistake; did, in fact, what we had never done before, ran aground on the very top of high water, and are now sitting hard and fast on the edge of the Rute Flat, south of the east spit of Langeoog. The light was bad, and a misplaced boom tricked us; kedging-off failed, and at 8 p.m. we were left on a perfect Ararat of sand, and only a yard or two from that accursed boom, which is perched on the very summit, as a lure to the unwary. It is going to blow hard too, though that is no great matter, as we are sheltered by banks on the sou'-west and nor'-west sides, the likely quarters. We hope to float at 6.15 to-morrow morning, but to make sure of being able to get her off, we have been transferring some ballast to the dinghy, by way of lightening the yacht—a horrid business handling the pigs of lead, heavy, greasy, and black. The saloon is an inferno, the deck like a collier's, and ourselves like sweeps.

"The anchors are laid out, and there is nothing more to be done.

"*18th Oct.*—Half a gale from the sou'west when we turned out, but it helped us to float off safely at six. The dinghy was very nearly swamped with the weight of lead in it, and getting the ballast back into the yacht was the toughest job of all. We got the dinghy alongside, and Davies jumped in (nearly sinking it for good), balanced himself, fended off, and, whenever he got a chance, attached the pigs one by one on to a bight of rope, secured to the peak halyards, on which I hoisted from the deck. It was touch and go for a few minutes, and then easier.

"It was nine before we had finished replacing the pigs in the hold, a filthy but delicate operation, as they fit like a puzzle, and if one is out of place the floor-boards won't shut down. Coming on deck after it, we saw to our surprise the *Blitz*, lying at anchor in the Schill Balje, inside Spiekeroog, about a mile and a half off. She must have entered the Otzumer Ee at high-water for shelter from the gale; a neat bit of work for a vessel of her size, as Davies says she draws nine-foot-ten, and there can't be more than twelve on the bar at high-water neaps. Several smacks had run in too, and there were two galliots farther up our channel, but we couldn't make out if the *Kormoran* was one.

"When the banks uncovered we lay more quietly, so landed and took a long, tempestuous walk over the Rute, with compass and notebooks. Returning at two, we found the glass tumbling down almost visibly.

"I suggested running for Bensersiel, one of the mainland villages southwest of us, on the evening flood, as it seemed just the right opportunity, if we were to visit one of those 'siels' at all. Davies was very lukewarm, but events overcame him. At 3.30 a black, ragged cloud, appearing to trail into the very sea, brought up a terrific squall. This passed, and there was a deathly pause of ten minutes while the whole sky eddied as with smoke-wreaths. Then an icy puff struck us from the northwest, rapidly veering till it reached northeast; there it settled and grew harder every moment.

"'Sou'-west to north-east—only the worst sort do that,' said Davies.

"The shift to the east changed the whole situation (as shifts often have before), making the Rute Flats a lee shore, while to windward lay the deep lagoons of the Otzumer Ee, bounded indeed by Spiekeroog, but still offering a big drift for wind and sea. We had to clear out sharp, to see the mizzen. It was out of the question to beat to windward, for it was blowing a hurricane in a few minutes. We must go to leeward, and Davies was for running farther in well behind the Jans sand, and not risking Bensersiel. A blunder of mine, when I went to the winch to get up anchor, settled the question. Thirty out of our forty fathoms of chain were out. Confused by the motion and a blinding sleet-shower that had come on, and forgetting the tremendous strain on the cable, I cast the slack off the bitts and left it loose. There was then only one turn of the chain round the drum, enough in ordinary weather to prevent it running out. But now my first heave on the winch-lever started it slipping, and in an instant it was whizzing out of the hawse-pipe and overboard. I tried to stop it with my foot, stumbled at a heavy plunge of the yacht, heard something snap below, and saw the last of it disappear. The yacht fell off the wind, and drifted astern. I shouted, and had the sense to hoist the reefed foresail at once. Davies had her in hand in no time, and was steering southwest. Going aft I found him cool and characteristic.

"'Doesn't matter,' he said; 'anchor's buoyed.\* We'll come back tomorrow and get it. Can't now. Should have had to slip it anyhow; wind and sea too strong. We'll try for Bensersiel. Can't trust to a warp and kedge out here.'

"An exciting run it was, across country, so to speak, over an unboomed watershed; but we had bearings from our morning's walk. Shoal water all the way and a hollow sea breaking everywhere. We soon made out the Bensersiel booms, but even under mizzen and foresail only we travelled too fast, and had to heave to outside them, for the channel looked too shallow still. We lowered half the centre-board and kept her just holding her own to windward, through a most trying period. In the end had to run for it sooner than we meant, as we were sagging to leeward in spite of all, and the light was failing. Bore up at 5.15, and raced up the channel with the booms on our left scarcely visible in the surf and rising water. Davies stood forward, signalling—port, starboard, or steady—with his arms, while I wrestled with the helm, flung from side to side and flogged by wave-tops. Suddenly found a sort of dyke on our right just covering with sea. The shore appeared through scud, and men on a quay shouting. Davies brandished his left arm furiously; I ported hard, and we were in smoother water. A few seconds more and we were whizzing through a slit between two wood jetties. Inside a small square harbour showed, but there was no room to round up properly and no time to lower sails. Davies just threw the kedge over, and it just got a grip in time to check our momentum and save our bowsprit from the quayside. A man threw us a rope and we brought up alongside, rather bewildered.

"Not more so than the natives, who seemed to think we had dropped from the sky. They were very friendly, with an undercurrent of disappointment, having expected salvage work outside, I think. All showed embarrassing helpfulness in stowing sails, etc. We were rescued by a

---

\*Ever since leaving the Elbe we had had a buoy-line on our anchor against the emergency of having to slip our cable and run. For the same reason the end of the chain was not made permanently fast below.

fussy person in uniform and spectacles, who swept them aside and announced himself as the custom-house officer (fancy such a thing in this absurd mud-hole!), marched down into the cabin, which was in a fearful mess and wringing wet, and producing ink, pen, and a huge printed form, wanted to know our cargo, our crew, our last port, our destination, our food, stores, and everything. No cargo (pleasure); captain, Davies; crew, me; last port, Brunsbüttel; destination, England. What spirits had we? Whisky, produced. What salt? Tin of Cerebos, produced, and a damp deposit in a saucer. What coffee? etc. Lockers searched, guns fingered, bunks rifled. Meanwhile the German charts and the log, the damning clues to our purpose, were in full evidence, crying for notice which they did not get. (We had forgotten our precautions in the hurry of our start from the Rute.) When the huge form was as full as he could make it, he suddenly became human, talkative, and thirsty; and, when we treated him, patronizing. It seemed to dawn on him that, under our rough clothes and crust of brine and grime, we were two mad and wealthy aristocrats, worthy *protégés* of a high official. He insisted on our bringing our cushions to dry at his house, and to get rid of him we consented, for we were wet, hungry, and longing to change and wash. He talked himself away at last, and we hid the log and charts; but he returned, in the postmaster's uniform this time before we had finished supper, and haled us and our cushions up through dark and mud to his cottage near the quay. To reach it we crossed a small bridge spanning what seemed to be a small river with sluice-gates, just as we had thought.

"He showed his prizes to his wife, who was quite flustered by the distinguished strangers, and received the cushions with awe; and next we were carried off to the Gasthaus and exhibited to the village circle, where we talked ducks and weather. (Nobody takes us seriously; I never felt less like a conspirator.) Our friend, who is a feather-headed chatterbox, is enormously important about his ridiculous little port, whose principal customer seems to be the Langeoog post-boat, a galliot running to and fro according to tide. A few lighters also come down the stream with bricks and produce from the interior, and are towed to the islands. The harbour has from five to seven feet in it for two hours out of twelve! Herr Schenkel talked us back to the yacht, which we found resting on the mud—and here we are. Davies pretends there are harbour smells, and says he won't be able to sleep; is already worrying about how to get away from here. Ashore, they were saying that it's impossible, under sail, in strong north-east winds, the channel being too narrow to tack in. For my part I find it a huge relief to be in any sort of harbour after a fortnight in the open. There are no tides or anchors to think about, and no bumping or rolling. Fresh milk to-morrow!"

# 16

## Commander von Brüning

To resume my story in narrative form.

I was awakened at ten o'clock on the 19th, after a long and delicious sleep, by Davies's voice outside, talking his unmistakable German. Looking out, in my pyjamas, I saw him on the quay above in conversation with a man in a long mackintosh coat and a gold-laced navy cap. He had a close-trimmed auburn beard, a keen, handsome face, and an animated manner. It was raining in a raw air.

They saw me, and Davies said: "Hullo, Carruthers! Here's Commander von Brüning from the *Blitz*—that's 'meiner Freund' Carruthers." (Davies was deplorably weak in terminations.)

The commander smiled broadly at me, and I inclined an uncombed head, while, for a moment, the quest was a dream, and I myself felt unutterably squalid and foolish. I ducked down, heard them parting, and Davies came aboard.

"We're to meet him at the inn for a talk at twelve," he said.

His news was that the *Blitz*'s steam-cutter had come in on the morning tide, and he had met von Brüning when marketing at the inn. Secondly, the *Kormoran* had also come in, and was moored close by. It was as clear as possible, therefore, that the latter *had* watched us, and was in touch with the *Blitz*, and that both had seized the opportunity of our being cooped up in Bensersiel to take further stock of us. What had passed hitherto? Nothing much. Von Brüning had greeted Davies with cordial surprise, and said he had wondered yesterday if it was the *Dulcibella* that he had seen anchored behind Langeoog. Davies had explained that we had left the Baltic and were on our way home; taking the shelter of the islands.

"Supposing he comes on board and asks to see our log?" I said.

"Pull it out," said Davies, "It's rot, this hiding, after all. I say, I rather funk this interview; what are we to say? It's not in my line."

We resolved abruptly on an important change of plan, replaced the log and charts in the rack as the first logical step. They contained nothing but bearings, courses, and the bare data of navigation. To Davies they were hard-won secrets of vital import, to be lied for, however hard and distasteful lying was. I was cooler as to their value, but in any case the same thing was now in both our minds. There would be great difficulties in the coming interview if we tried to be too clever and conceal the fact that we had been exploring. We did not know how much

von Brüning knew. When had our surveillance by the *Kormoran*
begun? Apparently at Wangeroog, but possibly in the estuaries, where
we had not fired a shot at duck. Perhaps he knew even more—
Dollmann's treachery, Davies's escape, and our subsequent movements—we could not tell. On the other hand, exploration was known
to be a fad of Davies's, and in September he had made no secret of it.
It was safer to be consistent now. After breakfast we determined to find
out something about the *Kormoran*, which lay on the mud at the other
side of the harbour, and accordingly addressed ourselves to two mighty
sailors, whose jerseys bore the legend "Post," and who towered conspicuous among a row of stolid Frisians on the quay, all gazing gravely
down at us as at a curious bit of marine bric-à-brac. The twins (for such
they proved to be) were most benignant giants, and asked us aboard the
post-boat galliot for a chat. It was easy to bring the talk naturally round
to the point we wished, and we soon gained some most interesting information, delivered in the broadest Frisian, but intelligible enough.
They called the *Kormoran* a Memmert boat, or "wreck-works" boat. It
seemed that off the western end of Juist, the island lying west of
Norderney, there lay the bones of a French war-vessel, wrecked ages
ago. She carried bullion which has never been recovered, in spite of
many efforts. A salvage company was trying for it now, and had works
on Memmert, an adjacent sand-bank. "That is Herr Grimm, the overseer himself," they said, pointing to the bridge above the sluice-gates. (I
call him "Grimm" because it describes him exactly.) A man in a pilot
jacket and peaked cap was leaning over the parapet.

"What's he doing here?" I asked.

They answered that he was often up and down the coast, work on the
wreck being impossible in rough weather. They supposed he was bringing cargo in his galliot from Wilhelmshaven, all the company's plant
and stores coming from that port. He was a local man from Aurich; an
ex-tug skipper.

We discussed this information while walking out over the sands to
see the channel at low water.

"Did you hear anything about this in September?" I asked.

"Not a word. I didn't go to Juist. I would have, probably, if I hadn't
met Dollmann."

What in the world did it mean? How did it affect our plans?

"Look at his boots if we pass him," was all Davies had to suggest.

The channel was now a ditch, with a trickle in it, running north by
east, roughly, and edged by a dyke of withies for the first quarter of a
mile. It was still blowing fresh from the north-east, and we saw that exit
was impossible in such a wind.

So back to the village, a paltry, bleak little place. We passed friend Grimm on the bridge; a dark, clean-shaved, saturnine man, wearing *shoes*. Approaching the inn:

"We haven't settled quite enough, have we?" said Davies. "What about our future plans?"

"Heaven knows, we haven't," I said. "But I don't see how we can. We must see how things go. It's past twelve, and it won't do to be late."

"Well, I leave it to you."

"All right, I'll do my best. All you've got to do is to be yourself and tell one lie, if need be, about the trick Dollmann played you."

The next scene: von Brüning, Davies, and I, sitting over coffee and Kümmel at a table in a dingy inn-parlour overlooking the harbour and the sea, Davies with a full box of matches on the table before him. The commander gave us a hearty welcome, and I am bound to say I liked him at once, as Davies had done; but I feared him, too, for he had honest eyes, but abominably clever ones.

I had impressed on Davies to talk and question as freely and naturally as though nothing uncommon had happened since he last saw von Brüning on the deck of the *Medusa*. He must ask about Dollmann—the mutual friend—at the outset, and, if questioned about that voyage in his company to the Elbe, must lie like a trooper as to the danger he had been in. This was the one clear and essential necessity, where much was difficult. Davies did his duty with precipitation, and blushed when he put his question, in a way that horrified me, till I remembered that his embarrassment was due, and would be ascribed, to another cause.

"Herr Dollmann is away still, I think," said von Brüning. (So Davies had been right at Brunsbüttel.) "Were you thinking of looking him up again?" he added.

"Yes," said Davies, shortly.

"Well, I'm sure he's away. But his yacht is back, I believe—and Fräulein Dollmann, I suppose."

"H'm!" said Davies; "she's a very fine boat that."

Our host smiled, gazing thoughtfully at Davies, who was miserable. I saw a chance, and took it mercilessly.

"We can call on Fräulein Dollmann, at least, Davies," I said, with a meaning smile at von Brüning.

"H'm!" said Davies; "will he be back soon, do you think?"

The commander had begun to light a cigar, and took his time in answering. "Probably," he said, after some puffing, "he's never away very long. But you've seen them later than I have. Didn't you sail to the Elbe together the day after I saw you last?"

"Oh, part of the way," said Davies, with great negligence. "I haven't seen him since. He got there first; outsailed me."

"Gave you the slip, in fact?"

"Of course he beat me; I was close-reefed. Besides—"

"Oh, I remember; there was a heavy blow—a devil of a heavy blow. I thought of you that day. How did you manage?"

"Oh, it was a fair wind; it wasn't far, you see."

"Grosse Gott! In *that*." He nodded towards the window whence the *Dulcibella*'s taper mast could be seen pointing demurely heavenwards.

"She's a splendid sea-boat," said Davies, indignantly.

"A thousand pardons!" said von Brüning, laughing.

"Don't shake my faith in her," I put in. "I've got to get to England in her."

"Heaven forbid; I was only thinking that there must have been some sea round the Scharhorn that day; a tame affair, no doubt, Herr Davies?"

"Scharhorn?" said Davies, who did not catch the idiom in the latter sentence. "Oh, we didn't go that way. We cut through the sands—by the Telte."

"The Telte! In a northwest gale!" The commander started, ceased to smile, and only stared. (It was genuine surprise; I could swear it. He had heard nothing of this before.)

"Herr Dollmann knew the way," said Davies, doggedly. "He kindly offered to pilot me through, and I wouldn't have gone otherwise." There was an awkward little pause.

"He led you well, it seems?" said von Brüning.

"Yes; there's a nasty surf there, though, isn't there? But it saves six miles—and the Scharhorn. Not that I saved distance. I was fool enough to run aground."

"Ah!" said the other, with interest.

"It didn't matter, because I was well inside then. Those sands are difficult at high water. We've come back that way, you know."

("And we run aground every day," I remarked, with resignation.)

"Is that where the *Medusa* gave you the slip?" asked von Brüning, still studying Davies with a strange look, which I strove anxiously to analyze.

"She wouldn't have noticed," said Davies. "It was very thick and squally—and she had got some way ahead. There was no need for her to stop, anyway. I got off all right; the tide was rising still. But, of course, I anchored there for the night."

"Where?"

"Inside there, under the Hohenhörn," said Davies, simply.

"Under the *what*?"

"The Hohenhörn."

"Go on—didn't they wait for you at Cuxhaven?"

"I don't know; I didn't go that way." The commander looked more and more puzzled.

"Not by the ship canal, I mean. I changed my mind about it, because the next day the wind was easterly. It would have been a dead beat across the sands to Cuxhaven, while it was a fair wind straight out to the Eider River. So I sailed there, and reached the Baltic that way. It was all the same."

There was another pause.

"Well done, Davies," I thought. He had told his story well, using no subtlety. I knew it was exactly how he would have told it to anyone else, if he had not had irrefutable proof of foul play.

The commander laughed, suddenly and heartily.

"Another liqueur?" he said. Then, to me: "Upon my word, your friend amuses me. It's impossible to make him spin a yarn. I expect he had a bad time of it."

"That's nothing to him," I said; "he prefers it. He anchored me the other day behind the Hohenhörn in a gale of wind; said it was safer than a harbour, and more sanitary."

"I wonder he brought you here last night. It was a fair wind for England; and not very far."

"There was no pilot to follow, you see."

"With a charming daughter—no."

Davies frowned and glared at me. I was merciful and changed the subject.

"Besides," I said, "we've left our anchor and chain out there." And I made confession of my sin.

"Well, as it's buoyed, I should advise you to pick it up as soon as you can," said von Brüning, carelessly; "or someone else will."

"Yes, by Jove! Carruthers," said Davies, eagerly, "we must get out on this next tide."

"Oh, there's no hurry," I said, partly from policy, partly because the ease of the shore was on me. To sit on a chair upright is something of a luxury, however good the cause in which you have crouched like a monkey over a table at the level of your knees, with a reeking oil-stove at your ear.

"They're honest enough about here, aren't they?" I added. While the words were on my lips I remembered the midnight visitor at Wangeroog, and guessed that von Brüning was leading up to a test. Grimm (if he was the visitor) would have told him of his narrow escape from detection, and reticence on our part would show we suspected something. I could have kicked myself, but it was not too late. I took the bull by the horns, and, before the commander could answer, added:

"By Jove! Davies, I forgot about that fellow at Wangeroog. The anchor might be stolen, as he says."

Davies looked blank, but von Brüning had turned to me.

"We never dreamed there would be thieves among these islands," I said, "but the other night I nearly caught a fellow in the act. He thought the yacht was empty."

I described the affair in detail, and with what humour I could. Our host was amused, and apologetic for the islanders.

"They're excellent folk," he said, "but they're born with predatory instincts. Their fathers made their living out of wrecks on this coast, and the children inherit a weakness for plunder. When Wangeroog lighthouse was built they petitioned the Government for compensation, in perfect good faith. The coast is well lighted now, and windfalls are rare, but the sight of a stranded yacht, with the owners ashore, would inflame the old passion; and, depend upon it, someone has seen that anchor-buoy."

The word "wrecks" had set me tingling. Was it another test? Impossible to say; but audacity was safer than reserve, and might save trouble in the future.

"Isn't there the wreck of a treasure-ship somewhere farther west?" I asked. "We heard of it at Wangeroog" (my first inaccuracy). "They said a company was exploiting it."

"Quite right," said the commander, without a sign of embarrassment. "I don't wonder you heard of it. It's one of the few things folk have to talk about in these parts. It lies on Juister Riff, a shoal off Juist.* She was a French frigate, the *Corinne*, bound from Hamburg to Havre in 1811, when Napoleon held Hamburg as tight as Paris. She carried a million and a half in gold bars, and was insured in Hamburg; foundered in four fathoms, broke up, and there lies the treasure."

"Never been raised?"

"No. The underwriters failed and went bankrupt, and the wreck came into the hands of your English Lloyd's. It remained their property till '75, but they never got at the bullion. In fact, for fifty years it was never scratched at, and its very position grew doubtful, for the sand swallowed every stick. The rights passed through various hands, and in '86 were held by an enterprising Swedish company, which brought modern appliances, dived, dredged, and dug, fished up a lot of timber and bric-à-brac, and then broke. Since then, two Hamburg firms have

*See Map B.

tackled the job and lost their capital. Scores of lives have been spent over it, all told, and probably a million of money. Still there are the bars, somewhere."

"And what's being done now?"

"Well, recently a small local company was formed. It has a depot at Memmert, and is working with a good deal of perseverance. An engineer from Bremen was the principal mover, and a few men from Norderney and Emden subscribed the capital. By the way, our friend Dollmann is largely interested in it."

Out of the corner of my eye I saw Davies's tell-tale face growing troubled with inward questionings.

"We mustn't get back to him," I said, laughing. "It's not fair to my friend. But all this is very interesting. Will they ever get those bars?"

"Ah! that's the point," said von Brüning, with a mysterious twinkle. "It's an undertaking of immense difficulty; for the wreck is wholly disintegrated, and the gold, being the heaviest part of it, has, of course, sunk the deepest. Dredging is useless after a certain point; and the divers have to make excavations in the sand, and shore them up as best they can. Every gale nullifies half their labour, and weather like this of the last fortnight plays the mischief with the work. Only this morning I met the overseer, who happens to be ashore here. He was as black as thunder over prospects."

"Well, it's a romantic speculation," I said. "They deserve a return for their money."

"I hope they'll get it," said the commander. "The fact is, I hold a few shares myself."

"Oh, I hope I haven't been asking indiscreet questions?"

"Oh, dear no; all the world knows what I've told you. But you'll understand that one has to be reticent as to results in such a case. It's a big stake, and the *title is none too sound.* There has been litigation over it. Not that I worry much about my investment; for I shan't lose much by it at the worst. But it gives one an interest in this abominable coast. I go and see how they're getting on sometimes, when I'm down that way."

"It *is* an abominable coast," I agreed, heartily, "though you won't get Davies to agree."

"It's a magnificent place for sailing," said Davies, looking wistfully out over the storm-speckled grey of the North Sea. He underwent some more chaff, and the talk passed to our cruising adventures in the Baltic and the estuaries. Von Brüning cross-examined us with the most charming urbanity and skill. Nothing he asked could cause us the slightest offence; and a responsive frankness was our only possible course. So, date after date, and incident after incident, were elicited in the most natural way. As we talked I was astonished to find how little there was that was worth concealing, and heartily thankful that we had decided on candour. My fluency gave me the lead, and Davies followed me; but his own personality was really our tower of strength. I realized that as I watched the play of his eager features, and heard him struggle for expression on his favourite hobby; all his pet phrases translated crudely into the most excruciating German. He was convincing, because he was himself.

"Are there many like you in England?" asked von Brüning once.

"Like me? Of course—lots," said Davies.

"I wish there were more in Germany; they play at yachting over here—on shore half the time, drinking and loafing; paid crews, clean hands, white trousers; laid up in the middle of September."

"We haven't seen many yachts about," said Davies, politely.

For my part, I made no pretence of being a Davies. Faithful to my lower nature, I vowed the Germans were right, and, not without a secret zest, drew a lurid picture of the horrors of crewless cruising, and the drudgery that my remorseless skipper inflicted on me. It was delightful to see Davies wincing when I described my first night at Flensburg, for I had my revenge at last, and did not spare him. He bore up gallantly under my jesting, but I knew very well by his manner that he had not forgiven me my banter about the "charming daughter."

"You speak German well," said von Brüning.

"I have lived in Germany," said I.

"Studying for a profession, I suppose?"

"Yes," said I, thinking ahead. "Civil Service," was my prepared answer to the next question, but again (morbidly, perhaps) I saw a pitfall. That letter from my chief awaiting me at Norderney? My name was known, and we were watched. It might be opened. Lord, how casual we have been!

"May I ask what?"

"The Foreign Office." It sounded suspicious, but there it was.

"Indeed—in the Government service? When do you have to be back?"

That was how the question of our future intentions was raised, prematurely by me; for two conflicting theories were clashing in my brain. But the contents of the letter dogged me now, and "when at a loss, tell the truth," was an axiom I was finding sound. So I answered, "Pretty soon, in about a week. But I'm expecting a letter at Norderney, which may give me an extension. Davies said it was a good address to give," I added, smiling.

"Naturally," said von Brüning, dryly; the joke had apparently ceased to amuse him. "But you haven't much time then, have you?" he added, "unless you leave your skipper in the lurch. It's a long way to England, and the season is late for yachts."

I felt myself being hurried.

"Oh, you don't understand," I explained; "*he's* in no hurry. He's a man of leisure; aren't you, Davies?"

"What?" said Davies.

I translated my cruel question.

"Yes," said Davies, with simple pathos.

"If I have to leave him I shan't be missed—as an able seaman, at least. He'll just potter on down the islands, running aground and kedging-off, and arrive about Christmas."

"Or take the first fair gale to Dover," laughed the commander.

"Or that. So, you see, we're in no hurry; and we never make plans. And as for a passage to England straight, I'm not such a coward as I was at first, but I draw the line at that."

"You're a curious pair of shipmates; what's your point of view, Herr Davies?"

"I like this coast," said Davies. "And—we want to shoot some ducks." He was nervous, and forgot himself. I had already satirized our sporting armament and exploits, and hoped the subject was disposed of. Ducks were pretexts, and might lead to complications. I particularly wanted a free hand.

"As to wild fowl," said our friend, "I would like to give you gentlemen some advice. There are plenty to be got, now that autumn weather has set in (you wouldn't have got a shot in September, Herr Davies; I remember your asking about them when I saw you last). And even now it's early for amateurs. In hard winter weather a child can pick them up; but they're wild still, and want crafty hunting. You want a local punt, and above all a local man (you could stow him in your fo'c'sle), and to go to work seriously. Now, if you really wish for sport, I could help you. I could get you a trustworthy—"

"Oh, it's too good of you," stammered Davies, in a more unhappy accent than usual. "We can easily find one for ourselves. A man at Wangeroog offered—"

"Oh, did he?" interrupted von Brüning, laughing. "I'm not surprised. You don't know the Frieslanders. They're guileless, as I said, but they cling to their little perquisites." (I translated to Davies.) "They've been cheated out of wrecks, and they're all the more sensitive about ducks, which are more lucrative than fish. A stranger is a poacher. Your man would have made slight errors as to time and place."

"You said they were odd in their manner, didn't you, Davies?" I put in. "Look here, this is very kind of Commander von Brüning; but hadn't we better be certain of my plans before settling down to shoot? Let's push on direct to Norderney and get that letter of mine, and then decide. But we shan't see you again, I suppose, commander?"

"Why not? I am cruising westwards, and shall probably call at Norderney. Come aboard if you're there, won't you? I should like to show you the *Blitz*."

"Thanks, very much," said Davies, uneasily.

"Thanks, very much," said I, as heartily as I could.

Our party broke up soon after this.

"Well, gentlemen, I must take leave of you," said our friend. "I have to drive to Esens. I shall be going back to the *Blitz* on the evening tide, but you'll be busy then with your own boat."

It had been a puzzling interview, but the greatest puzzle was still to come. As we went towards the door, von Brüning made a sign to me. We let Davies pass out and remained standing.

"One word in confidence with you, Herr Carruthers," he said, speaking low. "You won't think me officious, I hope. I only speak out of keen regard for your friend. It is about the Dollmanns—you see how the land lies? I wouldn't encourage him."

"Thanks," I said, "but really—"

"It's only a hint. He's a splendid young fellow, but if anything—you understand—too honest and simple. I take it you have influence with him, and I should use it."

"I was not in earnest," I said. "I have never seen the Dollmanns; I thought they were friends of yours," I added, looking him straight in the eyes.

"I know them, but"—he shrugged his shoulders—"I know everybody."

"What's wrong with them?" I said, point-blank.

"Softly! Herr Carruthers. Remember, I speak out of pure friendliness to you as strangers, foreigners, and young. You I take to have discretion, or I should not have said a word. Still, I will add this. We know very little of Herr Dollmann, of his origin, his antecedents. He is half a Swede, I believe, certainly not a Prussian; came to Norderney three years ago, appears to be rich, and has joined in various commercial undertakings. Little scope about here? Oh, there is more enterprise than you think—development of bathing resorts, you know, speculation in land on these islands. Sharp practice? Oh, no! he's perfectly straight in that way. But he's a queer fellow, of eccentric habits, and—and, well, as I say, little is known of him. That's all, just a warning. Come along."

I saw that to press him further was useless.

"Thanks; I'll remember," I said.

"And look here," he added, as we walked down the passage, "if you take my advice, you'll omit that visit to the *Medusa* altogether." He gave me a steady look, smiling gravely.

"How much do you know, and what do you mean?" were the questions that throbbed in my thoughts; but I could not utter them, so I said nothing and felt very young.

Outside we joined Davies, who was knitting his brow over prospects.

"It just comes of going into places like this," he said to me. "We may be stuck here for days. Too much wind to tow out with the dinghy, and too narrow a channel to beat in."

Von Brüning was ready with a new proposal.

"Why didn't I think of it before?" he said. "I'll tow you out in my launch. Be ready at 6.30; we shall have water enough then. My men will send you a warp."

It was impossible to refuse, but a sense of being personally conducted again oppressed me; and the last hope of a bed in the inn vanished. Davies was none too effusive either. A tug meant a pilot, and he had had enough of them.

"He objects to towage on principle," I said.

"Just like him!" laughed the other. "That's settled, then!"

A dogcart was standing before the inn door in readiness for von Brüning. I was curious about Esens and his business there. Esens, he said, was the principal town of the district, four miles inland.

"I have to go there," he volunteered, "about a poaching case—a Dutchman trawling inside our limits. That's my work, you know—police duty."

Had the words a deeper meaning?

"Do you ever catch an Englishman?" I asked, recklessly.

"Oh, very rarely; your countrymen don't come so far as this—except on pleasure." He bowed to us each and smiled.

"Not much of that to be got in Bensersiel," I laughed.

"I'm afraid you'll have a dull afternoon. Look here. I know you can't leave your boat altogether, and it's no use asking Herr Davies; but will *you* drive into Esens with me and see a Frisian town—for what it's worth? You're getting a dismal impression of Friesland." I excused myself, said I would stop with Davies; we would walk out over the sands and prospect for the evening's sail.

"Well, good-bye then," he said, "till the evening. Be ready for the warp at 6.30."

He jumped up, and the cart rattled off through the mud, crossed the bridge, and disappeared into the dreary hinterland.

# 17

### Clearing the Air

"HAS he gone to get the police, do you think?" said Davies, grimly.

"I don't think so," said I. "Let's go aboard before that customs fellow buttonholes us."

A diminished row of stolid Frisians still ruminated over the *Dulcibella*. Friend Grimm was visible smoking on his forecastle. We went on board in silence.

"First of all, where exactly is Memmert?" I said.

Davies pulled down the chart, said "There," and flung himself at full length on a sofa.

The reader can see Memmert for himself. South of Juist,* abutting on the Ems delta, lies an extensive sandbank called Nordland, whose extreme western rim remains uncovered at the highest tides; the effect being to leave a C-shaped island, a mere paring of sand like a boomerang, nearly two miles long but only 150 yards or so broad, of curiously symmetrical outline, except at one spot, where it bulges to the width of a quarter of a mile. On the English chart its nakedness was absolute, save for a beacon at the south; but the German chart marked a building at the point where the bulge occurs. This was evidently the depot. "Fancy living there!" I thought, for the very name struck cold. No wonder Grimm was grim; and no wonder he was used to seek change of air. But the advantages of the site were obvious. It was remarkably isolated, even in a region where isolation is the rule; yet it was conveniently near the wreck, which, as we had heard, lay two miles out on the Juister Reef. Lastly, it was clearly accessible at any state of the tide, for the six-fathom channel of the Ems estuary runs hard up to it on the south, and thence sends off an eastward branch which closely borders the southern horn, thus offering an anchorage at once handy, deep, and sheltered from seaward gales.

Such was Memmert, as I saw it on the chart, taking in its features mechanically, for while Davies lay there heedless and taciturn, a pretence of interest was useless. I knew perfectly well what was between us, but I did not see why I should make the first move; for I had a grievance too, an old one. So I sat back on my sofa and jotted down in my notebook the heads of our conversation at the inn while it was fresh in my memory, and strove to draw conclusions. But the silence

---

*See Map B.

continuing and becoming absurd, I threw my pride to the winds, and my notebook on the table.

"I say, Davies," I said, "I'm awfully sorry I chaffed you about Fräulein Dollmann." (No answer.) "Didn't you see I couldn't help it?"

"I wish to Heaven we had never come in here," he said, in a hard voice; "it comes of landing *ever*." (I couldn't help smiling at this, but he wasn't looking at me.) "Here we are, given away, moved on, taken in charge, arranged for like Cook's tourists. I couldn't follow your game — too infernally deep for me, but—" That stung me.

"Look here," I said, "I did my best. It was you that muddled it. Why did you harp on ducks?"

"We could have got out of that. Why did you harp on everything idiotic—your letter, the Foreign Office, the *Kormoran*, the wreck, the—?"

"You're utterly unreasonable. Didn't you see what traps there were? I was driven the way I went. We started unprepared, and we're jolly well out of it."

Davies drove on blindly. "It was bad enough telling all about the channels and exploring—"

"Why, you agreed to that yourself!"

"I gave in to you. We can't explore any more now."

"There's the wreck, though."

"Oh, hang the wreck! It's all a blind, or he wouldn't have made so much of it. There are all these channels to be—"

"Oh, hang the channels! I know we wanted a free hand, but we've got to go to Norderney some time, and if Dollmann's away—"

"Why did you harp on Miss Dollmann?" said Davies.

We had worked round, through idle recrimination, to the real point of departure. I knew Davies was not himself, and would not return to himself till the heart of the matter was reached.

"Look here," I said, "you brought me out here to help you, because, as you say, I was clever, talked German, and—liked yachting (I couldn't resist adding this). But directly you really *want* me you turn round and go for me."

"Oh, I didn't mean all that, really," said Davies; "I'm sorry—I was worried."

"I know; but it's your own fault. You haven't been fair with me. There's a complication in this business that you've never talked about. I've never pressed you because I thought you would confide in me. You—"

"I know I haven't," said Davies.

"Well, you see the result. Our hand was forced. To have said nothing about Dollmann was folly—to have said he tried to wreck you was equal folly. The story we agreed on was the best and safest, and you told it splendidly. But for two reasons I had to harp on the daughter—one because your manner when they were mentioned was so confused as to imperil our whole position. Two, because your story, though the safest, was, at the best, suspicious. Even on your own showing Dollmann treated you badly—discourteously, say; though you pretended not to have seen it. You want a motive to neutralize that, and induce you to revisit him in a friendly way. I supplied it, or rather I only encouraged von Brüning to supply it."

"Why revisit him, after all?" said Davies.

"Oh, come—"

"But don't you see what a hideous fix you've put me in? How caddish I feel about it?"

I did see, and I felt a cad myself, as his full distress came home to me. But I felt, too, that, whosesoever the fault, we had drifted into a ridiculous situation, and were like characters in one of those tiresome plays where misunderstandings are manufactured and so carefully sustained that the audience are too bored to wait for the *dénouement*. You can do that on the stage; but we wanted our *dénouement*.

"I'm very sorry," I said, "but I wish you had told me all about it. Won't you now? Just the bare, matter-of-fact truth. I hate sentiment, and so do you."

"I find it very difficult to tell people things," said Davies, "things like this." I waited. "I did like her—very much." Our eyes met for a second, in which all was said that need be said, as between two of our phlegmatic race. "And she's—separate from him. That was the reason of all my indecisions," he hurried on. "I only told you half at Schlei. I know I ought to have been open, and asked your advice. But I let it slide. I've been hoping all along that we might find what we want and win the game without coming to close quarters again."

I no longer wondered at his devotion to the channel theory, since, built on conviction, it was thus doubly fortified.

"Yet you always knew what might happen," I said. "At Schlei you spoke of 'settling with' Dollmann."

"I know. When I thought of him I was mad. I made myself forget the other part."

"Which recurred at Brunsbüttel?" I thought of the news we had there.

"Yes."

"Davies, we must have no more secrets. I'm going to speak out. Are you sure you've not misunderstood her? You say—and I'm willing to assume it—that Dollmann's a traitor and a murderer."

"Oh, hang the murder part!" said Davies, impatiently. "What does *that* matter?"

"Well, traitor. Very good; but in that case I suspect his daughter. No! let me go on. She was useful, to say the least. She encouraged you— you've told me that—to make that passage with them."

"Stop, Carruthers," said Davies, firmly. "I know you mean kindly; but it's no use. I believe in her."

I thought for a moment.

"In that case," I said, "I've something to propose. When we get out of this place let's sail straight away to England." ("There, Commander von Brüning," I thought, "you never can say I neglected your advice.")

"No!" exclaimed Davies, starting up and facing me. "I'm hanged if we will. Think what's at stake. Think of that traitor—plotting with Germans. My God!"

"Very good," I said. "I'm with you for going on. But let's face facts. We *must* scotch Dollmann. We can't do so without hurting *her*."

"Can't we *possibly*?"

"Of course not; be sensible, man. Face that. Next point; it's absurd to hope that we need not revisit them—it's ten to one that we must, if we're to succeed. His attempt on you is the whole foundation of our suspicions. And we don't even know for certain who he *is* yet. We're committed, I know, to going straight to Norderney now; but even if we weren't, should we do any good by exploring and prying? It's very doubtful. We know we're watched, if not suspected, and that disposes of nine-tenths of our power. The channels? Yes, but is it likely they'll let us learn them by heart, if they're of such vital importance, even if we are thought to be *bona fide* yachtsmen? And, seriously, apart from their value in war, which I don't deny, are they at the root of this business? But we'll talk about that in a moment. The point now is, what shall we do if we meet the Dollmanns?"

Beads of sweat stood on Davies's brow. I felt like a torturer, but it could not be helped. "Tax him with having wrecked you? Our quest would be at an end! We must be friendly. You must tell the story you told to-day, and chance his believing it. If he does, so much the better; if he doesn't, he won't dare say so, and we still have chances. We gain time, and have a tremendous hold on him—*if* we're friendly." Davies winced. I gave another turn to the screw. "Friendly with them *both*, of course. You were before, you know; you liked her very much—you must seem to still."

"Oh, stop your infernal logic."

"Shall we chuck it and go to England?" I asked again, as an inquisitor might say, "Have you had enough?" No answer. I went on: "To make it easier, you *do* like her still." I had roused my victim at last.

"What the devil do you mean, Carruthers? That I'm to trade on my liking for her—on her innocence, to—good God! what *do* you mean?"

"No, no, not that. I'm not such a cad, or such a fool, or so ignorant of you. If she knows nothing of her father's character and likes you—and you like her—and you are what you are—oh Heavens! man, face it, realize it! But what I mean is this: is she, *can* she be, what you think? Imagine his position if we're right about him; the vilest creature on God's earth—a disgraceful past to have been driven to this—in the pay of Germany. I want to spare you misery." I was going to add: "And if you're on your guard, to increase our chances." But the utter futility of such suggestions silenced me. What a plan I had foreshadowed! An enticing plan and a fair one, too, as against such adversaries; turning this baffling cross-current to advantage as many a time we had worked eddies of an adverse tide in these difficult seas. But Davies was Davies, and there was an end of it; his faith and simplicity shamed me. And the pity of it, the cruelty of it, was that his very qualities were his last torture, raising to the acutest pitch the conflict between love and patriotism. Remember that the latter was his dominant life-motive, and that here and now was his chance—if you would gauge the bitterness of that conflict.

It was in its last throes now. His elbows were on the table, and his twitching hands pressed on his forehead. He took them away.

"Of course we must go on. It can't be helped, that's all."

"And you believe in her?"

"I'll remember what you've said. There may be some way out. And—I'd rather not talk about that any more. What about the wreck?"

Further argument was futile. Davies by an effort seemed to sweep the subject from his thoughts, and I did my best to do the same. At any rate the air was cleared—we were friends; and it only remained to grapple with the main problem in the light of the morning's interview.

Every word that I could recollect of that critical conversation I reviewed with Davies, who had imperfectly understood what he had not been directly concerned in; and, as I did so, I began to see with what cleverness each succeeding sentence of von Brüning's was designed to suit both of two contingencies. If we were innocent travellers, he was the genial host, communicative and helpful. If we were spies, his tactics had been equally applicable. He had outdone us in apparent candour, hiding nothing which he knew we would discover for ourselves, and contriving at the same time both to gain knowledge and control of our movements, and to convey us warnings, which would only be understood if we were guilty, that we were playing an idle and perilous game, and had better desist. But in one respect we had had the advantage, and that was in the version Davies had given of his stranding on the Hohenhörn. Inscrutable as our questioner was, he let it appear not only that the incident was new to him, but that he conjectured at its sinister significance. A little cross-examination on detail would have been fatal to Davies's version; but that was where our strength lay; he dared not cross-examine for fear of suggesting to Davies suspicions which he might never have felt. Indeed, I thought I detected that fear underlying his whole attitude towards us, and it strengthened a conviction which had been growing in me since Grimm's furtive midnight visit, that the secret of this coast was of so important and delicate a nature that rather than attract attention to it at all, overt action against intruders would be taken only in the last resort, and on irrefragable proofs of guilty intention.

Now for our clues. I had come away with two, each the germ of a distinct theory, and both obscured by the prevailing ambiguity. Now, however, as we thumbed the chart and I gave full rein to my fancy, one of them, the idea of Memmert, gained precious and vigour every moment. True, such information as we had about the French wreck and his own connection with it was placed most readily at our disposal by von Brüning; but I took it to be information calculated only to forestall suspicion, since he was aware that we already associated him with Dollmann, possibly also with Grimm, and it was only likely that in the ordinary course we should learn that the trio were jointly concerned in Memmert. So much for the facts; as for the construction he wished us to put on them, I felt sure it was absolutely false. He wished to give us the impression that the buried treasure itself was at the root of any mystery we might have scented. I do not know if the reader fully appreciated that astute suggestion—the hint that secrecy as to results was necessary owing both to the great sum at stake and the flaw in the title, which he had been careful to inform us had passed through British hands. What he meant to imply was, "Don't be surprised if you have midnight visitors; Englishmen prowling along this coast are suspected of being Lloyd's agents." An ingenious insinuation, which, at the time it was made, had caused me to contemplate a new and much more commonplace solution of our enigma than had ever occurred to us; but it was only a passing doubt, and I dismissed it altogether now.

The fact was, it either explained everything or nothing. As long as we held to our fundamental assumption—that Davies had been decoyed into a death-trap in September—it explained nothing. It was too fantastic to suppose that the exigencies of a commercial speculation would lead to such extremities as that. We were not in the South Sea Islands; nor were we the puppets of a romance. We were in Europe, dealing not only with a Dollmann, but with an officer of the German Imperial Navy, who would scarcely be connected with a commercial enterprise which could conceivably be reduced to forwarding its objects in such a fashion. It was shocking enough to find him in relations with such a scoundrel at all, but it was explicable if the motive were imperial—not so if it were financial. No; to accept the suggestion we must declare the whole quest a mare's nest from beginning to end; the attempt on Davies a delusion of his own fancy, the whole structure we had built on it, baseless.

"Well," I can hear the reader saying, "why not? You, at any rate, were always a little sceptical."

Granted; yet I can truthfully say I scarcely faltered for a moment. Much had happened since Schlei Fiord. I had seen the mechanism of the death-trap; I had lived with Davies for a stormy fortnight, every hour of which had increased my reliance on his seamanship, and also, therefore, on his account of an event which depended largely for its correct interpretation on a balanced nautical judgement. Finally, I had been unconsciously realizing, and knew from his mouth to-day, that he had exercised and acted on that judgement in the teeth of personal considerations, which his loyal nature made overwhelming in their force.

What, then, was the meaning of Memmert? At the outset it riveted my attention on the Ems estuary, whose mouth it adjoins. We had always rather neglected the Ems in our calculations; with some excuse, too, for at first sight its importance bears no proportion to that of the three greater estuaries. The latter bear vessels of the largest tonnage and deepest draught to the very quays of Hamburg, Bremerhaven, and the naval dockyard of Wilhelmshaven; while two of them, the Elbe and the Weser, are commerce carriers on the vastest scale for the whole empire. The Ems, on the other hand, only serves towns of the second class. A glance at the chart explains this. You see a most imposing estuary on a grander scale than any of the other three taken singly, with a length of thirty miles and a frontage on the North Sea of ten miles, or one-seventieth, roughly, of the whole seaboard; encumbered by outlying shoals, and blocked in the centre by the island of Borkum, but presenting two fine deep-water channels to the incoming vessel. These roll superbly through enormous sheets of sand, unite and approach the mainland in one stately stream three miles in breadth. But then comes a sad falling off. The navigable fairway shoals and shrinks, middle grounds obstruct it, and shelving foreshores persistently deny it that easy access to the land that alone can create great seaboard cities. All the ports of the Ems are tidal; the harbour of Delfzyl, on the Dutch side, dries at low water, and Emden, the principal German port, can only be reached by a lock and a mile of canal.

But this depreciation is only relative. Judged on its merits, and not by the standard of the Elbe, it is a very important river. Emden is a flourishing and growing port. For shallow craft the stream is navigable far into the interior, where, aided by tributaries and allied canals (notably the connection with the Rhine at Dortmund, then approaching completion), it taps the resources of a great area. Strategically there was still less reason for underrating it. It is one of the great maritime gates of Germany; and it is the westernmost gate, the nearest to Great Britain and France, contiguous to Holland. Its great forked delta presents two yawning breaches in that singular rampart of islets and shoals which masks the German seaboard—a seaboard itself so short in proportion to the empire's bulk, that, as Davies used to say, "every inch of it must be important." Warships could force these breaches, and so threaten the mainland at one of its few vulnerable points. Quay accommodation is no object to such visitors; intricate navigation no deterrent. Even the heaviest battleships could approach within striking distance of the land, while cruisers and military transports could penetrate to the level of Emden itself. Emden, as Davies had often pointed out, is connected by canal with Wilhelmshaven on the Jade, a strategic canal, designed to carry gunboats as well as merchandise.

Now Memmert was part of the outer rampart; its tapering sickle of sand directly commanded the eastern breach; it *must* be connected with the defence of this breach. No more admirable base could be imagined; self-contained and isolated, yet sheltered, accessible—better than Juist and Borkum. And supposing it were desired to shroud the nature of the work in absolute secrecy, what a pretext lay to hand in the wreck and its buried bullion, which lay in the offing opposite the fairway!

On Memmert was the depot for the salvage operations. Salvage work, with its dredging and diving, offered precisely the disguise that was needed. It was submarine, and so are some of the most important defences of ports, mines, and dirigible torpedoes. All the details of the story were suggestive: the "small local company"; the "engineer from Bremen" (who, I wondered, was he?); the few shares held by von Brüning, enough to explain his visits; the stores and gear coming from Wilhelmshaven, a naval dockyard.

Try as I would I could not stir Davies's imagination as mine was stirred. He was bent on only seeing the objections, which, of course, were numerous enough. Could secrecy be ensured under pretext of salving a wreck? It must be a secret shared by many—divers, crews of tugs, employees of all sorts. I answered that trade secrets are often preserved under no less difficult conditions, and why not imperial secrets?

"Why the Ems and not the Elbe?" he asked.

"Perhaps," I replied, "the Elbe, too, holds similar mysteries." Neuerk Island might, for all we know, be another Memmert; when cruising in that region we had had no eyes for such things, absorbed in a preconceived theory of our own. Besides, we must not take ourselves too seriously. We were amateurs, not experts in coast defence, and on such vague grounds to fastidiously reject a clue which went so far as this one was to quarrel with our luck. There was a disheartening corollary to this latter argument that in my new-born zeal I shut my eyes to. As amateurs, were we capable of using our clue and gaining exact knowledge of the defences in question? Davies, I knew, felt this strongly, and I think it accounted for his lukewarm view of Memmert more than he was aware. He clung more obstinately than ever to his "channel theory," conscious that it offered the one sort of opportunity of which with his peculiar gifts he was able to take advantage. He admitted, however, that it was under a cloud at present, for if knowledge of the coastwise navigation were a crime in itself we should scarcely be sitting here now. "It's something to *do* with it, anyhow!" he persisted.

# 18

### Imperial Escort

MEMMERT gripped me, then, to the exclusion of a rival notion which had given me no little perplexity during the conversation with von Brüning. His reiterated advice that we should lose no time in picking up our anchor and chain had ended by giving me the idea that he was anxious to get us away from Bensersiel and the mainland. At first I had taken the advice partly as a test of our veracity (as I gave the reader to understand), and partly as an indirect method of lulling any suspicions which Grimm's midnight visit may have caused. Then it struck me that this might be over-subtlety on my part, and the idea recurred when the question of our future plans cropped up, and hampered me in deciding on a course. It returned again when von Brüning offered to tow us out in the evening. It was in my mind when I questioned him as to his business ashore, for it occurred to me that perhaps his landing here was not solely due to a wish to inspect the crew of the *Dulcibella*. Then came his perfectly frank explanation (with its sinister *double entente* for us), coupled with an invitation to me to accompany him to Esens. But, on the principle of *"timeo Danaos"* etc., I instantly smelt a ruse, not that I dreamt that I was to be decoyed into captivity; but if there was anything here which we two might discover in the few hours left to us, it was an ingenious plan to remove the most observant of the two till the hour of departure.

Davies scorned them, and I had felt only a faint curiosity in these insignificant hamlets, influenced, I am afraid, chiefly by a hankering after *terra firma* which the pitiless rigour of his training had been unable to cure.

But it was imprudent to neglect the slightest chance. It was three o'clock, and I think both our brains were beginning to be addled with thinking in close confinement. I suggested that we should finish our council of war in the open, and we both donned oilskins and turned out. The sky had hardened and banked into an even canopy of lead, and the wind drove before it a fine cold rain. You could hear the murmur of the rising flood on the sands outside, but the harbour was high above it still, and the *Dulcibella* and the other boats squatted low in a bed of black slime. Native interest seemed to be at last assuaged, for not a soul was visible on the bank (I cannot call it a quay); but the top of a black sou'wester with a feather of smoke curling round it showed above the forehatch of the *Kormoran*.

"I wish I could get a look at your cargo, my friend," I thought to myself.

We gazed at Bensersiel in silence.

"There can't be anything *here*?" I said.

"What *can* there be?" said Davies.

"What about that dyke?" I said, with a sudden inspiration.

From the bank we could see all along the coast-line, which is dyked continuously, as I have already said. The dyke was here a substantial brick-faced embankment, very similar, though on a smaller scale, to that which had bordered the Elbe near Cuxhaven, and over whose summit we had seen the snouts of guns.

"I say, Davies," I said, "do you think this coast could be invaded? Along here, I mean, behind these islands?"

Davies shook his head. "I've thought of that," he said. "There's nothing in it. It's just the very last place on earth where a landing would be possible. No transport could get nearer than where the *Blitz* is lying, four miles out."

"Well, you say every inch of this coast is important?"

"Yes, but it's the *water* I mean."

"Well, I want to see that dyke. Let's walk along it."

My mushroom theory died directly I set foot on it. It was the most innocent structure in the world—like a thousand others in Essex and Holland—topped by a narrow path, where we walked in single file with arms akimbo to keep our balance in the gusts of wind. Below us lay the sands on one side and rank fens on the other, interspersed with squares of pasture ringed in with ditches. After half a mile we dropped down and came back by a short circuit inland, following a mazy path—which was mostly right angles and minute plank bridges, till we came to the Esens road. We crossed this and soon after found our way barred by the stream I spoke of. This involved a *détour* to the bridge in the village, and a stealthy avoidance of the post-office, for dread of its garrulous occupant. Then we followed the dyke in the other direction, and ended by a circuit over the sands, which were fast being covered by the tide, and so back to the yacht.

Nobody appeared to have taken the slightest notice of our movements.

As we walked we had tackled the last question, "What are we to do?" and found very little to say on it. We were to leave to-night (unless the Esens police appeared on the scene), and were committed to sailing direct to Norderney, as the only alternative to duck shooting under the espionage of a "trustworthy" nominee of von Brüning's. Beyond that— vagueness and difficulty of every sort.

At Norderney I should be fettered by my letter. If it seemed to have been opened and it ordered my return, I was limited to a week, or must risk suspicion by staying. Dollmann was away (according to von Brüning), "would probably be back soon"; but how soon? Beyond Norderney lay Memmert. How to probe its secret? The ardour it had roused in me was giving way to a mortifying sense of impotence. The sight of the *Kormoran*, with her crew preparing for sea, was a pointed comment on my diplomacy, and most of all on my ridiculous survey of the dykes. When all was said and done we were *protégés* of von Brüning, and dogged by Grimm. Was it likely they would let us succeed?

The tide was swirling into the harbour in whorls of chocolate froth, and as it rose all Bensersiel, dominated as before by Herr Schenkel, straggled down to the quay to watch the movements of shipping during the transient but momentous hour when the mud-hole was a seaport. The captain's steam-cutter was already afloat, and her sailors busy with sidelights and engines. When it became known that we, too, were to sail, and under such distinguished escort, the excitement intensified.

Again our friend of the customs was spreading out papers to sign, while a throng of helpful Frisians, headed by the twin giants of the post-boat, thronged our decks and made us ready for sea in their own confused fashion. Again we were carried up to the inn and overwhelmed with advice, and warnings, and farewell toasts. Then back again to find the *Dulcibella* afloat, and von Brüning just arrived, cursing the weather and the mud, chaffing Davies, genial and *débonnaire* as ever.

"Stow that mainsail, you won't want it," he said. "I'll tow you right out to Spiekeroog. It's your only anchorage for the night in this wind— under the island, near the *Blitz*, and that would mean a dead beat for you in the dark."

The fact was so true, and the offer so timely, that Davies's faint protests were swept aside in a torrent of ridicule.

"And now I think of it," the commander ended, "I'll make the trip with you, if I may. It'll be pleasanter and drier."

We all three boarded the *Dulcibella*, and then the end came. Our tow-rope was attached, and at half-past six the little launch jumped into the collar, and amidst a demonstration that could not have been more hearty if we had been ambassadors on a visit to a friendly power, we sidled out through the jetties.

It took us more than an hour to cover the five miles to Spiekeroog, for the *Dulcibella* was a heavy load in the stiff head wind, and Davies, though he said nothing, showed undisguised distrust of our tug's capacities. He at once left the helm to me and flung himself on the gear, not resting till every rope was ready to hand, the mainsail reefed, the binnacle lighted, and all ready for setting sail or anchoring at a moment's notice. Our guest watched these precautions with infinite amusement. He was in the highest and most mischievous humour, raining banter on Davies and mock sympathy on me, laughing at our huge compass, heaving the lead himself, startling us with imaginary soundings, and doubting if his men were sober. I offered entertainment and warmth below, but he declined on the ground that Davies would be tempted to cut the tow-rope and makes us pass the night on a safe sandbank. Davies took the raillery unmoved. His work done, he took the tiller and sat bareheaded, intent on the launch, the course, the details, and chances of the present. I brought up cigars and we settled ourselves facing him, our backs to the wind and spray. And so we made the rest of the passage, von Brüning cuddled against me and the cabin-hatch, alternately shouting a jest to Davies and talking to me in a light and charming vein, with just that shade of patronage that the disparity in our ages warranted, about my time in Germany, places, people, and books I knew, and about life, especially young men's life, in England, a country he had never visited, but hoped to; I responding as well as I could, striving to meet his mood, acquit myself like a man, draw zest instead of humiliation from the irony of our position, but scarcely able to make headway against a numbing sense of defeat and incapacity. A queer thought was haunting me, too, that such skill and judgement as I possessed was slipping from me as we left the land and faced again the rigours of this exacting sea. Davies, I very well knew, was under exactly the opposite spell—a spell which even the reproach of the tow-rope could not annul. His face, in the glow of the binnacle, was beginning to wear that same look of contentment and resolve that I had seen on it that night we had sailed to Kiel from Schlei Fiord. Heaven knows he had more cause for worry than I—a casual comrade in an adventure which was peculiarly his, which meant everything on earth to him; but there he was, washing away perplexity in the salt wind, drawing counsel and confidence from the unfailing source of all his inspirations— the sea.

"Looks happy, doesn't he?" said the captain once. I grunted that he did, ashamed to find how irritated the remark made me.

"You'll remember what I said," he added in my ear.

"Yes," I said. "But I should like to see her. What *is* she like?"

"Dangerous." I could well believe it.

The hull of the *Blitz* loomed up, and a minute later our kedge was splashing overboard and the launch was backing alongside.

"Good-night, gentlemen," said our passenger. "You're safe enough here, and you can run across in ten minutes in the morning and pick up your anchor, if it's there still. Then you've a fair wind west—to England if you like. If you decide to stay a little longer in these parts, and I'm in reach, count on me to help you, to sport or anything else."

We thanked him, shook hands, and he was gone.

"He's a thundering good chap, anyhow," said Davies; and I heartily agreed.

The narrow vigilant life began again at once. We were "safe enough" in a sense, but a warp and a twenty-pound anchor were poor security if the wind backed or increased. Plans for contingencies had to be made, and deck-watches kept till midnight, when the weather seemed to improve, and stars appeared. The glass was rising, so we turned in and slept under the very wing, so to speak, of the Imperial Government.

"Davies," I said, when we were settled in our bunks, "it's only a day's sail to Norderney, isn't it?"

"With a fair wind, less, if we go outside the islands direct."

"Well, it's settled that we do that to-morrow?"

"I suppose so. We've got to get the anchor first. Good-night."

# 19

### The Rubicon

IT was a cold, vaporous dawn, the glass rising, and the wind fallen to a light air still from the north-east. Our creased and sodden sails scarcely answered to it as we crept across the oily swell to Langeoog. "Fogs and calms," Davies prophesied. The *Blitz* was astir when we passed her, and soon after steamed out to sea. Once over the bar, she turned westward and was lost to view in the haze. I should be sorry to have to explain how we found that tiny anchor-buoy, on the expressionless waste of grey. I only know that I hove the lead incessantly while Davies conned, till at last he was grabbing overside with the boat-hook, and there was the buoy on deck. The cable was soon following it, and finally the rusty monster himself, more loathsome than usual, after his long sojourn in the slime.

"That's all right," said Davies. "Now we can go anywhere."

"Well, it's Norderney, isn't it? We've settled that."

"Yes, I suppose we have. I was wondering whether it wouldn't be shortest to go inside the Langeoog after all."

"Surely not," I urged. "The tide's ebbing now, and the light's bad; it's new ground, with a 'watershed' to cross, and we're safe to get aground."

"All right—outside. Ready about." We swung lazily round and headed for the open sea. I record the fact, but in truth Davies might have taken me where he liked, for no land was visible, only a couple of ghostly booms.

"It seems a pity to miss over that channel," said Davies with a sigh; "just when the *Kormoran* can't watch us." (We had not seen her at all this morning.)

I set myself to the lead again, averse to reopening a barren argument. Grimm had done his work for the present, I felt certain, and was on his way by the shortest road to Norderney and Memmert.

We were soon outside and heading west, our boom squared away and the island sand-dunes just apparent under our lee. Then the breeze died to the merest draught, and left us rolling inert in a long swell. Consumed with impatience to get on I saw fatality in this failure of wind, after a fortnight of unprofitable meanderings, when we had generally had too much of it, and always enough for our purpose. I tried to read below, but the vile squirting of the centre-board drove me up.

"Can't we go any faster?" I burst out once. I felt that there ought to be a pyramid of gauzy canvas aloft, spinnakers, flying jibs, and what not.

"I don't go in for speed," said Davies, shortly. He loyally did his best to "shove her" along, but puffs and calms were the rule all day, and it was only by towing in the dinghy for two hours in the afternoon that we covered the length of Langeoog, and crept before dark to an anchorage behind Baltrum, its slug-shaped neighbour on the west. Strictly, I believe, we should have kept the sea all night; but I had not the grit to suggest that course, and Davies was only too glad of an excuse for threading the shoals of the Accumer Ee on a rising tide. The atmosphere had been slowly clearing as the day wore on; but we had scarcely anchored ten minutes before a blanket of white fog, rolling in from sea-ward, swallowed us up. Davies was already afield in the dinghy, and I had to guide him back with a foghorn, whose music roused hosts of sea birds from the surrounding flats, and brought them wheeling and com-plaining round us, a weird invisible chorus to my mournful solo.

The fog hung heavy still at daybreak on the 20th, but dispersed par-tially under a catspaw from the south about eight o'clock, in time for us to traverse the boomed channel behind Baltrum, before the tide left the watershed.

"We shan't get far to-day," said Davies, with philosophy. "And this sort of thing may go on for any time. It's a regular autumn anti-cyclone—glass thirty point five and steady. That gale was the last of a stormy equinox."

We took the inside route as a matter of course to-day. It was now the shortest to Norderney harbour, and scarcely less intricate than the Wichter Ee, which appeared to be almost totally blocked by banks, and is, in fact, the most impassable of all these outlets to the North Sea. But, as I say, this sort of navigation, always puzzling to me, was utterly be-wildering in hazy weather. Any attempt at orientation made me giddy. So I slaved at the lead, varying my labour with a fierce bout of kedge-work when we grounded somewhere. I had two rests before two o'clock, one of an hour, when we ran into a patch of windless fog; an-other of a few moments, when Davies said, "There's Norderney!" and I saw, surmounting a long slope of weedy sand, still wet with the re-ceding sea, a cluster of sandhills exactly like a hundred others I had seen of late, but fraught with a new and unique interest.

The usual formula, "What have you got now?" checked my reverie, and "Helm's a-lee," ended it for the time. We tacked on (for the wind had headed us) in very shoal water.

Suddenly Davies said: "Is that a boat ahead?"

"Do you mean that galliot?" I asked. I could plainly distinguish one of those familiar craft about half a mile away, just within the limit of vision.

"The *Kormoran*, do you think?" I added. Davies said nothing, but grew inattentive to his work. "Barely four," from me passed unnoticed, and we touched once, but swung off under some play of the current. Then came abruptly, "Stand by the anchor. Let go," and we brought up in mid-stream of the narrow creek we were following. I triced up the main-tack, and stowed the head-sails unaided. When I had done Davies was still gazing to windward through his binoculars, and, to my astonishment, I noticed that his hands were trembling violently. I had never seen this happen before, even at moments when a false turn of the wrist meant death on a surf-battered bank.

"What is it?" I asked; "are you cold?"

"That little boat," he said. I gazed to windward, too, and now saw a scrap of white in the distance, in sharp relief.

"Small standing lug and jib; it's her, right enough," said Davies to himself, in a sort of nervous stammer.

"Who? What?"

"*Medusa's* dinghy."

He handed, or rather pushed, me the glasses, still gazing.

"Dollmann?" I exclaimed.

"No, it's *hers*—the one she always sails. She's come to meet m——, us."

Through the glasses the white scrap became a graceful little sail, squared away for the light following breeze. An angle of the creek hid the hull, then it glided into view. Someone was sitting aft steering, man or woman I could not say, for the sail hid most of the figure. For full two minutes—two long, pregnant minutes—we watched it in silence. The damp air was fogging the lenses, but I kept them to my eyes; for I did not want to look at Davies. At last I heard him draw a deep breath, straighten himself up, and give one of his characteristic "h'ms." Then he turned briskly aft, cast off the dinghy's painter, and pulled her up alongside.

"You come too," he said, jumping in, and fixing the rowlocks. (His hands were steady again.) I laughed, and shoved the dinghy off.

"I'd rather you did," he said, defiantly.

"I'd rather stay. I'll tidy up, and put the kettle on." Davies had taken a half stroke, but paused.

"She oughtn't to come aboard," he said.

"She might like to," I suggested. "Chilly day, long way from home, common courtesy—"

"Carruthers," said Davies, "if she comes aboard, please remember that she's outside this business. There are no clues to be got from *her*."

A little lecture which would have nettled me more if I had not been exultantly telling myself that, once and for all, for good or ill, the Rubicon was passed.

"It's your affair this time," I said; "run it as you please."

He sculled away with vigorous strokes. "Just as he is," I thought to myself: bare head, beaded with fog-dew, ancient oilskin coat (only one button); grey jersey; grey woollen trousers (like a deep-sea fisherman's) stuffed into long boots. A vision of his antitype, the Cowes Philanderer, crossed me for a second. As to his face—well, I could only judge by it, and marvel, that he was gripping his dilemma by either horn, as firmly as he gripped his sculls.

I watched the two boats converging. They would meet in the natural course about three hundred yards away, but a hitch occurred. First, the sail-boat checked and slewed; "aground," I concluded. The row-boat leapt forward still; then checked, too. From both a great splashing of sculls floated across the still air, then silence. The summit of the watershed, a physical Rubicon, prosaic and slimy, had still to be crossed, it seemed. But it could be evaded. Both boats headed for the northern side of the creek: two figures were out on the brink, hauling on two painters. Then Davies was striding over the sand, and a girl—I could see her now—was coming to meet him. And then I thought it was time to go below and tidy up.

Nothing on earth could have made the *Dulcibella*'s saloon a worthy reception-room for a lady. I could only use hurried efforts to make it look its best by plying a bunch of cotton-waste and a floor-brush; by pitching into racks and lockers the litter of pipes, charts, oddments of apparel, and so on, that had a way of collecting afresh, however recently we had tidied up; by neatly arranging our demoralized library, and by lighting the stove and veiling the table under a clean white cloth.

I suppose about twenty minutes had elapsed, and I was scrubbing fruitlessly at the smoky patch on the ceiling, when I heard the sound of oars and voices outside. I threw the cotton-waste into the fo'c'sle, made an onslaught of my hands, and then mounted the companion ladder. Our own dinghy was just rounding up alongside, Davies sculling in the bows, facing him in the stern a young girl in a grey tam-o'-shanter, loose waterproof jacket and dark serge skirt, the latter, to be frigidly accurate, disclosing a pair of workman-like rubber boots which, *mutatis mutandis*, were very like those Davies was wearing. Her hair, like his, was spangled with moisture, and her rose-brown skin struck a note of delicious colour against the sullen Stygian background.

"There he is," said Davies. Never did his "meiner Freund, Carruthers," sound so pleasantly in my ears; never so discordantly the "Fräulein Dollmann" that followed it. Every syllable of the four was a lie. Two honest English eyes were looking up into mine; an honest English hand—is this insular nonsense? Perhaps so, but I stick to it—a brown, firm hand—no, not so very small, my sentimental reader—was clasping mine. Of course I had strong reasons, apart from the racial instinct, for thinking her to be English, but I believe that if I had had none at all I should at any rate have congratulated Germany on a clever bit of plagiarism. By her voice, when she spoke, I knew that she must have talked German habitually from childhood; diction and accent were faultless, at least to my English ear; but the native constitutional ring was wanting.

She came on board. There was a hollow discussion first about time and weather, but it ended as we all in our hearts wished it to end. None of us uttered our real scruples. Mine, indeed, were too new and rudimentary to be worth uttering, so I said commonsense things about tea and warmth; but I began to think about my compact with Davies.

"Just for a few minutes, then," she said.

I held out my hand and swung her up. She gazed round the deck and rigging with profound interest—a breathless, hungry interest—touching to see.

"You've seen her before, haven't you?" I said.

"I've not been on board before," she answered.

This struck me in passing as odd; but then I had only too few details from Davies about his days at Norderney in September.

"Of course, *that* is what puzzled me," she exclaimed, suddenly, pointing to the mizzen. "I knew there was something different."

Davies had belayed the painter, and now had to explain the origin of the mizzen. This was a cumbrous process, and his hearer's attention soon wandered from the subject and became centred in him—his was already more than half in her—and the result was a golden opportunity for the discerning onlooker. I was very brief, but I made the most of it; buried deep a few regrets, did a little heartfelt penance, told myself I had been a cynical fool not to have foreseen this, and faced the new situation with a sinking heart; I am not ashamed to admit that, for I was fond of Davies, and I was keen about the quest.

She had never been a guilty agent in that attempt on Davies. Had she been an unconscious tool or only an unwilling one? If the latter, did she know the secret we were seeking? In the last degree unlikely, I decided. But, true to the compact, whose importance I now fully appreciated, I flung aside my diplomatic weapons, recoiling, as strongly, or nearly as strongly, let us say, from any effort direct or indirect to gain information from such a source. It was not our fault if by her own conversation and behaviour she gave us some idea of how matters stood. Davies already knew more than I did.

We spent a few minutes on deck while she asked eager questions about our build and gear and seaworthiness, with a quaint mixture of professional acumen and personal curiosity.

"How *did* you manage alone that day?" she asked Davies, suddenly.

"Oh, it was quite safe," was the reply. "But it's much better to have a friend."

She looked at me; and—well, I would have died for Davies there and then.

"Father said you would be safe," she remarked, with decision—a slight excess of decision, I thought. And at that turned to some rope or block and pursued her questioning. She found the compass impressive, and the trappings of that hateful centre-board had a peculiar fascination for her. Was this the way we did it in England? was her constant query.

Yet, in spite of a superficial freedom, we were all shy and constrained. The descent below was a welcome diversion, for we should have been less than human if we had not extracted some spontaneous fun from the humours of the saloon. I went down first to see about the tea, leaving them struggling for mutual comprehension over the theory of an English lifeboat. They soon followed, and I can see her now stooping in at the doorway, treading delicately, like a kitten, past the obstructive centre-board to a place on the starboard sofa, then taking in her surroundings with a timid rapture that broke into delight at all the primitive arrangements and dingy amenities of our den. She explored the cavernous recesses of the Rippingille, fingered the duck-guns and the miscellany in the racks, and peeped into the fo'c'sle with dainty awe. Everything was a source of merriment, from our cramped attitudes to the painful deficiency of spoons and the "yachtiness" (there is no other word to describe it) of the bread, which had been bought at Bensersiel, and had suffered from incarceration and the climate. This fact came out, and led to some questions, while we waited for the water to boil, about the gale and our visit there. The topic, a pregnant one for us, appeared to have no special significance to her. At the mention of von Brüning she showed no emotion of any sort; on the contrary, she went out of her way, from an innocent motive that anyone could have guessed, to show that she could talk about him with dispassionate detachment.

"He came to see us when you were here last, didn't he?" she said to Davies. "He often comes. He goes with father to Memmert sometimes. You know about Memmert? They are diving for money out of an old wreck."

Yes, we had heard about it.

"Of course you have. Father is a director of the company, and Commander von Brüning takes great interest in it; they took me down in a diving-bell once."

I murmured, "Indeed!" and Davies sawed laboriously at the bread. She must have misconstrued our sheepish silence, for she stopped and drew herself up with just a touch of momentary hauteur, utterly lost on Davies. I could have laughed aloud at this transient little comedy of errors.

"Did you see any gold?" said Davies at last, with husky solemnity. Something had to be said or we should defeat our own end; but I let him say it. He had not my faith in Memmert.

"No, only mud and timber—oh, I forgot—"

"You mustn't betray the company's secrets," I said, laughing; "Commander von Brüning wouldn't tell us a word about the gold." ("There's self-denial!" I said to myself.)

"Oh, I don't think it matters much," she answered, laughing too. "You are only visitors."

"That's all," I remarked, demurely. "Just passing travellers."

"You will stop at Norderney?" she said, with naïve anxiety. "Herr Davies said—"

I looked at Davies; it was his affair. Fair and square came his answer, in blunt dog-German.

"Yes, of course, we shall. I should like to see your father again."

Up to this moment I had been doubtful of his final decision; for ever since our explanation at Bensersiel I had had the feeling that I was holding his nose to a very cruel grindstone. This straight word, clear and direct, beyond anything I had hoped for, brought me to my senses and showed me that his mind had been working far in advance of mine; and more, shaping a double purpose that I had never dreamt of.

"My father?" said Fräulein Dollmann; "yes, I am sure he will be very glad to see you."

There was no conviction in her tone, and her eyes were distant and troubled.

"He's not at home now, is he?" I asked.

"How did you know?" (a little maidenly confusion). "Oh, Commander von Brüning."

I might have added that it had been clear as daylight all along that this visit was in the nature of an escapade of which her father might not approve. I tried to say "I won't tell," without words, and may have succeeded.

"I told Mr. Davies when we first met," she went on. "I expect him back very soon—to-morrow in fact; he wrote from Amsterdam. He left me at Hamburg and has been away since. Of course, he will not know your yacht is back again. I think he expected Mr. Davies would stay in the Baltic, as the season was so late. But—but I am sure he will be glad to see you."

"Is the *Medusa* in harbour?" said Davies.

"Yes; but we are not living on her now. We are at our villa in the Schwannallée—my stepmother and I, that is." She added some details, and Davies gravely pencilled down the address on a leaf of the log-book; a formality which somehow seemed to regularize the present position.

"We shall be at Norderney to-morrow," he said.

Meanwhile the kettle was boiling merrily, and I made the tea—cocoa, I should say, for the menu was changed in deference to our visitor's tastes. "This *is* fun!" she said. And by common consent we abandoned ourselves, three youthful, hungry mariners, to the enjoyment of this impromptu picnic. Such a chance might never occur again—*carpamus diem.*

But the banquet was never celebrated. As at Belshazzar's feast, there was a writing on the wall; no supernatural inscription, but just a printed name; an English surname with title and initials, in cheap gilt lettering on the back of an old book; a silent, sneering witness of our snug party. The catastrophe came and passed so suddenly that at the time I had scarcely even an inkling of what caused it; but I know now that this is how it happened. Our visitor was sitting at the forward end of the starboard sofa, close to the bulkhead. Davies and I were opposite her. Across the bulkhead, on a level with our heads, ran the bookshelf, whose contents, remember, I had carefully straightened only half an hour ago, little dreaming of the consequence. Some trifle, probably the logbook which Davies had reached down from the shelf, called her attention to the rest of our library. While busied with the cocoa I heard her spelling out some titles, fingering leaves, and twitting Davies with the little care he took of his books. Suddenly there was a silence which made me look up, to see a startled and pitiful change in her. She was staring at Davies with wide eyes and parted lips, a burning flush mounting on her forehead, and such an expression on her face as a sleep-walker might wear, who wakes in fear he knows not where.

Half her mind was far away, labouring to construe some hideous dream of the past; half was in the present, cringing before some sickening reality. She remained so for perhaps ten seconds, and then—plucky girl that she was—she mastered herself, looked deliberately round and up with a circular glance, strangely in the manner of Davies himself, and spoke. How late it was, she must be going—her boat was not safe. At the same time she rose to go, or rather slid herself along the sofa, for rising was impossible. We sat like mannerless louts, in blank amazement. Davies at the outset had said, "What's the matter?" in plain English, and then relapsed into stupefaction. I recovered myself the first, and protested in some awkward fashion about the cocoa, the time, the absence of fog. In trying to answer, her self-possession broke down, poor child, and her retreat became a blind flight, like that of a wounded animal, while every sordid circumstance seemed to accentuate her panic.

She tilted the corner of the table in leaving the sofa and spilt cocoa over her skirt; she knocked her head with painful force against the sharp lintel of the doorway, and stumbled on the steps of the ladder. I was close behind, but when I reached the deck she was already on the counter hauling up the dinghy. She had even jumped in and laid hands on the sculls before any check came in her precipitate movements. Now there occurred to her the patent fact that the dinghy was ours, and that someone must accompany her to bring it back.

"Davies will row you over," I said.

"Oh no, thank you," she stammered. "If you will be so kind, Herr Carruthers. It is your turn. No, I mean, I want—"

"Go on," said Davies to me in English.

I stepped into the dinghy and motioned to take the sculls from her. She seemed not to see me, and pushed off while Davies handed down her jacket, which she had left in the cabin. Neither of us tried to better the situation by conventional apologies. It was left to her, at the last moment, to make a show of excusing herself, an attempt so brave and yet so wretchedly lame that I tingled all over with hot shame. She only made matters worse, and Davies interrupted her.

"*Auf Wiedersehen*," he said, simply.

She shook her head, did not even offer her hand, and pulled away; Davies turned sharp round and went below.

There was now no muddy Rubicon to obstruct us, for the tide had risen a good deal, and the sands were covering. I offered again to take the sculls, but she took no notice and rowed on, so that I was a silent passenger on the stern seat till we reached her boat, a spruce little yacht's gig, built to the native model, with a spoon-bow and tiny leeboards. It was already afloat, but riding quite safely to a rope and a little grapnel, which she proceeded to haul in.

"It was quite safe after all, you see," I said.

"Yes, but I could not stay. Herr Carruthers, I want to say something to you." (I knew it was coming; von Brüning's warning over again.) "I made a mistake just now; it is no use your calling on us to-morrow."

"Why not?"

"You will not see my father."

"I thought you said he was coming back?"

"Yes, by the morning steamer; but he will be very busy."

"We can wait. We have several days to spare, and we have to call for letters anyhow."

"You must not delay on our account. The weather is very fine at last. It would be a pity to lose a chance of a smooth voyage to England. The season—"

"We have no fixed plans. Davies wants to get some shooting."

"My father will be much occupied."

"We can see *you*."

I insisted on being obtuse, for though this fencing with an unstrung girl was hateful work, the quest was at stake. We were going to Norderney, come what might, and sooner or later we must see

Dollmann. It was no use promising not to. I had given no pledge to von Brüning, and I would give none to her. The only alternative was to violate the compact (which the present fiasco had surely weakened), speak out, and try and make an ally of her. Against her own father? I shrank from the responsibility and counted the cost of failure—certain failure, to judge by her conduct. She began to hoist her lugsail in a dazed, shiftless fashion, while our two boats drifted slowly to leeward.

"Father might not like it," she said, so low and from such tremulous lips that I scarcely caught her words. "He does not like foreigners much. I am afraid . . . he did not want to see Herr Davies again."

"But I thought—"

"It was wrong of me to come aboard—I suddenly remembered; but I could not tell Herr Davies."

"I see," I answered. "I will tell him."

"Yes, that he must not come near us."

"He will understand. I know he will be very sorry, but," I added, firmly, "you can trust him implicitly to do the right thing." And how I prayed that this would content her! Thank Heaven, it did.

"Yes," she said, "I am afraid I did not say good-bye to him. You will do so?" She gave me her hand.

"One thing more," I added, holding it, "nothing had better be said about this meeting?"

"No, no, nothing. It must never be known."

I let go the gig's gunwale and watched her tighten her sheet and make a tack or two to windward. Then I rowed back to the *Dulcibella* as hard as I could.

# 20

### The Little Drab Book

I FOUND Davies at the cabin table, surrounded with a litter of books. The shelf was empty, and its contents were tossed about among the cups and on the floor. We both spoke together.

"Well, what was it?"

"Well, what did she say?"

I gave way, and told my story briefly. He listened in silence, drumming on the table with a book which he held.

"It's not good-bye," he said. "But I don't wonder; look here!" and he held out to me a small volume, whose appearance was quite familiar to me, if its contents were less so. As I noted in an early chapter, Davies's library, excluding tide-tables, "pilots," etc., was limited to two classes of books, those on naval warfare, and those on his own hobby, cruising in small yachts. He had six or seven of the latter, including Knight's *Falcon in the Baltic*, Cowper's *Sailing Tours*, Macmullen's *Down Channel*, and other less-known stories of adventurous travel. I had scarcely done more than look into some of them at off-moments, for our life had left no leisure for reading. This particular volume was—no, I had better not describe it too fully; but I will say that it was old and unpretentious, bound in cheap cloth of a rather antiquated style, with a title which showed it to be a guide for yachtsmen to a certain British estuary. A white label partly scratched away bore the legend "3*d*." I had glanced at it once or twice with no special interest.

"Well?" I said, turning over some yellow pages.

"Dollmann!" cried Davies. "Dollmann wrote it." I turned to the title-page, and read: "By Lieut. X——, R.N." The name itself conveyed nothing to me, but I began to understand. Davies went on: "The name's on the back, too—and I'm certain it's the last she looked at."

"But how do you know?"

"And there's the man himself. Ass that I am not to have seen it before! Look at the frontispiece."

It was a sorry piece of illustration of the old-fashioned sort, lacking definition and finish, but effective notwithstanding; for it was evidently the reproduction, though a cheap and imperfect process, of a photograph. It represented a small yacht at anchor below some woods, with the owner standing on deck in his shirt sleeves: a well-knit, powerful man, young, of middle height, clean shaved. There appeared to be nothing remarkable about the face: the portrait being on too small a scale, and the expression, such as it was, being of the fixed "photographic" character.

"How do you know him? You said he was fifty, with a greyish beard."

"By the shape of his head; that hasn't changed. Look how it widens at the top, and then flattens—sort of wedge shaped—with a high, steep forehead; you'd hardly notice it in that" (the points were not very noticeable, but I saw what Davies meant). "The height and figure are right, too; and the dates are about right. Look at the bottom."

Underneath the picture was the name of a yacht and a date. The publisher's date on the title-page was the same.

"Sixteen years ago," said Davies. "He looks thirty odd in that, doesn't he? And fifty now."

"Let's work the thing out. Sixteen years ago he was still an Englishman, an officer in Her Majesty's Navy. Now he's a German. At some time between this and then, I suppose, he came to grief—disgrace, flight, exile. When did it happen?"

"They've been here three years; von Brüning said so."

"It was long before that. She has talked German from a child. What's her age, do you think—nineteen or twenty?"

"About that."

"Say she was four when this book was published. The crash must have come not long after."

"And they've been hiding in Germany since."

"Is this a well-known book?"

"I never saw another copy; picked this up on a second-hand bookstall for threepence."

"She looked at it, you say?"

"Yes, I'm certain of it."

"Was she never on board you in September?"

"No; I asked them both, but Dollmann made excuses."

"But *he—he* came on board? You told me so."

"Once; he asked himself to breakfast on the first day. By Jove! yes; you mean he saw the book?"

"It explains a good deal."

"It explains everything."

We fell into deep reflexion for a minute or two.

"Do you really mean *everything*?" I said. "In that case let's sail straight away and forget the whole affair. He's only some poor devil with a past, whose secret you stumbled on, and, half mad with fear, he tried to silence you. But you don't want revenge, so it's no business of ours. We can ruin him if we like; but is it worth it?"

"You don't mean a word you're saying," said Davies, "though I know why you say it; and many thanks, old chap. I didn't mean 'everything.' He's plotting with Germans, or why did Grimm spy on us, and von Brüning cross-examine us? We've got to find out what he's at, as well as who he is. And as to her—what do you think of her now?"

I made my *amende* heartily. "Innocent and ignorant," was my verdict. "Ignorant, that is, of her father's treasonable machinations; but aware, clearly, that they were English refugees with a past to hide." I said other things, but they do not matter. "Only," I concluded, "it makes the dilemma infinitely worse."

"There's no dilemma at all," said Davies. "You said at Bensersiel that we couldn't hurt him without hurting her. Well, all I can say is, we've *got* to. The time to cut and run, if ever, was when we sighted her dinghy. I had a baddish minute then."

"She's given us a clue or two after all."

"It wasn't our fault. To refuse to have her on board would have been to give our show away; and the very fact that she's given us clues decides the matter. She mustn't suffer for it."

"What will she do?"

"Stick to her father, I suppose."

"And what shall we do?"

"I don't know yet; how can I know? It depends," said Davies, slowly. "But the point is, that we have two objects, equally important—yes, equally, by Jove!—to scotch him, and save her."

There was a pause.

"That's rather a large order," I observed. "Do you realize that at this very moment we have probably gained the first object? If we went home now, walked into the Admiralty and laid our facts before them, what would be the result?"

"The Admiralty!" said Davies, with ineffable scorn.

"Well, Scotland Yard, too, then. Both of them want our man, I dare say. It would be strange if between them they couldn't dislodge him, and, incidentally, either discover what's going on here or draw such attention to this bit of coast as to make further secrecy impossible."

"It's out of the question to let her betray her father, and then run away! Besides, we don't know enough, and they mightn't believe us. It's a cowardly course, however you look at it."

"Oh! that settles it," I answered, hastily. "Now I want to go back over the facts. When did you first see her?"

"That first morning."

"She wasn't in the saloon the night before?"

"No; and he didn't mention her."

"You would have gone away next morning if he hadn't called?"

"Yes; I told you so."

"He allowed her to persuade you to make that voyage with them?"

"I suppose so."

"But he sent her below when the pilotage was going on?"

"Of course."

"She said just now, 'Father said you would be safe.' What had you been saying to her?"

"It was when I met her on the sand. (By the way, it wasn't a chance meeting; she had been making inquiries and heard about us from a skipper who had seen the yacht near Wangeroog, and she had been down this way before.) She asked at once about that day, and began apologizing, rather awkwardly, you know, for their rudeness in not having waited for me at Cuxhaven. Her father found he must get on to Hamburg at once."

"But you didn't go to Cuxhaven; you told her that? What exactly *did* you tell her? This is important."

"I was in a fearful fix, not knowing what *he* had told her. So I said something vague, and then she asked the very question von Brüning did, 'Wasn't there a *schrecklich* sea round the Scharhorn?'"

"She didn't know you took the short cut, then?"

"No; he hadn't dared to tell her."

"She knew that *they* took it?"

"Yes. He couldn't possibly have hidden that. She would have known by the look of the sea from the portholes, the shorter time, etc."

"But when the *Medusa* hove to and he shouted to you to follow him—didn't she understand what was happening?"

"No, evidently not. Mind you, she couldn't possibly have heard what we said, in that weather, from below. I couldn't cross-question her, but it was clear enough what she thought; namely, that he had hove to for exactly the opposite reason, to say *he* was taking the short cut, and that I wasn't to attempt to follow him."

"That's why she laid stress on *waiting* for you at Cuxhaven?"

"Of course; mine would have been the longer passage."

"She had no notion of foul play?"

"None—that I could see. After all, there I was, alive and well."

"But she was remorseful for having induced you to sail at all that day, and for not having waited to see you arrived safely."

"That's about it."

"Now what did you say about Cuxhaven?"

"Nothing. I let her understand that I went there, and, not finding them, went on to the Baltic by the Eider river, having changed my mind about the ship canal."

"Now, what about her voyage back from Hamburg? Was she alone?"

"No; the stepmother joined her."

"Did she say she had inquired about you at Brunsbüttel?"

"No; I suppose she didn't like to. And there was no need, because my taking the Eider explained it."

I reflected. "You're sure she hadn't a notion that you took the short cut?"

"Quite sure; but she may guess it now. She guessed foul play by seeing that book."

"Of course she did; but I was thinking of something else. There are two stories afloat now—yours to von Brüning, the true one, that you followed the *Medusa* to the short cut; and Dollmann's to her, that you went round the Scharhorn. That's evidently his version of the affair—the version he would have given if you had been drowned and inquiries were ever made; the version he would have sworn his crew to if they discovered the truth."

"But he must drop that yarn when he knows I'm alive and back again."

"Yes; but meanwhile, supposing von Brüning sees him *before* he knows you're back again, and wants to find out the truth about that incident. If I were von Brüning I should say, 'By the way, what's become of that young Englishman you decoyed away to the Baltic?' Dollmann would give his version, and von Brüning, having heard ours, would know he was lying, and had tried to drown you."

"Does it matter? He must know already that Dollmann's a scoundrel."

"So we've been supposing; but we may be wrong. We're still in the dark as to Dollmann's position towards these Germans. They may not even know he's English, or they may know that and not know his real name and past. What effect your story will have on their relations with him we can't forecast. But I'm clear about one thing, that it's our paramount interest to maintain the *status quo* as long as we can, to minimize the danger you ran that day, and act as witnesses in his defence. We can't do that if his story and yours don't tally. The discrepancy will not only damn him (that may be immaterial), but it will throw doubt on us."

"Why?"

"Because if the short cut was so dangerous that he dared not own to having led you to it, it was dangerous enough to make you suspect foul play; the very supposition we want to avoid. We want to be thought mere travellers, with no scores to wipe out, and no secrets to pry after."

"Well, what do you propose?"

"Hitherto I believe we stand fairly well. Let's assume we hoodwinked von Brüning at Bensersiel, and base our policy on that assumption. It follows that we must show Dollmann at the earliest possible moment that you *have* come back, and give him time to revise his tactics before he commits himself. Now—"

"But *she'll* tell him we're back," interrupted Davies.

"I don't think so. We've just agreed to keep this afternoon's episode a secret. She expects never to see us again."

"Now, he comes to-morrow by the morning boat, she said. What did that mean? Boat from where?"

"I know. From Norddeich on the mainland opposite. There's a railway there from Norden, and a steam ferry crosses to the island."

"At what time?"

"Your Bradshaw will tell us—here it is: 'Winter Service, 8.30 a.m., due at 9.5.'"

"Let's get away at once."

We had a tussle with the tide at first, but once over the watershed the channel improved, and the haze lightened gradually. A lighthouse appeared among the sand-dunes on the island shore, and before darkness fell we dimly saw the spires and roofs of a town, and two long black piers stretching out southwards. We were scarcely a mile away when we lost our wind altogether, and had to anchor. Determined to reach our destination that night we waited till the ebb stream made, and then towed the yacht with the dinghy. In the course of this a fog dropped on us suddenly, just as it had yesterday. I was towing at the time, and, of course, stopped short; but Davies shouted to me from the tiller to go on, that he could manage with the lead and compass. And the end of it was that, at about nine o'clock, we anchored safely in the five-fathom roadstead, close to the eastern pier, as a short reconnaissance proved to us. It had been a little masterpiece of adroit seamanship.

There was utter stillness till our chain rattled down, when a muffled shout came from the direction of the pier, and soon we heard a boat groping out to us. It was a polite but sleepy port-officer, who asked in a perfunctory way for our particulars, and when he heard them, remembered the *Dulcibella*'s previous visit.

"Where are you bound to?" he asked.

"England—sooner or later," said Davies.

The man laughed derisively. "Not this year," he said; "there will be fogs for another week; it is always so, and then storms. Better leave your yawl here. Dues will be only sixpence a month for you."

"I'll think about it," said Davies. "Good-night."

The man vanished like a ghost in the thick night.

"Is the post-office open?" I called after him.

"No; eight to-morrow," came back out of the fog.

We were too excited to sup in comfort, or sleep in peace, or to do anything but plan and speculate. Never till this night had we talked with absolute mutual confidence, for Davies broke down the last barriers of reserve and let me see his whole mind. He loved this girl and he loved his country, two simple passions which for the time absorbed his whole moral capacity. There was no room left for casuistry. To weigh one passion against the other, with the discordant voices of honour and expediency dinning in his ears, had too long involved him in fruitless torture. Both were right; neither could be surrendered. If the facts showed them irreconcilable, *tant pis pour les faits*. A way must be found to satisfy both or neither.

I should have been a spiritless dog if I had not risen to his mood. But in truth his cutting of the knot was at this juncture exactly what appealed to me. I, too, was tired of vicarious casuistry, and the fascination of our enterprise, intensified by the discovery of that afternoon, had never been so strong in me. Not to be insincere, I cannot pretend that I viewed the situation with his single mind. My philosophy when I left

London was of a very worldly sort, and no one can change his temperament in three weeks. I plainly said as much to Davies, and indeed took perverse satisfaction in stating with brutal emphasis some social truths which bore on this attachment of his to the daughter of an outlaw. Truths I call them, but I uttered them more by rote than by conviction, and he heard them unmoved. And meanwhile I snatched recklessly at his own solution. If it imparted into our adventure a strain of crazy chivalry more suited to knights-errant of the Middle Ages than to sober modern youths—well, thank Heaven, I was not too sober, and still young enough to snatch at that fancy with an ardour of imagination, if not of character; perhaps, too, of character, for Galahads are not so common but that ordinary folk must needs draw courage from their example and put something of a blind trust in their tenfold strength.

To reduce a romantic ideal to a working plan is a very difficult thing.

"We shall have to argue backwards," I said. "What is to be the final stage? Because that must govern the others."

There was only one answer—to get Dollmann, secrets and all, daughter and all, away from Germany altogether. So only could we satisfy the double aim we had set before us. What a joy it is, when beset with doubts, to find a bed-rock necessity, however unattainable! We fastened on this one and reasoned back from it. The first lesson was that, however many and strong were the enemies we had to contend with, our sole overt foe must be Dollmann. The issue of the struggle must be known only to ourselves and him. If we won, and found out "what he was at," we must at all costs conceal our success from his German friends, and detach him from them before he was compromised. (You will remark that to blithely accept this limitation showed a very sanguine spirit in us.) The next question, how to find out what he was at, was a deal more thorny. If it had not been for the discovery of Dollmann's identity, we should have found it as hard a nut to crack as ever. But this discovery was illuminating. It threw into relief two methods of action which hitherto we had been hazily seeking to combine, seesawing between one and the other, each of us influenced at different times by different motives. One was to rely on independent research; the other to extort the secret from Dollmann direct, by craft or threats. The moral of to-day was to abandon the first and embrace the second.

The prospects of independent research were not a whit better than before. There were only two theories in the field, the channel theory and the Memmert theory. The former languished for lack of corroboration; the latter also appeared to be weakened. To Fräulein Dollmann the wreck-works were evidently what they purported to be, and nothing more. This fact in itself was unimportant, for it was clear as crystal that she was no party to her father's treacherous intrigues, if he was engaged in such. But if Memmert was his sphere for them, it was disconcerting to find her so familiar with that sphere, lightly talking of a descent in a diving-bell—hinting, too, that the mystery as to results was only for local consumption. Nevertheless, the charm of Memmert as the place we had traced Grimm to, and as the only tangible clue we had obtained, was still very great. The really cogent objection was the insuperable difficulty, known and watched as we were, of learning its significance. If there was anything important to see there we should never be allowed to see it, while by trying and failing we risked everything. It was on this point that the last of all misunderstandings between me and Davies was dissipated. At Bensersiel he had been influenced more than he owned by my arguments about Memmert; but at that time (as I hinted) he was biased by a radical prejudice. The channel theory had become a sort of religion with him, promising double salvation—not only avoidance of the Dollmanns, but success in the quest by methods in which he was past master. To have to desert it and resort to spying on naval defences was an idea he dreaded and distrusted. It was not the morality of the course that bothered him. He was far too clear-headed to blink at the essential fact that at heart we were spies on a foreign power in time of peace, or to salve his conscience by specious distinctions as to our mode of operation. The foreign power to him was Dollmann, a traitor. There was his final justification, fearlessly adopted and held to the last. It was rather that, knowing his own limitations, his whole nature shrank from the sort of action entailed by the Memmert theory. And there was strong common sense in his antipathy.

So much for independent research.

On the other hand the road was now clear for the other method. Davies no longer feared to face the imbroglio at Norderney; and that day fortune had given us a new and potent weapon against Dollmann; precisely how potent we could not tell, for we had only a glimpse of his past, and his exact relations with the Government were unknown to us. But we knew who he was. Using this knowledge with address, could we not wring the rest from him? Feel our way, of course, be guided by his own conduct, but in the end strike hard and stake everything on the stroke? Such at any rate was our scheme to-night. Later, tossing in my bunk, I bethought me of the little drab book, lit a candle, and fetched it. A preface explained that it had been written during a spell of two months' leave from naval duty, and expressed a hope that it might be of service to Corinthian sailors. The style was unadorned, but scholarly and pithy. There was no trace of the writer's individuality, save a certain subdued relish in describing banks and shoals, which reminded me of Davies himself. For the rest, I found the book dull, and, in fact, it sent me to sleep.

## 21

### Blindfold to Memmert

"HERE she comes," said Davies. It was nine o'clock on the next day, 22nd October, and we were on deck waiting for the arrival of the steamer from Norddeich. There was no change in the weather—still the same stringent cold, with a high barometer, and only fickle flaws of air; but the morning was gloriously clear, except for a wreath or two of mist curling like smoke from the sea, and an attenuated belt of opaque fog on the northern horizon. The harbour lay open before us, and very commodious and civilized it looked, enclosed between two long piers which ran quite half a mile out from the land to the roadstead (Riff-Gat by name) where we lay. A stranger might have taken it for a deep and spacious haven; but this, of course, was an illusion, due to the high water. Davies knew that three-quarters of it was mud, the remainder being a dredged-out channel along the western pier. A couple of tugs, a dredger, and a ferry packet with steam up, were moored on that side—a small stack of galliots on the other. Beyond these was another vessel, a galliot in build, but radiant as a queen among sluts; her varnished sides and spars flashing orange in the sun. These, and her snow-white sail-covers and the twinkle of brass and gun-metal, proclaimed her to be a yacht. I had already studied her through the glasses and read on her stern *Medusa*. A couple of sailors were swabbing her decks; you could hear the slush of the water and the scratching of the deck-brooms. "*They* can see us anyway," Davies had said.

For that matter all the world could see us—certainly the incoming steamer must; for we lay as near to the pier as safety permitted, abreast of the berth she would occupy, as we knew by a gangway and a knot of sailors.

A packet boat, not bigger than a big tug, was approaching from the south.

"Remember, we're not supposed to know he's coming," I said; "let's go below." Besides the skylight, our "coach-house" cabin top had little oblong side windows. We wiped clean those on the port side and watched events from them, kneeling on the sofa.

The steamer backed her paddles, flinging out a wash that set us rolling to our scuppers. There seemed to be very few passengers aboard, but all of them were gazing at the *Dulcibella* while the packet was warped alongside. On the forward deck there were some market-women with baskets, a postman, and a weedy youth who might be an hotel waiter; on the after-deck, standing close together, were two men in ulsters and soft felt hats.

"There he is!" said Davies, in a tense whisper; "the tall one." But the tall one turned abruptly as Davies spoke and strode away behind the deck-house, leaving me just a lightning impression of a grey beard and a steep tanned forehead, behind a cloud of cigar smoke. It was perverse of me, but, to tell the truth, I hardly missed him, so occupied was I by the short one, who remained leaning on the rail, thoughtfully contemplating the *Dulcibella* through gold-rimmed pince-nez: a sallow, wizened old fellow, beetle-browed, with a bush of grizzled moustache and a jet-black tuft of beard on his chin. The most remarkable feature was the nose, which was broad and flat, merging almost imperceptibly in the wrinkled cheeks. Lightly beaked at the nether extremity, it drooped towards an enormous cigar which was pointing at us like a gun just discharged. He looked wise as Satan, and you would say he was smiling inwardly.

"Who's that?" I whispered to Davies. (There was no need to talk in whispers, but we did so instinctively.)

"Can't think," said Davies. "Hullo! she's backing off, and they've not landed."

Some parcels and mail-bags had been thrown up, and the weedy waiter and two market-women had gone up the gangway, which was now being hauled up, and were standing on the quay. I think one or two other persons had first come aboard unnoticed by us, but at the last moment a man we had not seen before jumped down to the forward deck. "Grimm!" we both ejaculated at once.

The steamer whistled sharply, circled backwards into the roadstead, and then steamed away. The pier soon hid her, but her smoke showed she was steering towards the North Sea.

"What does this mean?" I asked.

"There must be some other quay to stop at nearer the town," said Davies. "Let's go ashore and get your letters."

We had made a long and painful toilette that morning, and felt quite shy of one another as we sculled towards the pier, in much-creased blue suits, conventional collars, and brown boots. It was the first time for two years that I had seen Davies in anything approaching a respectable garb; but a fashionable watering-place, even in the dead season, exacts respect; and, besides, we had friends to visit.

We tied up the dinghy to an iron ladder, and on the pier found our inquisitor of the night before smoking in the doorway of a shed marked "Harbour Master." After some civilities we inquired about the steamer. The answer was that it was Saturday, and she had, therefore, gone on to Juist. Did we want a good hotel? The "Vier Jahreszeiten" was still open, etc.

"Juist, by Jove!" said Davies, as we walked on. "Why are those three going to Juist?"

"I should have thought it was pretty clear. They're on their way to Memmert."

Davies agreed, and we both looked longingly westward at a straw-coloured streak on the sea.

"Is it some meeting, do you think?" said Davies.

"Looks like it. We shall probably find the *Kormoran* here, wind-bound."

And find her we did soon after, the outermost of the stack of galliots, on the farther side of the harbour. Two men, whose faces we took a good look at, were sitting on her hatch, mending a sail.

Flooded with sun, yet still as the grave, the town was like a dead butterfly for whom the healing rays had come too late. We crossed some deserted public gardens commanded by a gorgeous casino, its porticos heaped with chairs and tables; so past kiosques and *cafés*, great white hotels with boarded windows, bazaars and booths, and all the stale lees of vulgar frivolity, to the post-office, which at least was alive. I received a packet of letters and purchased a local time-table, from which we learned that the steamer sailed daily to Borkum *via* Norderney, touching three times a week at Juist (weather permitting). On the return journey to-day it was due at Norderney at 7.30 p.m. Then I inquired the way to the "Vier Jahreszeiten." "For whatever your principles, Davies," I said, "we are going to have the best breakfast money can buy! We've got the whole day before us."

The "Four Seasons" Hotel was on the esplanade facing the northern beach. Living up to its name, it announced on an illuminated signboard, "Inclusive terms for winter visitors; special attention to invalids, etc." Here in a great glass restaurant, with the unruffled blue of ocean spread out before us, we ate the king of breakfasts, dismissed the waiter, and over long and fragrant Havanas examined my mail at leisure.

"What a waste of good diplomacy!" was my first thought, for nothing had been tampered with, so far as we could judge from the minutest scrutiny, directed, of course, in particular to the franked official letters (for to my surprise there were two) from Whitehall.

The first in order of date (6th Oct.) ran: "Dear Carruthers.—Take another week by all means.—Yours, etc."

The second (marked "urgent") had been sent to my home address and forwarded. It was dated 15th October, and cancelled the previous letter, requesting me to return to London without delay—"I am sorry to abridge your holiday, but we are very busy, and, at present, short-handed.—Yours, etc." There was a dry postscript to the effect that another time I was to be good enough to leave more regular and definite information as to my whereabouts when absent.

"I'm afraid I never got this!" I said, handing it to Davies.

"You won't go, will you?" said he, looking, nevertheless, with unconcealed awe at the great man's handwriting under the haughty official crest. Meanwhile I discovered an endorsement on a corner of the envelope: "Don't worry; it's only the chief's fuss.—M——" I promptly tore up the envelope. There are domestic mysteries which it would be indecent and disloyal to reveal, even to one's best friend. The rest of my letters need no remark; I smiled over some and blushed over others—all were voices from a life which was infinitely far away. Davies, meanwhile, was deep in the foreign intelligence of a newspaper, spelling it out line by line, and referring impatiently to me for the meaning of words.

"Hullo!" he said, suddenly; "same old game! Hear that siren?"

A curtain of fog had grown on the northern horizon and was drawing shorewards slowly but surely.

"It doesn't matter, does it?" I said.

"Well, we must get back to the yacht. We can't leave her alone in the fog."

There was some marketing to be done on the way back, and in the course of looking for the shops we wanted we came on the Schwannallée and noted its position. Before we reached the harbour the fog was on us, charging up the streets in dense masses. Happily a tramline led right up to the pier-head, or we should have lost our way and wasted time, which, in the event, was of priceless value. Presently we stumbled up against the Harbour Office, which was our landmark for the steps where we had tied up the dinghy. The same official appeared and good-naturedly held the painter while we handed in our parcels. He wanted to know why we had left the flesh-pots of the "Vier Jahreszeiten." To look after our yacht, of course. There was no need, he objected; there would be no traffic moving while the fog lasted, and the fog, having come on at that hour, had come to stay. If it did clear he would keep an eye on the yacht for us. We thanked him, but thought we would go aboard.

"You'll have a job to find her now," he said.

The distance was eighty yards at the most, but we had to use a scientific method, the same one, in fact, that Davies had used last night in the approach to the eastern pier.

"Row straight out at right angles to the pier," he said now. I did so, Davies sounding with his scull between the strokes. He found the bottom after twenty yards, that being the width of the dredged-out channel at this point. Then we turned to the right, and moved gently forward, keeping touch with the edge of the mud-bank (for all the world like blind men tapping along a kerb-stone) and taking short excursions from it, till the *Dulcibella* hove in view. "That's partly luck," Davies commented; "we ought to have had the compass as well."

We exchanged shouts with the man on the pier to show we had arrived.

"It's very good practice, that sort of thing," said Davies, when we had disembarked.

"You've got a sixth sense," I observed. "How far could you go like that?"

"Don't know. Let's have another try. I can't sit still all day. Let's explore this channel."

"*Why not go to Memmert?*" I said, in fun.

"To Memmert?" said Davies, slowly; "by Jove! that's an idea!"

"Good Heavens, man! I was joking. Why, it's ten mortal miles."

"More," said Davies, absently. "It's not so much the distance—what's the time? Ten fifteen; quarter ebb—What am I talking about? We made our plans last night."

But seeing him, to my amazement, serious, I was stung by the splendour of the idea I had awakened. Confidence in his skill was second nature to me. I swept straight on to the logic of the thing, the greatness, the completeness of the opportunity, if by a miracle it could be seized and used. Something was going on at Memmert to-day: our men had gone there; here were we, ten miles away, in a smothering, blinding fog. It was known we were here—Dollmann and Grimm knew it; the crew of the *Medusa* knew it; the crew of the *Kormoran* knew it; the man on the pier, whether he cared or not, knew it. But none of them knew Davies as I knew him. Would anyone dream for an instant—?

"Stop a second," said Davies; "give me two minutes." He whipped out the German chart. "Where exactly should we go?" ("Exactly!" The word tickled me hugely.)

"To the depot, of course; it's our only chance."

"Listen then—there are two routes: the outside one by the open sea, right round Juist, and doubling south*—the simplest, but the longest; the depot's at the south point of Memmert, and Memmert's nearly two miles long."

"How far would that way be?"

"Sixteen miles good. And we should have to row in a breaking swell most of the way, close to land."

"Out of the question; it's too public, too, if it clears. The steamer

*See Chart B.

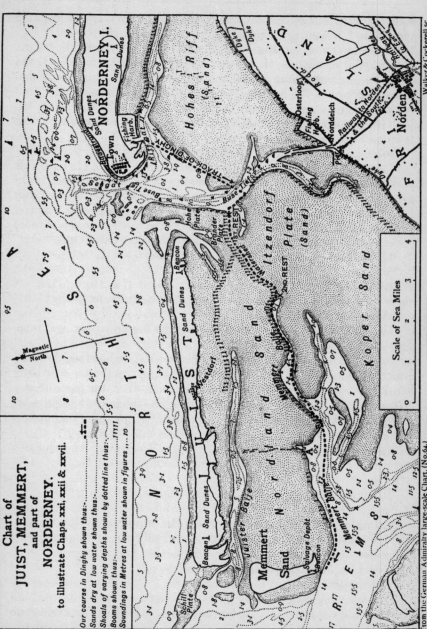

went that way, and will come back that way. We must go inside over the sands. Am I dreaming, though? Can you possibly find the way?"

"I shouldn't wonder. But I don't believe you see the hitch. It's the *time* and the falling tide. High water was about 8.15; it's now 10.15, and all those sands are drying off. We must cross the See-Gat and strike that boomed channel, the Memmert Balje; strike it, freeze on to it—can't cut off an inch—and pass that 'watershed' you see there before it's too late. It's an infernally bad one, I can see. Not even a dinghy will cross it for an hour each side of low water."

"Well, how far is the 'watershed'?"

"Good Lord! What are we talking for? Change, man, change! Talk while we're changing." (He began flinging off his shore clothes, and I did the same.) "It's at least five miles to the end of it; six, allowing for bends; hour and a half hard pulling; two, allowing for checks. Are you fit? You'll have to pull the most. Then there are six or seven more miles—easier ones. And then—What are we to do when we get there?"

"Leave that to me," I said. "You get me there."

"Supposing it clears?"

"After we get there? Bad; but we must risk that. If it clears on the way there it doesn't matter by this route; we shall be miles from land."

"What about getting back?"

"We shall have a rising tide, anyway. If the fog lasts—can you manage in a fog *and* dark?"

"The dark makes it no more difficult, if we've a light to see the compass and chart by. You trim the binnacle lamp—no, the riding-light. Now give me the scissors, and don't speak a word for ten minutes. Meanwhile, think it out, and load the dinghy—(by Jove! though, don't make a sound)—some grub and whisky, the boat-compass, lead, riding-light, matches, *small* boat-hook, grapnel and line."

"Foghorn?"

"Yes, and the whistle too."

"A gun?"

"What for?"

"We're after ducks."

"All right. And muffle the rowlocks with cotton-waste."

I left Davies absorbed in the charts, and softly went about my own functions. In ten minutes he was on the ladder, beckoning.

"I've done," he whispered. "Now *shall* we go?"

"I've thought it out. Yes," I answered.

This was only roughly true, for I could not have stated in words all the pros and cons that I had balanced. It was an impulse that drove me forward; but an impulse founded on reason, with just a tinge, perhaps, of superstition; for the quest had begun in a fog and might fitly end in one.

It was twenty-five minutes to eleven when we noiselessly pushed off. "Let her drift," whispered Davies, "the ebb'll carry her past the pier."

We slid by the *Dulcibella*, and she disappeared. Then we sat without speech or movement for about five minutes, while the gurgle of tide through piles approached and passed. The dinghy appeared to be motionless, just as a balloon in the clouds may appear to its occupants to be motionless, though urged by a current of air. In reality we were driving out of the Riff-Gat into the See-Gat. The dinghy swayed to a light swell.

"Now, pull," said Davies, under his breath; "keep it long and steady, above all steady— both arms with equal force."

I was on the bow-thwart; he *vis-à-vis* to me on the stern seat, his left hand behind him on the tiller, his right forefinger on a small square of paper which lay on his knees; this was a section cut out from the big German chart (Chart B). On the midship-thwart between us lay the compass and a watch. Between these three objects—compass, watch, and chart—his eyes darted constantly, never looking up or out, save occasionally for a sharp glance over the side at the flying bubbles, to see if I was sustaining a regular speed. My duty was to be his automaton, the human equivalent of a marine engine whose revolutions can be counted and used as data by the navigator. My arms must be regular as twin pistons; the energy that drove them as controllable as steam. It was a hard ideal to reach, for the complex mortal tends to rely on all the senses God has given him, so unfitting himself for mechanical exactitude when a sense (eyesight, in my case) fails him. At first it was constantly "left" or "right" from Davies, accompanied by a bubbling from the rudder.

"This won't do, too much helm," said Davies, without looking up. "Keep your stroke, but listen to me. Can you see the compass card?"

"When I come forward."

"Take your time, and don't get flurried, but each time you come forward have a good look at it. The course is sou'-west half-west. You take the opposite, north-east half-east, and keep her *stern* on that. It'll be rough, but it'll save some helm, and give me a hand free if I want it."

I did as he said, not without effort, and our progress gradually became smoother, till he had no need to speak at all. The only sound now was one like the gentle simmer of a saucepan away to port—the lisp of surf I knew it to be—and the muffled grunt of the rowlocks. I broke the silence once to say "It's very shallow." I had touched sand with my right scull.

"Don't talk," said Davies.

About half an hour passed, and then he added sounding to his other occupations. "Plump" went the lead at regular intervals, and he steered with his hip while pulling in the line. Very little of it went out at first, then less still. Again I struck bottom, and, glancing aside, saw weeds. Suddenly he got a deep cast, and the dinghy, freed from the slight drag which shallow water always inflicts on a small boat, leapt buoyantly forward. At the same time, I knew by boils on the smooth surface that we were in a strong tideway.

"The Buse Tief,"* muttered Davies. "Row hard now, and steady as a clock."

For a hundred yards or more I bent to my sculls and made her fly. Davies was getting six fathom casts, till, just as suddenly as it had deepened, the water shoaled—ten feet, six, three, one—the dinghy grounded.

"Good!" said Davies. "Back her off! Pull your right only." The dinghy spun round with her bow to N.N.W. "Both arms together! Don't you worry about the compass now; just pull, and listen for orders. There's a tricky bit coming."

He put aside the chart, kicked the lead under the seat, and, kneeling on the dripping coils of line, sounded continuously with the butt-end of the boat-hook, a stumpy little implement, notched at intervals of a foot, and often before used for the same purpose. All at once I was aware that a check had come, for the dinghy swerved and doubled like a hound ranging after scent.

"Stop her," he said, suddenly, "and throw out the grapnel."

I obeyed and we brought up, swinging to a slight current, whose direction Davies verified by the compass. Then for half a minute he gave himself up to concentrated thought. What struck me most about him was that he never for a moment strained his eyes through the fog; a useless exercise (for five yards or so was the radius of our vision) which, however, I could not help indulging in, while I rested. He made up his mind, and we were off again, straight and swift as an arrow this time, and in water deeper than the boat-hook. I could see by his face that he was taking some bold expedient whose issue hung in the balance . . . Again we touched mud, and the artist's joy of achievement shone in his eyes. Backing away, we headed west, and for the first time he began to gaze into the fog.

"There's one!" he snapped at last. "Easy all!"

A boom, one of the usual upright saplings, glided out of the mist. He caught hold of it, and we brought up.

---

*See Chart B.

"Rest for three minutes now," he said. "We're in fairly good time."

It was 11.10. I ate some biscuits and took a nip of whisky while Davies prepared for the next stage.

We had reached the eastern outlet of Memmert Balje, the channel which runs east and west behind Juist Island, direct to the south point of Memmert. How we had reached it was incomprehensible to me at the time, but the reader will understand by comparing my narrative with the dotted line on the chart. I add this brief explanation, that Davies's method had been to cross the channel called the Buse Tief, and strike the other side of it at a point well *south* of the outlet of the Memmert Balje (in view of the northward set of the ebb-tide), and then to drop back north and feel his way to the outlet. The check was caused by a deep indentation in the Itzendorf Flat; a *cul-de-sac*, with a wide mouth, which Davies was very near mistaking for the Balje itself. We had no time to skirt dents so deep as that; hence the dash across its mouth with the chance of missing the upper lip altogether, and of either being carried out to sea (for the slightest error was cumulative) or straying fruitlessly along the edge.

The next three miles were the most critical of all. They included the "watershed," whose length and depth were doubtful; they included, too, the crux of the whole passage, a spot where the channel forks, our own branch continuing west, and another branch diverging from it north-westward. We must row against time, and yet we must negotiate that crux. Add to this that the current was against us till the watershed was crossed; that the tide was just at its most baffling stage, too low to allow us to risk short cuts, and too high to give definition to the banks of the channel; and that the compass was no aid whatever for the minor bends. "Time's up," said Davies, and on we went. I was hugging the comfortable thought that we should now have booms on our starboard for the whole distance; on our starboard, I say, for experience had taught us that all channels running parallel with the coast and islands were uniformly boomed on the northern side. Anyone less confident than Davies would have succumbed to the temptation of slavishly relying on these marks, creeping from one to the other, and wasting precious time. But Davies knew our friend the "boom" and his eccentricities too well; and preferred to trust to his sense of touch, which no fog in the world could impair. If we happened to sight one, well and good, we should know which side of the channel we were on. But even this contingent advantage he deliberately sacrificed after a short distance, for he crossed over to the *south* or unboomed side and steered and sounded along it, using the Itzendorf Flat as his handrail, so to speak. He was compelled to do this, he told me afterwards, in view of the crux, where the converging lines of booms would have involved us in irremediable confusion. Our branch was the southern one, and it followed that we must use the southern bank, and defer obtaining any help from booms until sure we were past that critical spot.

For an hour we were at the extreme strain, I of physical exertion, he of mental. I could not get into a steady swing, for little checks were constant. My right scull was for ever skidding on mud or weeds, and the backward suck of shoal water clogged our progress. Once we were both of us out in the slime tugging at the dinghy's sides; then in again, blundering on. I found the fog bemusing, lost all idea of time and space, and felt like a senseless marionette kicking and jerking to a mad music without tune or time. The misty form of Davies as he sat with his right arm swinging rhythmically forward and back, was a clockwork figure as mad as myself, but didactic and gibbering in his madness. Then the boat-hook he wielded with a circular sweep began to take grotesque shapes in my heated fancy; now it was the antenna of a groping insect, now the crank of a cripple's self-propelled perambulator, now the alpenstock of a lunatic mountaineer, who sits in his chair and climbs and climbs to some phantom "watershed." At the back of such mind as was left me lodged two insistent thoughts: "we must hurry on," "we are going wrong." As to the latter, take a link-boy through a London fog and you will experience the same thing; he always goes the way you think is wrong. "We're rowing *back*!" I remember shouting to Davies once, having become aware that it was now my left scull which splashed against obstructions. "Rubbish," said Davies, "I've crossed over"; and I relapsed.

By degrees I returned to sanity, thanks to improved conditions. It is an ill wind that blows nobody good, and the state of the tide, though it threatened us with total failure, had the compensating advantage that the lower it fell the more constricted and defined became our channel; till the time came when the compass and boat-hook were alike unnecessary, because our hand-rail, the muddy brink of the channel, was visible to the eye, close to us; on our right hand always now, for the crux was far behind, and the northern side was now our guide. All that remained was to press on with might and main ere the bed of the creek dried.

What a race it was! Homeric, in effect; a struggle of men with gods, for what were the gods but forces of nature personified? If the God of the Falling Tide did not figure in the Olympian circle he is none the less a mighty divinity. Davies left his post, and rowed stroke. Under our united efforts the dinghy advanced in strenuous leaps, hurling miniature-rollers on the bank beside us. My palms, seasoned as they were, were smarting with watery blisters. The pace was too hot for my strength and breath.

"I must have a rest," I gasped.

"Well, I think we're over it," said Davies.

We stopped the dinghy dead, and he stabbed over the side with the boat-hook. It passed gently astern of us, and even my bewildered brain took in the meaning of that.

"Three feet and the current with us. *Well* over it," he said. "I'll paddle on while you rest and feed."

It was a few minutes past one and we still, as he calculated, had eight miles before us, allowing for bends.

"But it's a mere question of muscle," he said.

I took his word for it, and munched at tongue and biscuits. As for muscle, we were both in hard condition. He was fresh, and what distress I felt was mainly due to spasmodic exertion culminating in that desperate spurt. As for the fog, it had more than once shown a faint tendency to lift, growing thinner and more luminous, in the manner of fogs, always to settle down again, heavy as a quilt.

Note the spot marked "second rest" (approximately correct, Davies says) and the course of the channel from that point westward. You will see it broadening and deepening to the dimensions of a great river, and finally merging in the estuary of the Ems. Note, too, that its northern boundary, the edge of the now uncovered Nordland Sand, leads, with one interruption (marked A), direct to Memmert, and is boomed throughout. You will then understand why Davies made so light of the rest of his problem. Compared with the feats he had performed, it was child's play, for he always had that visible margin to keep touch with if he chose, or to return to in case of doubt. As a matter of fact—observe our dotted line—he made two daring departures from it, the first purely to save time, the second partly to save time and partly to avoid the very awkward spot marked A, where a creek with booms and a little delta of its own interrupts the even bank. During the first of these departures—the shortest but most brilliant—he let me do the rowing, and devoted himself to the niceties of the course; during the second, and through both the intermediate stages, he rowed himself, with occasional pauses to inspect the chart. We fell into a long, measured stroke, and covered the miles rapidly, scarcely exchanging a single word till, at the end of a long pull through vacancy, Davies said suddenly:

"Now where are we to land?"

A sandbank was looming over us crowned by a lonely boom.

"Where are we?"

"A quarter of a mile from Memmert."

"What time is it?"

"Nearly three."

# 22

### The Quartette

His *tour de force* was achieved, and for the moment something like collapse set in.

"What in the world have we come here for?" he muttered; "I feel a bit giddy."

I made him drink some whisky, which revived him; and then, speaking in whispers, we settled certain points.

I alone was to land. Davies demurred to this out of loyalty, but common sense, coinciding with a strong aversion of his own, settled the matter. Two were more liable to detection than one. I spoke the language well, and if challenged could cover my retreat with a gruff word or two; in my woollen overalls, seaboots, oilskin coat, with a sou'wester pulled well over my eyes, I should pass in a fog for a Frisian. Davies must mind the dinghy; but how was I to regain it? I hoped to do so without help, by using the edge of the sand; but if he heard a long whistle he was to blow the foghorn.

"Take the pocket-compass," he said. "Never budge from the shore without using it, and lay it on the ground for steadiness. Take this scrap of chart, too—it may come in useful; but you can't miss the depot, it looks to be close to the shore. How long will you be?"

"How long have I got?"

"The young flood's making—has been for nearly an hour—that bank (he measured it with his eye) will be covering in an hour and a half."

"That ought to be enough."

"Don't run it too fine. It's steep here, but it may shelve farther on. If you have to wade you'll never find me, and you'll make a deuce of a row. Got your watch, matches, knife? No knife? Take mine; never go anywhere without a knife." (It was his seaman's idea of efficiency.)

"Wait a bit, we must settle a place to meet at in case I'm late and can't reach you here."

"*Don't* be late. We've got to get back to the yacht before we're missed."

"But I may have to hide and wait till dark—the fog may clear."

"We were fools to come, I believe," said Davies, gloomily. "There *are* no meeting-places in a place like this. Here's the best I can see on the chart—a big triangular beacon marked on the very point of Memmert. You'll pass it."

"All right. I'm off."

"Good luck," said Davies, faintly.

I stepped out, climbed a miry glacis of five or six feet, reached hard wet sand, and strode away with the sluggish ripple of the Balje on my left hand. A curtain dropped between me and Davies, and I was alone—alone, but how I thrilled to feel the firm sand rustle under my boots; to know that it led to dry land, where, whatever befell, I could give my wits full play. I clove the fog briskly.

Good Heavens! what was that? I stopped short and listened. From over the water on my left there rang out, dulled by fog, but distinct to the ear, three double strokes on a bell or gong. I looked at my watch.

"Ship at anchor," I said to myself. "Six bells in the afternoon watch." I knew the Balje was here a deep roadstead, where a vessel entering the Eastern Ems might very well anchor to ride out a fog.

I was just stepping forward when another sound followed from the same quarter, a bugle-call this time. Then I understood—only men-of-war sound bugles—the *Blitz* was here then; and very natural, too, I thought, and strode on. The sand was growing drier, the water farther beneath me; then came a thin black ribbon of weed—high-water mark. A few cautious steps to the right and I touched tufts of marram grass. It was Memmert. I pulled out the chart and refreshed my memory. No! there could be no mistake; keep the sea on my left and I must go right. I followed the ribbon of weed, keeping it just in view, but walking on the verge of the grass for the sake of silence. All at once I almost tripped over a massive iron bar; others, a rusty network of them, grew into being above and around me, like the arms of a ghostly polyp.

"What infernal spider's web is this?" I thought, and stumbled clear. I had strayed into the base of a gigantic tripod, its gaunt legs stayed and cross-stayed, its apex lost in fog; the beacon, I remembered. A hundred yards farther and I was down on my knees again, listening with might and main; for several little sounds were in the air—voices, the rasp of a boat's keel, the whistling of a tune. There were straight ahead. More to the left, seaward, that is, I had aural evidence of the presence of a steamboat—a small one, for the hiss of escaping steam was low down. On my right front I as yet heard nothing, but the depot must be there.

I prepared to strike away from my base, and laid the compass on the ground—N.W. roughly I made the course. ("Southeast—southeast for coming back," I repeated inwardly, like a child learning a lesson.) Then of my two allies I abandoned one, the beach, and threw myself wholly on the fog.

"Play the game," I said to myself. "Nobody expects you; nobody will recognize you."

I advanced in rapid stages of ten yards or so, while grass disappeared and soft sand took its place, pitted everywhere with footmarks. I trod carefully, for obstructions began to show themselves—an anchor, a heap of rusty cable; then a boat bottom upwards, and, lying on it, a foul old meerschaum pipe. I paused here and strained my ears, for there were sounds in many directions; the same whistling (behind me now), heavy footsteps in front, and somewhere beyond—fifty yards away, I reckoned—a buzz of guttural conversation; from the same quarter there drifted to my nostrils the acrid odour of coarse tobacco. Then a door banged.

I put the compass in my pocket (thinking "southeast, southeast"), placed the pipe between my teeth (ugh! the rank savour of it!), rammed my sou'wester hard down, and slouched on in the direction of the door that had banged. A voice in front called, "Karl Schicker"; a nearer voice, that of the man whose footsteps I had heard approaching, took it up and called "Karl Schicker"; I, too, took it up, and, turning my back, called "Karl Schicker" as gruffly and gutturally as I could. The footsteps passed quite close to me, and glancing over my shoulder I saw a young man passing, dressed very like me, but wearing a sealskin cap instead of a sou'wester. As he walked he seemed to be counting coins in his palm. A hail came back from the beach and the whistling stopped.

I now became aware that I was on a beaten track. These meetings were hazardous, so I inclined aside, but not without misgivings, for the path led towards the buzz of talk and the banging door, and these were my only guides to the depot. Suddenly, and much before I expected it, I knew rather than saw that a wall was in front of me; now it was visible, the side of a low building of corrugated iron. A pause to reconnoitre was absolutely necessary; but the knot of talkers might have heard my footsteps, and I must at all costs not suggest the groping of a stranger. I lit a match—two—and sucked heavily (as I had seen navvies do) at my pipe, studying the trend of the wall by reference to the sounds. There was a stale dottle wedged in the bowl, and loathsome fumes resulted. Just then the same door banged again; another name, which I forget, was called out. I decided that I was at the end of a rectangular building which I pictured as like an Aldershot "hut," and that the door I heard was round the corner to my left. A knot of men must be gathered there, entering it by turns. Having expectorated noisily, I followed the tin wall to my *right*, and turning a corner strolled leisurely on, passing signs of domesticity, a washtub, a water-butt, then a tiled approach to an open door. I now was aware of the corner of a second building, also of zinc, parallel to the first, but taller, for I could only just see the eave. I was just going to turn off to this as a more promising field for exploration, when I heard a window open ahead of me in my original building.

I am afraid I am getting obscure, so I append a rough sketch of the scene, as I partly saw and chiefly imagined it. It was window (A) that I

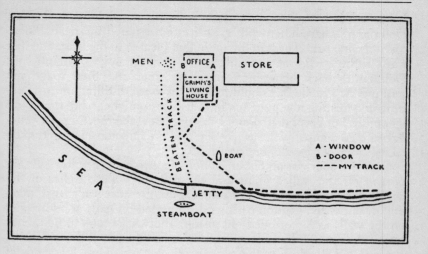

heard open. From it I could just distinguish through the fog a hand
protrude, and throw something out—cigar-end? The hand, a clean one
with a gold signet-ring, rested for an instant afterwards on the sash, and
then closed the window.

My geography was clear now in one respect. That window belonged
to the same room as the banging door (B); for I distinctly heard the latter open and shut again, opposite me on the other side of the building.
It struck me that it might be interesting to see into that room. "Play the
game," I reminded myself, and retreated a few yards back on tiptoe,
then turned and sauntered coolly past the window, puffing my villainous pipe and taking a long deliberate look into the interior as I
passed—the more deliberate that at the first instant I realized that nobody inside was disturbing himself about me. As I had expected (in
view of the fog and the time) there was artificial light within. My mental photograph was as follows: a small room with varnished deal walls
and furnished like an office; in the far right-hand corner a counting-
house desk, Grimm sitting at it on a high stool, side-face to me, counting money; opposite him in an awkward attitude a burly fellow in
seaman's dress holding a diver's helmet. In the middle of the room a
deal table, and on it something big and black. Lolling on chairs near
it, their backs to me and their faces turned towards the desk and the
diver, two men—von Brüning and an older man with a bald yellow
head (Dollmann's companion on the steamer, beyond a doubt). On another chair, with its back actually tilted against the window, Dollmann.

Such were the principal features of the scene; for details I had to
make another inspection. Stooping low, I crept back, quiet as a cat, till

I was beneath the window, and, as I calculated, directly behind Dollmann's chair. Then with great caution I raised my head. There was only one pair of eyes in the room that I feared in the least, and that was Grimm's, who sat in profile to me, farthest away. I instantly put Dollmann's back between Grimm and me, and then made my scrutiny. As I made it, I could feel a cold sweat distilling on my forehead and tickling my spine; not from fear or excitement, but from pure ignominy. For beyond all doubt I was present at the meeting of a *bona-fide* salvage company. It was pay-day, and the directors appeared to be taking stock of work done; that was all.

Over the door was an old engraving of a two-decker under full sail; pinned on the wall a chart and the plan of a ship. Relics of the wrecked frigate abounded. On a shelf above the stove was a small pyramid of encrusted cannon-balls, and supported on nails at odd places on the walls were corroded old pistols, and what I took to be the remains of a sextant. In a corner of the floor sat a hoary little carronade, carriage and all. None of these things affected me so much as a pile of lumber on the floor, not firewood but unmistakable wreck-wood, black as bog-oak, still caked in places with the mud of ages. Nor was it the mere sight of this lumber that dumbfounded me. It was the fact that a fragment of it, a balk of curved timber garnished with some massive bolts, lay on the table, and was evidently an object of earnest interest. The diver had turned and was arguing with gestures over it; von Brüning and Grimm were pressing another view. The diver shook his head frequently, finally shrugged his shoulders, made a salutation, and left the room. Their movements had kept me ducking my head pretty frequently, but I now grew almost reckless as to whether I was seen or not. All the weaknesses of my theory crowded on me—the arguments Davies had used at Bensersiel; Fräulein Dollmann's thoughtless talk; the ease (comparatively) with which I had reached this spot, not a barrier to cross or a lock to force; the publicity of their passage to Memmert by Dollmann, his friend, and Grimm; and now this glimpse of business-like routine. In a few moments I sank from depth to depth of scepticism. Where were my mines, torpedoes, and submarine boats, and where my imperial conspirators? Was gold after all at the bottom of this sordid mystery? Dollmann after all a commonplace criminal? The ladder of proof I had mounted tottered and shook beneath me. "Don't be a fool," said the faint voice of reason. "There are your four men. Wait."

Two more *employés* came into the room in quick succession and received wages; one looking like a fireman, the other of a superior type, the skipper of a tug, say. There was another discussion with this latter over the balk of wreck-wood, and this man, too, shrugged his shoulders. His departure appeared to end the meeting. Grimm shut up a ledger, and I shrank down on my knees, for a general shifting of chairs began. At the same time, from the other side of the building, I heard my knot of men retreating beachwards, spitting and chatting as they went. Presently someone walked across the room towards my window. I sidled away on all fours, rose and flattened myself erect against the wall, a sickening despondency on me; my intention to slink away southeast as soon as the coast was clear. But the sound that came next pricked me like an electric shock; it was the tinkle and scrape of curtain-rings.

Quick as thought I was back in my old position, to find my view barred by a cretonne curtain. It was in one piece, with no chink for my benefit, but it did not hang straight, bulging towards me under the pressure of something—human shoulders by the shape. Dollmann, I concluded, was still in his old place. I now was exasperated to find that I could scarcely hear a word that was said, not even by pressing my ear against the glass. It was not that the speakers were of set purpose hushing their voices—they used an ordinary tone for intimate discussion—but the glass and curtain deadened the actual words. Still, I was soon able to distinguish general characteristics. Von Brüning's voice—the only one I had ever heard before—I recognized at once; he was on the left of the table, and Dollmann's I knew from his position. The third was a harsh croak, belonging to the old gentlemen whom, for convenience, I shall prematurely begin to call Herr Böhme. It was too old a voice to be Grimm's; besides, it had the ring of authority, and was dealing at the moment in sharp interrogations. Three of its sentences I caught in their entirety. "When was that?" "They went no farther?" and "Too long; out of the question." Dollmann's voice, though nearest to me, was the least audible of all. It was a dogged monotone, and what was that odd movement of the curtain at his back? Yes, his hands were behind him clutching and kneading a fold of the cretonne. "You are feeling uncomfortable, my friend," was my comment. Suddenly he threw back his head—I saw the dent of it—and spoke up so that I could not miss a word. "Very well, sir, you shall see them at supper to-night; I will ask them both."

(You will not be surprised to learn that I instantly looked at my watch—though it takes long to write what I have described—but the time was only a quarter to four.) He added something about the fog, and his chair creaked. Ducking promptly I heard the curtain-rings jar, and: "Thick as ever."

"Your report, Herr Dollmann," said Böhme, curtly. Dollmann left the window and moved his chair up to the table; the other two drew in theirs and settled themselves.

"*Chatham*," said Dollmann, as if announcing a heading. It was an easy word to catch, rapped out sharp, and you can imagine how it startled me. "That's where you've been for the last month!" I said to myself. A map crackled and I knew they were bending over it, while Dollmann explained something. But now my exasperation became acute, for not a syllable more reached me. Squatting back on my heels, I cast about for expedients. Should I steal round and try the door? Too dangerous. Climb to the roof and listen down the stove-pipe? Too noisy, and generally hopeless. I tried for a downward purchase on the upper half of the window, which was of the simple sort in two sections, working vertically. No use; it resisted gentle pressure, would start with a sudden jar if I forced it. I pulled out Davies's knife and worked the point of the blade between sash and frame to give it play—no result; but the knife was a nautical one, with a marlin-spike as well as a big blade.

Just now the door within opened and shut again, and I heard steps approaching round the corner to my right. I had the presence of mind not to lose a moment, but moved silently away (blessing the deep Frisian sand) round the corner of the big parallel building. Someone whom I could not see walked past till his boots clattered on tiles, next resounded on boards. "Grimm in his living-room," I inferred. The precious minutes ebbed away—five, ten, fifteen. Had he gone for good? I dared not return otherwise. Eighteen—he was coming out! This time I stole forward boldly when the man had just passed, dimly saw a figure, and clearly enough the glint of a white paper he was holding. He made his circuit and re-entered the room.

Here I felt and conquered a relapse to scepticism. "If this is an important conclave why don't they set guards?" Answer, the only possible one, "Because they stand alone. Their *employés*, like *everyone* we had met hitherto, know nothing. The real object of this salvage company (a poor speculation, I opined) is solely to afford a pretext for the conclave." "Why the curtain, even?" "Because there are maps, stupid!"

I was back again at the window, but as impotent as ever against that even stream of low confidential talk. But I would not give up. Fate and the fog had brought me here, the one solitary soul perhaps who by the chain of circumstances had both the will and the opportunity to wrest their secret from these four men.

The marlin-spike! Where the lower half of the window met the sill it sank into a shallow groove. I thrust the point of the spike down into the interstice between sash and frame and heaved with a slowly increasing force, which I could regulate to the fraction of an ounce, on this powerful lever. The sash gave, with the faintest possible protest, and by imperceptible degrees I lifted it to the top of the groove, and the least bit

above it, say half an inch in all; but it made an appreciable difference
to the sounds within, as when you remove your foot from a piano's soft
pedal. I could do no more, for there was no further fulcrum for the
spike, and I dared not gamble away what I had won by using my hands.

Hope sank again when I placed my cheek on the damp sill, and my
ear to the chink. My men were close round the table referring to papers which I heard rustle. Dollmann's "report" was evidently over, and
I rarely heard his voice; Grimm's occasionally, von Brüning's and
Böhme's frequently; but, as before, it was the latter only that I could
ever count on for an intelligible word. For, unfortunately, the villains
of the piece plotted without any regard to dramatic fitness or to my interests. Immersed in a subject with which they were all familiar, they
were allusive, elliptic, and persistently technical. Many of the words I
did catch were unknown to me. The rest were, for the most part, either
letters of the alphabet or statistical figures, of depth, distance, and, once
or twice, of time. The letters of the alphabet recurred often, and
seemed, as far as I could make out, to represent the key to the cipher.
The numbers clustering round them were mostly very small, with dec-
imals. What maddened me most was the scarcity of plain nouns.

To report what I heard to the reader would be impossible; so chaotic
was most of it that it left no impression on my own memory. All I can
do is to tell him what fragments stuck, and what nebulous classifica-
tion I involved. The letters ran from A to G, and my best continuous
chance came when Böhme, reading rapidly from a paper, I think,
went through the letters, backwards, from G, adding remarks to each;
thus: "G . . . completed." "F . . . bad . . . 1.3 (metres?) . . . 2.5 (kilometres?)." "E . . . thirty-two . . . 1.2." "D . . . 3 weeks . . . thirty." "C . . ."
and so on.

Another time he went through this list again, only naming each letter himself, and receiving laconic answers from Grimm—answers
which seemed to be numbers, but I could not be sure. For minutes together I caught nothing but the scratching of pens and inarticulate
mutterings. But out of the muck-heap I picked five pearls—four sibilant nouns and a name that I knew before. The nouns were "Schleppboote" (tugs); "Wassertiefe" (depth of water); "Eisenbahn" (railway);
"Lotsen" (pilots). The name, also sibilant and thus easier to hear, was
"Esens."

Two or three times I had to stand back and ease my cramped neck,
and on each occasion I looked at my watch, for I was listening against
time, just as we had rowed against time. We were going to be asked to
supper, and must be back aboard the yacht in time to receive the invitation. The fog still brooded heavily and the light, always bad, was
growing worse. How would *they* get back? How had they come from

Juist? Could we forestall them? Questions of time, tide, distance—just the odious sort of sums I was unfit to cope with—were distracting my attention when it should have been wholly elsewhere. 4.20—4.25—now it was past 4.30, when Davies said the bank would cover. I should have to make for the beacon; but it was fatally near that steamboat path, etc., and I still at intervals heard voices from there. It must have been about 4.35 when there was another shifting of chairs within. Then someone rose, collected papers, and went out; someone else, *without* rising (therefore Grimm), followed him.

There was silence in the room for a minute, and after that, for the first time, I heard some plain colloquial German, with no accompaniment of scratching or rustling. "I must wait for this," I thought, and waited.

"He insists on coming," said Böhme.

"Ach!" (an ejaculation of surprise and protest from von Brüning).

"I said the 25th."

"Why?"

"The tide serves well. The night-train, of course. Tell Grimm to be ready—" (An inaudible question from von Brüning.) "No, any weather." A laugh from von Brüning and some words I could not catch.

"Only one, with half a load."

". . . meet?"

"At the station."

"So—how's the fog?"

This appeared to be really the end. Both men rose and steps came towards the window. I leapt aside as I heard it thrown up, and covered by the noise backed into safety. Von Brüning called "Grimm!" and that, and the open window, decided me that my line of advance was now too dangerous to retreat by. The only alternative was to make a circuit round the bigger of the two buildings—and an interminable circuit it seemed—and all the while I knew my compass-course "southeast" was growing nugatory. I passed a padlocked door, two corners, and faced the void of fog. Out came the compass, and I steadied myself for the sum. "Southeast before—I'm farther to the eastward now—east will about do"; and off I went, with an error of four whole points, over tussocks and deep sand. The beach seemed much farther off than I had thought, and I began to get alarmed, puzzled over the compass several times, and finally realized that I had lost my way. I had the sense not to make matters worse by trying to find it again, and, as the lesser of two evils, blew my whistle, softly at first, then louder. The bray of a foghorn sounded right *behind* me. I whistled again and then ran for my life, the horn sounding at intervals. In three or four minutes I was on the beach and in the dinghy.

## 23

### A Change of Tactics

WE pushed off without a word, and paddled out of sight of the beach. A voice was approaching, hailing us. "Hail back," whispered Davies; "pretend we're a galliot."

"Ho-a," I shouted, "where am I?"

"Off Memmert," came back. "Where are you bound?"

"Delfzyl," whispered Davies.

"Delf-zyl," I bawled.

A sentence ending with "anchor" was returned.

"The flood's tearing east," whispered Davies; "sit still."

We heard no more, and, after a few minutes' drifting "What luck?" said Davies.

"One or two clues, and an invitation to supper."

The clues I left till later; the invitation was the thing, and I explained its urgency.

"How will *they* get back?" said Davies; "if the fog lasts the steamer's sure to be late."

"We can count on nothing," I answered. "There was some little steamboat off the depot, and the fog may lift. Which is our quickest way?"

"At this tide, a bee-line to Norderney by compass; we shall have water over all the banks."

He had all his preparations made, the lamp lit in advance, the compass in position, and we started at once; he at the bow-oar, where he had better control over the boat's nose; lamp and compass on the floor between us. Twilight thickened into darkness—a choking, pasty darkness—and still we sped unfalteringly over that trackless waste, sitting and swinging in our little pool of stifled orange light. To drown fatigue and suspense I conned over my clues, and tried to carve into my memory every fugitive word I had overheard.

"What are there seven of round here?" I called back to Davies once (thinking of A to G). "Sorry," I added, for no answer came.

"I see a star," was my next word, after a long interval. "Now it's gone. There it is again! Right aft!"

"That's Borkum light," said Davies, presently; "the fog's lifting."

A keen wind from the west struck our faces, and as swiftly as it had come the fog rolled away from us, in one mighty mass, stripping clean and pure the starry dome of heaven, still bright with the western afterglow, and beginning to redden in the east to the rising moon.

Norderney light was flashing ahead, and Davies could take his tired eyes from the pool of light.

"Damn!" was all he uttered in the way of gratitude for this mercy, and I felt very much the same; for in a fog Davies in a dinghy was a match for a steamer; in a clear he lost his handicap.

It was a quarter to seven. "An hour'll do it, if we buck up," he pronounced, after taking a rough bearing with the two lights. He pointed out a star to me, which we were to keep exactly astern, and again I applied to their labour my aching back and smarting palms.

"What did you say about seven of something?" said Davies.

"What are there seven of hereabouts?"

"Islands, of course," said Davies. "Is that the clue?"

"Maybe."

Then followed the most singular of all our confabulations. Two memories are better than one, and the sooner I carved the cipher into his memory as well as mine the better record we should have. So, with rigid economy of breath, I snapped out all my story, and answered his breathless questions. It saved me from being mesmerized by the star, and both of us from the consciousness of over-fatigue.

"Spying at Chatham, the blackguard?" he hissed.

"What do you make of it?" I asked.

"Nothing about battleships, mines, forts?" he said.

"No."

"Nothing about the Ems, Emden, Wilhelmshaven?"

"No."

"Nothing about transports?"

"No."

"I believe—I was right—after all—something to do—with the channels—behind islands."

And so that outworn creed took a new lease of life; though for my part the words that clashed with it were those that had sunk the deepest.

"Esens," I protested; "that town behind Bensersiel."

"Wassertiefe, Lotsen, Schleppboote," spluttered Davies.

"Kilometre—Eisenbahn," from me, and so on.

I should earn the just execration of the reader if I continued to report such a dialogue. Suffice to say that we realized very soon that the substance of the plot was still a riddle. On the other hand, there was fresh scent, abundance of it; and the question was already taking shape—were we to follow it up or revert to last night's decision and strike with what weapons we had? It was a pressing question, too, the last of many—was there to be no end to the emergencies of this crowded day?—pressing for reasons I could not define, while

convinced that we must be ready with an answer by supper-time
to-night.

Meantime, we were nearing Norderney; the See-Gat was crossed,
and with the last of the flood tide fair beneath us, and the red light on
the west pier burning ahead, we began insensibly to relax our efforts.
But I dared not rest, for I was at that point of exhaustion when mechanical movement was my only hope.

"Light astern," I said, thickly. "Two—white and red."

"Steamer," said Davies; "going south though."

"Three now."

A neat triangle of gems—topaz, ruby, and emerald—hung steady
behind us.

"Turned east," said Davies. "Buck up—steamer from Juist. No, by
Jove! too small. What is it?"

On we laboured, while the gems waxed in brilliancy as the steamer
overhauled us.

"Easy," said Davies, "I seem to know those lights—the *Blitz's*
launch—don't let's be caught rowing like madmen in a muck sweat.
Paddle inshore a bit." He was right, and, as in a dream, I saw hurrying
and palpitating up the same little pinnace that had towed us out of
Bensersiel.

"We're done for now," I remember thinking, for the guilt of the runaway was strong in me; and an old remark of von Brüning's about "police" was in my ears. But she was level with and past us before I could
sink far into despair.

"Three of them behind the hood," said Davies; "what are we to do?"

"Follow," I answered, and essayed a feeble stroke, but the blade scut-
tered over the surface.

"Let's wait about for a bit," said Davies. "We're late anyhow. If they
go to the yacht they'll think we're ashore."

"Our shore clothes—lying about."

"Are you up to talking?"

"No; but we must. The least suspicion'll do for us now."

"Give me your scull, old chap, and put on your coat."

He extinguished the lantern, lit a pipe, and then rowed slowly on,
while I sat on a slack heap in the stern and devoted my last resources
of will to the emancipation of the spirit from the tired flesh.

In ten minutes or so we were rounding the pier, and there was the
yacht's top-mast against the sky. I saw, too, that the launch was alongside of her, and told Davies so. Then I lit a cigarette, and made a la-
mentable effort to whistle. Davies followed suit, and emitted a strange
melody which I took to be "Home, Sweet Home," but he has not the
slightest ear for music.

"Why, they're on board, I believe," said I; "the cabin's lighted. Ahoy there!" I shouted as we came up. "Who's that?"

"Good evening, sir," said a sailor, who was fending off the yacht with a boat-hook. "It's Commander von Brüning's launch. I think the gentlemen want to see you."

Before we could answer, an exclamation of: "Why, here they are!" came from the deck of the *Dulcibella*, and the dim form of von Brüning himself emerged from the companion-way. There was something of a scuffle down below, which the commander nearly succeeded in drowning by the breeziness of his greeting. Meanwhile, the ladder creaked under fresh weight, and Dollmann appeared.

"Is that you, Herr Davies?" he said.

"Hullo! Herr Dollmann," said Davies; "how are you?"

I must explain that we had floated up between the yacht and the launch, whose sailors had passed her a little aside in order to give us room. Her starboard side-light was just behind and above us, pouring its green rays obliquely over the deck of the *Dulcibella*, while we and the dinghy were in deep shadow between. The most studied calculation could not have secured us more favourable conditions for a moment which I had always dreaded—the meeting of Davies and Dollmann. The former, having shortened his sculls, just sat where he was, half turned towards the yacht and looking up at his enemy. No lineament of his own face could have been visible to the latter, while those pitiless green rays—you know their ravaging effect on the human physiognomy—struck full on Dollmann's face. It was my first fair view of it at close quarters, and, secure in my background of gloom, I feasted with a luxury of superstitious abhorrence on the livid smiling mask that for a few moments stooped peering down towards Davies. One of the caprices of the crude light was to obliterate, or at any rate so penetrate, beard and moustache, as to reveal in outline lips and chin, the features in which defects of character are most surely betrayed, especially when your victim smiles. Accuse me, if you will, of stooping to melodramatic embroidery; object that my own prejudiced fancy contributed to the result; but I can, nevertheless, never efface the impression of malignant perfidy and base passion, exaggerated to caricature, that I received in those few instants. Another caprice of the light was to identify the man with the portrait of him when younger and clean-shaven, in the frontispiece of his own book; and another still, the most repulsively whimsical of all, was to call forth a strong resemblance to the sweet young girl who had been with us yesterday.

Enough! I shall never offend again in this way. In reality I am much more inclined to laugh than shudder over this meeting; for meanwhile the third of our self-invited guests had with stertorous puffing risen to the stage, for all the world like a demon out of a trap-door, specially when he entered the zone of that unearthly light. And there they stood in a row, like delinquents at judgement, while we, the true culprits, had only passively to accept explanations. Of course these were plausible enough. Dollmann having seen the yacht in port that morning had called on his return from Memmert to ask us to supper. Finding no one aboard, and concluding we were ashore, he had meant to leave a note for Davies in the cabin. His friend, Herr Böhme, *the distinguished engineer*, was anxious to see over the little vessel that had come so far, and he knew that Davies would not mind the intrusion. Not at all, said Davies; would not they stop and have drinks? No, but would we come to supper at Dollmann's villa? With pleasure, said Davies, but we had to change first. Up to this point we had been masters of the situation; but here von Brüning, who alone of the three appeared to be entirely at his ease, made the *retour offensif.*

"Where have you been?" he asked.

"Oh, rowing about since the fog cleared," said Davies.

I suppose he thought that evasion would pass muster, but as he spoke, I noticed to my horror that a stray beam of light was playing on the bunch of white cotton-waste that adorned one of the rowlocks; for we had forgotten to remove these tell-tale appendages. So I added: "After ducks again"; and, lifting one of the guns, let the light flash on its barrel. To my own ears my voice sounded husky and distant.

"Always ducks," laughed von Brüning. "No luck, I suppose?"

"No," said Davies; "but it ought to be a good time after sunset—"

"What, with a rising tide and the banks covered?"

"We saw some," said Davies, sullenly.

"I tell you what, my zealous young sportsmen, you're rash to leave your boat at anchor here after dark without a light. I came aboard to find your lamp and set it."

"Oh, thanks," said Davies; "we took it with us."

"To see to shoot by?"

We laughed uncomfortably, and Davies compassed a wonderful German phrase to the effect that "it might come in useful." Happily the matter went no farther, for the position was a strained one at the best, and would not bear lengthening. The launch went alongside, and the invaders evacuated British soil, looking, for all von Brüning's flippant nonchalance, a rather crestfallen party. So much so, that, acute as was my anxiety, I took courage to whisper to Davies, while the transhipment of Herr Böhme was proceeding: "Ask Dollmann to stay while we dress."

"Why?" he whispered.

"Go on."

"I say, Herr Dollmann," said Davies, "won't you stay on board with us while we dress? There's a lot to tell you, and—and we can follow on with you when we're ready."

Dollmann had not yet stepped into the launch. "With pleasure," he said; but there followed an ominous silence, broken by von Brüning.

"Oh, come along, Dollmann, and let them alone," he said brusquely. You'll be horribly in the way down there, and we shall never get any supper if you keep them yarning."

"And it's now a quarter-past eight o'clock," grumbled Herr Böhme from his corner behind the hood. Dollmann submitted, and excused himself, and the launch steamed away.

"I think I twig," said Davies, as he helped, almost hoisted, me aboard. "Rather risky though—eh?"

"I knew they'd object—only wanted to make sure."

The cabin was just as we had left it, our shore clothes lying in disorder on the bunks, a locker or two half open.

"Well, I wonder what they did down here," said Davies.

For my part I went straight to the bookshelf.

"Does anything strike you about this?" I asked, kneeling on the sofa.

"Logbook's shifted," said Davies. "I'll swear it was at the end before."

"That doesn't matter. Anything else?"

"By Jove!—where's Dollmann's book?"

"It's here all right, but not where it should be." I had been reading it, you remember, overnight, and in the morning had replaced it in full view among the other books. I now found it behind them, in a wrenched attitude, which showed that someone who had no time to spare had pushed it roughly inwards.

"What do you make of that?" said Davies.

He produced long drinks, and we allowed ourselves ten minutes of absolute rest, stretched at full length on the sofas.

"They don't trust Dollmann," I said. "I spotted that at Memmert even."

"How?"

"First, when they were talking about you and me. He was on his defence, and in a deuce of a funk, too. Böhme was pressing him hard. Again, at the end, when he left the room followed by Grimm, who I'm certain was sent to watch him. It was while he was away that the other two arranged that rendezvous for the night of the 25th. And again just now, when you asked him to stay. I believe it's working out as I thought it would. Von Brüning, and through him Böhme (who is the 'engineer from Bremen'), know the story of that short cut and suspect that it was an attempt on your life. Dollmann daren't confess to that, because, morality apart, it could only have been prompted by extreme necessity—that is, by the knowledge that you were really dangerous, and not merely an inquisitive stranger. Now *we* know his motive; but they don't yet. The position of that book proves it."

"He shoved it in?"

"To prevent them seeing it. There's no earthly reason why *they* should have hidden it."

"Then we're getting on," said Davies. "That shows they know his real name, or why should he shove the book in? But they don't know he wrote a book, and that I have a copy."

"At any rate he *thinks* they don't; we can't say more than that."

"And what does he think about me—and you?"

"That's the point. Ten to one he's in tortures of doubt, and would give a fortune to have five minutes' talk alone with you to see how the land lies and get your version of the short-cut incident. But they won't let him. They want to watch him in our company and us in his; you see it's an interesting reunion for you and him."

"Well, let's get into these beastly clothes for it," groaned Davies. "I shall have a plunge overboard."

Something drastic was required, and I followed his example, curious as the hour was for bathing.

"I believe I know what happened just now," said I, as we plied rough towels in the warmth below. "They steamed up and found nobody on board. 'I'll leave a note,' says Dollmann. 'No independent communications,' say they (or think they), 'we'll come too, and take the chance of inspecting this hornets' nest.' Down they go, and Dollmann, who knows what to look for first, sees that damning bit of evidence staring him in the face. They look casually at the shelf among other things—examine the logbook, say—and he manages to push his own book out of sight. But he couldn't replace it when the interruption came. The action would have attracted attention *then*, and Böhme made him leave the cabin in advance, you know."

"This is all very well," said Davies, pausing in his toilet, "but do they guess how we've spent the day? By Jove, Carruthers, that chart with the square cut out; there it is on the rack!"

"We must chance it, and bluff for all we're worth," I said. The fact was that Davies could not be brought to realize that he had done anything very remarkable that day; yet those fourteen sinuous miles traversed blindfold, to say nothing of the return journey and my own exploits, made up an achievement audacious and improbable enough to out-distance suspicion. Nevertheless, von Brüning's banter had been disquieting, and if an inkling of our expedition had crossed his mind or theirs, there were ways of testing us which it would require all our effrontery to defeat.

"What are you looking for?" said Davies. I was at the collar and stud stage, but had broken off to study the time-table which we had bought that morning.

"Somebody insists on coming by the night train to somewhere, on the 25th," I reminded him. "Böhme, von Brüning, and Grimm are to meet the Somebody."

"Where?"

"At a railway station! I don't know where. They seemed to take it for granted. But it must be somewhere on the sea, because Böhme said, 'the tide serves.'"

"It may be anywhere from Emden to Hamburg."*

"Ho, there's a limit; it's probably somewhere near. Grimm was to come, and he's at Memmert."

"Here's the map . . . Emden and Norddeich are the only coast stations till you get to Wilhelmshaven—no, to Carolinensiel; but those are a long way east."

"And Emden's a long way south. Say Norddeich then; but according to this there's no train there after 6.15 p.m.; that's hardly 'night.' When's high tide on the 25th?"

"Let's see—8.30 here to-night—Norddeich'll be the same. Somewhere between 10.30 and 11 on the 25th."

"There's a train at Emden at 9.22 from Leer and the south, and one at 10.50 from the north."

"Are you counting on another fog?" said Davies, mockingly.

"No; but I want to know what our plans are."

"Can't we wait till this cursed inspection's over?"

"No, we can't; we should come to grief." This was no barren truism, for I was ready with a plan of my own, though reluctant to broach it to Davies.

Meanwhile, ready or not, we had to start. The cabin we left as it was, changing nothing and hiding nothing; the safest course to take, we thought, in spite of the risk of further search. But, as usual, I transferred my diary to my breast-pocket, and made sure that the two official letters from England were safe in a compartment of it.

"What do you propose?" I asked, when we were in the dinghy again.

"It's a case of 'as you were'," said Davies. "To-day's trip was a chance we shall never get again. We must go back to last night's decision—tell them that we're going to stay on here for a bit. Shooting, I suppose we shall have to say."

"And courting?" I suggested.

"Well, they know all about that. And then we must watch for a

---

*See Map B.

chance of tackling Dollmann privately. Not to-night, because we want time to consider those clues of yours."

"'Consider'?" I said: "that's putting it mildly."

We were at the ladder, and what a languid stiffness oppressed me I did not know till I touched its freezing rungs, each one of which seared my sore palms like red-hot iron.

The overdue steamer was just arriving as we set foot on the quay.

"And yet, by Jove! why not to-night?" pursued Davies, beginning to stride up the pier at a pace I could not imitate.

"Steady on," I protested; "and, look here, I disagree altogether. I believe to-day has doubled our chances, but unless we alter our tactics it has doubled our risks. We've involved ourselves in too tangled a web. I don't like this inspection, and I fear that foxy old Böhme who prompted it. The mere fact of their inviting us shows that we stand badly; for it runs in the teeth of Brüning's warning at Bensersiel, and smells uncommonly like arrest. There's a rift between Dollmann and the others, but it's a ticklish matter to drive our wedge in; as to *to-night*, hopeless; they're on the watch, and won't give us a chance. And after all, do we know enough? We don't know why he fled from England and turned German. It may have been an extraditable crime, but it may not. Supposing he defies us? There's the girl, you see—she ties our hands, and if he once gets wind of that, and trades on our weakness, the game's up."

"What are you driving at?"

"We want to detach him from Germany, but he'll probably go to any lengths rather than abandon his position here. His attempt on you is the measure of his interest in it. Now, is to-day to be wasted?" We were passing through the public gardens, and I dropped on to a seat for a moment's rest, crackling dead leaves under me. Davies remained standing, and pecked at the gravel with his toe.

"We have got two valuable clues," I went on; "that rendezvous on the 25th is one, and the name Esens is the other. We may consider them to eternity; I vote we act on them."

"How?" said Davies. "We're under a searchlight here; and if we're caught—"

"Your plan—ugh!—it's as risky as mine, and more so," I replied, rising with a jerk, for a spasm of cramp took me. "We must separate," I added, as we walked on. "We want, at one stroke, to prove to them that we're harmless, and to get a fresh start. I go back to London."

"To London!" said Davies. We were passing under an arc lamp, and, for the dismay his face showed, I might have said Kamchatka.

"Well, after all, it's where I ought to be at this moment," I observed.

"Yes, I forgot. And me?"

"You can't get on without me, so you lay up the yacht here—taking your time."

"While you?"

"After making inquiries about Dollmann's past I double back as somebody else, and follow up the clues."

"You'll have to be quick," said Davies, abstractedly.

"I can just do it in time for the 25th."

"When you say 'making inquiries,'" he continued, looking straight before him, "I hope you don't mean setting other people on his track?"

"He's fair game!" I could not help saying; for there were moments when I chafed under this scrupulous fidelity to our self-denying ordinance.

"He's our game, or nobody's," said Davies, sharply.

"Oh, I'll keep the secret," I rejoined.

"Let's stick together," he broke out. "I shall make a muck of it without you. And how are we to communicate—meet?"

"Somehow—that can wait. I know it's a leap in the dark, but there's safety in darkness."

"Carruthers! what are we talking about? If they have the ghost of a notion where we have been to-day, you give us away by packing off to London. They'll think we know their secret and are clearing out to make use of it. *That* means arrest, if you like!"

"Pessimist! Haven't I written proof of good faith in my pocket—official letters of recall, received to-day? It's one deception the less, you see; for those letters *may* have been opened; skilfully done it's impossible to detect. When in doubt, tell the truth!"

"It's a rum thing how often it pays in this spying business," said Davies, thoughtfully.

We had been tramping through deserted streets under the glare of electricity, I with my leaden shuffle, he with the purposeful forward stoop and swinging arms that always marked his gait ashore.

"Well, what's it to be?" I said. "Here's the Schwannallée."

"I don't like it," said he; "but I trust your judgement."

We turned slowly down, running over a few last points where prior agreement was essential. As we stood at the very gate of the villa: "Don't commit yourself to dates," I said; "say nothing that will prevent you from being here at least a week hence with the yacht still afloat." And my final word, as we waited at the door for the bell to be answered, was: "Don't mind what *I* say. If things look queer we may have to lighten the ship."

"Lighten?" whispered Davies; 'oh, I hope I shan't bosh it."

"I hope I shan't get cramp," I muttered between my teeth.

It will be remembered that Davies had never been to the villa before.

# 24

**Finesse**

THE door of a room on the ground floor was opened to us by a man-servant. As we entered the rattle of a piano stopped, and a hot wave of mingled scent and cigar smoke struck my nostrils. The first thing I noticed over Davies's shoulder, as he preceded me into the room, was a woman—the source of the perfume I decided—turning round from the piano as he passed it and staring him up and down with a disdainful familiarity that I at once hotly resented. She was in evening dress, pronounced in cut and colour; had a certain exuberant beauty, not wholly ascribable to nature, and a notable lack of breeding. Another glance showed me Dollmann putting down a liqueur glass of brandy, and rising from a low chair with something of a start; and another, von Brüning, lying back in a corner of a sofa, smoking; on the same sofa, *vis-à-vis* to him, was—yes, of course it was—Clara Dollmann; but how their surroundings alter people, I caught myself thinking. For the rest, I was aware that the room was furnished with ostentation, and was stuffy with stove-engendered warmth. Davies steered a straight course for Dollmann, and shook his hand with businesslike resolution. Then he tacked across to the sofa, abandoning me in the face of the enemy.

"Mr——?" said Dollmann.

"Carruthers," I answered, distinctly. "I was with Davies in the boat just now, but I don't think he introduced me. And now he has forgotten again," I added, dryly, turning towards Davies, who, having presented himself to Fräulein Dollmann, was looking feebly from her to von Brüning, the picture of tongue-tied awkwardness. (The commander nodded to me and stretched himself with a yawn.)

"Von Brüning told me about you," said Dollmann, ignoring my allusion, "but I was not quite sure of the name. No; it was not an occasion for formalities, was it?" He gave a sudden, mirthless laugh. I thought him flushed and excitable; yet, seen in a normal light, he was in some respects a pleasant surprise, the remarkable conformation of the head giving an impression of intellectual power and restless, almost insanely restless, energy.

"What need?" I said. "I have heard so much about you from Davies—and Commander von Brüning—that we seem to be old friends already."

He shot a doubtful look at me, and a diversion came from the piano.

"And now, for Heaven's sake," cried the lady of the perfume, "let us join Herr Böhme at supper!"

"Let me present you to my wife," said Dollmann.

So this was the stepmother; unmistakably German, I may add. I made my bow, and underwent much the same sort of frank scrutiny as Davies, only that it was rather more favourable to me, and ended in a carmine smile.

There was a general movement and further introductions. Davies was led to the stepmother, and I found myself confronting the daughter with quickened pulses, and a sudden sense of added complexity in the issues. I had, of course, made up my mind to ignore our meeting of yesterday, and had assumed that she would do the same. And she did ignore it—we met as utter strangers; nor did I venture (for other eyes were upon us) to transmit any sign of intelligence to her. But the next moment I was wondering if I had not fallen into a trap. She had promised not to tell, but under what circumstances? I saw the scene again; the misty flats, the spruce little sail-boat and its sweet young mistress, fresh as a dewy flower, but blanched and demoralized by a horrid fear, appealing to my honour so to act that we three should never meet again, promising to be silent, but as much in her own interest as ours, and under that implied condition which I had only equivocally refused. The condition was violated, not by her fault or ours, but violated. She was free to help her father against us, and was she helping him? What troubled me was the change in her; that she—how can I express it without offence?—was less in discord with her surroundings than she should have been; that in dress, pose and manner (as we exchanged some trivialities) she was too near reflecting the style of the other woman; that, in fact, she in some sort realized my original conception of her, so brutally avowed to Davies, so signally, as I had thought, falsified. In the sick perplexity that this discovery caused me I dare say I looked as foolish as Davies had done, and more so, for the close heat of the room and its tainted atmosphere, succeeding so abruptly to the wholesome nip of the outside air, were giving me a faintness which this moral check lessened my power to combat. Von Brüning's face wore a sneering smile that I winced under; and, turning, I found another pair of eyes fixed on me, those of Herr Böhme, whose squat figure had appeared at a pair of folding doors leading to an adjoining room. Napkin in hand, he was taking in the scene before him with fat benevolence, but exceeding shrewdness. I instantly noticed a faint red weal relieving the ivory of his bald head; and I had suffered too often in the same quarter myself to mistake its origin, namely, our cabin doorway.

"This is the other young explorer, Böhme," said von Brüning. "Herr Davies kidnapped him a month ago, and bullied and starved him into submission; they'll drown together yet. I believe his sufferings have been terrible."

"His sufferings are over," I retorted. "I've mutinied—deserted—haven't I, Davies?" I caught Davies gazing with solemn *gaucherie* at Miss Dollmann.

"Oh, what?" he stammered. I explained in English. "Oh, yes, Carruthers has to go home," he said, in his vile lingo.

No one spoke for a moment, and even von Brüning had no persiflage ready.

"Well, are we never going to have supper?" said madame, impatiently; and with that we all moved towards the folding doors. There had been little formality in the proceedings so far, and there was less still in the supper-room. Böhme resumed his repast with appetite, and the rest of us sat down apparently at random, though an underlying method was discernible. As it worked out, Dollmann was at one end of the small table, with Davies on his right and Böhme on his left; Frau Dollmann at the other, with me on her right and von Brüning on her left. The seventh personage, Fräulein Dollmann, was between the commander and Davies on the side opposite to me. No servants appeared, and we waited on ourselves. I have a vague recollection of various excellent dishes, and a distinct one of abundance of wine. Someone filled me a glass of champagne, and I confess that I drained it with honest avidity, blessing the craftsman who coaxed forth the essence, the fruit that harboured it, the sun that warmed it.

"Why are you going so suddenly?" said von Brüning to me across the table.

"Didn't I tell you we had to call here for letters? I got mine this morning, and among others a summons back to work. Of course I must obey." (I found myself speaking in a frigid silence.) "The annoying thing was that there were two letters, and if I had only come here two days sooner I should have only got the first, which gave me an extension."

"You are very conscientious. How will they know?"

"Ah, but the second's rather urgent."

There was another uncomfortable silence, broken by Dollmann.

"By the way, Herr Davies," he began, "I ought to apologize to you for—"

This was no business of mine, and the less interest I took in it the better; so I turned to Frau Dollmann and abused the fog.

"Have you been in the harbour all day?" she asked, "then how was it you did not visit us? Was Herr Davies so shy?" (Curiosity or malice?)

"Quite the contrary; but I was," I answered coldly; "you see, we knew Herr Dollmann was away, and we really only called here to get my letters; besides, we did not know your address." I looked at Clara and found her talking gaily to von Brüning, deaf seemingly to our little dialogue.

"Anyone would have told you it," said madame, raising her eyebrows.

"I dare say; but directly after breakfast the fog came on, and—well, one cannot leave a yacht alone in a fog," I said, with professional solidity.

Von Brüning pricked up his ears at this. "I'll be hanged if that was *your* maxim," he laughed; "you're too fond of the shore!"

I sent him a glance of protest, as though to say: "What's the use of your warning if you won't let me act on it?"

For, of course, my excuses were meant chiefly for his consumption, and Fräulein Dollmann's. That the lady I addressed them to found them unpalatable was not my fault.

"Then you sat in your wretched little cabin all day?" she persisted.

"All day," I said, brazenly; "it was the safest thing to do." And I looked again at Fräulein Dollmann, frankly and squarely. Our eyes met, and she dropped hers instantly, but not before I had learnt something; for if ever I saw misery under a mask it was on her face. No; she had not told.

I think I puzzled the stepmother, who shrugged her white shoulders, and said in that case she wondered we had dared to leave our precious boat and come to supper. If we knew Frisian fogs as well as she did—

Oh, I explained, we were not so nervous as that; and as for supper on shore, if she only knew what a Spartan life we led—

"Oh, for mercy's sake, don't tell me about it!" she cried, with a grimace; "I hate the mention of yachts. When I think of that dreadful *Medusa* coming from Hamburg—" I sympathized with half my attention, keeping one strained ear open for developments on my right. Davies, I knew, was in the thick of it, and none too happy under Böhme's eye, but working manfully. "My fault"—"sudden squall"—"quite safe," were some of the phrases I caught; while I was aware, to my alarm, that he was actually drawing a diagram of something with bread-crumbs and table-knives. The subject seemed to gutter out to an awkward end, and suddenly Böhme, who was my right-hand neighbour, turned to me. "You are starting for England to-morrow morning?" he said.

"Yes," I answered; "there is a steamer at 8.15, I believe."

"That is good. We shall be companions."

"Are you going to England, too, sir?" I asked, with hot misgivings.

"No, no! I am going to Bremen; but we shall travel together as far as—you go by Amsterdam, I suppose?—as far as Leer, then. That will be very pleasant." I fancied there was a ghoulish gusto in his tone.

"Very," I assented. "You are making a short stay here, then?"

"As long as usual. I visit the work at Memmert once a month or so, spend a night with my friend Dollmann and his charming family" (he leered round him), "and return."

Whether I was right or wrong in my next step I shall never know, but obeying a strong instinct, "Memmert," I said; "do tell me more about Memmert. We heard a good deal about it from Commander von Brüning; but—"

"He was discreet, I expect," said Böhme.

"He left off at the most interesting part."

"What's that about me?" joined in von Brüning.

"I was saying that we're dying to know more about Memmert, aren't we, Davies?"

"Oh, I don't know," said Davies, evidently aghast at my temerity; but I did not mind that. If he roughed my suit, so much the better; I intended to rough his.

"You gave us plenty of history, commander, but you did not bring it up to date." The triple alliance laughed, Dollmann boisterously.

"Well," said von Brüning; "I gave you very good reasons, and you acquiesced."

"And now he is trying to pump *me*," said Böhme, with his rasping chuckle.

"Wait a bit, sir; I have an excuse. The commander was not only mysterious but inaccurate. I appeal to you, Herr Dollmann, for it was *apropos* of you. When we fell in with him at Bensersiel, Davies asked him if you were at home, and he said 'No.' When would you be back? Probably soon; *but he did not know when.*"

"Oh, he said that?" said Dollmann.

"Well, only three days later we arrive at Norderney, and find you have returned that very day, but have gone to Memmert. Again (by the way) the mysterious Memmert! But more than ever mysterious now, for in the evening, not only you and Herr Böhme—"

"What penetration!" laughed von Brüning.

"But also Commander von Brüning, pay us a visit in *his* launch, all coming from Memmert!"

"And you infer?" said von Brüning.

"Why, that you must have known at Bensersiel—only three days ago—exactly when Herr Dollmann was coming back, having an appointment at Memmert with him for to-day."

"Which I wished to conceal from you?"

"Yes, and that's why I'm so inquisitive; it's entirely your own fault."

"So it seems," said he, with mock humility; "but fill your glass and go on, young man. Why should I want to deceive you?"

"That's just what I want to know. Come, confess now; wasn't there something important afoot to-day at Memmert? Something to do with the gold? You were inspecting it, sorting it, weighing it? Or *I* know! You were transporting it secretly to the mainland?"

"Not a very good day for that! But softly, Herr Carruthers; no fishing for admissions. Who said we had found any gold?"

"Well, have you? There!"

"That's better! Nothing like candour, my young investigator. But I am afraid, having no authority, I cannot assist you at all. Better try Herr Böhme again. I'm only a casual onlooker."

"With shares."

"Ah! you remember that? (He remembers everything!) With a few shares, then; but with no expert knowledge. Now, Böhme is the consulting engineer. Rescue me, Böhme."

"I cannot disclaim expert knowledge," said Böhme, with humorous gravity; "but I disclaim responsibility. Now, Herr Dollmann is chairman of the company."

"And I," said Dollmann, with a noisy laugh, "must fall back on the shareholders, whose interests I have to guard. One can't be too careful in these confidential matters."

"Here's one who gives his consent," I said. "Can't he represent the rest?"

"Extorted by torture," said von Brüning. "I retract."

"Don't mind them, Herr Carruthers," cried Frau Dollmann, "they are making fun of you; but I will give you a hint; no woman can keep a secret—"

"Ah!" I cried, triumphantly, "you have been there?"

"I? Not I; I detest the sea! But Clara has." Everyone looked at Clara, who in her turn looked in naïve bewilderment from me to her father.

"Indeed?" I said, more soberly, "but perhaps she is not a free agent."

"Perfectly free!" said Dollmann.

"I have only been there once, some time ago," said she, "and I saw no gold at all."

"Guarded," I observed. "I beg your pardon; I mean that perhaps you only saw what you were allowed to see. And, in any case, the fräulein has no expert knowledge and no responsibility, and, perhaps, no shares. Her province is to be charming, not to hold financial secrets."

"I have done my best to help you," said the stepmother.

"They're all against us, Davies."

"Oh, chuck it, Carruthers!" said Davies, in English.

"He's insatiable," said von Brüning, and there was a pause; clearly, they meant to elicit more.

"Well, I shall draw my own conclusions," I said.

"This is interesting," said von Brüning, "in what sense?"

"It begins to dawn on me that you made fools of us at Bensersiel.

Don't you remember, Davies, what an interest he took in all our doings? I wonder if he feared our exploring propensities might possibly lead us to Memmert?"

"Upon my word, this is the blackest ingratitude. I thought I made myself particularly agreeable to you."

"Yes, indeed; especially about the duck shooting! How useful your local man would have been—both to us and to you!"

"Go on," said the commander, imperturbably.

"Wait a moment; I'm thinking it out." And thinking it out I was in deadly earnest, for all my levity, as I pressed my hand on my burning forehead and asked myself where I was to stop in this seductive but perilous fraud. To carry it too far was to court complete exposure; to stop too soon was equally compromising.

"What is he talking about, and why go on with this ridiculous mystery?" said Frau Dollmann.

"I was thinking about this supper party, and the way it came about," I pursued, slowly.

"Nothing to complain of, I hope?" said Dollmann.

"Of course not! Impromptu parties are always the pleasantest, and this one was delightfully impromptu. Now I bet you I know its origin! Didn't you discuss us at Memmert? And didn't one of you suggest—"

"One would almost think you had been there," said Dollmann.

"You may thank your vile climate that we weren't," I retorted, laughing. "But, as I was saying, didn't one of you suggest—which of you? Well, I'm sure it wasn't the commander—"

"Why not?" said Böhme.

"It's difficult to explain—an intuition, say—I am sure he stood up for us; and I don't think it was Herr Dollmann, because he knows Davies already, and he's always on the spot; and, in short I'll swear it was Herr Böhme, who is leaving early to-morrow, and had never seen either of us. It was you, sir, who proposed that we should be asked to supper to-night—for inspection?"

"Inspection?" said Böhme; "what an extraordinary idea!"

"You can't deny it, though! And one thing more; in the harbour just now—no—this is going too far; I shall mortally offend you." I gave way to hearty laughter.

"Come, let's have it. Your hallucinations are diverting."

"If you insist; but this is rather a delicate matter. You know we were a little surprised to find you *all* on board; and you, Herr Böhme, did you always take such a deep interest in small yachts? I am afraid that it was at a certain sacrifice of comfort that you *inspected* ours!" And I glanced at the token he bore of his encounter with our lintel. There was a burst of pent-up merriment, in which Dollmann took the loudest share.

"I warned you, Böhme," he said.

The engineer took the joke in the best possible part. "We owe you apologies," he conceded.

"Don't mention it," said Davies.

"*He* doesn't mind," I said; "I'm the injured one. I'm sure you never suspected Davies, who could?" (Who indeed? I was on firm ground there.)

"The point is, what did you take *me* for?"

"Perhaps we take you for it still," said von Brüning.

"Oho! Still suspicious? Don't drive me to extremities."

"What extremities?"

"When I get back to London I shall go to Lloyd's! I haven't forgotten the flaw in the title." There was an impressive silence.

"Gentlemen," said Dollmann, with exaggerated solemnity, "we must come to terms with this formidable young man. What do you say?"

"Take me to Memmert," I exclaimed. "Those are my terms!"

"Take you to Memmert? But I thought you were starting for England to-morrow?"

"I ought to; but I'll stay for that."

"You said it was urgent. Your conscience is very elastic."

"That's my affair. Will you take me to Memmert?"

"What do you say, gentlemen?" Böhme nodded. "I think we owe some reparation. Under promise of absolute secrecy, then?"

"Of course, now that you trust me. But you'll show me everything—honour bright—wreck, depot, and all?"

"Everything; if you don't object to a diver's dress."

"Victory!" I cried, in triumph. "We've won our point, Davies. And now, gentlemen, I don't mind saying that as far as I am concerned the joke's at an end; and, in spite of your kind offer, I must start for England to-morrow under the good Herr Böhme's wing. And in case my elastic conscience troubles you (for I see you think me a weather-cock) here are the letters received this morning, establishing my identity as a humble but respectable clerk in the British Civil Service, summoned away from his holiday by a tyrannical superior." (I pulled out my letters and tossed them to Dollmann.) "Ah, you don't read English easily, perhaps? I dare say Herr Böhme does."

Leaving Böhme to study dates, post-marks, and contents to his heart's content, and unobserved, I turned to sympathize with my fair neighbour, who complained that her head was going round; and no wonder. But at this juncture, and very much to my surprise, Davies struck in.

"*I* should like to go to Memmert," he said.

"You?" said von Brüning. "Now I'm surprised at that."

"But you won't be staying here either, Davies," I objected.

"Yes, I shall," said Davies. "Why, I told you I should. If you leave me in the lurch like this I must have time to look round."

"You needn't pretend that you cannot sail alone," said von Brüning.

"It's much more fun with two; I think I shall wire for another friend. Meanwhile, I should like to see Memmert."

"That's only an excuse, I'm afraid," said I.

"I want to shoot ducks too," pursued Davies, reddening. "I always have wanted to; and you promised to help in that, commander."

"You can't get out of it now," I laughed.

"Certainly not," said he, unmoved; "but, honestly, I should advise Herr Davies, if he is ever going to get home this season, to make the best of this fine weather."

"It's too fine," said Davies; "I prefer wind. If I cannot get a friend I think I shall stop cruising, leave the yacht here, and come back for her next year."

There was some mute telegraphy between the allies.

"You can leave her in my charge," said Dollmann, "and start with your friend to-morrow."

"Thanks; but there is no hurry," said Davies, growing redder than ever. "I like Norderney—and we might have another sail in your dinghy, fräulein," he blurted out.

"Thank you," she said, in that low dry voice I had heard yesterday; "but I think I shall not be sailing again—it is getting too cold."

"Oh, no!" said Davies, "it's splendid." But she had turned to von Brüning, and took no notice.

"Well, send me a report about Memmert, Davies," I laughed, with the idea of drawing attention from his rebuff. But Davies, having once delivered his soul, seemed to have lost his shyness, and only gazed at his neighbour with the placid, dogged expression that I knew so well. That was the end of those delicate topics; and conviviality grew apace.

I am not indifferent at any time to good wine and good cheer, nor was it for lack of pressing that I drank as sparingly as I was able, and pretended to a greater elation than I felt. Nor certainly was it from any fine scruples as to the character of the gentleman whose hospitality we were receiving—scruples which I knew affected Davies, who ate little and drank nothing. In any case he was adamant in such matters, and I verily believe would at any time have preferred our own little paraffin-flavoured messes to the best dinner in the world. It was a very wholesome caution that warned me not to abuse the finest brain tonic ever invented by the wit of man. I had finessed Memmert, as one finesses a low card when holding a higher; but I had too much respect for our adversaries to trade on any fancied security we had won thereby. They had allowed me to win the trick, but I credited them with a better knowledge of my hand than they chose to show. On the other hand I hugged the axiom that in all conflicts it is just as fatal to underrate the difficulties of your enemy as to overrate your own. Their chief one—and it multiplied a thousandfold the excitement of the contest—was, I felt sure, the fear of striking in error; of using a sledge-hammer to break a nut. In breaking it they risked publicity, and publicity, I felt convinced, was death to their secret. So, even supposing they had detected the finesse, and guessed that we had in fact got wind of imperial designs; yet, even so, I counted on immunity so long as they thought we were on the wrong scent, with Memmert, and Memmert alone, as the source of our suspicions.

Had it been necessary I was prepared to encourage such a view, admitting that the cloth von Brüning wore had made his connexion with Memmert curious, and had suggested to Davies, for I should have put it on him, with his naval enthusiasms, that the wreck-works were really naval-defence works. If they went farther, and suspected that we had tried to go to Memmert that very day, the position was worse, but not desperate; for the fear that they would take the final step and suppose that we had actually got there and overheard their talk, I flatly refused to entertain, until I should find myself under arrest.

Precisely how near we came to it I shall never rightly know; but I have good reason to believe that we trembled on the verge. The main issue was fully enough for me, and it was only in passing flashes that I followed the play of the warring under-currents. And yet, looking back on the scene, I would warrant there was no party of seven in Europe that evening where a student of human documents would have found so rich a field, such noble and ignoble ambitions, such base and holy fears, aye, and such pitiful agonies of the spirit. Roughly divided though we were into separate camps, no two of us were wholly at one. Each wore a mask in the grand imposture; excepting, I am inclined to think, the lady on my left, who, outside her own well-being, which she cultivated without reserve, had, as far as I could see, but one axe to grind—the intimacy of von Brüning and her stepdaughter—and ground it openly.

Not even Böhme and von Brüning were wholly at one; and as moral distances are reckoned, Davies and I were leagues apart. Sitting between Dollmann and Dollmann's daughter, the living and breathing symbols of the two polar passions he had sworn to harmonize, he kept an equilibrium which, though his aims were nominally mine, I could not attain to. For me the man was the central figure; if I had attention to spare it was on him that I bestowed it; groping disgustfully after his hidden springs of action, noting the evidences of great gifts squandered and prostituted; questioning where he was most vulnerable; whom he feared most, us or his colleagues; whether he was open to remorse or shame; or whether he meditated further crime. The girl was incidental. After the first shock of surprise I had soon enough discovered that she, like the rest, had assumed a disguise; for she was far too innocent to sustain the deception; and yesterday was fresh in my memory. I was forced to continue turning her assumed character to account; but it would be pharisaical in me to say that I rose to any moral heights in her regard—wine and excitement had deadened my better nature to that extent. I thought she looked prettier than ever, and, as time passed, I fell into a cynical carelessness about her. This glimpse of her home life, and the desperate expedients to which she was driven (whether by compulsion or from her own regard for Davies) to repel and dismiss him, did not strike me as they might have done as the crowning argument in favour of the course we had adopted the night before, that of compassing our end without noise and scandal, disarming Dollmann, but aiding him to escape from the allies he had betrayed. To Davies, the man, if not a pure abstraction, was at most a noxious vermin to be trampled on for the public good; while the girl, in her blackguardly surroundings, and with her sinister future, had become the very source of his impulse.

And the other players? Böhme was *my* abstraction, the fortress whose foundations we were sapping, the embodiment of that systematized force which is congenital to the German people. In von Brüning, the personal factor was uppermost. Callous as I was this evening, I could not help wondering occasionally, as he talked and laughed with Clara Dollmann, what in his innermost thoughts, knowing her father, he felt and meant. It is a point I cannot and would not pursue, and, thank Heaven, it does not matter now; yet, with fuller knowledge of the facts, and, I trust, a mellower judgement, I often return to the same debate, and, by I know not what illogical bypaths, always arrive at the same conclusion, that I liked the man and like him still.

We behaved as sportsmen in the matter of time, giving them over two hours to make up their minds about us. It was only when tobacco smoke and heat brought back my faintness, and a twinge of cramp warned me that human strength has limits, that I rose and said we must go; that I had to make an early start to-morrow. I am hazy about the farewells, but I think that Dollmann was the most cordial, to me at any rate, and I augured good therefrom. Böhme said he should see me again. Von Brüning, though bound for the harbour also, considered it was far too early to be going yet, and said good-bye.

"You want to talk us over," I remember saying, with the last flicker of gaiety I could muster.

We were in the streets again, under a silver, breathless night; dizzily footing the greasy ladder again; in the cabin again, where I collapsed on a sofa just as I was, and slept such a deep and stringent sleep that the men of the *Blitz's* launch might have handcuffed and trussed and carried me away, without incommoding me in the least.

## 25

### I Double Back

"GOOD-BYE, old chap," called Davies.

"Good-bye," the whistle blew and the ferry-steamer forged ahead, leaving Davies on the quay, bareheaded and wearing his old Norfolk jacket and stained grey flannels, as at our first meeting in Flensburg station. There was no bandaged hand this time, but he looked pinched and depressed; his eyes had black circles round them; and again I felt that same indefinable pathos in him.

"Your friend is in low spirits," said Böhme, who was installed on a seat beside me, voluminously caped and rugged against the biting air. It was a still, sunless day.

"So am I," I grunted, and it was the literal truth. I was only half awake, felt unwashed and dissipated, heavy in head and limbs. But for Davies I should never have been where I was. It was he who had patiently coaxed me out of my bunk, packed my bag, fed me with tea and an omelette (to which I believe he had devoted peculiarly tender care), and generally mothered me for departure. While I swallowed my second cup he was brushing the mould and smoothing the dents from my felt hat, which had been entombed for a month in the sail-locker; working at it with a remorseful concern in his face. The only initiative I am conscious of having shown was in the matter of my bag. "Put in my sea clothes, oils, and all," I had said; "I may want them again." There was mortal need of a thorough consultation, but this was out of the question. Davies did not badger or complain, but only timidly asked me how we were to meet and communicate, a question on which my mind was an absolute blank.

"Look out for me about the 26th," I suggested feebly.

Before we left the cabin he gave me a scrap of pencilled paper and saw that it went safely into my pocket-book. "Look at it in the train," he said.

Unable to cope with Böhme, I paced the deck aimlessly as we swung round the See-Gat into the Buse Tief, trying to identify the point where we crossed it yesterday blindfold. But the tide was full, and the waters blank for miles round till they merged in haze. Soon I drifted down into the saloon, and crouching over a stove pulled out that scrap of paper. In a crabbed, boyish hand, and much besmudged with tobacco ashes, I found the following notes:

(1) *Your journey.** Norddeich 8.58, Emden 10.32, Leer 1.16 (Böhme changes for Bremen), Rheine 1.8 (change), Amsterdam 7.17 p.m. Leave again *via* Hook 8.52, London 9 a.m.

(2) The coast-station—*their* rondezvous—querry is it *Norden*? (You pass it 9.13)—there is a tidal creek up to it. High-water there on 25th, say 10.30 to 11 p.m. It cannot be Norddeich, which I find has a dredged-out low-water channel for the steamer, so tide "serves" would not apply.

(3) *Your other clews* (tugs, pilots, depths, railway, Esens, seven of something). Querry: Scheme of defence by land and sea for North Sea Coast?

*Sea*—7 islands, 7 channels between (counting West Ems), very small depths (what you said) in most of them. Tugs and pilots for patrol work behind islands, as I always said. Querry: Rondezvous is for inspecting channels?

*Land*—Look at railway (map in ulster pocket) running in a loop all round Friesland, a few miles from coast. Querry: To be used as line of communication for army corps. Troops could be quickly sent to any threatened point. *Esens* the base? It is in top centre of loop. Von Brooning dished us fairly over that at Bensersiel.

*Chatham*—D. was spying after our naval plans for war with Germany.

Von Brooning runs naval part over here.

Where does Burmer come in? Querry—you go to Breman and find out about him?

I nodded stupidly over this document—so stupidly that I found myself wondering whether Burmer was a place or a person. Then I dozed, to wake with a violent start and find the paper on the floor. Panic-stricken, I hid it away, and went on deck, when I found we were close to Norddeich, running up to the bleakest of bleak jetties thrown out from the dyke-bound polders of the mainland. Böhme and I landed together, and he was at my elbow as I asked for a ticket for Amsterdam, and was given one as far as Rheine, a junction near the Dutch frontier. He was ensconced in an opposite corner to me in the railway carriage, looking like an Indian idol. "Where do you come in?" I pondered, dreamily. Too sleepy to talk, I could only blink at him, sitting bolt upright with my arms folded over my precious pocket-book. Finally, I gave up the struggle, buttoned my ulster tightly up, and turning my back upon him with an apology, lay down to sleep, the precious pocket

---

*See Maps A and B.

nethermost. He was at liberty to rifle my bag if he chose, and I dare say he did. I cannot say, for from this point till Rheine, for the best part of four hours, that is, I had only two lucid intervals.

The first was at Emden, where we both had to change. Here, as we pushed our way down the crowded platform, Böhme, after being greeted respectfully by several persons, was at last button-holed without means of escape by an obsequious gentleman, whose description is of no moment, but whose conversation is. It was about a canal; what canal I did not gather, though, from a name dropped, I afterwards identified it as one in course of construction as a feeder to the Ems. The point is that the subject was canals. At the moment it was seed dropped in un-receptive soil, but it germinated later. I passed on, mingling with the crowd, and was soon asleep again in another carriage where Böhme this time did not follow me.

The second occasion was at Leer, when I heard myself called by name, and woke to find him at the window. He had to change trains, and had come to say good-bye. "Don't forget to go to Lloyd's," he grated in my ear. I expect it was a wan smile that I returned, for I was at a very low ebb, and my fortress looked sarcastically impregnable. But the sapper was free; "free" was my last conscious thought.

Even after Rheine, where I changed for the last time, a brutish drowsiness enchained me, and the afternoon was well advanced before my faculties began to revive.

The train crept like a snail from station to station. I might, so a fellow-passenger told me, have waited three hours at Rheine for an express which would have brought me to Amsterdam at about the same time; or, if I had chosen to break the journey farther back, two hours at either Emden or Leer would still have enabled me to catch the said express at Rheine. These alternatives had escaped Davies, and, I surmised, had been suppressed by Böhme, who doubtless did not want me behind him, free either to double back or to follow him to Bremen.

The pace, then, was execrable, and there were delays; we were behind time at Hengelo, thirty minutes late at Apeldoorn; so that I might well have grown nervous about my connexions at Amsterdam, which were in some jeopardy. But as I battled out of my lethargy and began to take account of our position and prospects, quite a different thought at the outset affected me. Anxiety to reach London was swamped in re-luctance to quit Germany, so that I found myself grudging every mile that I placed between me and the frontier. It was the old question of ur-gency. To-day was the 23rd. The visit to London meant a minimum ab-sence of forty-eight hours, counting from Amsterdam; that is to say, that by travelling for two nights and one day, and devoting the other day to investigating Dollmann's past, it was humanly possible for me to be

back on the Frisian coast on the evening of the 25th. Yes, I could be at
Norden, if that was the "rendezvous," at 7 p.m. But what a scramble!
No margin for delays, no physical respite. Some pasts take a deal of rak-
ing up—other persons may be affected; men are cautious, they trip you
up with red tape; or the man who knows is out at lunch—a protracted
lunch; or in the country—a protracted week-end. Will you see Mr. So-
and-so, or leave a note? Oh! I know those public departments—from
the inside! And the Admiralty! . . . I saw myself baffled and racing back
the same night to Germany, with two days wasted, arriving, good for
nothing, at Norden, with no leisure to reconnoitre my ground; to be
baffled again there, probably, for you cannot always count on fogs (as
Davies said). Esens was another clue, and "to follow Burmer"—there
was something in that notion. But I wanted time, and had I time? How
long could Davies maintain himself at Norderney? Not so very long,
from what I remembered of last night. And was he ever safe there? A
feverish dream recurred to me—a dream of Davies in a diving-dress; of
a regrettable hitch in the air-supply—Stop, that was nonsense! . . . Let
us be sane. What matter if he had to go? What matter if I took my time
in London? Then with a flood of shame I saw Davies's wistful face on
the quay, heard his grim ejaculation: "He's our game or no one's"; and
my own sullen "Oh, I'll keep the secret!" London was utterly impossible. If I found my informant, what credentials had I, what claim to con-
fidences? None, unless I told the whole story. Why, my mere presence
in Whitehall would imperil the secret; for, once on my native heath, I
should be recognized—possibly haled to judgement; at the best should
escape in a cloud of rumour—"last heard of at Norderney"; "only this
morning was raising Cain at the Admiralty about a mythical lieutenant." No! Back to Friesland, was the word. One night's rest—I must
have that—between sheets, on a feather bed; one long, luxurious night,
and then back refreshed to Friesland, to finish our work in our own
way, and with none but our own weapons.

Having reached this resolve, I was nearly putting it into instant execution, by alighting at Amersfoort, but thought better of it. I had a transformation to effect before I returned North, and the more populous
centre I made it in the less it was likely to attract notice. Besides, I had
in my mind's eye a perfect bed in a perfect hostelry hard by the Amstel
River. It was an economy in the end.

So, at half-past eight I was sipping my coffee in the aforesaid hostelry,
with a London newspaper before me, which was unusually interesting,
and some German journals, which, "in hate of a wrong not theirs,"
were one and all seething with rancorous Anglophobia. At nine I was
in the Jewish quarter, striking bargains in an infamous marine slop-
shop. At half-past nine I was despatching this unscrupulous telegram to

my chief—"Very sorry, could not call Norderney; hope extension all right; please write to Hôtel du Louvre, Paris." At ten I was in the perfect bed, rapturously flinging my limbs abroad in its glorious redundancies. And at 8.28 on the following morning, with a novel chilliness about the upper lip, and a vast excess of strength and spirits, I was sitting in a third-class carriage, bound for Germany, and dressed as a young seaman, in a pea-jacket, peaked cap, and comforter.

The transition had not been difficult. I had shaved off my moustache and breakfasted hastily in my bedroom, ready equipped for a journey in my ulster and cloth cap. I had dismissed the hotel porter at the station, and left my bag at the cloak-room, after taking out of it an umber bundle and substituting the ulster. The umber bundle, which consisted of my oilskins, and within them my sea-boots and a few other garments and necessaries, the whole tied up with a length of tarry rope, was now in the rack above me, and (with a stout stick) represented my luggage. Every article in it—I shudder at their origin—was in strict keeping with my humble *métier*, for I knew they were liable to search at the frontier custom-house; but there was a Baedeker of Northern Germany in my jacket pocket.

For the nonce, if questions were asked, I was an English seaman, going to Emden to join a ship, with a ticket as far as the frontier. Beyond that a definite scheme of action had still to be thought out. One thing, however, was sure. I was determined to be at Norden tomorrow night, the 25th. A word about Norden, which is a small town seven miles south of Norddeich. When hurriedly scanning the map for coast stations in the cabin yesterday, I had not thought of Norden, because it did not appear to be on the coast, but Davies had noticed it while I slept, and I now saw that his pencilled hint was a shrewd one. The creek he spoke of, though barely visible on the map,* flowed into the Ems Estuary in a south-westerly direction. The "night train" tallied to perfection, for high tide in the creek would be, as Davies estimated, between 10.30 and 11 p.m. on the night of the 25th; and the time-table showed that the only night train arriving at Norden was one from the south at 10.46 p.m. This looked promising. Emden, which I had inclined to on the spur of the moment, was out of court in comparison, for many reasons; not the least being that it was served by three trains between 9 p.m. and 1 a.m., so that the phrase "night train" would be ambiguous and not decisive as with Norden.

So far good; but how was I to spend the intervening time? Should I act on Davies's "querry" and go to Bremen after Böhme? I soon dismissed that idea. It was one to act upon if others failed; for the present

*See Map B.

it meant another scramble. Bremen is six hours from Norden by rail. I should spend a disproportionate amount of my limited time in trains, and I should want a different disguise. Besides, I had already learnt something fresh about Böhme; for the seed dropped at Emden Station yesterday had come to life. A submarine engineer I knew him to be before; I now knew that canals were another branch of his labours—not a very illuminating fact; but could I pick up more in a single day?

There remained Esens, and it was thither I resolved to go to-night— a tedious journey, lasting till past eight in the evening; but there I should only be an hour from Norden by rail.

And at Esens?

All day long I strove for light on the central mystery, collecting from my diary, my memory, my imagination, from the map, the time-table, and Davies's grubby jottings, every elusive atom of material. Sometimes I issued from a reverie with a start, to find a phlegmatic Dutch peasant staring strangely at me over his china pipe. I was more careful over the German border. Davies's paper I soon knew by heart. I pictured him writing it with his cramped fist in his corner by the stove, fighting against sleep, absently striking salvos of matches, while I snored in my bunk; absently diverging into dreams, I knew, of a rose-brown face under dewy hair and a grey tam-o'-shanter; though not a word of her came into the document. I smiled to see his undying faith in the "channel theory" reconciled at the eleventh hour, with new data touching the neglected "land."

The result was certainly interesting, but it left me cold. That there existed in the German archives some such scheme of defence for the North Sea coast was very likely indeed. The seven islands, with their seven shallow channels (though, by the way, two of them, the twin branches of the Ems, are by no means so shallow), were a very fair conjecture, and fitted in admirably with the channel theory, whose intrinsic merits I had always recognized; my constant objection having been that it did not go nearly far enough to account for our treatment. The ring of railway round the peninsula, with Esens at the apex, was suggestive, too; but the same objection applied. Every country with a maritime frontier has, I suppose, secret plans of mobilization for its defence, but they are not such as could be discovered by passing travellers, not such as would warrant stealthy searches, or require for their elaboration so recondite a meeting-place as Memmert. Dollmann was another weak point; Dollmann in England, spying. All countries, Germany included, have spies in their service, dirty though necessary tools; but Dollmann in such intimate association with the principal plotters on this side; Dollmann rich, influential, a power in local affairs—it was clear he was no ordinary spy.

And here I detected a hesitation in Davies's rough sketch, a reluctance, as it were, to pursue a clue to its logical end. He spoke of a German scheme of coast defence, and in the next breath of Dollmann spying for English plans in the event of war with Germany, and there he left the matter; but what sort of plans? Obviously (if he was on the right track) plans of attack on the German coast as opposed to those of strategy on the high seas. But what sort of an attack? Obviously again, if his railway-ring meant anything, an attack by invasion on that remote and desolate littoral which he had so often himself declared to be impregnably secure behind its web of sands and shallows. My mind went back to my question at Bensersiel, "Can this coast be invaded?" to his denial and our fruitless survey of the dykes and polders. Was he now reverting to a fancy we had both rejected, while shrinking from giving it explicit utterance? The doubt was tantalizing.

A brief digression here about the phases of my journey. At Rheine I changed trains, turned due north and became a German seaman. There was little risk in a defective accent—sailors are so polyglot; while an English sailor straying about Esens might excite curiosity. Yesterday I had paid no heed to the landscape; to-day I neglected nothing that could conceivably supply a hint.

From Rheine to Emden we descended the valley of the Ems; at first through a land of thriving towns and fat pastures, degenerating farther north to spaces of heathery bog and moorland—a sad country, but looking at its best, such as that was, for I should mention here that the weather, which in the early morning had been as cold and misty as ever, grew steadily milder and brighter as the day advanced; while my newspaper stated that the glass was falling and the anticyclone giving way to pressure from the Atlantic.

At Emden, where we entered Friesland proper, the train crossed a big canal, and for the twentieth time that day (for we had passed numbers of them in Holland, and not a few in Germany), I said to myself, "Canals, canals. Where does Böhme come in?" It was dusk, but light enough to see an unfamiliar craft, a torpedo-boat in fact, moored to stakes at one side. In a moment I remembered that page in the *North Sea Pilot* where the Ems-Jade Canal is referred to as deep enough to carry gun-boats, and as used for that strategic purpose between Wilhelmshaven and Emden, along the base, that is, of the Frisian peninsula. I asked a peasant opposite; yes, that was the Ems-Jade Canal. Had Davies forgotten it? It would have greatly strengthened his halting sketch.

At the bookstall at Emden I bought a pocket ordnance map* of

---

*There is, of course, no space to reproduce this, but here and henceforward the reader is referred to Map B.

Friesland, on a much larger scale than anything I had used before, and when I was unobserved studied the course of the canal, with an impatience which, alas! quickly cooled. From Emden northwards I used the same map to aid my eyesight, and with its help saw in the gathering gloom more heaths and bogs once a great glimmering lake, and at intervals cultivated tracts; a watery land as ever; pools, streams and countless drains and ditches. Extensive woods were marked also, but farther inland. We passed Norden at seven, just dark. I looked out for the creek, and sure enough, we crossed it just before entering the station. Its bed was nearly dry, and I distinguished barges lying aground in it. This being the junction for Esens, I had to wait three-quarters of an hour, and then turned east through the uttermost northern wilds, stopping at occasional village stations and keeping five or six miles from the sea. It was during this stage, in a wretchedly lit compartment, and alone for the most part, that I finally assembled all my threads and tried to weave them into a cable whose core should be Esens; "a town," so Baedeker said, "of 3,500 inhabitants, the centre of a rich agricultural district. Fine spire."

Esens is four miles inland from Bensersiel. I reviewed every circumstance of that day at Bensersiel, and boiled to think how von Brüning had tricked me. He had driven to Esens himself, and read me so well that he actually offered to take me with him, and I had refused from excess of cleverness. Stay, though; if I had happened to accept he would have taken very good care that I saw nothing important. The secret, therefore, was not writ large on the walls of Esens. Was it connected with Bensersiel too, or the country between? I searched the ordnance map again, standing up to get a better light and less jolting. There was the road northwards from Esens to Bensersiel, passing through dots and chess-board squares, the former meaning fen, the latter fields, so the reference said. Something else, too, immediately caught my eye, and that was a stream running to Bensersiel. I knew it at once for the muddy stream or drain we had seen at the harbour, issuing through the sluice or *siel* from which Bensersiel took its name. But it arrested my attention now because it looked more prominent than I should have expected. Charts are apt to ignore the geography of the mainland, except in so far as it offers sea-marks to mariners. On the chart this stream had been shown as a rough little corkscrew, like a sucking-pig's tail. On the ordnance map it was marked with a dark blue line, was labelled "Benser Tief," and was given a more resolute course; bends became angles, and there were what appeared to be artificial straightnesses at certain points. One of the threads in my skein, the canal thread, tingled sympathetically, like a wire charged with current. Standing astraddle on both seats, with the map close to the lamp, I greedily followed the course of the "tief" southward. It inclined away from the road to Esens and passed the town about a mile to the west, diving underneath the railway. Soon after it took angular tacks to the eastward, and joined another blue line trending south-east, and lettered "Esens-Wittmunde *Canal.*" This canal, however, came to an abrupt end halfway to Wittmund, a neighbouring town.

For the first time that day there came to me a sense of genuine inspiration. Those shallow depths and short distances, fractions of metres and kilometres, which I had overheard from Böhme's lips at Memmert, and which Davies had attributed to the outside channels—did they refer to a canal? I remembered seeing barges in Bensersiel harbour. I remembered conversations with the natives in the inn, scraps of the post-master's pompous loquacity, talks of growing trade, of bricks and grain passing from the interior to the islands; from another source— was it the grocer of Wangeroog?—of expansion of business in the islands themselves as bathing resorts; from another source again—von Brüning himself, surely—of Dollmann's personal activity in the development of the islands. In obscure connexion with these things, I saw the torpedo-boat in the Ems-Jade Canal.

It was between Dornum and Esens that these ideas came, and I was still absorbed in them when the train drew up, just upon nine o'clock, at my destination, and after ten minutes' walk, along with a handful of other passengers, I found myself in the quiet cobbled streets of Esens, with the great church steeple, that we had so often seen from the sea, soaring above me in the moonlight.

# 26

## The Seven Siels

SELECTING the very humblest *Gasthaus* I could discover, I laid down my bundle and called for beer, bread, and *Wurst*. The landlord, as I had expected, spoke the Frisian dialect, so that though he was rather difficult to understand, he had no doubts about the purity of my own German high accent. He was a worthy fellow, and hospitably interested: "Did I want a bed?" "No; I was going on to Bensersiel," I said, "to sleep there, and take the morning *Postschiff* to Langeoog Island." (I had not forgotten our friends the twin giants and their functions.) "I was not an islander myself?" he asked. "No, but I had a married sister there; had just returned from a year's voyaging, and was going to visit her." "By the way," I asked, "how are they getting on with the Benser Tief?" My friend shrugged his shoulders; it was finished, he believed. "And the connexion to Wittmund?" "Under construction still." "Langeoog would be going ahead then?" "Oh! he supposed so, but he did not believe in these new-fangled schemes." "But it was good for trade, I supposed? Esens would benefit in sending goods by the 'tief'—what was the traffic, by the way?" "Oh, a few more barge-loads than before of bricks, timber, coals, etc., but it would come to nothing *he* knew; *Aktiengesellschaften* (companies) were an invention of the devil. A few speculators got them up and made money themselves out of land and contracts, while the shareholders they had hoodwinked starved." "There's something in that," I conceded to this bigoted old conservative; "my sister at Langeoog rents her lodging-house from a man named Dollmann; they say he owns a heap of land about. I saw his yacht once—pink velvet and electric light inside, they say—"

"That's the name," said mine host, "that's one of them—some sort of foreigner, I've heard; runs a salvage concern, too, Juist way."

"Well, he won't get any of my savings!" I laughed, and soon after took my leave, and inquired from a passer-by the road to Dornum. "Follow the railway," I was told.

With a warm wind in my face from the south-west, fleecy clouds and a half-moon overhead, I set out, not for Bensersiel but for Benser Tief, which I knew must cross the road to Dornum somewhere. A mile or so of cobbled causeway flanked with ditches and willows, and running cheek by jowl with the railway track; then a bridge, and below me the "Tief"; which was, in fact, a small canal. A rutty track left the road, and sloped down to it one side; a rough siding left the railway, and sloped down to it on the other.

I lit a pipe and sat on the parapet for a little. No one was stirring, so with great circumspection I began to reconnoitre the left bank to the north. The siding entered a fenced enclosure by a locked gate—a gate I could have easily climbed, but I judged it wiser to go round by the bridge again and look across. The enclosure was a small coal-store, nothing more; there were gaunt heaps of coal glittering in the moonlight; a barge half loaded lying alongside, and a deserted office building. I skulked along a sandy towpath in solitude. Fens and field were round me, as the map had said; willows and osier-beds; the dim forms of cattle; the low melody of wind roaming unfettered over a plain; once or twice the flutter and quack of a startled wild-duck.

Presently I came to a farmhouse, dark and silent; opposite it, in the canal, a couple of empty barges. I climbed into one of these, and sounded with my stick on the off-side—barely three feet; and the torpedo-boat melted out of my speculations. The stream, I observed also, was only just wide enough for two barges to pass with comfort. Other farms I saw, or thought I saw, and a few more barges lying in side-cuts linked by culverts to the canal, but nothing noteworthy; and mindful that I had to explore the Wittmund side of the railway too, I turned back, already a trifle damped in spirits, but still keenly expectant.

Passing under the road and railway, I again followed the towpath, which, after half a mile, plunged into woods, then entered a clearing and another fenced enclosure; a timber-yard by the look of it. This time I stripped from the waist downward, waded over, dressed again, and climbed the paling. (There was a cottage standing back, but its occupants evidently slept.) I was in a timber-yard, by the stacks of wood and the steam saw-mill; but something more than a timber-yard, for as I warily advanced under the shadow of the trees at the edge of the clearing I came to a long tin shed which strangely reminded me of Memmert, and below it, nearer the canal, loomed a dark skeleton framework, which proved to be a half-built vessel on stocks. Close by was a similar object, only nearly completed — a barge. A paved slipway led to the water here, and the canal broadened to a siding or back-water in which lay seven or eight more barges in tiers. I scaled another paling and went on, walking, I should think, three miles by the side of the canal, till the question of bed and ulterior plans brought me to a halt. It was past midnight, and I was adding little to my information. I had encountered a brick-field, but soon after that there was increasing proof that the canal was as yet little used for traffic. It grew narrower, and there were many signs of recent labour for its improvement. In one place a dammed-off deviation was being excavated, evidently to abridge an impossible bend. The path had become atrocious, and my boots were heavy with clay. Bearing in mind the abruptly-ending blue line on the map, I considered it useless to go farther, and retraced my steps, trying to concoct a story which would satisfy an irritable Esens inn-keeper that it was a respectable wayfarer, and not a tramp or a lunatic, who knocked him up at half-past one or thereabouts.

But a much more practical resource occurred to me as I approached the timber-yard; for lodging, free and accessible, lay there ready to hand. I boarded one of the empty barges in the backwater, and surveyed my quarters for the night. It was of a similar pattern to all the others I had seen; a lighter, strictly, in the sense that it had no means of self-propulsion, and no separate quarters for a crew, the whole interior of the hull being free for cargo. At both bow and stern there were ten feet or so of deck, garnished with bitts and bollards. The rest was an open well, flanked by waterways of substantial breadth; the whole of stout construction and, for a humble lighter, of well-proportioned and even graceful design, with a marked forward sheer, and, as I had observed in the specimen on the stocks, easy lines at the stern. In short, it was apparent, even to an ignorant landsman like myself, that she was designed not merely for canal work but for rough water; and well she might be, for, though the few miles of sea she had to cross in order to reach the islands were both shallow and sheltered, I knew from experience what a vicious surf they could be whipped into by a sudden gale. It must not be supposed that I dwelt on this matter. On limited lines I was making progress, but the wings of imagination still drooped nervelessly at my sides. Otherwise I perhaps should have examined this lighter more particularly, instead of regarding it mainly as a convenient hiding-place. Under the stern-deck was stored a massive roll of tarpaulin, a corner of which made an excellent blanket, and my bundle a good pillow. It was a descent from the luxury of last night; but a spy, I reflected philosophically, cannot expect a feather bed two nights running, and this one was at any rate airier and roomier than the coffin-like bunk of the *Dulcibella*, and not so very much harder.

When snugly ensconced, I studied the map by intermittent match-light. It had been dawning on me in the last half-hour that this canal was only one of several; that in concentrating myself on Esens and Bensersiel, I had forgotten that there were other villages ending in *siel*, also furnished on the chart with corkscrew streams; and, moreover, that Böhme's statistics of depth and distance had been marshalled in seven categories, A to G. The very first match brought full recollection as to the villages. The suffix *siel* repeated itself all round the coast-line. Five miles eastward of Bensersiel was Neu-harlingersiel, and farther on Carolinensiel. Four miles westward was Dornumersiel; and farther on Nessmersiel and Hilgenriedersiel. That was six on the north coast of the peninsula alone. On the west coast, facing the Ems, there was only one, Greetsiel, a good way south of Norden. But on the east, facing the Jade, there were no less than eight, at very close intervals. A moment's thought and I disregarded this latter group; they had nothing to do with Esens, nor had they any imaginable *raison d'être* as veins for commerce; differing markedly in this respect from the group of six on the north coast, whose outlook was the chain of islands, and whose inland centre, almost exactly, was Esens. I still wanted one to make seven, and as a working hypothesis added the solitary Greetsiel. At all seven villages streams debouched, as at Bensersiel. From all seven points of issue dotted lines were marked seaward, intersecting the great tidal sands and leading towards the islands. And on the mainland behind the whole sevenfold system ran the loop of railway. But there were manifold minor points of difference. No stream boasted so deep and decisive a blue lintel as did Benser Tief; none penetrated so far into the Hinterland. They varied in length and sinuosity. Two, those belonging to

Hilgenriedersiel and Greetsiel, appeared not to reach the railway at all. On the other hand, Carolinensiel, opposite Wangeroog Island, had a branch line all to itself.

Match after match waxed and waned as I puzzled over the mystic seven. In the end I puzzled myself to sleep, with the one fixed idea that to-morrow, on my way back to Norden, I must see more of these budding canals, if such they were. My dreams that night were of a mighty chain of redoubts and masked batteries couching *perdus* among the sand-dunes of desolate islets; built, coral-like, by infinitely slow and secret labour; fed by lethal cargoes borne in lighters and in charge of stealthy mutes who, one and all, bore the likeness of Grimm. I was up and away at daylight (the weather mild and showery), meeting some navvies on my way back to the road, who gave me good morning and a stare. On the bridge I halted and fell into torments of indecision. There was so much to do and so little time to do it in. The whole problem seemed to have been multiplied by seven, and the total again doubled and redoubled—seven blue lines on land, seven dotted lines on the sea, seven islands in the offing. Once I was near deciding to put my pretext into practice, and cross to Langeoog; but that meant missing the rendezvous, and I was loth to do that.

At any rate, I wanted breakfast badly; and the best way to get it, and at the same time to open new ground, was to walk to Dornum. Then I should find a blue line called the *Neues Tief*, leading to Dornumersiel, on the coast. That explored, I could pass on to Nesse, where there was another blue line to Nessmersiel. All this was on the way to Norden, and I should have the railway constantly at my back, to carry me there in the evening. The last train (my time-table told me) was one reaching Norden at 7.15 p.m. I could catch this at Hage Station at 7.5.

A brisk walk of six miles brought me, ravenously hungry, to Dornum. Road and railway had clung together all the time, and about half-way had been joined on the left by a third companion in the shape of a puny stream which I knew from the map to be the upper portion of Neues Tief. Wriggling and doubling like an eel, choked with sedges and reeds, it had no pretensions to being navigable. At length it looped away into the fens out of sight, only to reappear again close to Dornum in a much more dignified guise.

There was no siding where the railway crossed it, but at the town itself, which it skirted on the east, a towpath began, and a piled wharf had been recently constructed. Going on to this was a red-brick building with the look of a warehouse, roofless as yet, and with workmen on its scaffolds. It sharpened the edge of my appetite.

If I had been wise I should have been content with a snack bought at a counter, but a thirst for hot coffee and clues induced me to repeat the experiment of Esens and seek a primitive beerhouse. I was less lucky on this occasion. The house I chose was obscure enough, but its proprietor was no simple Frisian, but an ill-looking rascal with shifty eyes and a debauched complexion, who showed a most unwelcome curiosity in his customer. As a last fatality, he wore a peaked cap like my own, and turned out to be an ex-sailor. I should have fled at the sight of him had I had the chance, but I was attended to first by a slatternly girl who, I am sure, called him up to view me. To explain my muddy boots and trousers I said I had walked from Esens, and from that I found myself involved in a tangle of impromptu lies. Floundering down an old groove, I placed my sister this time on Baltrum Island, and said I was going to Dornumersiel (which is opposite Baltrum) to cross from there. As this was drawing a bow at a venture, I dared not assume local knowledge, and spoke of the visit as my first. Dornumersiel was a lucky shot; there *was* a ferry-galliot from there to Baltrum; but he knew, or pretended to know, Baltrum, and had not heard of my sister. I grew the more nervous in that I saw from the first that he took me to be of better condition than most merchant seamen; and, to make matters worse, I was imprudent enough in pleading haste to pull out from an inner pocket my gold watch with the chain and seals attached. He told me there was no hurry, that I should miss the tide at Dornumersiel, and then fell to pressing strong waters on me, and asking questions whose insinuating grossness gave me the key to his biography. He must have been at one stage in his career a dock-side crimp, one of those foul sharks who prey on discharged seamen, and as often as not are exseamen themselves, versed in the weaknesses of the tribe. He was now keeping his hand in with me, who, unhappily, purported to belong to the very class he was used to victimize, and, moreover, had a gold watch, and, doubtless, a full purse. Nothing more ridiculously inopportune could have befallen me, or more dangerous; for his class are as cosmopolitan as waiters and *concierges*, with as facile a gift for language and as unerring a scent for nationality. Sure enough, the fellow recognized mine, and positively challenged me with it in fairly fluent English with a Yankee twang. Encumbered with the mythical sister, of course I stuck to my lie, said I had been on an English ship so long that I had picked up the accent, and also gave him some words in broken English. At the same time I showed I thought him an impertinent nuisance, paid my score and walked out—quit of him? Not a bit of it! He insisted on showing me the way to Dornumersiel, and followed me down the street. Perceiving that he was in liquor, in spite of the early hour, I dared not risk a quarrelsome scene with a man who already knew so much about me, and might at any moment elicit more. So I melted, and humoured him; treated him in a ginshop in the hope of giving him the slip—a disastrous resource, which was made a precedent for further potations elsewhere. I would gladly draw a veil over our scandalous progress through peaceable Dornum, of the terrors I experienced when he introduced me as his friend, and as his English friend, and of the abasement I felt, too, as, linked arm in arm, we trod the three miles of road coastwards. It was his malicious whim that we should talk English; a fortunate whim, as it turned out, because I knew no fo'c'sle German, but had a smattering of fo'c'sle English, gathered from Cutcliffe Hyne and Kipling. With these I extemporized a disreputable hybrid, mostly consisting of oaths and blasphemies, and so yarned of imaginary voyages. Of course he knew every port in the world, but happily was none too critical, owing to repeated *schnappsen*.

Nevertheless, it was a deplorable *contretemps* from every point of view. I was wasting my time, for the road took a different direction to the Neues Tief, so that I had not even the advantage of inspecting the canal and only met with it when we reached the sea. Here it split into two mouths, both furnished with locks, and emptying into two little mud-hole harbours, replicas of Bensersiel, each owning its cluster of houses. I made straight for the *Gasthaus* at Dornumersiel, primed my companion well, and asked him to wait while I saw about a boat in the harbour; but, needless to say, I never rejoined him. I just took a cursory look at the left-hand harbour, saw a lighter locking through (for the tide was high), and then walked as fast as my legs would carry me to the outermost dyke, mounted it, and strode along the sea westwards in the teeth of a smart shower of rain, full of deep apprehensions as to the stir and gossip my disappearance might cause if my odious crimp was sober enough to discover it. As soon as I deemed it safe, I dropped on to the sand and ran till I could run no more. Then I sat on my bundle with my back to the dyke in partial shelter from the rain, watching the sea recede from the flats and dwindle into slender meres, and the laden clouds fly weeping over the islands till those pale shapes were lost in mist.

The barge I had seen locking through was creeping across towards Langeoog behind a tug and a wisp of smoke.

No more exploration by daylight! That was my first resolve, for I felt as if the country must be ringing with reports of an Englishman in disguise. I must remain in hiding till dusk, then regain the railway and slink into that train to Norden. Now directly I began to resign myself to temporary inaction, and to centre my thoughts on the rendezvous, a new doubt assailed me. Nothing had seemed more certain yesterday than that Norden was the scene of the rendezvous, but that was before the seven *siels* had come into prominence. The name Norden now sounded naked and unconvincing. As I wondered why, it suddenly occurred to me that *all* the stations along this northern line, though farther inland than Norden, were equally "coast stations," in the sense that they were in touch with harbours (of a sort) on the coast. Norden had its tidal creek, but Esens and Dornum had their "tiefs" or canals. Fool that I had been to put such a narrow and literal construction on the phrase "the tide serves!" Which was it more likely that my conspirators would visit—Norden, whose intrusion into our theories was purely hypothetical, or one of these *siels* to whose sevenfold systems all my latest observations gave such transcendent significance?

There was only one answer; and it filled me with profound discouragement. Seven possible rendezvous!—eight, counting Norden. Which to make for? Out came the time-table and map, and with them hope. The case was not so bad after all; it demanded no immediate change of plan, though it imported grave uncertainties and risks. Norden was still the objective, but mainly as a railway junction, only remotely as a seaport. Though the possible rendezvous were eight, the possible stations were reduced to five—Norden, Hage, Dornum, Esens, Wittmund—all on one single line. Trains from east to west along this line were negligible, because there were none that could be called night trains, the latest being the one I had this morning fixed on to bring me to Norden, where it arrived at 7.15. Of trains from west to east there was only one that need be considered, the same one that I had travelled by last night, leaving Norden at 7.43 and reaching Esens at 8.50, and Wittmund at 9.13. This train, as the reader who was with me in it knows, was in correspondence with another from Emden and the south, and also, I now found, with services from Hanover, Bremen, and Berlin. He will also remember that I had to wait three-quarters of an hour at Norden, from 7 to 7.43.

The platform at Norden Junction, therefore, between 7.15, when I should arrive at it *from* the east, and 7.43, when Böhme and his unknown friend should leave it *for* the east; there, and in that half-hour, was my opportunity for recognizing and shadowing two at least of the conspirators. I must take the train they took, and alight where they alighted. If I could not find them at all I should be thrown back on the rejected view that Norden itself was the rendezvous, and should wait there till 10.46.

In the meantime it was all very well to resolve on inaction till dusk; but after an hour's rest, damp clothes and feet, and the absence of pursuers, tempted me to take the field again. Avoiding roads and villages as long as it was light, I cut across country south-westwards—a dismal and laborious journey, with oozy fens and knee-deep drains to course, with circuits to be made to pass clear of peasants, and many furtive crouchings behind dykes and willows. What little I learnt was in harmony with previous explorations, for my track cut at right angles the line of the Harke Tief, the stream issuing at Nessmersiel. It, too, was in the nature of a canal, but only in embryo at the point I touched it, south of Nesse. Works on a deviation were in progress, and in a short digression down stream I sighted another lighter-building yard. As for Hilgenriedersiel, the fourth of the seven, I had no time to see anything of it at all. At seven o'clock I was at Hage Station, very tired, wet, and footsore, after covering nearly twenty miles all told since I left my bed in the lighter.

From here to Norden it was a run in the train of ten minutes, which I spent in eating some rye bread and smoked eel, and in scraping the mud off my boots and trousers. Fatigue vanished when the train drew up at the station, and the momentous twenty-eight minutes began to run their course. Having donned a bulky muffler and turned up the collar of my pea-jacket, I crossed over immediately to the up-platform, walked boldly to the booking-office, and at once sighted—von Brüning—yes, von Brüning in mufti; but there was no mistaking his tall athletic figure, pleasant features, and neat brown beard. He was just leaving the window, gathering up a ticket and some coins. I joined a *queue* of three or four persons who were waiting their turn, flattened myself between them and the partition till I heard him walk out. Not having heard what station he had booked for, I took a fourth-class ticket to Wittmund, which covered all chances. Then, with my chin buried in my muffler, I sought the darkest corner of the ill-lit combination of bar and waiting-room where, by the tiresome custom in Germany, would-be travellers are penned till their train is ready. Von Brüning I perceived sitting in another corner, with his hat over his eyes and a cigar between his lips. A boy brought me a tankard of tawny Munich beer, and, sipping it, I watched. People passed in and out, but nobody spoke to the sailor in mufti. When a quarter of an hour elapsed, a platform door opened, and a raucous voice shouted: "Hage, Dornum, Esens, Wittmund!" A knot of passengers jostled out to the platform, showing their tickets. I was slow over my beer, and was last of the knot, with von Brüning immediately ahead of me, so close that his cigar smoke curled into my face. I looked over his shoulder at the ticket he showed, missed the name, but caught a muttered double sibilant from the official who checked it; ran over the stations in my head, and pounced on *Esens*. That was as much I wanted to know for the present; so I made my way to a fourth-class compartment, and lost sight of my quarry, not venturing, till the last door had banged, to look out of the window. When I did so two late arrivals were hurrying up to a carriage—one tall, one of middle height; both in cloaks and comforters. Their features I could not distinguish, but certainly neither of them was

Böhme. They had not come through the waiting-room door, but, plainly, from the dark end of the platform, where they had been waiting. A guard, with some surly remonstrances, shut them in, and the train started.

Esens—the name had not surprised me; it fulfilled a presentiment that had been growing in strength all the afternoon. For the last time I referred to the map, pulpy and blurred with the day's exposure, and tried to etch it into my brain. I marked the road to Bensersiel, and how it converged by degrees on the Benser Tief until they met at the sea. "The tide serves!" Longing for Davies to help me, I reckoned, by the aid of my diary, that high tide at Bensersiel would be about eleven, and for two hours, I remembered (say from ten to twelve to-night), there were from five to six feet of water in the harbour.

We should reach Esens at 8.50. Would they drive, as von Brüning had done a week ago? I tightened my belt, stamped my mud-burdened boots, and thanked God for the Munich beer. Whither were they going from Bensersiel, and in what; and how was I to follow them? These were nebulous questions, but I was in fettle for anything; boat-stealing was a bagatelle. Fortune, I thought, smiled; Romance beckoned; even the sea looked kind. Ay, and I do not know but that Imagination was already beginning to unstiffen and flutter those nerveless wings.

## 27

### The Luck of the Stowaway

AT ESENS Station I reversed my Norden tactics, jumped out smartly, and got to the door of egress first of all, gave up my ticket, and hung about the gate of the station under cover of darkness. Fortune smiled still; there was no vehicle in waiting at all, and there were only half a dozen passengers. Two of these were the cloaked gentlemen who had been so nearly left behind at Norden, and another was von Brüning. The latter walked well in advance of the first pair, but at the gate on to the high road the three showed a common purpose, in that, unlike the rest, who turned towards Esens town, they turned southwards; much to my perplexity, for this was the contrary direction to Bensersiel and the sea. I, with my bundle on my shoulder, had been bringing up the rear, and, as their faithful shadow, turned to the right too, without foreseeing the consequence. When it was too late to turn back I saw that, fifty yards ahead, the road was barred by the gates of a level crossing, and that the four of us must inevitably accumulate at the barrier till the train had steamed away. This, in fact, happened, and for a minute or two we were all in a group, elaborately indifferent to one another, silent, but I am sure very conscious. As for me, "secret laughter tickled all my soul." When the gates were opened the three seemed disposed to lag, so I tactfully took my cue, trudged briskly on ahead, and stopped after a few minutes to listen. Hearing nothing I went cautiously back and found that they had disappeared; in which direction was not long in doubt, for I came on a grassy path leading into the fields on the left or west of the road, and though I could see no one I heard the distant murmur of receding voices.

I took my bearings collectedly, placed one foot on the path, thought better of it, and turned back towards Esens. I knew without reference to the map that that path would bring them to the Benser Tief at a point somewhere near the timber-yard. In a fog I might have followed them there; as it was, the night was none too dark, and I had my strength to husband; and stamped on my memory were the words "the tide serves." I judged it a wiser use of time and sinew to anticipate them at Bensersiel by the shortest road, leaving them to reach it by way of the devious Tief, to examine which was, I felt convinced, one of their objects.

It was nine o'clock of a fresh wild night, a halo round the beclouded moon. I passed through quiet Esens, and in an hour I was close to Bensersiel, and could hear the sea. In the rooted idea that I should find Grimm on the outskirts, awaiting visitors, I left the road short of the village, and made a circuit to the harbour by way of the sea-wall. The lower windows of the inn shed a warm glow into the night, and within I could see the village circle gathered over cards, and dominated as of old by the assertive little postmaster, whose high-pitched, excitable voice I could clearly distinguish, as he sat with his cap on the back of his head and a "feine schnapps" at his elbow. The harbour itself looked exactly the same as I remembered it a week ago. The post-boat lay in her old berth at the eastern jetty, her mainsail set and her twin giants spitting over the rail. I hailed them boldly from the shore (without showing them who I was), and was told they were starting for Langeoog in a few minutes; the wind was off-shore, the mails aboard, and the water just high enough. "Did I want a passage?" "No, I thought I would wait." Positive that my party could never have got here so soon, I nevertheless kept an eye on the galliot till she let go her stern-rope and slid away. One contingency was eliminated. Some loiterers dispersed, and all port business appeared to be ended for the night.

Three-quarters of an hour of strained suspense ensued. Most of it I spent on my knees in a dark angle between the dyke and the western jetty, whence I had a strategic survey of the basin; but I was driven at times to relieve inaction by sallies which increased in audacity. I scouted on the road beyond the bridge, hovered round the lock, and peered in at the inn parlour; but nowhere could I see a trace of Grimm. I examined every floating object in the harbour (they were very few), dropped on to two lighters and pried under tarpaulins, boarded a deserted tug and two or three clumsy rowboats tied up to a mooring-post. Only one of these had the look of readiness, the rest being devoid of oars and rowlocks; a discouraging state of things for a prospective boat-lifter. It was the sight of these rowboats that suggested a last and most distracting possibility, namely, that the boat in waiting, if boat there were, might be not in the harbour at all, but somewhere on the sands outside the dyke, where, at this high state of the tide, it would have water and to spare. Back to the dyke then; but as I peered seaward on the way, contingencies evaporated and a solid fact supervened, for I saw the lights of a steamboat approaching the harbour mouth. I had barely time to gain my coign of vantage before she had swept in between the piers, and with a fitful swizzling of her screw was turning and backing down to a berth just ahead of one of the lighters, and not fifty feet from my hiding-place. A deck-hand jumped ashore with a rope, while the man at the wheel gave gruff directions. The vessel was a small tug, and the man at the wheel disclosed his identity when, having rung off his engines, he jumped ashore also, looked at his watch in the beam of the side-light, and walked towards the village. It was Grimm, by the height and build—Grimm clad in a long tarpaulin coat and a sou'wester. I watched him cross the shaft of light from the inn window and disappear in the direction of the canal.

Another sailor now appeared and helped his fellow to tie up the tug. The two together then went aft and began to set about some job whose nature I could not determine. To emerge was perilous, so I set about a job of my own, tearing open my bundle and pulling an oilskin jacket and trousers over my clothes, and discarding my peaked cap for a sou'-wester. This operation was prompted instantaneously by the garb of two sailors, who in hauling on the forward warp came into the field of the mast-head light.

It was something of a gymnastic masterpiece, since I was lying—or, rather, standing aslant—on the rough sea-wall, with crannies of brick for foothold and the water plashing below me; but then I had not lived in the *Dulcibella* for nothing. My chain of thought, I fancy, was this— the tug is to carry my party; I cannot shadow a tug in a rowboat, yet I intend to shadow my party; I must therefore go with them in the tug, and the first and soundest step is to mimic her crew. But the next step was a hard matter, for the crew having finished their job sat side by side on the bulwarks and lit their pipes. However, a little pantomime soon occurred, as amusing as it was inspiriting. They seemed to consult together, looking from the tug to the inn and from the inn to the tug. One of them walked a few paces inn-wards and beckoned to the other, who in his turn called something down the engine-room skylight, and then joined his mate in a scuttle to the inn. Even while I watched the pantomime I was sliding off my boots, and it had not been consummated a second before I had them in my arms and was tripping over the mud in my stocking feet. A dozen noiseless steps and I was over the bulwarks between the wheel and the smoke-stack, casting about for a hiding-place. The conventional stowaway hides in the hold, but there was only a stokehold here, occupied moreover; nor was there an empty apple-barrel, such as Jim of *Treasure Island* found so useful. As far as I could see—and I dared not venture far for fear of the skylight—the surface of the deck offered nothing secure. But on the farther or starboard side, rather abaft the beam, there was a small boat in davits, swung outboard, to which common sense, and perhaps a vague prescience of its after utility, pointed irresistibly. In any case, discrimination was out of place, so I mounted the bulwark and gently entered my refuge. The tackles creaked a trifle, oars and seats impeded me; but well before the thirsty truants had returned I was settled on the floor boards between two thwarts, so placed that I could, if necessary, peep over the gunwale.

The two sailors returned at a run, and very soon after voices approached, and I recognized that of Herr Schenkel chattering volubly. He and Grimm boarded the tug and went down a companion-way aft, near which, as I peeped over, I saw a second skylight, no bigger than the *Dulcibella*'s, illuminated from below. Then I heard a cork drawn, and the kiss of glasses, and in a minute or two they re-emerged. It was apparent that Herr Schenkel was inclined to stay and make merry, and that Grimm was anxious to get rid of him, and none too courteous in showing it. The former urged that to-morrow's tide would do, the latter gave orders to cast off, and at length observed with an angry oath that the water was falling, and he must start; and, to clinch matters, with a curt good-night, he went to the wheel and rang up his engines. Herr Schenkel landed and strutted off in high dudgeon, while the tug's screw began to revolve. We had only glided a few yards on when the engines stopped, a short blast of the whistle sounded, and, before I had had time to recast the future, I heard a scurry of footsteps from the direction of the dyke, first on the bank, next on the deck. The last of these new arrivals panted audibly as he got aboard and dropped on the planks with an unelastic thud.

Her complement made up, the tug left the harbour, but not alone. While slowly gathering way the hull checked all at once with a sharp

jerk, recovered, and increased its speed. We had something in tow—
what? The lighter, of course, that had been lying astern of us.

Now I knew what was in that lighter, because I had been to see, half
an hour ago. It was no lethal cargo, but coal, common household coal;
not a full load of it, I remembered—just a good-sized mound amidships, trimmed with battens fore and aft to prevent shifting. "Well,"
thought I, "this is intelligible enough. Grimm was ostensibly there to
call for a load of coal for Memmert. But does that mean we are going
to Memmert?" At the same time I recalled a phrase overheard at the
depot, "Only one—half a load." Why half a load?

For some few minutes there was a good deal of movement on deck,
and of orders shouted by Grimm and answered by a voice from far
astern on the lighter. Presently, however, the tug warmed to her work,
the hull vibrated with energy, and an ordered peace reigned on board.
I also realized that having issued from the boomed channel we had
turned westward, for the wind, which had been blowing us fair, now
blew strongly over the port beam.

I peeped out of my eyrie and was satisfied in a moment that as long
as I made no noise, and observed proper prudence, I was perfectly safe
*until the boat was wanted*. There were no deck lamps; the two skylights
diffused but a sickly radiance, and I was abaft the side-lights. I was abaft
the wheel also, though thrillingly near it in point of distance—about
twelve feet, I should say; and Grimm was steering. The wheel, I should
mention here, was raised, as you often see them, on a sort of pulpit, approached by two or three steps and fenced by a breast-high arc of board-
ing. Only one of the crew was visible, and he was acting as look-out in
the extreme bows, the rays of the masthead lights—for a second had
been hoisted in sign of towage—glistening on his oilskin back. The
other man, I concluded, was steering the lighter, which I could dimly
locate by the pale foam at her bow.

And the passengers? They were all together aft, three of them, leaning over the taffrail, with their backs turned to me. One was short and
stout—Böhme unquestionably; the panting and the thud on the planks
had prepared me for that, though where he had sprung from I did not
know. Two were tall, and one of these must be von Brüning. There
ought to be four, I reckoned; but three were all I could see. And what
of the third? It must be he who "insists on coming," the unknown superior at whose instance and for whose behoof this secret expedition
had been planned. And who could he be? Many times, needless to say,
I had asked myself that question, but never till now, when I had found
the rendezvous and joined the expedition, did it become one of burning import.

"Any weather" was another of those stored-up phrases that were *apropos*. It was a dirty, squally night, not very cold, for the wind still hung in the S.S.W.—an off-shore wind on this coast, causing no appreciable sea on the shoal spaces we were traversing. In the matter of our bearings, I set myself doggedly to overcome that paralysing perplexity, always induced in me by night or fog in these intricate waters; and, by screwing round and round, succeeded so far as to discover and identify two flashing lights—one alternately red and white, far and faint astern; the other right ahead and rather stronger, giving white flashes only. The first and least familiar was, I made out, from the lighthouse on Wangeroog; the second, well known to me as our beacon star in the race from Memmert, was the light on the centre of Norderney Island, about ten miles away.

I had no accurate idea of the time, for I could not see my watch, but I thought we must have started about a quarter-past eleven. We were travelling fast, the funnel belching out smoke and the bow-wave curling high; for the tug appeared to be a powerful little craft, and her load was comparatively light.

So much for the general situation. As for my own predicament, I was in no mood to brood on the hazards of this mad adventure, a hundredfold more hazardous than my fog-smothered eavesdropping at Memmert. The crisis, I knew, had come, and the reckless impudence that had brought me here must serve me still and extricate me. Fortune loves rough wooing. I backed my luck and watched.

The behaviour of the passengers struck me as odd. They remained in a row at the taffrail, gazing astern like regretful emigrants, and sometimes, gesticulating and pointing. Now no vestige of the low land was visible, so I was driven to the conclusion that it was the lighter they were discussing; and I date my awakening from the moment that I realized this. But the thread broke prematurely; for the passengers took to pacing the deck, and I had to lie low. When next I was able to raise my head they were round Grimm at the wheel, engaged, as far as I could discover from their gestures, in an argument about our course and the time, for Grimm looked at his watch by the light of a hand-lantern.

We were heading north, and I knew by the swell that we must be near the Accumer Ee, the gap between Langeoog and Baltrum. Were we going out to open sea? It came over me with a rush that we *must*, if we were to drop this lighter at Memmert. Had I been Davies I should have been quicker to seize certain rigid conditions of this cruise, which no human power could modify. We had left after high tide. The water therefore was falling everywhere; and the tributary channels in rear of the islands were slowly growing impassable. It was quite thirty miles to Memmert, with three watersheds to pass; behind Baltrum, Norderney, and Juist. A skipper with nerve and perfect confidence might take us

over one of these in the dark, but most of the run would infallibly have
to be made outside. I now better understood the protests of Herr
Schenkel to Grimm. Never once had we seen a lighter in tow in the
open sea, though plenty behind the barrier of islands; indeed it was the
very existence of the sheltered byways that created such traffic as there
was. It was only Grimm's *métier* and the incubus of the lighter that had
suggested Memmert as our destination at all, and I began to doubt it
now. That tricky hoop of sand had befooled us before.

At this moment, and as if to corroborate my thought, the telegraph
rang and the tug slowed down. I effaced myself and heard Grimm
shouting to the man on the lighter to starboard his helm, and to the
look-out to come aft. The next order froze my very marrow; it was
"lower away." Someone was at the davits of my boat fingering the tackles; the forward fall-rope actually slipped in the block and tilted the
boat a fraction. I was just wondering how far it was to swim to
Langeoog, when a strong, imperious voice (unknown to me) rang out,
"No, no! We don't want the boat. The swell's nothing; we can jump!
Can't we, Böhme?" The speaker ended with a jovial laugh. "Mercy!"
thought I, "are *they* going to swim to Langeoog?" but I also gasped for
relief. The tug rolled lifelessly in the swell for a little, and footsteps retreated aft. There were cries of "Achtung!" and some laughter, one big
bump and a good deal of grinding; and on we moved again, taking the
strain of the tow-rope gingerly, and then full-speed ahead. The passengers, it seemed, preferred the lighter to the tug for cruising in; coal-dust
and exposure to clean planks and a warm cuddy. When silence reigned
again I peeped out. Grimm was at the wheel still, impassively twirling
the spokes, with a glance over his shoulder at his precious freight. And,
after all, we *were* going outside.

Close on the port hand lay a black foam-girt shape, the east of spit
Baltrum. It fused with the night, while we swung slowly round to wind-
ward over the troubled bar. Now we were in the spacious deeps of the
North Sea; and feeling it too in increase of swell and volleys of spray.

At this point evolutions began. Grimm gave the wheel up to the
look-out, and himself went to the taffrail, whence he roared back orders
of "Port!" or "Starboard!" in response to signals from the lighter. We
made one complete circle, steering on each point of the wind in succession, after that worked straight out to sea till the water was a good
deal rougher, and back again at a tangent, till in earshot of the surf on
the island beach. There the manoeuvres, which were clearly in the nature of a trial trip, ended, and we hove to, to transship our passengers.
They, when they came aboard, went straight below, and Grimm, having steadied the tug on a settled course and entrusted the wheel to the
sailor again, stripped off his dripping oilskin coat, threw it down on the

cabin skylight, and followed them. The course he had set was about west, with Norderney light a couple of points off the port bow. The course for Memmert? Possibly; but I cared not, for my mind was far from Memmert to-night. *It was the course for England too.* Yes, I understood at last. I was assisting at an experimental rehearsal of a great scene, to be enacted, perhaps, in the near future—a scene when multitudes of sea-going lighters, carrying full loads of soldiers, not half loads of coals, should issue simultaneously, in seven ordered fleets, from seven shallow outlets, and, under escort of the Imperial Navy, traverse the North Sea and throw themselves bodily upon English shores.

Indulgent reader, you may be pleased to say that I have been very obtuse; and yet, with humility, I protest against that verdict. Remember that, recent as are the events I am describing, it is only since they happened that the possibility of an invasion of England by Germany has become a topic of public discussion. Davies and I had never—I was going to say had never considered it; but that would not be accurate, for we had glanced at it once or twice; and if any single incident in his or our joint cruise had provided a semblance of confirmation, he, at any rate, would have kindled to that spark. But you will see how perversely from first to last circumstances drove us deeper and deeper into the wrong groove, till the idea became inveterate that the secret we were seeking was one of defence and not offence. Hence a complete mental somersault was required, and, as an amateur, I found it difficult; the more so that the method of invasion, as I darkly comprehended it now, was of such a strange and unprecedented character; for orthodox invasions start from big ports and involve a fleet of ocean transports, while none of our clues pointed that way. To neglect obvious methods, to draw on the obscure resources of an obscure strip of coast, to improve and exploit a quantity of insignificant streams and tidal outlets, and thence, screened by the islands, to despatch an armada of light-draught barges, capable of flinging themselves on a correspondingly obscure and therefore unexpected portion of the enemy's coast; that was a conception so daring, aye, and so quixotic in some of its aspects, that even now I was half incredulous. Yet it must be the true one. Bit by bit the fragments of the puzzle fell into order till a coherent whole was adumbrated.*

The tug surged on into the night; a squall of rain leapt upon us and swept hissing astern. Baltrum vanished and the strands of Norderney beamed under transient moonlight. Drunk with triumph, I cuddled in my rocking cradle and ransacked every unvisited chamber of the memory, tossing out their dusty contents, to make a joyous bonfire of some,

---

*The reader will find the whole matter dealt with in the Epilogue.

and to see the residue take life and meaning in the light of the great revelation.

My reverie was of things, not persons; of vast national issues rather than of the poignant human interests so closely linked with them. But on a sudden I was recalled, with a shock, to myself, Davies, and the present.

We were changing our course, as I knew by variations in the whirl of draughts which whistled about me. I heard Grimm afoot again, and, choosing my moment, surveyed the scene. Broad on the port-beam were the garish lights of Norderney town and promenade, and the tug, I perceived, was drawing in to enter the See-Gat.* Round she came, hustling through the broken water of the bar, till her nose was south and the wind was on the starboard bow. Not a mile from me were the villa and the yacht, and the three persons of the drama—three, that is, if Davies were safe.

Were we to land at Norderney harbour? Heavens, what a magnificent climax!—if only I could rise to it. My work here was done. At a stroke to rejoin Davies and be free to consummate our designs!

A desperate idea of cutting the davit-tackles—I blush to think of the stupidity—was rejected as soon as it was born, and instead, I endeavoured to imagine our approach to the pier. My boat hung on the starboard side; that would be the side away from the quay, and the tide would be low. I could swarm down the davits during the stir of arrival, drop into the sea and swim the few yards across the dredged-out channel, wade through the mud to within a short distance of the *Dulcibella*, and swim the rest. I rubbed the salt out of my eyes and wriggled my cramped legs . . . Hullo! why was Grimm leaving the helm again? Back he went to the cabin, leaving the sailor at the helm . . . We ought to be turning to port now; but no—on we went, south, for the mainland.

Though one plan was frustrated, the longing to get to Davies, once implanted, waxed apace.

Our destination was at last beyond dispute.† The channel we were in was the same that we had cut across on our blind voyage to Memmert, and the same my ferry-steamer had followed two days ago. It was a *cul-de-sac* leading to one place only, the landing stage at Norddeich. The only place on the whole coast, now I came to think of it, where the tug could land at this tide. There the quay would be on the starboard side, and I saw myself tied to my eyrie while the passengers landed and the tug and lighter turned back for Memmert; at Memmert, dawn, and discovery.

There was some way out—some way out, I repeated to myself; some

*See Chart B.      †See Chart.

way to reap the fruit of Davies's long tutelage in the lore of this strange region. What would *he* do?

For answer there came the familiar *frou-frou* of gentle surf on drying sands. The swell was dying away, the channel narrowing; dusky and weird on the starboard hand stretched leagues of new-risen sand. Two men only were on deck; the moon was quenched under the vanguard clouds of a fresh squall.

A madcap scheme danced before me. The time, I *must* know the time! Crouching low and cloaking the flame with my jacket I struck a match; 2.30 a.m. — the tide had been ebbing for about three hours and a half. Low water about five; they would be aground till 7.30. Danger to life? None. Flares and rescuers? Not likely, with "him who insists" on board; besides, no one could come, there being no danger. I should have a fair wind and a fair tide for *my* trip. Grimm's coat was on the skylight; we were both clean shaved.

The helmsman gazed ahead, intent on his difficult course, and the wind howled to perfection. I knelt up and examined one of the davit-tackles. There was nothing remarkable about it, a double and a single block (like our own peak halyards), the lower one hooked into a ring in the boat, the hauling part made fast to a cleat on the davit itself. Something there must be to give lateral support or the boat would have racketed abroad in the roll outside. The support, I found, consisted of two lanyards spliced to the davits and rove through holes in the keel. These I leaned over and cut with my pocket-knife; the result being a barely perceptible swaying of the boat, for the tug was under the lee of sands and on an even keel. Then I left my hiding-place, climbing out of the stern sheets by the after-davit, and preparing every successive motion with exquisite tenderness, till I stood on the deck. In another moment I was at the cabin skylight, lifting Grimm's long oilskin coat. (A second's yielding to temptation here; but no, the skylight was ground glass, fastened from below. So, on with the coat, up with the collar, and forward to the wheel on tiptoe.) As soon as I was up to the engine-room skylight (that is to say, well ahead of the cabin roof) I assumed a natural step, went up to the pulpit and touched the helmsman on the arm, as I had seen Grimm do. The man stepped aside, grunting something about a light, and I took the wheel from him. Grimm was a man of few words, so I just jogged his satellite, and pointed forward. He went off like a lamb to his customary place in the bows, not having dreamt — why should he? — of examining me, but in him I had instantly recognized one of the crew of the *Kormoran*.

My ruse developed in all its delicious simplicity. We were, I estimated, about half-way to Norddeich, in the Buse Tief, a channel of a navigable breadth, at the utmost of two hundred yards at this period of the tide. Two faint lights, one above the other, twinkled far ahead. What they meant I neither knew nor cared, since the only use I put them to was to test the effect of the wheel, for this was the first time I had ever tasted the sweets of command on a steamboat. A few cautious essays taught me the rudiments, and nothing could hinder the catastrophe now.

I edged over to starboard—that was the side I had selected—and again a little more, till the glistening back of the look-out gave a slight movement; but he was a well-drilled minion, with implicit trust in the "old man." Now, hard over! and spoke by spoke I gave her the full pressure of the helm. The look-out shouted a warning, and I raised my arm in calm acknowledgement. A cry came from the lighter, and I remember I was just thinking "What the dickens'll happen to her?" when the end came; a *euthanasia* so mild and gradual (for the sands are fringed with mud) that the disaster was on us before I was aware of it. There was just the tiniest premonitory shuddering as our keel clove the buttery medium, a cascade of ripples from either beam, and the wheel jammed to rigidity in my hands, as the tug nestled up to her resting-place.

In the scene of panic that followed, it is safe to say that I was the only soul on board who acted with methodical tranquillity. The look-out flew astern like an arrow, bawling to the lighter. Grimm, with the passengers tumbling up after him, was on deck in an instant, storming and cursing; flung himself on the wheel which I had respectfully abandoned, jangled the telegraph, and wrenched at the spokes. The tug listed over under the force of the tide; wind, darkness, and rain aggravated the confusion.

For my part, I stepped back behind the smoke stack, threw off my robe of office, and made for the boat. Long and bitter experience of running aground had told me that that was sure to be wanted. On the way I cannoned into one of the passengers and pressed him into my service; incidentally seeing his face, and verifying an old conjecture. It was one who, in Germany, has a better right to insist than anyone else.

As we reached the davits there was a report like a pistol-shot from the port-side—the tow-rope parting, I believe, as the lighter with her shallower draught swung on past the tug. Fresh tumult arose, in which I heard: "Lower the boat," from Grimm; but the order was already executed. My ally the Passenger and I had each cast off a tackle, and slacked away with a run; that done, I promptly clutched the wire guy to steady myself, and tumbled in. (It was not far to tumble, for the tug listed heavily to starboard; think of our course, and the set of the ebb stream, and you will see why.) The forward fall unhooked sweetly; but the after one lost play. "Slack away," I called, peremptorily, and felt for my knife. My helper above obeyed; the hook yielded; I filliped away the loose tackle, and the boat floated away.

# 28

## We Achieve Our Double Aim

WHEN, exactly, the atmosphere of misunderstanding on the stranded tug was dissipated, I do not know, for by the time I had fitted the rowlocks and shipped sculls, tide and wind had caught me, and were sweeping me merrily back on the road to Norderney, whose lights twinkled through the scud in the north. With my first few strokes I made towards the lighter—which I could see sagging helplessly to leeward—but as soon as I thought I was out of sight of the tug, I pulled round and worked out my own salvation. There was an outburst of shouting which soon died away. Full speed on a falling tide! They were pinned there for five hours sure. It was impossible to miss the way, and with my stout allies heaving me forward, I made short work of the two-mile passage. There was a sharp tussle at the last, where the Riff-Gat poured its stream across my path, and then I was craning over my shoulder, God knows with what tense anxiety, for the low hull and taper mast of the *Dulcibella*. Not there! No, not where I had left her. I pulled furiously up the harbour past a sleeping ferry-steamer and—praise Heaven!—came on her warped alongside the jetty.

"Who's that?" came from below, as I stepped on board.

"Hush! it's me." And Davies and I were pawing one another in the dark of the cabin.

"Are you all right, old chap?" said he.

"Yes; are you? A match! What's the time? Quick!"

"Good Heavens, Carruthers, what the blazes have you done to yourself?" (I suspect I cut a pretty figure after my two days' outing.)

"Ten past three. It's the invasion of England! Is Dollmann at the villa?"

"Invasion?"

"Is Dollmann at the villa?"

"Yes."

"Is the *Medusa* afloat?"

"No, on the mud."

"The devil! Are *we* afloat?"

"I think so still, but they made me shift."

"Think! Track her out! Pole her out! Cut those warps!"

For a few strenuous minutes we toiled at the sweeps till the *Dulcibella* was berthed ahead of the steamer, in deeper water. Meanwhile I had whispered a few facts.

"How soon can you get under way?" I asked.

"Ten minutes."

"When's daylight?"

"Sunrise about seven, first dawn about five. Where are we bound?"

"Holland, or England."

"Are they invading it now?" said Davies, calmly.

"No, only rehearsing!" I laughed, wildly.

"Then we can wait."

"We can wait exactly an hour and a half. Come ashore and knock up Dollmann; we must denounce him, and get them both aboard; it's now or never. Holy Saints! man, not as you are!" (He was in pyjamas.) "Sea clothes!"

While he put on Christian attire, I resumed my facts and sketched a plan. "Are you watched?" I asked.

"I think so; by the *Kormoran's* men."

"Is the *Kormoran* here?"

"Yes."

"The men?"

"Not to-night. Grimm called for them in that tug. I was watching. And, Carruthers, the *Blitz* is here."

"Where?"

"In the roads outside—didn't you see her?"

"Wasn't looking. Her skipper's safe anyway; so's Böhme, so's the Tertium Quid, and so are the *Kormoran's* men. The coast's clear—it's now or never."

Once more we were traversing the long jetty and the silent streets, rain driving at our backs. We trod on air, I think; I remember no fatigue. Davies sometimes broke into a little run, muttering "scoundrel" to himself.

"I was right—only upside down," he murmured more than once. "Always really right—those channels are the key to the whole concern. Chatham, our only eastern base—no North Sea base or squadron—they'll land at one of those God-forsaken flats off the Crouch and Blackwater."

"It seems a wild scheme," I observed.

"Wild? In a way. So is *any* invasion. But it's thorough; it's German. No other country could do it. It's all dawning on me—by Jove! It will be at the *Wash*—much the nearest, and as sandy as this side."

"How's Dollmann been?" I asked.

"Polite, but queer and jumpy. It's too long a story."

"Clara?"

"*She's* all right. By Jove! Carruthers—never mind."

We found a night-bell at the villa door and rang it lustily. A window aloft opened, and "A message from Commander von Brüning—urgent," I called up.

The window shut, and soon after the hall was lighted and the door opened by Dollmann in a dressing-gown.

"Good morning, Lieutenant X——," I said, in English. "Stop, we're friends, you fool!" as the door was flung nearly to. It opened very slowly again, and we walked in.

"Silence!" he hissed. The sweat stood on his steep forehead and a hectic flush on either cheek, but there was a smile—what a smile!—on his lips. Motioning us to tread noiselessly (a vain ideal for me), he led the way to the sitting-room we knew, switched on the light, and faced us.

"Well?" he said, in English, still smiling.

I consulted my watch, and I may say that if my hand was an index to my general appearance, I must have looked the most abject ruffian under heaven.

"We probably understand one another," I said, "and to explain is to lose time. We sail for Holland, or perhaps England, at five at the latest, and we want the pleasure of your company. We promise you immunity—on certain conditions, which can wait. We have only two berths, so that we can only accommodate Miss Clara besides yourself." He smiled on through this terse harangue, but the smile froze, as though beneath it raged some crucial debate. Suddenly he laughed (a low, ironical laugh).

"You fools," he said, "you confounded meddlesome young idiots; I thought I had done with you. Promise me immunity? Give me till five? By God, I'll give you five minutes to be off to England and be damned to you, or else to be locked up for spies! What the devil do you take me for?"

"A traitor in German service," said Davies, none too firmly. We were both taken aback by this slashing attack.

"A tr——? You pig-headed young marplots! I'm in *British* service! You're wrecking the work of years—and on the very threshold of success."

For an instant Davies and I looked at one another in stupefaction. He lied—I could swear he lied; but how make sure?

"Why did you try to wreck Davies?" said I, mechanically.

"Pshaw! They made me clear him out. I knew he was safe, and safe he is."

There was only one thing for it—a last finesse, to put him to the proof.

"Very well," I said, after a moment or two, "we'll clear out—silence, Davies!—as it appears we have acted in error; but it's right to tell you that we know everything."

"Not so loud, curse you! What do you know?"

"I was taking notes at Memmert the other night."

"Impossible!"

"Thanks to Davies. Under difficulties, of course, but I heard quite enough. You were reporting your English tour—Chatham, you know, and the English scheme of attack, a mythical one, no doubt, as you're on the right side! Böhme and the rest were dealing with the German scheme of defence A to G—I heard it all—the seven islands and the seven channels between them (Davies knows every one of them by heart); and then on land, the ring of railway, Esens the centre, the army corps to mobilize and entrench—all nugatory, wasted, ha! ha!—as you're on the right s—"

"Not so loud, you fiend of mischief!" He turned his back, and made an irresolute pace or two towards the door, his hands kneading the folds of his dressing-gown as they had kneaded the curtain at Memmert. Twice he began a question and twice broke off. "I congratulate you, gentlemen," he said, finally, and with more composure, facing us again, "you have done marvels in your misplaced zeal; but you have compromised me too much already. I shall have to have you arrested— purely for form's sake—"

"Thank you," I broke in. "We have wasted five minutes, and time presses. We sail at five, and—purely for form's sake—would rather have you with us."

"What do you mean?" he snarled.

"I had the advantage of *you* at Memmert, in spite of acoustic obstacles. Your friends made an appointment behind your back, and I, in my misplaced zeal, have taken some trouble to attend it; so that I've had a working demonstration on another matter, the invasion of England from the seven *siels*." (Davies nudged me.) "No, I should let that pistol alone; and no, I wouldn't ring the bell. You can arrest us if you like, but the secret's in safe hands."

"You lie!" He was right there; but he could not know it.

"Do you suppose I haven't taken that precaution? But no names are mentioned." He gave a sort of groan, sank into a chair, and seemed to age and grizzle before our very eyes.

"What did you say about immunity, and Clara?" he muttered.

"We're friends—we're friends!" burst out Davies, with a gulp in his voice. "We want to help you both." (Through a sudden mist that filmed my eyes I saw him impetuously walk over and lay his hand on the other's shoulder.) "Those chaps are on our track and yours. Come with us. Wake her, tell her. It'll be too late soon."

X—— shrank from his touch. "Tell her? I can't tell her. You tell her, boy." He was huddling back into his chair. Davies turned to me.

"Where's her room?" I said, sharply.

"Above this one."

"Go up, Carruthers," said Davies.

"Not I—I shall frighten her into a fit."

"I don't like to."

"Nonsense, man! We'll both go then."

"Don't make a noise," said a dazed voice. We left that huddled figure and stole upstairs—thickly carpeted stairs, luckily. The door we wanted was half open, and the room behind it lighted. On the threshold stood a slim white figure, bare-footed, bare-throated.

"What is it, father?" she called in a whisper. "Whom have you been talking to?" I pushed Davies forward, but he hung back.

"Hush, don't be frightened," I said, "it's I, Carruthers, and Davies— and Davies. May we come in, just for one moment?"

I gently widened the opening of the door, while she stepped back and put one hand to her throat.

"Please come to your father," I said. "We are going to take you both to England in the *Dulcibella*—now, at once."

She had heard me, but her eyes wandered to Davies.

"I understand not," she faltered, trembling and cowering in such touching bewilderment that I could not bear to look at her.

"For God's sake, say something, Davies," I muttered.

"Clara!" said Davies, "will you not trust us?"

I heard a little gasp from her. There was a flutter of lace and cambric and she was in his arms, sobbing like a tired child, her little white feet between his great clumsy sea-boots—her rose-brown cheek on his rough jersey.

"It's past four, old chap," I remarked, brutally. "I'm going down to him again. No packing to speak of, mind. They must be out of this in half an hour." I stumbled awkwardly on the stairs (again that tiresome film!) and found him stuffing some papers pell-mell into the stove. There were only slumbering embers in it, but he did not seem to notice that. "You must be dressed in half an hour," I said, furtively pocketing a pistol which lay on the table.

"Have you told her? Take her to England, you two boys. I think I'll stay." He sank into a chair again.

"Nonsense, she won't go without you. You must, for her sake—in half an hour, too."

I prefer to pass that half-hour lightly over. Davies left before me to prepare the yacht for sea, and I had to bear the brunt of what followed, including (as a mere episode) a scene with the stepmother, the memory of which rankles in me yet. After all, she was a sensible woman.

As for the other two, the girl when I saw her next, in her short boating skirt and tam-o'-shanter, was a miracle of coolness and pluck. But for her I should never have got him away. And ah! how good it was to be out in the wholesome rain again, hurrying to the harbour with my two charges, hurrying them down the greasy ladder to that frail atom of English soil, their first guerdon of home and safety.

Our flight from the harbour was unmolested, unnoticed. Only the first ghastly evidences of dawn were mingling with the strangled moon-light, as we tacked round the pier-head and headed close-reefed down the Riff-Gat on the lees of the ebb-tide. We had to pass under the very quarter of the *Blitz*, so Davies said; for, of course, he alone was on deck till we reached the open sea. Day was breaking then. It was dead low water, and, far away to the south, between dun swathes of sand, I thought I saw—but probably it was only a fancy—two black stranded specks. Rail awash, and decks streaming, we took the outer swell and clawed close-hauled under the lee of Juist, westward, hurrying westward.

"Up the Ems on the flood, and to Dutch Delfzyl," I urged. No, thought Davies; it was too near Germany, and there was a tidal cut through from Buse Tief. Better to dodge in behind Rottum Island. So on we pressed, past Memmert, over the Juister Reef and the *Corinne's* buried millions, across the two broad and yeasty mouths of the Ems, till Rottum, a wee lonesome wafer of an islet, the first of the Dutch archi-pelago, was close on the weather-bow.

"We must get in behind that," said Davies, "then we shall be safe; I think I know the way, but get the next chart; and then take a rest, old chap. Clara and I can manage." (She had been on deck most of the time, as capable a hand as you could wish for, better far than I in my present state of exhaustion.) I crawled along the slippery sloping planks and went below.

"Where are we?" cried Dollmann, starting up from the lee sofa, where he seemed to have been lying in a sort of trance. A book, his own book, slipped from his knees, and I saw the frontispiece lying on the floor in a pool of oil; for the stove had gone adrift, and the saloon was in a wretched state of squalor and litter.

"Off Rottum," I said, and knelt up to find the chart. There was a look in his eyes that I suppose I ought to have understood, but I can scarcely blame myself, for the accumulated strain, not only of the last three days and nights, but of the whole arduous month of my cruise with Davies, was beginning to tell on me, now that safety and success were at hand. I handed up the chart through the companion, and then crept into the reeling fo'c'sle and lay down on the spare sail-bags, with the thunder and thump of the seas around and above me.

I must quote Davies for the event that happened now; for by the time

I had responded to the alarm and climbed up through the fore-hatch, the whole tragedy was over and done with.

"X—— came up the companion," he says, "soon after you went down. He held on by the runner, and stared to windward at Rottum, as though he knew the place quite well. And then he came towards us, moving so unsteadily that I gave Clara the tiller, and went to help him. I tried to make him go down again, but he wouldn't, and came aft.

"'Give me the helm,' he said, half to himself. 'Sea's too bad outside—there's a short cut here.'

"'Thanks,' I said, 'I know this one.' (I don't think I meant to be sarcastic.) He said nothing, and settled himself on the counter behind us, safe enough, with his feet against the lee-rail, and then, to my astonishment, began to talk over my shoulder jolly sensibly about the course, pointing out a buoy which is wrong on the chart (as I knew), and telling me it was wrong, and so on. Well, we came to the bar of the Schild, and had to turn south for that twisty bit of beating between Rottum and Bosch Flat. Clara was at the jib-sheet, I had the chart and the tiller (you know how absent I get like that); there was a bobble of sea, and we both had heaps to do, and—well—I happened to look round, and he was gone. He hadn't spoken for a minute or two, but I believe the last thing I heard him say (I was hardly attending at the time, for we were in the thick of it) was something about a 'short cut' again. He must have slipped over quietly . . . He had an ulster and big boots on."

We cruised about for a time, but never found him.

That evening, after threading the maze of shoals between the Dutch mainland and islands, we anchored off the little hamlet of Ostmahorn,* gave the yacht in charge of some astonished fishermen, and thence by road and rail, hurrying still, gained Harlingen, and took passage on a steamer to London. From that point our personal history is of no concern to the outside world, and here, therefore, I bring this narrative to an end.

## Epilogue†

### BY THE EDITOR

AN interesting document, somewhat damaged by fire, lies on my study table.

It is a copy (in cipher) of a confidential memorandum to the German Government embodying a scheme for the invasion of

---

*See Map A.     †For this chapter see Map A.

England by Germany. It is unsigned, but internal evidence, and the fact that it was taken by Mr. "Carruthers" from the stove of the villa at Norderney, leave no doubt as to its authorship. For many reasons it is out of the question to print the textual translation of it, as deciphered; but I propose to give an outline of its contents.

Even this must strain discretion to its uttermost limits, and had I only to consider the instructed few who follow the trend of professional opinion on such subjects, I should leave the foregoing narrative to speak for itself. But, as was stated in the preface, our primary purpose is to reach everyone; and there may be many who, in spite of able and authoritative warnings frequently uttered since these events occurred, are still prone to treat the German danger as an idle "bogey," and may be disposed, in this case, to imagine that a baseless romance has been foisted on them.

A few persons (English as well as German) hold that Germany is strong enough now to meet us single-handed, and throw an army on our shores. The memorandum rejects this view, deferring isolated action for at least a decade; and supposing, for present purposes, a coalition of three Powers against Great Britain. And subsequent researches through the usual channels place it beyond dispute that this condition was relied on by the German Government in adopting the scheme. They realized that even if, owing to our widely scattered forces, they gained that temporary command of the North Sea which would be essential for a successful landing, they would inevitably lose it when our standing fleets were concentrated and our reserve ships mobilized. With its sea-communications cut, the prospects of the invading army would be too dubious. I state it in that mild way, for it seems not to have been held that failure was absolutely certain; and rightly, I think, in spite of the dogmas of the strategists—for the case transcends all experience. No man can calculate the effect on our delicate economic fabric of a well-timed, well-planned blow at the industrial heart of the kingdom, the great northern and midland towns, with their teeming populations of peaceful wage-earners. In this instance, however, joint action (the occasion for which is perhaps not difficult to guess) was distinctly contemplated, and Germany's *rôle* in the coalition was exclusively that of invader. Her fleet was to be kept intact, and she herself to remain ostensibly neutral until the first shock was over, and our own battle-fleets either beaten, or, the much more likely event, so crippled by a hard-won victory as to be incapable of withstanding compact and unscathed forces. Then, holding the balance of power, she would strike. And the blow? It was not till I read this memorandum that I grasped the full merits of that daring scheme, under which every advantage, moral, material, and geographical, possessed by Germany, is utilized to the utmost, and every disadvantage of our own turned to account against us.

Two root principles pervade it: perfect organization; perfect secrecy. Under the first head come some general considerations. The writer (who is intimately conversant with conditions on both sides of the North Sea) argued that Germany is pre-eminently fitted to undertake an invasion of Great Britain. She has a great army (a mere fraction of which would suffice) in a state of high efficiency, but a useless weapon, as against us, unless transported over seas. She has a peculiar genius for organization, not only in elaborating minute detail, but in the grasp of a coherent whole. She knows the art of giving a brain to a machine, of transmitting power to the uttermost cog-wheel, and at the same time of concentrating responsibility in a supreme centre. She has a small navy, but very effective for its purpose, built, trained, and manned on methodical principles, for defined ends, and backed by an inexhaustible reserve of men from her maritime conscription. She studies and practises co-operation between her army and navy. Her hands are free for offence in home waters, since she has no distant network of coveted colonies and dependencies on which to dissipate her defensive energies. Finally, she is, compared with ourselves, economically independent, having commercial access through her land frontiers to the whole of Europe. She has little to lose and much to gain.

The writer pauses here to contrast our own situation, and I summarize his points. We have a small army, dispersed over the whole globe, and administered on a gravely defective system. We have no settled theory of national defence, and no competent authority whose business it is to give us one. The matter is still at the stage of civilian controversy. Co-operation between the army and navy is not studied and practised; much less do there exist any plans, worthy of the name, for the repulse of an invasion, or any readiness worth considering for the prompt equipment and direction of our home forces to meet a sudden emergency. We have a great and, in many respects, a magnificent navy, but not great enough for the interests it insures, and with equally defective institutions; not built or manned methodically, having an utterly inadequate reserve of men, all classes of which would be absorbed at the very outset, without a vestige of preparation for the enrolment of volunteers; distracted by the multiplicity of its functions in guarding our colossal empire and commerce, and conspicuously lacking a brain, not merely for the smooth control of its own unwieldy mechanism, but for the study of rival aims and systems. We have no North Sea naval base, no North Sea Fleet, and no North Sea policy. Lastly, we stand in a highly dangerous economical position.

The writer then deals with the method of invasion, and rejects the obvious one at once, that of sending forth a fleet of transports from one or more of the North Sea ports. He combats especially the idea of making Emden (the nearest to our shores) the port of departure. I mention this because, since his own scheme was adopted, it is instructive to note that Emden had been used (with caution) as a red herring by the inspired German press, when the subject was mentioned at all, and industriously dragged across the trail. His objections to the North Sea ports apply, he remarks, in reality to all schemes of invasion, whether the conditions be favourable or not. One is that secrecy is rendered impossible—and secrecy is vital. The collection of the transports would be known in England weeks before the hour was ripe for striking; for all large ports are cosmopolitan and swarm with potential spies. In Germany's case, moreover, suitable ships are none too plentiful, and the number required would entail a large deduction from her mercantile marine. The other reason concerns the actual landing. This must take place on an open part of the east coast of England. No other objective is even considered. Now the difficulty of transshipping and landing troops by boats from transports anchored in deep water, in a safe, swift, and orderly fashion, on an open beach, is enormous. The most hastily improvised resistance might cause a humiliating disaster. Yet the first stage is the most important of all. It is imperative that the invaders should seize and promptly intrench a pre-arranged line of country, to serve as an initial base. This once done, they can use other resources; they can bring up transports, land cavalry and heavy guns, pour in stores, and advance. But unless this is done, they are impotent, be their sea-communications never so secure.

The only logical alternative is then propounded: to despatch an army of infantry with the lightest type of field-guns in big sea-going lighters, towed by powerful but shallow-draught tugs, under escort of a powerful composite squadron of warships; and to fling the flotilla, at high tide, if possible, straight upon the shore.

Such an expedition could be prepared in absolute secrecy, by turning to account the natural features of the German coast. No great port was to be concerned in any way. All that was required was sufficient depth of water to float the lighters and tugs; and this is supplied by seven insignificant streams, issuing from the Frisian littoral, and already furnished with small harbours and sluice-gates, with one exception, namely, the tidal creek at Norden; for this, it appeared, was one of the chosen seven, and not, as "Carruthers" supposed, Hilgenriedersiel, which, if you remember, he had no time to visit, and which has, in fact, no stream of any value at all, and no harbour. All of these streams would have to be improved, deepened, and generally canalized; ostensibly with a commercial end, for purposes of traffic with the islands, which are growing health resorts during a limited summer season.

The whole expedition would be organized under seven distinct

sub-divisions—not too great a number in view of its cumbrous character. Seawards, the whole of the coast is veiled by the fringe of islands
and the zone of shoals. Landwards, the loop of railway round the
Frisian peninsula would form the line of communication in rear of the
seven streams. Esens was to be the local centre of administration when
the scheme grew to maturity, but not till then. Every detail for the
movement of troops under the seven different heads was to be arranged
for with secrecy and exactitude many months in advance, and from
headquarters at Berlin. It was not expected that nothing would leak out,
but care was to be taken that anything that did do so should be attributed to defensive measures—a standing feature in German mobilization being the establishment of a corps of observation along the Frisian
coast; in fact, the same machinery was to be used, and its conversion
for offence concealed up to the latest possible moment. The same precautions were to be taken in the preliminary work on the spot. There,
four men only (it was calculated) need be in full possession of the secret. One was to represent the Imperial Navy (a post filled by our friend
von Brüning). Another (Böhme) was to superintend the six canals and
the construction of the lighters. The functions of the third were two-
fold. He was to organize what I may call the local labour—that is, the
helpers required for embarkation, the crews of the tugs, and, most important of all, the service of pilots for the navigation of the seven flotillas through the corresponding channels to the open sea. He must be a
local man, thoroughly acquainted with the coast, of a social standing
not much above the average of villagers and fishermen, and he must be
ready when the time was ripe with lists of the right men for the right
duties, lists to which the conscription authorities could, when required,
give instant legal effect. His other function was to police the coast for
spies, and to report anything suspicious to von Brüning, who would
never be far away. On the whole I think that they found the grim
Grimm a jewel for their purpose.

As fourth personage, the writer designates himself, the promoter of
the scheme, the indispensable link between the two nations. He un-
dertakes to furnish reliable information as to the disposition of troops in
England, as to the hydrography of the coast selected for the landing, as
to the supplies available in its vicinity, and the strategic points to be
seized. He proposes to be guide-in-chief to the expedition during transit. And in the meantime (when not otherwise employed) he was to re-
side at Norderney, in close touch with the other three, and controlling
the commercial undertakings which were to throw dust in the eyes of
the curious. (Memmert, by the way, is not mentioned in this memorandum.)

He speaks of the place "selected for the landing," and proceeds to consider this question in detail. I cannot follow him in his review, deeply interesting though it is, and shall say at once that he reduces possible landing-places to two, the flats on the Essex coast between Foulness and Brightlingsea, and the Wash—with a decided preference for the latter. Assuming that the enemy, if they got wind of an invasion at all, would expect transports to be employed, he chooses the sort of spot which they would be least likely to defend, and which, nevertheless, was suitable to the character of the flotillas, and similar to the region they started from. There is such a spot on the Lincolnshire coast, on the north side of the Wash,* known as East Holland. It is low-lying land, dyked against the sea, and bordered like Frisia with sand-flats which dry off at low water. It is easy of access from the east, by way of Boston Deeps, a deep-water channel formed by a detached bank, called the Long Sand, lying parallel to the shore for ten miles. This bank makes a natural breakwater against the swell from the east (the only quarter to be feared); and the Deeps behind it, where there is an average depth of thirty-four feet at low-water, would form an excellent roadstead for the covering squadron, whose guns would command the shore within easy range. It is noted in passing that this is just the case where German first-class battleships would have an advantage over British ships of the same calibre. The latter are of just too heavy a draught to navigate such waters without peril, if, indeed, they could enter this roadstead at all, for there is a bar at the mouth of it with only thirty-one feet at high water, spring tides. The former, built as they were with a view to manoeuvring in the North Sea, are just within the margin of safety. East Holland is within easy striking distance of the manufacturing districts, a vigorous raid on which is, the writer urges, the true policy of an invader. He reports positively that there exist (in a proper military sense) no preparations whatever to meet such an attack. East Holland is also the nearest point on the British shores to Germany, excepting the coast of Norfolk; much nearer, indeed, than the Essex flats alluded to, and reached by a simple deep-sea passage, without any dangerous region to navigate, like the mouth of the Channel and the estuary of the Thames from Harwich westwards. The distance is 240 sea-miles, west by south roughly, from Borkum Island, and 280 from Wangeroog. The time estimated for transit after the flotillas had been assembled outside the islands is from thirty to thirty-four hours.

Embarkation is the next topic. This could and must be effected in one tide. At the six *siels* there was a mean period of two and a half hours in every twelve, during which the water was high enough. At Norden a rather longer time was available. But this should be amply sufficient if

---

*See Map A.

the machinery were in good working order and were punctually set in motion. High water occurs approximately at the same time at all seven outlets, the difference between the two farthest apart, Carolinensiel and Greetsiel, being only half an hour.

Lastly, the special risks attendant on such an expedition are dispassionately weighed. X——, though keenly anxious to recommend his scheme, writes in no blindly sanguine spirit. There are no modern precedents for any invasion in the least degree comparable to that of England by Germany. Any such attempt will be a hazardous experiment. But he argues that the advantages of his method outweigh the risks, and that most of the risks themselves would attach equally to any other method. Whatever skill in prediction was used, bad weather might overtake the expedition. Yes; but if transports were used transhipment into boats for landing would in bad weather be fraught with the same and a greater peril. But transports could stand off and wait. Delay is fatal in any case; unswerving promptitude is the essence of such an enterprise. The lighters would be in danger of foundering? Beside the point; if the end is worth gaining the risks must be faced. Soldiers' lives are sacrificed in tens of thousands on battlefields. The flotilla would be demoralized during transit by the assault of a few torpedo-boats? Granted; but the same would apply to a fleet of transports, with the added certainty that one lucky shot would send to the bottom ten times the number of soldiers, with less hope of rescue. In both cases reliance must be placed on the efficiency and vigilance of the escort. It is admitted, however, in a passage which might well make my two adventurers glow with triumph, that if by any mischance the British discovered what was afoot in good time, and were able to send over a swarm of light-draught boats, which could elude the German warships and get amongst the flotillas while they were still in process of leaving the *siels*; it is admitted that in that case the expedition was doomed. But it is held that such an event was not to be feared. Reckless pluck is abundant in the British Navy, but expert knowledge of the tides and shoals in these waters is utterly lacking. The British charts are of no value, and there is no evidence (he reports) that the subject has been studied in any way by the British Admiralty. Let me remark here, that I believe Mr. "Davies's" views, as expressed in the earlier chapters, when they were still among the great estuaries, are all absolutely sound. The "channel theory," though it only bore indirectly on the grand issue before them, was true, and should be laid to heart, or I should not have wasted space on it.

One word more, in conclusion. There is an axiom, much in fashion now, that there is no fear of an invasion of the British Isles, because if we lose command of the sea, we can be starved—a cheaper and surer way of reducing us to submission. It is a loose, valueless axiom, but by sheer repetition it is becoming an article of faith. It implies that "command of the sea" is a thing to be won or lost definitely; that we may have it to-day and lose it for ever to-morrow. On the contrary, the chances are that in anything like an even struggle the command of the sea will hang in the balance for an indefinite time. And even against great odds, it would probably be impossible for our enemies so to bar the avenues of our commerce, so to blockade the ports of our extensive coast-line, and so to overcome the interest which neutrals will have in supplying us, as to bring us to our knees in less than two years, during which time we can be recuperating and rebuilding from our unique internal resources, and endeavouring to regain command.

No; the better axiom is that nothing short of a successful invasion could finally compel us to make peace. Our hearts are stout, we hope; but facts are facts; and a successful raid, such as that here sketched, if you will think out its consequences, must appal the stoutest heart. It was checkmated, but others may be conceived. In any case, we know the way in which they look at these things in Germany.

### Postscript (March 1903)

IT SO happens that while this book was in the press a number of measures have been taken by the Government to counteract some of the very weaknesses and dangers which are alluded to above. A Committee of National Defence has been set up, and the welcome given to it was a truly extraordinary comment on the apathy and confusion which it is designed to supplant. A site on the Forth has been selected for a new North Sea naval base—an excellent if tardy decision; for ten years or so must elapse before the existing anchorage becomes in any sense a "base." A North Sea fleet has also been created—another good measure; but it should be remembered that its ships are not modern, or in the least capable of meeting the principal German squadrons under the circumstances supposed above.

Lastly, a Manning Committee has (among other matters) reported vaguely in favour of a Volunteer Reserve. There is no means of knowing what this recommendation will lead to; let us hope not to the fiasco of the last badly conceived experiment. Is it not becoming patent that the time has come for training all Englishmen systematically either for the sea or for the rifle?

THE END

# DOVER · THRIFT · EDITIONS

## POETRY

"MINIVER CHEEVY" AND OTHER POEMS, Edwin Arlington Robinson. 64pp. 28756-4 $1.00

EARLY POEMS, Ezra Pound. 80pp. (Available in U.S. only) 28745-9 $1.00

EARLY POEMS, William Carlos Williams. 64pp. (Available in U.S. only) 29294-0 $1.00

"THE WASTE LAND" AND OTHER POEMS, T. S. Eliot. 64pp. (Available in U.S. only) 40061-1 $1.00

RENASCENCE AND OTHER POEMS, Edna St. Vincent Millay. 64pp. (Available in U.S. only) 26873-X $1.00

SELECTED POEMS, John Milton. 128pp. 27554-X $1.50

SELECTED CANTERBURY TALES, Geoffrey Chaucer. 144pp. 28241-4 $1.00

GREAT SONNETS, Paul Negri (ed.). 96pp. 28052-7 $1.00

CIVIL WAR POETRY: An Anthology, Paul Negri. 128pp. 29883-3 $1.50

WAR IS KIND AND OTHER POEMS, Stephen Crane. 64pp. 40424-2 $1.00

THE RAVEN AND OTHER FAVORITE POEMS, Edgar Allan Poe. 64pp. 26685-0 $1.00

ESSAY ON MAN AND OTHER POEMS, Alexander Pope. 128pp. 28053-5 $1.50

GOBLIN MARKET AND OTHER POEMS, Christina Rossetti. 64pp. 28055-1 $1.00

CHICAGO POEMS, Carl Sandburg. 80pp. 28057-8 $1.00

THE SHOOTING OF DAN McGREW AND OTHER POEMS, Robert Service. 96pp. (Available in U.S. only) 27556-6 $1.00

COMPLETE SONNETS, William Shakespeare. 80pp. 26686-9 $1.00

SELECTED POEMS, Percy Bysshe Shelley. 128pp. 27558-2 $1.50

100 BEST-LOVED POEMS, Philip Smith (ed.). 96pp. 28553-7 $1.00

101 GREAT AMERICAN POEMS, The American Poetry & Literacy Project (ed.). (Available in U.S. only) 40158-8 $1.00

NATIVE AMERICAN SONGS AND POEMS: An Anthology, Brian Swann (ed.). 64pp. 29450-1 $1.00

SELECTED POEMS, Alfred Lord Tennyson. 112pp. 27282-6 $1.00

LITTLE ORPHANT ANNIE AND OTHER POEMS, James Whitcomb Riley. 80pp. 28260-0 $1.00

CHRISTMAS CAROLS: COMPLETE VERSES, Shane Weller (ed.). 64pp. 27397-0 $1.00

GREAT LOVE POEMS, Shane Weller (ed.). 128pp. 27284-2 $1.00

LOVE: A Book of Quotations, Herb Galewitz (ed.). 64pp. 40004-2 $1.00

EVANGELINE AND OTHER POEMS, Henry Wadsworth Longfellow. 64pp. 28255-4 $1.00

CIVIL WAR POETRY AND PROSE, Walt Whitman. 96pp. 28507-3 $1.00

SELECTED POEMS, Walt Whitman. 128pp. 26878-0 $1.00

THE BALLAD OF READING GAOL AND OTHER POEMS, Oscar Wilde. 64pp. 27072-6 $1.00

FAVORITE POEMS, William Wordsworth. 80pp. 27073-4 $1.00

WORLD WAR ONE BRITISH POETS: Brooke, Owen, Sassoon, Rosenberg and Others, Candace Ward (ed.). (Available in U.S. only) 29568-0 $1.00

THE CAVALIER POETS: An Anthology, Thomas Crofts (ed.). 80pp. 28766-1 $1.00

ENGLISH ROMANTIC POETRY: An Anthology, Stanley Appelbaum (ed.). 256pp. 29282-7 $2.00

EARLY POEMS, William Butler Yeats. 128pp. 27808-5 $1.50

"EASTER, 1916" AND OTHER POEMS, William Butler Yeats. 80pp. (Available in U.S. only) 29771-3 $1.00

# DOVER · THRIFT · EDITIONS

## FICTION

THE STRANGE CASE OF DR. JEKYLL AND MR. HYDE, Robert Louis Stevenson. 64pp. 26688-5 $1.00

TREASURE ISLAND, Robert Louis Stevenson. 160pp. 27559-0 $1.50

THE LOST WORLD, Arthur Conan Doyle. 176pp. 40060-3 $1.50

GULLIVER'S TRAVELS, Jonathan Swift. 240pp. 29273-8 $2.00

ROBINSON CRUSOE, Daniel Defoe. 288pp. 40427-7 $2.00

THE KREUTZER SONATA AND OTHER SHORT STORIES, Leo Tolstoy. 144pp. 27805-0 $1.50

THE IMMORALIST, André Gide. 112pp. (Available in U.S. only) 29237-1 $1.50

ADVENTURES OF HUCKLEBERRY FINN, Mark Twain. 224pp. 28061-6 $2.00

THE ADVENTURES OF TOM SAWYER, Mark Twain. 192pp. 40077-8 $2.00

THE MYSTERIOUS STRANGER AND OTHER STORIES, Mark Twain. 128pp. 27069-6 $1.00

HUMOROUS STORIES AND SKETCHES, Mark Twain. 80pp. 29279-7 $1.00

YOU KNOW ME AL, Ring Lardner. 128pp. 28513-8 $1.00

MOLL FLANDERS, Daniel Defoe. 256pp. 29093-X $2.00

CANDIDE, Voltaire (François-Marie Arouet). 112pp. 26689-3 $1.00

"THE COUNTRY OF THE BLIND" AND OTHER SCIENCE-FICTION STORIES, H. G. Wells. 160pp. (Available in U.S. only) 29569-9 $1.00

THE ISLAND OF DR. MOREAU, H. G. Wells. (Available in U.S. only) 29027-1 $1.00

THE INVISIBLE MAN, H. G. Wells. 112pp. (Available in U.S. only) 27071-8 $1.00

THE TIME MACHINE, H. G. Wells. 80pp. (Available in U.S. only) 28472-7 $1.00

LOOKING BACKWARD, Edward Bellamy. 160pp. 29038-7 $2.00

THE WAR OF THE WORLDS, H. G. Wells. 160pp. (Available in U.S. only) 29506-0 $1.00

ETHAN FROME, Edith Wharton. 96pp. 26690-7 $1.00

SHORT STORIES, Edith Wharton. 128pp. 28235-X $1.00

THE AGE OF INNOCENCE, Edith Wharton. 288pp. 29803-5 $2.00

THE MOON AND SIXPENCE, W. Somerset Maugham. 176pp. (Available in U.S. only) 28731-9 $2.00

THE PICTURE OF DORIAN GRAY, Oscar Wilde. 192pp. 27807-7 $1.50

MONDAY OR TUESDAY: Eight Stories, Virginia Woolf. 64pp. (Available in U.S. only) 29453-6 $1.00

JACOB'S ROOM, Virginia Woolf. 144pp. (Available in U.S. only) 40109-X $1.50

## NONFICTION

THE DEVIL'S DICTIONARY, Ambrose Bierce. 144pp. 27542-6 $1.00

DE PROFUNDIS, Oscar Wilde. 64pp. 29308-4 $1.00

OSCAR WILDE'S WIT AND WISDOM: A Book of Quotations, Oscar Wilde. 64pp. 40146-4 $1.00

THE SOULS OF BLACK FOLK, W. E. B. Du Bois. 176pp. 28041-1 $2.00

NARRATIVE OF THE LIFE OF FREDERICK DOUGLASS, Frederick Douglass. 96pp. 28499-9 $1.00

NARRATIVE OF SOJOURNER TRUTH, Sojourner Truth. 80pp. 29899-X $1.00

UP FROM SLAVERY, Booker T. Washington. 160pp. 28738-6 $2.00

A VINDICATION OF THE RIGHTS OF WOMAN, Mary Wollstonecraft. 224pp. 29036-0 $2.00

THE SUBJECTION OF WOMEN, John Stuart Mill. 112pp. 29601-6 $1.50

TAO TE CHING, Lao Tze. 112pp. 29792-6 $1.00

THE ANALECTS, Confucius. 128pp. 28484-0 $2.00

SELF-RELIANCE AND OTHER ESSAYS, Ralph Waldo Emerson. 128pp. 27790-9 $1.00

SELECTED ESSAYS, Michel de Montaigne. 96pp. 29109-X $1.50

# DOVER·THRIFT·EDITIONS

## NONFICTION

A MODEST PROPOSAL AND OTHER SATIRICAL WORKS, Jonathan Swift. 64pp. 28759-9 $1.00

UTOPIA, Sir Thomas More. 96pp. 29583-4 $1.50

THE AUTOBIOGRAPHY OF BENJAMIN FRANKLIN, Benjamin Franklin. 144pp. 29073-5 $1.50

COMMON SENSE, Thomas Paine. 64pp. 29602-4 $1.00

THE STORY OF MY LIFE, Helen Keller. 80pp. 29249-5 $1.00

GREAT SPEECHES, Abraham Lincoln. 112pp. 26872-1 $1.00

THE PRINCE, Niccolò Machiavelli. 80pp. 27274-5 $1.00

PRAGMATISM, William James. 128pp. 28270-8 $1.50

TOTEM AND TABOO, Sigmund Freud. 176pp. (Available in U.S. only) 40434-X $2.00

POETICS, Aristotle. 64pp. 29577-X $1.00

NICOMACHEAN ETHICS, Aristotle. 256pp. 40096-4 $2.00

MEDITATIONS, Marcus Aurelius. 128pp. 29823-X $1.50

SYMPOSIUM AND PHAEDRUS, Plato. 96pp. 27798-4 $1.50

THE TRIAL AND DEATH OF SOCRATES: Four Dialogues, Plato. 128pp. 27066-1 $1.00

THE BIRTH OF TRAGEDY, Friedrich Nietzsche. 96pp. 28515-4 $1.50

BEYOND GOOD AND EVIL: Prelude to a Philosophy of the Future, Friedrich Nietzsche. 176pp. 29868-X $1.50

CONFESSIONS OF AN ENGLISH OPIUM EATER, Thomas De Quincey. 80pp. 28742-4 $1.00

CIVIL DISOBEDIENCE AND OTHER ESSAYS, Henry David Thoreau. 96pp. 27563-9 $1.00

SELECTIONS FROM THE JOURNALS (Edited by Walter Harding), Herny David Thoreau. 96pp. 28760-2 $1.00

WALDEN; OR, LIFE IN THE WOODS, Henry David Thoreau. 224pp. 28495-6 $2.00

THE LAND OF LITTLE RAIN, Mary Austin. 96pp. 29037-9 $1.50

THE THEORY OF THE LEISURE CLASS, Thorstein Veblen. 256pp. 28062-4 $2.00

## PLAYS

PROMETHEUS BOUND, Aeschylus. 64pp. 28762-9 $1.00

THE ORESTEIA TRILOGY: Agamemnon, The Libation-Bearers and The Furies, Aeschylus. 160pp. 29242-8 $1.50

LYSISTRATA, Aristophanes. 64pp. 28225-2 $1.00

WHAT EVERY WOMAN KNOWS, James Barrie. 80pp. (Available in U.S. only) 29578-8 $1.50

THE CHERRY ORCHARD, Anton Chekhov. 64pp. 26682-6 $1.00

THE THREE SISTERS, Anton Chekhov. 64pp. 27544-2 $1.00

UNCLE VANYA, Anton Chekhov. 64pp. 40159-6 $1.50

THE INSPECTOR GENERAL, Nikolai Gogol. 80pp. 28500-6 $1.50

THE WAY OF THE WORLD, William Congreve. 80pp. 27787-9 $1.50

BACCHAE, Euripides. 64pp. 29580-X $1.00

MEDEA, Euripides. 64pp. 27548-5 $1.00

THE MIKADO, William Schwenck Gilbert. 64pp. 27268-0 $1.50

FAUST, PART ONE, Johann Wolfgang von Goethe. 192pp. 28046-2 $2.00

SHE STOOPS TO CONQUER, Oliver Goldsmith. 80pp. 26867-5 $1.50

A DOLL'S HOUSE, Henrik Ibsen. 80pp. 27062-9 $1.00

HEDDA GABLER, Henrik Ibsen. 80pp. 26469-6 $1.50

GHOSTS, Henrik Ibsen. 64pp. 29852-3 $1.50

VOLPONE, Ben Jonson. 112pp. 28049-7 $1.50

DR. FAUSTUS, Christopher Marlowe. 64pp. 28208-2 $1.00

THE MISANTHROPE, Molière. 64pp. 27065-3 $1.00

# DOVER · THRIFT · EDITIONS

## PLADS

THE EMPEROR JONES, Eugene O'Neill. 64pp. 29268-1 $1.50

BEYOND THE HORIZON, Eugene O'Neill. 96pp. 29085-9 $1.50

ANNA CHRISTIE, Eugene O'Neill. 80pp. 29985-6 $1.50

THE LONG VOYAGE HOME AND OTHER PLAYS, Eugene O'Neill. 80pp. 28755-6 $1.00

RIGHT YOU ARE, IF YOU THINK YOU ARE, Luigi Pirandello. 64pp. (Available in U.S. only) 29576-1 $1.50

SIX CHARACTERS IN SEARCH OF AN AUTHOR, Luigi Pirandello. 64pp. (Available in U.S. only) 29992-9 $1.50

HANDS AROUND, Arthur Schnitzler. 64pp. 28724-6 $1.00

ANTONY AND CLEOPATRA, William Shakespeare. 128pp. 40062-X $1.50

HAMLET, William Shakespeare. 128pp. 27278-8 $1.00

HENRY IV, William Shakespeare. 96pp. 29584-2 $1.00

RICHARD III, William Shakespeare. 112pp. 28747-5 $1.00

OTHELLO, William Shakespeare. 112pp. 29097-2 $1.00

JULIUS CAESAR, William Shakespeare. 80pp. 26876-4 $1.00

KING LEAR, William Shakespeare. 112pp. 28058-6 $1.00

MACBETH, William Shakespeare. 96pp. 27802-6 $1.00

THE MERCHANT OF VENICE, William Shakespeare. 96pp. 28492-1 $1.00

A MIDSUMMER NIGHT'S DREAM, William Shakespeare. 80pp. 27067-X $1.00

MUCH ADO ABOUT NOTHING, William Shakespeare. 80pp. 28272-4 $1.00

AS YOU LIKE IT, William Shakespeare. 80pp. 40432-3 $1.50

THE TAMING OF THE SHREW, William Shakespeare. 96pp. 29765-9 $1.00

TWELFTH NIGHT; OR, WHAT YOU WILL, William Shakespeare. 80pp. 29290-8 $1.00

ROMEO AND JULIET, William Shakespeare. 96pp. 27557-4 $1.00

ARMS AND THE MAN, George Bernard Shaw. 80pp. (Available in U.S. only) 26476-9 $1.50

PYGMALION, George Bernard Shaw. 96pp. (Available in U.S. only) 28222-8 $1.00

HEARTBREAK HOUSE, George Bernard Shaw. 128pp. (Available in U.S. only) 29291-6 $1.50

THE SCHOOL FOR SCANDAL, Richard Brinsley Sheridan. 96pp. 26687-7 $1.50

ANTIGONE, Sophocles. 64pp. 27804-2 $1.00

OEDIPUS REX, Sophocles. 64pp. 26877-2 $1.00

ELECTRA, Sophocles. 64pp. 28482-4 $1.00

MISS JULIE, August Strindberg. 64pp. 27281-8 $1.50

THE PLAYBOY OF THE WESTERN WORLD AND RIDERS TO THE SEA, J. M. Synge. 80pp. 27562-0 $1.50

THE IMPORTANCE OF BEING EARNEST, Oscar Wilde. 64pp. 26478-5 $1.00

LADY WINDERMERE'S FAN, Oscar Wilde. 64pp. 40078-6 $1.00

## BOXED SETS

FIVE GREAT POETS: Poems by Shakespeare, Keats, Poe, Dickinson and Whitman, Dover. 416pp. 26942-6 $5.00

NINE GREAT ENGLISH POETS: Poems by Shakespeare, Keats, Blake, Coleridge, Wordsworth, Mrs. Browning, FitzGerald, Tennyson and Kipling, Dover. 704pp. 27633-3 $9.00

FIVE GREAT ENGLISH ROMANTIC POETS, Dover. 496pp. 27893-X $5.00

SEVEN GREAT ENGLISH VICTORIAN POETS: Seven Volumes, Dover. 592pp. 40204-5 $7.50

SIX GREAT AMERICAN POETS: Poems by Poe, Dickinson, Whitman, Longfellow, Frost and Millay, Dover. 512pp. (Available in U.S. only) 27425-X $6.00